ALSO BY ALI

The Spare Who Became the Heir and Other Stories

THE HEAD, THE HEART, AND THE HEIR

THE HEAD, THE HEART, AND THE HEIR

ALICE HANOV

Gryphon
Press

Gryphon Press

Published by Gryphon Press
Waterloo, Ontario

First Edition

Paperback: 978-1-7780476-1-9
Hardcover: 978-1-7780476-0-2
Ebook: 978-1-7780476-2-6

Edited by Lauren Taylor Shute Editorial
Cover design by The Book Designers

Dedicated to my husband, Steve, and my kids, Lillian, Katrina, and Zack, for encouraging me to follow my dream.

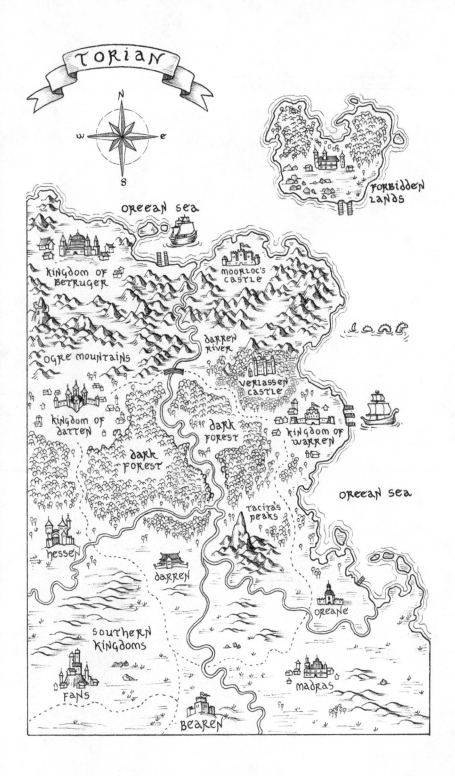

PROLOGUE

"With your father's temper? Diplomacy isn't a strong suit," Princess Victoria said. "Is Matthias joining you?"

"He's waiting outside. We'll leave once I've resolved the merchant disputes. Are we packed? Once I return, we can load the coaches and head for Datten. Elizabeth, are you excited to see Aaron and Daniel?" Crown Prince Edward asked. "Elizabeth?"

Sunlight shone through the second-floor balcony doors onto the polished throne room floor as Princess Elizabeth hopped from one lit marble square to another. She could see her reflection in each one; her eyes sparkled like emeralds, and her wild chestnut hair bounced on her shoulders as she played her game to pass the time. When she landed on the last illuminated square, she looked up and smiled at her mother.

"Need more?" Victoria asked, releasing Edward's hand. Her mother's emerald eyes flashed gold, and she waved her hand. A new path glowed on the marble before Elizabeth.

Elizabeth giggled and resumed her journey across the

1

throne room, ignoring her parents' dull conversation as best she could. *Why didn't Matthias bring Percival? He's silly.*

Edward snatched her, planting a big kiss on her cheek when she jumped too close. "Princesses don't run."

"Maybe she'll listen to you. I've told her a hundred times, but she insists on chasing after the Datten princes every chance she gets. She's only four. When she comes of age ..." Victoria sighed, tucking a loose curl behind Elizabeth's ear.

"It might be easier keeping Aaron from chasing her. By then, I'll be king, and my godson listens to me."

Elizabeth clung tighter as her father shifted her to his hip. He kissed her before tapping his cheek. Elizabeth kissed him, and his black hair tickled her cheek.

"Excited for Datten?"

"Yes," Elizabeth replied, nodding.

Edward pressed his forehead against hers and stared at her with his sea-blue eyes. "That's a pretty necklace you're wearing. It matches your eyes."

"It's not just pretty. It's very special," Victoria said.

Elizabeth reached for her mother, and Victoria took her. Edward kissed them both. Before he could leave, Victoria pulled him close, kissing him deeply.

"Ewww," said Elizabeth.

"Are you all right?" Edward asked, still holding onto Victoria.

"Just tired. We'll be here when you get back," Victoria said, putting Elizabeth down.

Elizabeth looked up, and Edward winked before he marched out of the room. She twirled around, trying to keep her skirt spinning. When she looked up, her mother's back was to her—she was looking toward the thrones. Elizabeth then noticed that the guards were no longer there. She spun—the room was empty.

"Mommy?" Elizabeth grabbed her mother's trembling hand.

The great doors banged shut, and her mother's hand squeezed hers so hard it hurt. *They never close those doors.*

Before she could turn to look, Victoria snatched up Elizabeth in her arms and ran for the paintings on the wall behind the thrones. Elizabeth clung to her mother but peeked over her shoulder. King Arthur, her grandfather, stalked across the cold marble. He pursed his lips, furrowed his brows, and set his steely gaze directly on her mother. He looked like a monster. The torches in the room reflected off his sword's strange red blade. Victoria put Elizabeth down, hiding her in her flowing skirts. Victoria pulled a corner of the painting, and to Elizabeth's surprise, the painting opened, revealing a dark tunnel.

"Are you there?" Victoria called into the darkness.

A voice echoed from down the tunnel. "Yes."

Elizabeth heard footsteps on dirt. Victoria picked her up, kissed her on her forehead, and placed her into the passage. "I love you. Be brave!"

The painting slammed shut, leaving Elizabeth engulfed in near total darkness except for the light filtering through the painting itself. She could see the throne room. Victoria ran her hand along the frame and whispered words Elizabeth couldn't make out. A hand suddenly gripped her shoulder and tried to pull her away, but Elizabeth fought it as she continued looking through the enchanted canvas at her mother. Then Victoria's voice rang out.

"You're still holding that grudge, Arthur? Even after I provided *two* generations for your line? Your revenge ends with me. You'll never find her. I've made sure of it."

Victoria didn't run. She stood tall and proud.

"You assume I'm acting alone," Arthur snarled. "You were

always such a silly girl. I could never figure out what my stupid son ever saw in you—other than your figure, of course."

Victoria glanced back at the painting and nodded. Turning back to Arthur, she froze. In the next instant, there was a flash of red steel and the sound of her mother's body meeting the stone floor. Elizabeth couldn't breathe. She stared as her mother's beautiful eyes turned swampy green and a pool of blood spread out beneath her. As the scream finally left Elizabeth's lungs, a pair of powerful arms grabbed her and pulled her deeper into the black tunnel.

CHAPTER I

ALEX

TWELVE YEARS LATER

"**M**ichael! Could you walk any louder?" Alex asked, picking up the arrow that had missed yet another rabbit. "It's hard enough to see them this early in the morning without you *stomping*."

Michael rubbed his face before slapping his cheeks as he tried to wake himself up. His messy black hair and beard stood out against his light copper-colored skin. The large bags under his dark blue eyes highlighted how exhausted he was. "It's not my fault. You know how bad Oliver snores when he's drunk."

"Of course I do. The entire camp heard him. After that performance, he should stop complaining about my nightmares. At least my screams aren't self-inflicted."

"The giant with the red hair was paying—we're lucky we got Oliver home at all. Does Stefan know?"

"He was asleep when I got back to our hut. I'm sure we'll hear about it when we get back to camp." Alex slung her bow on her shoulder and wiped the bloody arrows on her pants before returning them to her quiver. She held up the two rabbits they'd finally caught after an hour of hunting. "Is this enough for an apology?"

"From you? Yes. Stefan's your brother. So can we go back?" Michael asked. Then he whipped his head toward Alex. "Wait. You *told* Stefan we were going hunting, right?"

"Of course." *If telling him in his sleep counts.*

Michael's eyes narrowed, but Alex tossed him the rabbits and strolled up the trail back to camp.

When they arrived, everyone was awake and busy with chores. Beside the kitchen, Thomas was talking to Graham with the supply list in his hands. George had already pulled the old wagon to the stable for the weekly supply run to town, but the horses were inside. The moss-covered huts nearby were silent except for a thundering from the armory that made Alex's teeth chatter and drowned out the sound of the river rushing by the other side of the camp.

"How is Oliver making that much noise? Isn't he hungover?" Alex wondered aloud.

"No, he's still drunk, thanks to you two," a familiar voice said from behind.

Ferflucs.

Alex and Michael turned to find Stefan glaring at them. Michael held up the rabbits. "I'll bring these to Thomas."

"Coward!" Alex shouted as Michael fled.

"Hut. *Now,*" Stefan said, brushing past Alex.

Alex groaned and dropped the bow and arrows off at the armory with Oliver. Walking to the hut, she nodded to her ghostly guardian, someone only she could see. Prince Daniel of Datten had died to protect her and had been with her ever since. She was so used to his ghostly presence that she'd mastered acknowledging him without anyone noticing. At the hut, Stefan held the door and closed it the moment she entered. His usually pale skin was turning red with anger.

"I can explain," Alex said.

"Take off your pendant. I hate yelling at you when you look like a boy."

"How chivalrous of you—yelling at a girl."

Alex reached into her shirt and removed her oval emerald pendant, tossing it on her bed. Stefan glared as the soft green fog did its work, turning her gangly boy body into a curvy feminine one; because she was disguised as a boy so often, her feminine side felt foreign to her. The fog shifted her pale skin back to a natural pinkish hue and finished by replacing short rust-colored hair with flowing chestnut locks. Alex shook her head until they gathered down her back.

"Now tell me: What were you thinking, sneaking into town to get drunk?"

Alex picked at the hem of her shirt, gaze averted. "You know what day it is." *Don't make me say it.*

"Getting drunk won't bring your mother back, Elizabeth."

Alex stiffened. "I *hate* it when you call me that."

"I know, but it gets you talking," Stefan said, his tone softening. He motioned for her to sit on her bed. "You can't get drunk to avoid your nightmares, even if they're bad. People notice. We live out here to keep you safe, so either this reckless behavior stops, or I'll lock you in here at night."

"You wouldn't!" Alex growled.

Stefan leaned down toward her. The sun coming through the window made his brown eyes glisten. His short, fire-red hair stayed perfectly in place as his giant frame stopped mere inches from her face. "I'm the son of Datten's general, and I will do anything to protect you, even if you hate me for it."

I could never hate you.

Alex opened her mouth, but a shout from nearby interrupted her. Stefan bolted for the doorway, Alex following close behind. In an instant, they saw a black-haired man leap off his horse and rush into the camp.

"Ian?" Michael asked, greeting the rider.

"Where's Alex?" Ian asked, panting.

Alex stepped out from behind Stefan.

"Thank goodness!" Ian exclaimed, pulling Alex into a hug upon reaching her. Alex noticed Ian's body was trembling as much as his voice. "A group of Datten knights arrived last night in Kirsh. I didn't worry about it until they weren't in their rooms this morning. Irma overheard—they're looking for someone. Stefan, you have to lock down the camp. Hide her."

"Ferflucs. Could they have followed you?" Stefan asked.

A strong wind surged by, sending Alex's loose hair into her face. Despite trying to keep his voice light with Ian, Stefan's shoulders tightened, and his forehead was sweating. Alex lost track of what Stefan was saying as she struggled to get her hair under control enough to braid it. Her heart pounded so loudly in her ears it was all she could hear until Stefan grabbed her.

"I'm going with Ian to hunt for these men. Put on your pendant, get your bow, and stay with Michael. If anyone comes, don't get scared—get angry. You're more dangerous when you're angry. Last resort—*run*." He turned to Michael, who'd appeared with his and Alex's bows and quivers. "Understand?"

"Yeah. If someone shows up, piss her off so she burns something."

Alex would normally have smacked him for that, but she took the quiver of arrows he handed her.

"I'll take Flash; he's faster," Stefan said.

Breathe. Alex grabbed Stefan's arm. Her voice trembled as her throat went bone dry. "Stefan?" *I'm scared. Don't go.*

He pulled her close. "It'll be fine. This is why you have your pendant, why we practice. Together, you and Michael are lethal. I still think mind reading is one of your gifts because you two seem to share a brain."

I wish. Alex forced a smile.

Stefan kissed the top of her head. "I'll rush back."

George had already fetched her horse. Stefan mounted Flash, followed Ian, and vanished into the Dark Forest.

"What now, Alex?" Thomas asked, joining them.

Alex cracked her knuckles.

Calm down. No more wind.

"Lock down the camp. Thomas, Benjamin, get the fire put out. Hunter, secure the huts. George, William, handle the horses. The rest of us are on patrol. Oliver, you take the deep forest with Graham. Michael and I will take the riverside."

THEY STALKED along the Darren River, which flowed past the camp behind the stable. As Alex played with the pendant around her neck, heavy winds made it hard for them to listen for anything out of the ordinary.

"It's always weird when you wear that," Michael commented.

"Why?"

"Because you're not you. My best friend is a strong and beautiful maiden. This boy doesn't cut it."

"Thank you," Alex said, smiling. "You always know how to make me feel better."

They padded through the trees.

"Do you sense anything?"

"No," Alex said. She appreciated how accepting the lads were now about her *gifts,* as Stefan called them. She'd inherited them from her mother, and she suspected they were the reason her mother had been killed. It was the only explanation she'd ever come up with that made any sense. The powers had first manifested when she was nine. One new power appeared each year, as if they spaced themselves out to allow her to adjust to each one. She could predict things through dreams, control weather, grow plants, and even start fires. Whenever she lost control of her emotions, in a good or bad way, unusual things happened.

"*Stop* being scared. Your powers are distracting me," Michael teased, poking her.

To the camp, Stefan was her brother, but Michael always behaved more like her actual brother. He was the only person she trusted as much as Stefan. Alex was thankful to have him, especially today. The reason Stefan could run to town was because he knew Michael would protect her—with his life if needed.

Alex patted Michael's arm, and they stilled when a branch snapped. Michael pulled her behind a bunch of old-growth pine trees, and from there, they watched a fair-skinned blond man wander into the area.

"Was he at the inn last night?" Michael asked.

Alex shook her head. *I'd have remembered him.* The man was tall and muscular, and though his clothing appeared to be of high quality, it was as disheveled as his beard. He'd been traveling for some time.

Suddenly, the man spun around and glanced toward the pine trees.

Does he see us?

His eyes were a brighter blue than anyone else's in town, but there was something familiar about them. Alex's breathing quickened, and a gust of wind rushed by and tousled their hair.

"Calm down. You're getting worked up, and that means you're losing your grip on your magic. If you don't get your powers under control, you'll give us away," Michael said, patting Alex's leg.

She motioned for him to flank their uninvited visitor from behind then returned her gaze to the man.

His sword had a golden handle, but his satchel was made of simple worn leather. He moved stealthily—like Stefan had taught her to do when stalking a target. He had to be one of the knights. *I can do this.* Alex drew an arrow from her quiver, nocked it, and slid the bow between two trees, breathing sharply.

"You're trespassing," Alex barked. "Identify yourself and we might let you live."

The man turned in a full circle before stopping to face the trees. He raised his hands in surrender. "Please, don't hurt me. I lost my way when I argued with my friends. One is a rather angry drunk. If you could point me to town, I'll be on my way."

Alex looked him up and down—his legs stood sturdy, and his hand hovered over his sword. She could see that their conversation was distracting him, so she kept going while Michael sneaked around behind him.

"What's your name?"

"Come out and I'll tell you."

Alex exhaled. Michael shook his head at her, warning her to stay put. Ignoring him, Alex let her bowstring go slack and sidestepped out into view, keeping her arrow nocked on her bow.

"Now," Alex said evenly, "tell me your name."

"Aaron. You're small for a sentry."

Sentry? You are *a knight.*

"Why are you here, *Aaron*? We're a half day's walk from Kirsh in the daylight, so I doubt you ended up here on foot after drinking."

Aaron smirked. "Maybe I'm good in the woods." He

11

whipped around and drew his sword as Michael crept out of the bushes. "Two against one? That doesn't seem like an honorable fight. Well ... one and a half." Aaron pointed his sword at Michael as Alex drew back her bowstring.

"Drop the sword or I'll shoot."

Aaron turned and stared at her. Even though Alex *knew* Aaron could only see the boy version of her, his eyes never left hers—the only part of her that didn't change.

Stop staring at me.

He continued to do so until Alex's arm trembled from the bowstring. She blinked, and in that instant, he struck Michael's sword. The hit was hard enough to make Michael yip and drop it before Aaron returned his attention to Alex.

Wind suddenly began whipping around so that Aaron and Michael were forced to shield their eyes. Even as Alex's loose hair drifted across her face, she released the bowstring. Aaron shouted as he reeled, staring wide-eyed at the arrow protruding from his shoulder. When he didn't drop the sword, Alex nocked another arrow.

"You shot me!" Aaron exclaimed, incredulous, his features marked by pain and something else Alex couldn't identify. "I know who you're *hiding*. We don't want to hurt her."

Alex felt her face drain of color, and her palms became slick. She struggled to keep her bow up. As Aaron stepped toward her, she lost her grip on the bowstring and fired again. Before either could make another move, Michael struck Aaron on the head with a thick branch, and he collapsed. Alex tossed her bow and arrows aside and caught Aaron before he could further impale himself on the arrows sticking out of his body.

"Are you okay?" Michael asked.

Alex could only stare at Aaron as she replied, "Michael, what were you thinking? Now we have to carry him back to camp."

CHAPTER 2

ALEX

Alex and Michael lugged an unconscious Aaron back to camp, only to find it was already locked. Potted bushes and trees now covered the unnatural coloring and open spaces, the stable was closed up, and they'd extinguished the central fire pit and hidden the cooking rack.

It's always so creepy locked down.

The stable door rattled slightly as George and Thomas slipped out and rushed to Michael and Alex.

"Ferflucs. What did you do?" Thomas asked.

Alex and Michael looked at each other while George took Alex's place supporting Aaron.

"He knows who we're hiding, so she shot him," Michael said, letting Thomas take his side. Standing rigid as a tree trunk, Michael clutched Alex's bow, knuckles white.

"What do we do with him?" George asked.

Alex pointed. "Stick him in the empty hut and watch him until I get there. I need my supplies to get those arrows out before they get infected. It'll be easier while he's unconscious."

Alex sprinted to gather her healing supplies from under her

bed, and in minutes, she was in the hut with Aaron. George had laid Aaron on a bed, making sure his wounded shoulder was near the edge and therefore easily accessible.

"Thank you," Alex said as George left the hut.

"Are you sure you're safe?" Thomas asked, running his finger on Alex's forearm. Alex sighed; they'd been down this road before, and it hadn't ended well for Thomas when Stefan found out.

"I'll be fine." Alex pointed to the door where Michael had walked in with a pail of fresh water and a shirt. Thomas nodded and closed the door behind him.

Alex laid her bundle of supplies on the second bed and grabbed her hunting knife. She cut down the center of Aaron's shirt and along the sleeves, taking extra care to not snag any of the fabric around the arrows as she removed the pieces. When she kneeled to examine the arrows, Aaron jerked violently as her fingers grazed the shaft of the first arrow.

"I hope he's right-handed," Michael said, squatting beside Alex.

You're making jokes now? Despite herself, she grinned.

"Which arrows did you use?"

"Bodkins. This was defense—not dinner."

"*Still,* everyone here runs when they see you with a bow." Michael stood up and positioned himself at Aaron's head.

Alex rolled her eyes. "That was an accident. I was seven when I shot Graham. He should be over it by now."

Alex scanned Aaron's chest for injuries; a few new scratches and some old scars. Next, Alex ran her hands through his soft golden hair and checked his head where there was blood. She found an old scar on his hairline and a fresh cut from where Michael hit him. *It isn't too bad.* She soaked a rag and rubbed the wound clean before moving back to the arrows.

Uncorking the bottle of whiskey among her supplies, Alex took a swig before exhaling and dumping some on Aaron's shoulder.

"This will get messy."

"I know." Michael grimaced, placing one hand on Aaron's uninjured shoulder and the other on his bicep to hold him down.

Alex successfully removed the first arrow. Aaron moaned and shuddered under Michael's grip. Alex grabbed some clean rags and moved Michael's hand into position over the first wound.

One down.

Alex cracked her neck and moved on to the second arrow. Aaron wrenched beneath her when she gave it a gentle tug, but it didn't budge. He moaned and stilled. *Couldn't have dropped the sword.*

"It's stuck against the bone," Alex said, frowning at Michael.

"Can you get it?"

"I *think* so—but you're going to have to hold him still."

Michael leaned on Aaron, pressing him into the bed. Alex rested her knee on his bicep, placed her fist flush with his skin, and gripped the shaft. She could feel the heat of his body and wondered if it was always that hot or if she was taking too long. Alex braced herself against his other bicep. Squeezing, Alex pulled hard, and the arrow came out. Michael quickly applied pressure to slow the bleeding, and Alex mixed up some herbs and placed them into the wounds before wrapping it tightly.

Shoulder handled for the moment, Alex moved to check his head again for more blood but paused at the scars on his arms and torso: a line of small circular scars on his hip and back, a gash on his bicep, a healed burn on his shoulder and chest. As she studied his face, something stirred deep inside her. A memory appeared of a giant garden and a smiling blond boy with sky-blue eyes. He handed her a bouquet with a lily in the middle.

Lilies ... my favorite.

She had thanked him—kissed him.

No, it can't be.

Alex brought her fingers to her lips as she stared at the man. When she looked up, Daniel was hovering over Aaron with a mischievous smile. She was so used to his ghostly presence that she hadn't noticed they had the same hair and eyes. Daniel looked at her, still smiling, and pointed to the floor.

Daniel, no.

Michael, unaware of Alex's phantom guard, grabbed the pieces of shirt and Aaron's satchel off the floor.

"Alex, feel this!" He held the shirt bits out to her, snapping her back to reality. Rubbing the soft, expensive fabric between her fingers, she looked at Aaron again. With Daniel watching, Alex traced the line of circle scars on his hip. She gently rolled him over to count them. As her fingers grazed the fourth scar, another memory flooded her mind.

I was four. You were seven. We were playing in the stables, and Daniel wanted to scare us, but he scared the horse instead. You fell on a pitchfork, and Daniel rushed you to the doctor. Our mothers were furious. Aaron—my Aaron.

"Let me see his bag." Alex laid him down then ripped the bag from Michael's hand a moment later. Her hands trembled, and she struggled with the clasps.

Calm down and focus.

Succeeding, Alex opened the satchel. Her heart hammered, knowing what she'd find. She pulled out a book, a carrot, a clean shirt. Then she stopped and let loose a long, shaky breath.

"What's wrong?" Michael asked. He went ashen when she pulled a gold crown out of the satchel.

"Alex! You shot the Crown Prince of Datten. That's treason. They'll hang you."

Alex swallowed as she stuffed the crown back into the bag and tossed it under the bed as if it had bitten her. She began organizing her supplies and clenched the bundle to stop her hands from shaking.

Alex demanded her courage to come as she turned to Michael. "It'll be fine. We'll worry about it when Stefan gets back. For now, I need to stitch—"

Shouting outside diverted Alex's attention. She dropped her supplies back on the spare bed and hurried outside with Michael, but before they could catch their breath, there was more shouting.

Oliver and Graham had arrived and were dragging a disheveled man behind them. They'd bound his wrists with rope. His robe was filthy, his brown hair as overgrown and snarled as the woods surrounding them. Alex looked at Michael, but he shrugged.

How many of them are there?

"Where is Stefan when I need him?" Alex muttered.

"We found him stalking the edge of the camp," Oliver said.

Alex strode toward the man but stopped in her tracks when she saw his tanned face. The man had her emerald eyes.

"Hello, Elizabeth," he said.

"Alex, why did he call you *Elizabeth*?" Oliver asked, pushing the prisoner toward her. "Who are you, and what do you want?"

"My name is Megesti, and I'm looking for her." His eyes remained fixed on Alex. She froze. Daniel's words of warning from twelve years ago echoed in her brain.

"Wait," Michael said, suddenly leaving his post to flank Alex. "You're wearing the pendant. How does he *know*?"

"Megesti? As in Datten's apprentice sorcerer?" Alex asked.

"What does the royal sorcerer want with you?" Oliver asked, tightening his grip on the prisoner.

"Hopefully, he's come to take her back," Graham said, staring at Alex. "She belongs with them so things stop catching on fire."

"Catch your tongue, Graham. No one asked you," Michael spat as he squeezed Alex's shoulder.

If we have the prince and the sorcerer, then there's at least one more. Time for a family reunion, Stefan.

"Put him in the hut so he can watch over his friend. Michael and I will go out again," Alex said. "I doubt they came alone."

CHAPTER 3
ALEX

No king would send their only heir out without a guard, even to a town like Kirsh. He'll have the general with him, and even here we know Datten's general is the most fearsome man in all of Torian.

Alex tugged her necklace chain as they walked in silence for what felt like hours, afraid she might stir up emotions that would give them away. It was challenging enough to move through the forest unseen, but, given who they were hunting, now it was doubly challenging.

They'd stopped at the river for a drink when Michael gripped Alex's arm and pulled her behind some bushes. The raging river would mask their ragged breaths as they crouched. A minute later, another man appeared, moving with a stealthy agility the likes of which Alex had never seen before. Her hiding spot felt woefully inadequate. His clothes matched those of Aaron, but his appearance differed from the others. He was immense and intimidating even from behind. His graying red hair was so thick it stayed in place despite his movements. After surveying the area, he followed the river downstream.

"He wasn't that intimidating in the bar last night," Michael whispered.

"No one is when they're buying your drinks."

"Does he look a bit like Stefan? Same coloring and unusual red hair."

"He should," Alex replied, her voice strained.

"What?"

He deserves the truth. "Stefan's last name *is* Wafner."

"Wafner," Michael repeated. For a moment, his face remained blank, impassive. Then he understood all too well. His eyes widened. "Stefan's father is General Wafner? But that means he's here for you, for revenge. We have to get you away."

"It's a lie. I'll explain later, but for now, you have to trust me."

Michael squeezed her arm and nodded. Alex sighed in relief.

They crept out as silently as possible. Rising, Alex wiped her sweaty palms on her pants just as a branch snapped behind her. She spun to shush Michael but found herself staring instead at the general, who stood between them.

Before she could scream, he ripped her bow from her shoulder and shoved her into a nearby bush. Michael tried to unsheathe his blade, but in the blink of an eye, the general had grabbed him by the shirt collar and thrust him up in the air. Alex struggled to free herself from the branches holding her.

"Where is she?" The general's voice came out more like an animal growl than a human voice. It made Alex consider staying in the bush.

"I don't know!" Michael spat.

"Where is she?" the general demanded again. His face was stiff and calculating as he tightened his grip on Michael's shirt.

At the sound of the gasping and spluttering that followed,

Alex took courage, longing to protect Michael, and struggled to her feet.

"Alex. Run!" Michael gasped.

"General, stop!" Alex begged.

Michael fought to release himself, but the general was unyielding.

"Jerome, you're killing him," Alex said.

Lip trembling, she walked toward him. The general thrust his blade at Alex as he glared at her carefully. She dug her fingernails into her palms, eyes glistening as she met his gaze. Then, swallowing her terror and straightening her back, she reached beneath her shirt and clutched her pendant.

Fine. You need proof? Here it is.

"He ordered you to hide me. Tell no one where I was. Never breathe a word. When the time was right, Datten would come for me."

It was Daniel's last order to her and the Wafners on the day he left her in their protection. His father's general was the ideal place to hide her, and for twelve years, she'd recited those words every night, knowing she might need them one day.

"Princess," he whispered. His sword and Michael's knees hit the forest floor simultaneously. Michael coughed and gasped as Alex rushed to his side, dropping to the ground.

"Are you all right?" Alex asked, brushing the leaves off him.

"What did you mean, '*Datten would come*'?" Michael wheezed, eyes on Alex, though his question was directed at the general. Then, without waiting for the general's reply, he added, "He called you princess. What's going on?"

Alex tried to block out the sounds of the general moving closer to her, taking a protective stance at her side as Stefan would. She focused on Michael. Trembling, she reached for the words she had known she might someday need to recite. "I'm sorry. Everything you've been told about my past is a lie."

Heart racing, she had expected Michael to storm off, to leave her. Instead, she soon felt hands squeezing hers. When she dared to look up, prepared to plead for forgiveness, she met his dark blue eyes and saw warmth in them.

Michael tugged her hands. "What's my past?"

Alex hiccupped. "We don't know. I found you hurt ... and alone."

"Right."

"What does that have to do with my past?" Alex wondered aloud. "I've betrayed you, betrayed your trust."

"It means," Michael began, "I won't hold your past against you because you never held mine against me. No matter what happens—today, tomorrow, forever—we're family. Whatever this is, you're not alone."

Alex sobbed, and Michael pulled her to him. Kneeling on the cold, wet ground, Alex released the burden of twelve years of lying, relieved to know that even if the others hated her, she'd survive because Michael didn't.

When she pulled back from Michael, she saw the general standing to her left, hand outstretched.

"Still a man of few words?" Alex asked, accepting his hand before he pulled her to her feet.

"You hear more when you talk less," he said.

Jerome held his hand out to Michael next. Michael shot Alex an uncertain look, but she quickly nodded reassuringly. A few seconds later, Michael was beside Alex, gathering up her bow and arrows. In all the commotion, Alex had allowed several of the arrow shafts to get damaged.

"Graham's going to throw a fit," Alex said, as she refilled her quiver.

"Why are you here?" Michael asked, holding Alex's bow for her.

"It's a long story and not mine to tell. We should find my companions."

"We're holding them captive in our camp," Alex said.

"Pardon?" Jerome asked.

Michael smirked. "Your companions weren't as skilled as you. Though Alex did shoot one."

Jerome's head snapped toward Alex, his eyes wide. "Whom did you shoot?"

Alex avoided his gaze.

"The blond one," Michael said.

Jerome gasped, furious.

"I didn't know who he was when I shot him," Alex said. "Aaron attacked us. I reacted. It's what *my* Wafner taught me."

Alex felt the general's eyes bore into her as they marched back to the camp. Alex entered first, and the moment the general stepped out of the woods, everyone rushed out of their huts carrying half the armory.

STEFAN'S ARM ran across Alex's shoulders as he steered her toward the fire pit. Michael appeared on her other side. Megesti, Aaron, and Jerome sat on the opposite side. Thomas appeared with a big pot, and Alex got up to help, but when she reached for the handle, another pair of hands beat her to it.

"I can help," Aaron said, holding the pot while Thomas set up the cooking spit. Then Aaron hooked it to the spit and swung it over the fire.

"You didn't come here for a quiet stroll in the woods. What's changed?" Stefan asked.

Never one for small talk, are you, Stefan? You barely said hello to your father after twelve years because you're too busy keeping the prince at least an arm's length away from me. As if I care about how handsome he is despite that stupid beard.

"Her grandfather died last week," Aaron said, glaring at Stefan. "We left months ago to find you, Elizabeth. Arthur's been sick for years, but it was clear he wouldn't last much longer. King Edward, your father, sent us to find you—hopefully before your seventeenth birthday."

He's dead? Alex wondered whether he had taken his secret to the grave with him.

"Why this birthday?" Michael asked.

"It's an important age for sorcerers," Megesti explained. "It's when our powers manifest."

"You're late." Alex laughed. "I've had my powers since I was nine."

"*Nine?*" Megesti's mouth dropped open. "How? What happened?"

Alex and Michael looked at each other in silence then at the ground, avoiding Stefan.

"She died," Stefan said.

"I *almost* died," Alex said.

Thanks to a certain royal apparition who is always in the right place at the right time when I get into trouble.

"You didn't see yourself." Stefan turned back to Megesti. "Alex and Michael were playing on the ice of the Darren River, and she fell through. We found them quickly, but Alex's heart had stopped, and she was turning blue. Ian revived her, but after we warmed her up, she was ... different. Every year, another gift manifested, and now any time she gets emotional, something happens."

"The way the fire erupted when she yelled at the others for fighting when you arrived?" Aaron asked.

"Yes. If she's scared, the wind comes. Sad, it rains suddenly.

Happy, plants around her bloom or grow—even in the dead of winter," Michael said.

"Sometimes I vanish too, but you have to watch my temper. When I get mad, things catch on fire."

Stefan groaned. "That we learned the hard way. We got into a fight in town. A storm appeared out of nowhere, lightning hit the mill, and it burned to the ground."

"That isn't surprising," Megesti said. "Your mother was talented. We knew you'd become powerful too, which is why we wanted to find you. However, we never considered you'd have powers already."

"There's more, isn't there?" Aaron asked, looking at Alex.

"Spend the night; you'll experience her nightmares first-hand," Michael said.

"Experience is putting it mildly." Oliver laughed, coming over with some vegetables for the pot. "This time of year, they're terrifying. The screams wake the entire camp."

"At least my snoring doesn't keep the camp up," Alex said.

Oliver glared at Alex before turning back to Megesti and Aaron. "It isn't just the screaming. Everyone gets nightmares, but, knowing who she is—what she saw—I think hers are worse than ours. It's the knowing things. It's disturbing."

"Knowing things?" Jerome asked.

"That's enough talking about me," Alex said, crossing her arms and giving her friends a warning look, which they ignored.

"We want to hear about the predictions," Aaron said. He gave Alex a wide smile.

"Alex knows things," Michael said. "She'll have these weird dreams, sometimes the same one for weeks at a time, and then one day, she'll know something she shouldn't. That's why we moved the camp. She went on about it for weeks until Ian ordered us to move. Not a week later, a tremendous storm came down from the mountains, and the old camp was underwater for months. We'd have drowned."

"That's enough," Stefan ordered.

Thank you, Alex thought, squirming where she sat. "I'd like to hear more about why you're here." Alex turned her attention to the Datten men.

"I thought that was *obvious*. We're taking you home," Aaron said.

"With your grandfather dead, we believe Warren is safe," Jerome said.

"How'd you find us?" Stefan asked.

"As we said, we've been searching for months. When we left St. Clement, Megesti sensed something," Aaron said.

"Sensed?" Michael asked.

"Sorcerers can sense other sorcerers with the same powers. We call them lines. Some can also sense kin," Megesti explained. "Her mother was my aunt."

"Why didn't you sense her at the inn last night?" Michael asked.

"I was asleep," Megesti said, making Aaron snort.

"If you could sense me, why did you wait?"

"Our line doesn't have the power to find people. As kin, I could sense you but only if you had your powers and were nearby. You shouldn't have had powers until recently."

Alex stared at Megesti, and recognition hit her like a charging steed. "You were there that day. You took me to Prince Daniel."

Megesti nodded.

Aaron's head whipped to the side. "You did what?"

Jerome moved to grab Aaron but missed. Aaron leaped from the log he was on and tackled Megesti. "You witnessed the ferflucsing murder?"

"Now is not the time, Aaron," Megesti replied as he tried to free himself.

"Not the time? You let Edward stand beside that man for twelve years! How do you live with yourself?" Aaron gripped Megesti's shoulders to the point of leaving bruises.

"Not here," Jerome snapped, and at this, a silence fell over the camp.

This is your fault. Say something.

"When do we leave?" Alex asked. "I'd like one last night here. We need to assign new leaders and organize everything."

"That will be fine," Megesti said.

Alex opened her mouth to speak, but then she looked away.

Aaron groaned, avoiding looking at Megesti. "Whatever it is, ask."

Alex hesitated. "What's he like?"

"What is who like?"

Alex squeezed her hands between her knees. "My father."

Aaron grimaced, and then his features softened. "Edward is fantastic."

"You catch Her Highness up on King Edward while Megesti and I go find the horses," Jerome said.

"We'll help," George said. He looked at Stefan, who nodded and patted Alex's shoulder before following George.

CHAPTER 4
ALEX

The more Aaron told Alex about her father, the more questions she had. Aaron obliged, answering every question and telling her endless stories about Warren and Datten. As they talked, Alex inched closer to Aaron. He spoke so openly with her and knew so much about her father; she felt unusually at ease with him already. When Alex started laughing at a funny story of Aaron's, Stefan wedged himself between them.

"What's so funny?" Stefan asked, turning to Aaron.

"Aaron was telling me about the time he let the royal pigs into the castle. It took them a week to find them."

"Was your father there?" Stefan asked Alex.

"No. Edward was in Warren. This was in Datten," Aaron said.

"Then I don't see why you're telling it." Stefan gave Aaron a scowl Alex knew too well.

Behave, Stefan. She pinched him.

"I should go see if Jerome needs help." Aaron stood and

marched toward where Jerome was looking over the camp's weapons, frowning.

"That was rude," Alex said, pushing Stefan off the log as she stood up.

"We need to pick a new leader. Come on," Stefan said, gripping her elbow before pulling her toward their hut. Once inside, Alex dropped onto her bed while Stefan shut the door.

"I think Oliver should be the leader," she said. "He's not afraid to make hard decisions, and he gets along with Graham. For a second-in-command, I was thinking about Michael or Thomas, though selfishly I want Michael to come with us."

Alex's bed groaned under Stefan's weight as he sat down beside her. "You need to stay away from Aaron."

"I thought we were here to pick the next leaders."

"We will. As soon as you promise to stay away from him."

Alex stared at Stefan. "In what dream world did you think I was going to keep listening to you once everyone found out you aren't my brother?"

"I don't trust him."

"We were children together. Our parents are friends. I know him fine."

"I don't like the way he looks at you," Stefan insisted. "He's a prince. They don't ask. *They take.*"

"Yes, he's a prince, but he's also my father's godson. I'm not concerned about Aaron. This conversation is over."

"You mean His Highness," Stefan said.

Alex laughed. "I'm not worried about Crown Prince Aaron Edward Johnathon Arthur of Datten, especially with your father five steps away. Why aren't we picking new leaders so you can bond with your father? Or did you do that when you were looking for the horses? Did you cry?" Alex poked his shoulder.

"Wafner men don't cry," Stefan said, rising from the bed.

29

"Ian said you cried after you saved me when I fell through the ice," Alex teased, narrowing her eyes.

"Crying from relief doesn't count."

"Admit it—that scared you." Stefan opened his mouth to reply, but Alex pointed at him. "And I don't mean being scared about failing at your duty."

"Fine," Stefan sighed, exasperated. "I cried when you survived your ice swim because I care about you after raising you. You're not blood, but you'll be my sister until we die. Which is why I need you to stay away from Aaron."

Alex covered her face and groaned as she fell back onto her bed.

"Fine. I promise to be careful around him."

That's all you're getting.

Stefan took Alex's hand and pulled her to her feet before kissing the top of her head.

"Softie," she said.

A metal clang rang out through the camp.

"Dinnertime," Stefan said.

"But we didn't pick leaders," Alex said.

"Of course we did—Oliver and Michael. I agree. Now let's go eat your last meal at the camp before you become a *beautiful* princess."

Alex threw a pillow at him before he fled from the hut, laughing over his shoulder as she emerged. Alex stuck her tongue out at him before moving to sit between Michael and Thomas. Dinner was longer and louder than usual as the lads talked over each other to ask questions of their Datten guests about castle life, the town of Datten, and even what the king was like. Aaron, Jerome, and Megesti answered everyone's questions while Alex watched.

All those years worrying for nothing.

Once dinner finished, the hair on Alex's neck stood at

attention. She had expected Thomas to be staring at her, but when she turned around, she discovered someone else watching her: Aaron. Her cheeks flushed from the intensity of his gaze.

Just then, Stefan whistled to the lads. Once everyone gathered, he spoke. "I have decided the one who is best suited for the job is Oliver, with Michael as his second." Everyone started talking at once. "None of that," Stefan continued. He beckoned Oliver and Michael to come with him and left.

Alex walked over to where Aaron, Jerome, and Megesti stood some ways away from the rest of the group. "Thank you for agreeing to leave tomorrow. There are two empty huts for you near the stable. They aren't fancy, but they have clean beds. It'll give Stefan time to explain everything to Oliver and His *Highness* time to finish the wish list for the rewards he promised."

"Your tone seems to imply I won't be able to get the goods," Aaron remarked.

"Hey, you're the one making promises you have no authority to make," Alex said, shrugging.

Aaron playfully nudged her with his elbow. "Next time, I'll let the horde have you."

Alex laughed and shook her head. "General, is he always this difficult?"

"No. This is his best behavior," Megesti replied with a chuckle before the general could speak.

Aaron clenched his jaw, turning to Megesti. "Not all of us can keep our truths hidden as easily as you. I'm going to check on Thunder."

"Is he going to be like this the whole way to Warren?" Alex asked, brows furrowed.

"It's fine. My father will take us with a spell. Mortals call it 'cracking,'" Megesti said.

"Because of the sound," Jerome said.

"Whenever you're ready," Megesti continued, "Aaron will summon my father, and then we'll be there in mere moments. The royal family of Datten can summon my father."

Alex's eyes widened.

"Don't worry, it doesn't hurt," Jerome reassured her.

"But I suspect Aaron's anger will last much longer," Megesti said. "He hides it well, but Datten's legendary temper is a part of our crown prince. I wish he'd let me check his shoulder."

"What do you mean?" Alex asked.

"He wouldn't let me help him. I healed his head because he was still unconscious. Stubborn as an ox, that one," Megesti said.

"Let me try. I've dealt with many stubborn patients here. I had planned to stitch it but got interrupted when you arrived."

"Good luck!" Megesti chuckled.

Everyone was off doing their chores, so Alex returned to her hut. They'd scattered their meager possessions on their beds to pack. Alex had a worn copy of *The Iliad* that Stefan had gifted her for her thirteenth birthday, her favorite cloak, and a few books on Warren's history and laws, the culture of Torian kingdoms, and, her least favorite, *Etiquette for the Noble Lady*. Picking up her healer supplies, she tossed her books into her satchel and left the hut. A short while later, Alex found Aaron in the stable. Stopping just outside, she watched him for several seconds.

He's different here—normal—like a boy from town. Cute even.

"It's rude to stare, princess."

Alex leaned against the doorway, smiling nervously. "Sorry. It startled me how normal you look brushing your horse."

"Normal?" he asked, mirroring her smile. "Do I look *strange* to you?"

"I never imagined a prince would come to Kirsh. You aren't what I expected," Alex said.

Aaron's smile vanished. "I'm usually not what people expect of a prince." He turned back to his horse. Alex stepped closer and reached for his arm but stopped.

"Aaron—" *Can I call you Aaron?* "I didn't mean it like that. I'll never be the princess people expect to see, so I understand what that feels like. I guess I just expected a prince to be more pompous, afraid to get his hands dirty. You seem perfectly capable of doing things for yourself. Prefer it even."

"Thunder's important to me. I'm ... particular about my horse."

"I understand." Alex dug out a carrot from the bin and held it out to him. Aaron accepted it.

Alex patted Thunder, and he nudged her appreciatively. Then she headed a few stalls down to where Flash was already stamping and whinnying.

"Calm down, boy. You're still my favorite," Alex whispered, pressing her head to Flash's and feeding him his carrot.

"What brought you in here after me?" This time, Aaron was leaning against a beam, watching her. "Dying to be alone with me again?"

"There he is," Alex said, rolling her eyes.

"Who?"

"The pompous prince I expected to see when you first spoke. Do the maidens in Datten find this act appealing?"

"They do," Aaron replied. He tossed his head back, sending his hair flying around.

"What sheltered lives they must lead. But, no, your *royal full-of-yourselfness,* Megesti informed me you refused medical attention, so I came to invite you to see our healer. Your shoulder needs stitches."

"Fine, seeing as it was your camp that injured me. I'll allow your healer to see me."

Alex smiled. "Perfect. We'll go to your hut."

"Wait, *you're* the healer?"

Alex pointed at him. "If you make a joke about me having a soft touch, I'll skewer you like a rabbit."

Aaron was silent for a moment, regarding her. "I've never had a girl healer."

Alex blinked. "There are no women healers?" she asked.

"Warren has them but not Datten. There are limitations to what a woman may do in Datten."

"*May* do?" Alex spat, failing to hide her scowl.

"I don't agree with it. That's just how Datten is."

"Well, I've lived out here for years. You'll find I have a rather diverse skill set. I'm more than a mere princess."

"Interesting." Aaron stepped closer. "What sort of skill set?"

Stefan's words hit her. *Stay away from Aaron.*

"All *you* need to know is that I can help with your shoulder."

"Not even a hint?"

Alex effected a look of stoic disinterest for several moments until Aaron took the hint. "You're no fun. Lead the way, healer."

Alex sent Aaron, laden with her bundle of supplies, to the hut he and Jerome would sleep in while she fetched a pail of hot water. Arriving, she sighed, thankful someone had changed the bloody sheets. Aaron was watching her from the bed.

"Shirt off," she instructed.

"If I don't comply, will you cut it off?"

Alex almost dropped the mortar as she ground up some herbs. "I'm sorry about that. And for shooting you."

Aaron dropped his shirt on the bed, and Alex began examining his shoulder. Aaron winced when Alex's fingers touched his skin, but she quickly removed the bloody bandage and dipped a clean one into the hot water.

"This will sting," she warned before pressing against the wound. Aaron sucked his teeth and clenched his jaw. "Sorry," Alex whispered.

Alex pretended not to see the pain on his face as she continued working on him. Aaron frequently gripped the bed while Alex cleaned out the wound. As Alex stitched his wound shut, pressed the ground-up herbs around it, and replaced the bandage, Aaron clenched his teeth and looked away.

Afterward, Aaron examined his shoulder and thanked her.

"It's the least I could do," Alex replied, "since *I* shot you."

"You had good reason to," Aaron said, resting his hand on her arm. The look in his eyes simultaneously made Alex feel hot and queasy. The touch of his hand somehow burned like fire and sent a shiver through her entire body.

"I should go pack," she said, stumbling out of the hut.

CHAPTER 5
ALEX

The horizon glowed orange as the sun rose over the tree-lined mountaintops, casting golden rays throughout the camp. Alex pulled Aaron's cloak tighter to ward off the chilly morning air. He'd put it on her when she shivered during their late-night talk. She couldn't sleep after her nightmare, and Aaron had been happy to answer all her questions about her father in private. Stefan didn't comment about the cloak and just slid his arm around her shoulders.

"We should go before it gets late," Alex said to Stefan. They'd spent the previous night saying goodbye to everyone, and she couldn't handle any more. The Datten men brought all the horses over.

"I'll take your bag," Stefan said, reaching for Alex's satchel, but Jerome beat him to it.

"Thank you, General Wafner," Alex said.

"You may call me Jerome, Your Highness." He tied her bag to his horse.

"Alex, Elizabeth, Your Highness. What do I call you now?" Stefan asked.

"If you remain in Warren, you'll address her as Her Highness Princess Elizabeth Katrina Alexandria," Megesti said.

"Um, no, he won't. I'll always be Alex to you. In formal settings, we can go with Your Highness."

"In a castle, most settings are formal," Jerome said.

"Not for me," Alex said.

"You'll do many great things, princess," Megesti said. "But some traditions are unavoidable. Your choice of clothing, having guards, a lady's maid—"

"Oh, I know," Alex gasped.

Michael laughed, startling the horses. "Sorry. I'm still adjusting to you being royalty. Picturing you in a dress—even the plain dresses the lower nobility wear when they come through Kirsh—is too much."

Alex noticed Aaron and Jerome looking Michael up and down. He was dressed in his best clothes and carrying a bag. He'd even brushed his hair.

"You don't laugh at the princess," Jerome scolded.

"Michael, what are you doing?" Alex handed Flash's reins to Stefan and went to Michael.

"Coming with you," Michael replied. "I've known you since we were little. You saved my life. I'm not about to abandon you because you're royalty. You're still Alex to me. You'll have to act proper now, but you already boss me around as it is. So, if you'll have me, I'd like to come."

Alex hugged Michael with such force that she almost knocked him over. "Yes! You're my best friend. I wanted you to come but couldn't ask that of you."

"I'm not Stefan, but I'll find some way to be useful."

Alex recognized the look of relief and excitement on

Michael's face. She squeezed him harder as tears rolled down her cheek.

I won't let anyone send you away.

"You and Oliver assigned a new second, right?" Stefan asked.

"We picked Graham," Michael said.

Alex wrinkled her nose and scowled. "Of all people, you pick Graham?"

Michael shrugged.

Megesti nodded to Aaron. "One more."

"Merlock, as Crown Prince of Datten, I summon you," Aaron ordered.

A loud crack erupted through the camp, causing the horses to stomp and act up. A man dressed in a worn gray cloak appeared. He spoke in a deep, rumbling voice. "You summoned me, Your Highness?"

Why do you feel familiar? Is that what Megesti meant about sensing kin? Alex swallowed as she released Michael. Aaron had told her Merlock was over a century old, but the man looked young enough to be Megesti's brother.

"Elizabeth." Merlock bowed and then gazed at her. "I should have known; daughters of the Cassandra line all look identical."

The daughters of who?

Stefan brought Flash to Alex.

"We're all from the lines of Cassandra and Merlin," Megesti said.

Even more confused, Alex looked at Merlock and Megesti. *Who are Cassandra and Merlin?*

"History lessons can wait," Merlock said. He stepped toward Alex, but Stefan blocked his path. Stefan's protection calmed her. After a few moments, she mounted Flash and tried to emulate Aaron's stance.

The next thing she knew, Aaron squeezed his horse between hers and Stefan's. "Are you ready?"

I don't think I'll ever be ready.

Alex nodded anyway.

"Merlock, take us to Warren," Aaron said.

Megesti cleared his throat and pointed at Aaron. He took his crown out and placed it on his head. Then Aaron leaned toward Alex. "You're going to love this."

Alex exhaled, and then a crack sounded, taking them all away.

ALEX SQUINTED at the sunlight reflecting off the seawater below. The Dark Forest was gone. Merlock had brought them to an escarpment on the opposite side of Torian that overlooked Warren and the Oreean Sea. Alex and Michael gasped at the sight of the city leading to the sea. The sprawling town was filled with colorful and unique houses at the base of the escarpment, and a lighthouse sat off to one side on a lower cliff face. Alex's gaze followed the lines of streets, halting at a ship bobbing in the sea. Only then did she spot the four massive piers that jutted into the water, each with large boats tied to them.

I remember the pier.

"Welcome home, Your Highness," Megesti said.

Home. My home with my father and my people.

Alex's heart quickened, but then a hand patted her leg, and she looked up—Michael. Smiling gratefully, her gaze then shifted to the castle behind him. It was immense, and the sunlight reflecting from the sea painted bright undulating patterns on massive towers. Alex shut her eyes and breathed. Even on the escarpment, she smelled the sea.

Remember.

Alex heard the waves crashing against the rocky shores below, heard the waters calling to her, and felt her gifts stirring within her. The cries of the seabirds surrounded her; something about them had felt familiar and comforting since childhood. Alex smelled lilies and heard laughter. As she exhaled and opened her eyes, she found the escarpment filled with grass and flowers.

"Merlock," Aaron said, "would you notify our fathers?"

"Of course." Merlock bowed and cracked away.

Alex's hand hurt from gripping the saddle horn so tight. As Alex gazed upon the kingdom, Aaron's hand slid over her own. "Do you need another minute?"

She nodded. He squeezed her hand, and after a moment, she released the horn and squeezed his back, taking in the breathtaking view.

The pier. The garden. The sea.

When she had stared long enough at her old home, letting her memories come in waves, Alex stammered, "I'm ready."

Aaron nudged his horse forward, and Alex gave Flash an encouragement to keep pace. The others followed at a distance as Aaron led them down the winding cobblestone roads into the town. They'd have to cross the entire town of Warren to get to the castle. The homes on either side of the road were a stark juxtaposition of dark stone walls set against doors and roofs of every color imaginable, each window's flower box filled with rapturous beauty.

All the houses in the Dark Forest had been low and wide. Here the weatherworn stone houses filled the skies over her head. *How do they stay up like that?* Despite their age, the stones glistened in the early morning light. Most of the windows were dark, though a smattering of people roamed the cobblestone streets. Warren was just waking up.

"I thought there'd be more knights and guards," Alex said as they neared the castle.

"Warren is wealthy, and we train the guards in Datten."

"Why?"

"Warren and Datten are allies. It's tradition," Jerome said.

"For generations we've been friends. Datten's protection has allowed Warren to become a safe and progressive kingdom," Aaron said.

Alex and Michael looked up at the massive stone structure that stood at the entrance to the castle as they passed through the gates. Her ancestors had built ornate obsidian walls to protect the castle from the sea. A group of guards bowed and stepped aside so they could enter. The castle spires stood as tall as the trees in the Dark Forest. Despite the early hour, there were people everywhere. Guards and squires appeared in the yard to take their horses. Alex hesitated after dismounting, but Aaron took Flash's reins and handed them to the squire.

"He'll be okay," he reassured her.

CHAPTER 6
ALEX

Aaron and Jerome marched to the giant doors, and a pair of intimidating guards opened them. As they entered the castle, Alex gawked at the enormous steps that led up to a massive hallway whose ceilings made the town's houses feel small. The Datten men climbed the stairs, but Alex stalled. Intricate paintings of people and places filled the torch-lined walls, and on wooden tables sat all manner of treasures, including vases, statues, and a few other things she couldn't immediately identify. Alex couldn't move. *What sort of treasure do they tuck away in the castle if they leave this at the door?*

Just then, a breeze hit her. When she looked up, all her companions were staring.

You can do this.

Stefan and Michael returned to her while Aaron and Jerome flanked another knight. He was dressed in a blue tunic, and stitched across the chest was an ornate crest: two sea dragons holding up a shield emblazoned with a boat and a lighthouse.

Warren's crest. My crest.

The knight was middle-aged but younger than Jerome. His black hair stood out against his tawny skin while his sandy eyes sparkled. Alex tilted her head as he smiled at her.

You look familiar.

"Welcome home, princess," he said, still smiling as he descended the stairs toward the spot where Alex now stood. "My name is Sir Randal Nial. I'm your father's general, personal guard, and head of castle security. I've watched your father most of my adult life, and I also watched you when you were young." When he reached Alex, he dropped to a knee before her.

What do I do? Alex looked at Aaron.

He smiled, raised his palm, and mouthed, "Rise."

"Please rise, General Nial. I look forward to getting better acquainted," she replied before curtsying.

"A princess does not curtsy to a general," General Wafner said. "You nod."

Alex flushed, but Aaron quickly appeared at her side. When she looked at him, he gave a slight nod to General Wafner. Understanding, she nodded at General Nial.

"Perfect. Are you ready?" Aaron motioned to the doors ahead.

Trembling, Alex's heart beat so violently she suspected everyone could hear. She squeezed the life out of the hand Aaron proffered, but he didn't make a sound. Instead, he led her up the stone steps toward the doors. The generals each pushed one open.

With the vise grip still on Aaron's hand, Alex walked into the throne room. It was larger than Alex remembered. Two stories high, it could hold hundreds of people, maybe even a thousand. She craned her neck and saw the balcony running along the wall on three sides. At the far end of the throne room sat an obsidian dais. It was a work of art with several steps leading up to the two thrones. On either side of the dais was a row of seats.

The walls in this room were filled with more exquisite paintings, but the ones behind the thrones stole Alex's attention. They were so massive she could make them out from the middle of the hall. Suddenly, she dropped Aaron's hand as recognition welled up inside her.

That's me. Her father had commissioned it to be completed ahead of her fifth birthday—before she fled. *It's so lifelike. Ugh, I hated that gown.* Beside it was a portrait of her grandparents. Then there was her father's coronation, her parents on their wedding day, and last, a family portrait painted at the same time as the one of her. Looking at her father, she frowned. No matter how often her mother had explained that the women in their family all looked alike, Alex always wished she had something from her father.

As she studied the paintings, she felt underdressed. Unconsciously, she played with the necklace chain in her pocket as her gaze swept across the room. She noticed the Datten royal family on the next wall. It appeared as if Datten was watching over Warren. There was a painting of the royals when Aaron was young, his brother at his side, followed by a newer one of Aaron and his parents. In the middle of the wall was a lone portrait of a prince. *Daniel.* The prince who'd brought her from Warren to Datten. Even in death, he still protected her.

Thank you.

Alex watched Michael and Stefan taking in the room until she heard murmuring. She'd expected her father and Aaron's parents, but there were at least fifty people standing at the dais here—staring and whispering. Alex's eyes darted to the ground beside the dais. The memory of her mother's bloodied body hit her. Her heart stopped, and all the air left her.

Don't panic. You'll crack if you panic. No vanishing.

It was too late, however, as wind soon rushed through the crowd, sending hair and skirts flying.

The murmurs and whispers grew louder, and she wanted to scream. Alex's hands flew to her mouth; shaking her head, she stepped back, trying in vain to block the sight, to stifle the flood of memories that came unbidden.

No, no, no. Don't look. Breathe. No rain or fire.

Turning to flee, Alex hit Stefan.

He pulled her against him. "Elizabeth?"

"I see her. I can't be in here." Alex pushed him away and fled the room.

ALEX CLUTCHED Aaron's arm to keep herself moving forward despite her nerves. Jerome, Michael, and Stefan were behind them as they walked down a never-ending hallway. Even in the early morning, the castle buzzed with activity, and every single person recognized Aaron.

Even dirty and disheveled. How does everyone like you? Will they like me? What if they don't?

"The library is just down here. It'll give you some privacy to meet your father and godparents again after all these years. Your father is going to be ecstatic when he sees you."

"Godparents? Your parents are in Warren?" Alex asked.

"Of course. My mother didn't trust your father to remember everything needed to set up a princess in a castle, and my father probably doesn't believe we found the correct maiden. Is that a problem?"

"Of course not." Alex turned her head and looked at Stefan. He just nodded at her reassuringly. "As long as I can bring Stefan and Michael in with me."

General Nial stood guard at the library door. As their group arrived, General Wafner moved from behind the young royals and took the second guard position.

Aaron murmured into her ear as they came to a stop, "If General Nial is standing at a door, it means your father is inside. If General Wafner—it means my father is."

"Who guards the queen?"

"The safety of the Queen of Datten falls to the king or prince. It's the same for princesses and queens of former kings. In their absence, they assign someone. In Warren, a queen or princess has her own guards."

Alex exhaled and stepped toward the door, but she stopped when a woodsy, musky smell hit her. She gripped the hem of her shirt and tried to back away, but instead she bumped into Stefan. Alex turned and looked up at him, and when he put his hands on her shoulders, he gave them a squeeze. "You can do this. You're smart, strong, and were second in command because of your exceptional tactical planning. One thing you've never been is a coward."

Alex spied a grin on Jerome's face.

"You're usually angry when you face your fears. Would you like me to make you angry?" Michael asked. "Maybe we can find you one of those poufy dresses to wear."

Daniel subtly appeared beside Michael, erupting in silent laughter.

There you are! I was worried I'd left you behind.

Alex narrowed her eyes at Michael. "If you find one, *you'll* be wearing it."

Michael smirked at the threat that might be a promise. Alex then gave Aaron a quick nod, and a moment later, he opened the door.

Alex took a step forward and stalled.

I can't.

She grabbed Stefan's hand and dragged him through the door with her as Michael followed with Aaron.

The library was immense—at least five times larger than she remembered. Floor-to-ceiling bookshelves lined the room and held history books, classics, novels, and more. In the corner, a spiral staircase led to another floor, and the main floor finished with a gigantic fireplace, a large bear rug, and four large reading couches positioned in a circle.

Sitting on one couch were two fair-haired royals from Datten. Aaron's hand slipped into her free one, pulling her from Stefan. Michael came up behind them and stood beside Stefan, looking around. One general pulled the door shut, and though Alex startled, Aaron's grip held firm.

Alex spotted her father standing behind the couch. Aaron had described Edward as calm, modern thinking, patient, and, above all else, kind. He'd described his own father as a loud, bad-tempered lush who was too comfortable with violence and barking commands. Alex couldn't comment on his descriptions yet, but, physically, the kings were opposites. Edward's slim build, dark hair, and dark brown complexion reminded Alex of the figurehead carvings on the ships at the pier. Emmerich's heavy build, pale skin, and thinning blond hair brought to mind an image of a cooking pot: rotund, prone to overheating, emitting strange gurgles, and you never knew what might spew out of it. At first glance, the only thing they had in common was their bright blue eyes.

Queen Guinevere was more beautiful than Alex remembered. Her blonde hair, lightening with age, was lovely, and her blue eyes sparkled with the same mischievousness Aaron's did. They even had the same warm pink skin. She sat with perfect posture, her hands folded in her lap. Alex knew she would get along well with her godmother even if Emmerich already scared her.

Alex's eyes darted back to her father, who stared at her agape.

This is real. You're here. He was kind—that doesn't vanish.

Aaron squeezed her hand to draw her attention back to him.

"Elizabeth—your father. The two on the couch are your godparents, King Emmerich and Queen Guinevere."

"Your parents," Alex said to Aaron, though her eyes remained on the trio of royals before her. At this, Edward nodded.

"Edward. Father. Mother." Aaron motioned behind him. "You remember Patrick *Stefan* Wafner—Jerome's oldest son. He's responsible for having kept the princess safe these past twelve years. And this is their friend Michael."

Edward edged toward Alex. At this, Aaron released her hand and stepped aside. Alex gazed at her father's face, and traces of a smile developed on his lips as he took her in. Long-forgotten memories rushed to the surface, and she struggled to know whether she ought to revel in them or tamp them down. Edward reached for her face, paused briefly, exhaled, and then finally touched her cheek.

You're nervous too. What are you nervous about?

"You look like your mother."

"I'm sure there's some of you in me somewhere," Alex replied, looking downward for a second.

Edward laughed, and the tears came as he quickly enveloped her in an embrace so tight she could hardly breathe.

I'm home. The monster's dead, my father's fine, and I'm home.

A high-pitched whimper sounded. Alex turned to see the queen crying and fanning herself.

"I'm sorry. I worried this day wouldn't come. And now Jerome has Patrick back too." Emmerich put his arm around his wife, and Guinevere patted his leg. "I'll be fine. It's just so much."

For a few seconds, there was silence as Guinevere shook her head in wonder. "Elizabeth, you are stunning, and now you're home where you belong."

Edward squeezed Alex tightly and kissed the top of her head.

"Let the girl *breathe,* Edward. She's not going anywhere," Emmerich said.

"Except maybe for a bath," Aaron muttered.

"Aaron brings up a good point," said Edward. "I'll have to find you some proper lady's maids. And all of you should get settled—then we'll have a tour."

"That won't be necessary, Edward," Guinevere said, standing up. "I brought Lady Jessica Wafner. She's Elizabeth's age, and I thought she might make a good fit. Now, learning Elizabeth is familiar with the Wafner family, I'm sure they'll become friends. To assist Jessica, I suggested to Randal he fetch his youngest daughter, Lady Edith."

Edward nodded to Guinevere. "Thank you." He turned back to Alex. "I'll send the generals to fetch your ladies and get your guards settled. I presume you wish to keep them both. Should we add them to your palace guard?"

Alex found herself speechless as her chest swelled with too many feelings. After a moment, she managed to nod.

"Then welcome to Warren, gentlemen," Edward said.

CHAPTER 7
ALEX

W hat happened next felt like a dream. Aaron took Michael and Stefan away while the generals escorted Alex to a two-floor suite that made her gasp. The first floor alone was massive. They had filled the walls with paintings of places Alex didn't recognize, shelves of books, and more beautiful treasures. Three couches faced an elaborate stone fireplace on one side while on the other side were three small doors and a spiral staircase similar to the one in the library.

One door opened, revealing two ladies. Lady Jessica was easy to identify, having the same fiery red hair as her father and brother. Her delicate build and porcelain skin shocked Alex, considering Wafner men were built with muscles to spare. Lady Edith's genuine smile put Alex at ease—the same way Edith's father, General Nial, had. Her tawny skin sparkled in the light, her hair color matched Flash's midnight mane, and her beautiful sandy eyes twinkled. Both wore beautiful but simple blue gowns that fit them impeccably. *I've never had lady friends.*

"Hello, princess." They curtsied in unison.

"We've drawn you a bath," Jessica said as Edith closed the door to the hallway where the generals remained.

"Would you like us to help you?" Edith asked.

"No," Alex said, holding her shirt down.

"It would be our honor, Your Highness. You are royalty, and we serve you. It's our duty," Edith said.

There it is—duty—*a burden forced on them.*

Alex sighed. "I'd rather you help me because you think I'm *worthy* and not because your fathers' positions require it. If you'd rather leave, you are free to go. You'll learn soon enough I'm not like other princesses." She looked away, waiting for them to leave.

No footsteps.

Alex looked up, and both ladies smiled.

"Well, that's obvious," Jessica said. "No royal would speak to us as though we were equals."

"I grew up in the woods. I'm not above anyone here," Alex said.

"You have nothing to fear, princess. Our job is to help with proper etiquette, royal matters, and your attire. You'll never set a foot out of place," Edith said.

Alex exhaled happily, causing a bouquet of roses next to her to bloom.

"We should get you into the bath before it gets cold," Jessica said. "We'll leave if you wish and find something suitable for you to wear."

ALEX STEPPED into her room alone, wrapped in the softest towel she'd ever felt, and crept upstairs to explore the rest of her suite. Even more paintings filled the walls, but the one next to her bed—a beautiful woman dressed in regal clothing—caught her attention. The portrait was of her mother, and it was like looking in a mirror. After a time, she crept out on her balcony overlooking the courtyard, careful to not allow anyone to spy her in a towel. Alex soaked up the sound of children laughing while playing nearby and breathed deeply.

Sea air.

Then she heard a gasp behind her. "Princesses do *not* go outside in towels," Jessica said, holding up a blue dress.

Alex regarded the poufy skirt with giant sleeves with disdain, wrinkling her nose. "I can't wear that."

"It's the finest one we have."

"What about this one?" Edith arrived with an emerald dress embroidered with gold details. "The green matches your eyes."

Alex smiled. *I do like green, and it looks simple enough. Compromise.*

"That I can wear."

Jessica and Edith set about getting Alex into the dress. Never having been around other ladies, Alex spent the entire time unsure of what to do with her limbs, and even after they had her dress on, she still felt exposed. Alex was accustomed to shirts and pants; it didn't matter that the dress was composed of more fabric than either of those articles of clothing. Goosebumps now appeared on her legs, and the plunging neckline exposed more of her breasts than Alex would ever have dared show.

This is clothing? I feel naked.

Jessica appeared with a crown and handed it to Alex. The crown was a thin golden band with fat spikes protruding from the top. Rather than being covered in gems, it had been etched, with sections removed from the spikes to lighten it.

It's so beautiful—and somehow familiar.

They headed down the stairs, arriving on the main floor.

"Since we've finished, I'll ask my father to summon His Highness," Edith said.

"That won't be necessary," said a voice.

Aaron stood up from the couch, and Alex's breath caught. Gone were the stubble, dirty hair, and ratty clothes. In their stead stood a proper prince—crown and all. Alex swallowed hard, and she suddenly wished Michael were there.

Were you always that handsome?

Alex's eyes widened as Aaron grinned—he'd noticed her staring. Alex thought her cheeks were bursting into flames as he closed the distance between them, so she tried to focus on the pair of lions on his shirt. The magnificently stitched crest of Datten glittered like gold. He bowed when he arrived in front of her.

"Princess Elizabeth—may I escort you to your father?"

Alex glanced at Edith and Jessica, who pantomimed the motion for her. She extended her hand out to Aaron. He took it, kissed it, and then looped his arm through hers and led her out. In the hall, Alex could hear Edith giggling.

"Is that how maidens usually react to you?"

"Yes. That's why it was strange when I had no effect on you in the stable."

"I'm sorry about the arrows," she replied, trying to change the subject.

"Only the arrows? Not about wounding my pride?"

"*Fine.* Arrows, your overconfidence, Michael knocking you unconscious, your brother's death." She looked at the wall to avoid looking at Aaron. "All of it."

"You don't owe me an apology for Daniel. It wasn't your fault. Took me forever to realize it wasn't mine either. Everyone who protected you chose to. Now you can honor them by living."

Alex stilled. "Do you think they'll ever forgive me?"

I wouldn't forgive myself.

"Who?" Aaron asked, squeezing her arm to make her look at him.

"Your parents. Jerome. My father. All that death because of me." She paused, her next words—her great fear—both inevitable and paralyzing. "How could they not hate me?"

They reached a door just then, but instead of knocking, Aaron turned to Alex and leaned close. "I'm sorry for everything that happened to you, but I promise, *no one* blames you, no one is angry with you, and no one hates you. You were four when everything happened. All everyone has ever wanted is you back home. I hope you can find some peace now that you're home."

He was so close she could feel his breath, his warmth. His gaze was friendly yet unnerving, and after a few moments, she forced herself to look away, nodding her thanks. At this, Aaron turned and knocked on the door. Edward answered it.

"Where are Michael and Stefan?" Alex asked as they began the tour.

"The generals are giving them a more appropriate tour. It involves other parts of the castle that you needn't concern yourself with," Emmerich said.

Alex's stomach dropped. *Without Michael, who'll keep me from embarrassing myself?* Glancing at Aaron, he nodded as though he could read her thoughts and was happy to offer himself in Michael's stead. Alex decided he'd suffice.

"Don't worry, Elizabeth," Guinevere said. "They'll be back for dinner."

Aaron whispered, "Later, I'll show you the places he leaves off."

Edward took them all around the castle, explaining the layout. As they strolled through hall after hall, the paintings on the walls mesmerized Alex—some of them seemed to be alive. Alex's favorite spots were the massive library and the elaborate gardens. She'd always had a knack for growing things, and she couldn't wait to get lost in some new books after years of rereading her and Stefan's tiny collection. Her least favorite part of the tour—by far—was the crypts. All the former kings and queens of Warren were buried beneath the castle in the hopes that their combined knowledge and strength would help guide the current king and queen.

But Alex knew what this really meant—they stayed in the castle even after their death, having seen their ghosts all over during the tour. At least most of the ghosts only nodded and vanished. Edward was explaining how to get there should she wish to visit her mother's resting place, but Alex knew the fear of having to pass her grandfather would keep her away for a long time.

The best part of the tour had nothing to do with the castle at all. Just being around her father filled Alex with joy and a sense of safety. The more he talked, the more Alex relaxed. She hadn't expected to feel so comfortable so soon, especially without Stefan and Michael nearby. The description Aaron had given her back at the camp had been entirely true. When he wasn't busy answering every question she asked about the castle, the people, and kingdom, Edward asked Alex about growing up in the forest. She told him about the trouble she'd get into with Michael, her love of climbing trees and riding, her archery skills, and how her powers had already arrived.

Shortly after the tour, the Datten royals excused themselves. "We'll head back to our rooms to freshen up for dinner. You two carry on," Guinevere said.

"Are you sure?" Edward asked, but Alex suspected the royals wanted them to have time alone, and Guinevere's nod in response confirmed this before they continued down the garden path.

Alex was struck by how many strange flowers were already blooming. In May, the forest had wildflowers, but here there were roses, irises, violets, and so many more. Alex wanted to know everything about her father, but at that moment, she struggled to find the words.

"Your garden is beautiful," she finally managed to say.

"Thank you. My father had it planted for my mother as a wedding gift, but then your mother brought it to life. She had a gift for plants."

Alex smiled. *At least I have one gift in common with her.*

"What happens now?"

"After dinner, I'll meet with my council of advisers, and we'll choose tutors to teach you everything you need to know to become a Princess of Warren. Can you read?"

"Yes. I can read, write, ride, and fight."

"Those are important skills, but we need to teach you how to rule a kingdom," Edward said. "In Warren, we teach a princess the same skills as a prince, with one or two additions. Since a *Wafner* raised you, I expected you to know how to ride and use a sword or bow, but you will need to learn proper etiquette and how to dance as well as our laws, history, and the names of the noble families—hence the tutors."

Alex swallowed and looked up at her father.

"You can say *anything* you want when we're alone," he said, his regal voice a mix of strength and compassion. "In front of the council, I'd appreciate it if you let me speak until you have your bearings. But with me, I'd like you to be honest."

"Patrick goes by Stefan now," she said after a pause. "He's been Stefan, and I've been Alexandria for the last twelve years. Is there any way we ..." Alex fidgeted, twisting her skirts. "Is there any way I could go by Alexandria instead, and Patrick by Stefan? Michael has always been Michael."

Edward chuckled and grabbed her hands. "Elizabeth was my mother's name, but Alexandria is your maternal grandmother's name. I think your mother would love you to use it. But you'll have to forgive me if it takes time for me to adjust, and in formal settings, we should use Elizabeth to announce you. After that, you can go by any name you wish."

CHAPTER 8
AARON

Aron followed his parents to their usual guest suite. The royal guest suites were identical to Alex's room but on the other side of the castle, closer to the king's suite. With their frequent visits, Edward had given Aaron and Daniel their own dedicated rooms when they were children. Aaron still insisted on using his.

"Edward looks ecstatic," Guinevere said, sitting down on one of the blue velvet couches that faced the elaborate obsidian fireplace. "Elizabeth's so beautiful and full of life."

"You forgot fire and wit," Aaron said, leaning against the wall next to the fireplace. "Edward's going to have his hands full with her."

"I can sympathize," Emmerich said, sitting beside his wife.

Aaron felt his father's emphatic glare. "At least I never shot another royal."

"Emmerich," Guinevere said in a tone she rarely used with his father. "We agreed. He brought her back. Now end this successor nonsense."

58

"*They* brought her back. I thought Edward was sending them on a fool's errand."

Aaron shifted and turned to his father.

"Don't look at me like that," Emmerich said. "It's been twelve years. She was a child when she disappeared. We thought she was alone. I assumed she was dead, but you brought home a lovely young woman. We couldn't have asked for better. At last, the council will leave Edward alone about a new heir; although, with her being back now, they will probably demand a wedding next."

"Why would the council need Edward to marry?" Aaron asked.

Emmerich groaned at his son. "The princess. Warren is progressive, but she's about to turn seventeen and has spent most of her life away from here. They'll want her settled into her role and married off as quickly as possible."

Guinevere smiled. "Wait for word to spread. Once it does, the betrothal offers will come. And when the nobility finds out how beautiful she is, they'll increase their offers."

"Won't do them any good. Edward plans to refuse everyone," Emmerich said.

"How do you know?" Aaron asked.

"I asked Edward to move Daniel's betrothal to you, but he refused."

"Emmerich, she's not even home a day."

"He didn't tell me 'not now,' Guinevere. Edward reminded me that Arthur and I betrothed Elizabeth to Daniel. That decision wasn't his. Apparently, he and Victoria had intended to leave the choice up to the princess, and that is what he intends to do now."

Sounds like Edward to me. Aaron shrugged at his mother.

"That sounds like Victoria and Edward, dear."

"Spouted some nonsense about Elizabeth, only giving her

hand to a man she decides is worthy. What does a girl know about picking a husband? Someone who can rule?" Emmerich moaned, throwing up his arms. "We've waited centuries to unite our kingdoms, and for what? So Edward can throw it all away on a little girl's idea of love?"

"She can't pick worse than Wesley," Aaron muttered.

"Young man, if you don't like the successor I have put in line for *my* throne, then maybe you should shape up enough so I can entrust my crown to you. Strength and dominance—things you are lacking—rule Datten. Kindness won't keep our people in line. Until I know someone won't assassinate you your first month on the throne, I'm keeping my options open. Finding Elizabeth was a start, so keep it up."

Aaron turned away and clenched his teeth.

I'm not my brother, and I have no intention of ruling like you.

"The problem *we* have now is Elizabeth doesn't need to marry a prince," Emmerich continued. "She is the heir and will rule, so she can marry anyone. A nobleman, a merchant, a knight, that boy she found in the woods. Through marriage, that person will be prince or king when she takes the throne as queen," Emmerich said.

"But why so soon?" Aaron asked.

"She'll be seventeen in June," said Guinevere. "I was sixteen when I married your father, and I had Daniel when I was seventeen. We're getting the same pressure in Datten. You'll be twenty in a few weeks. Kingdoms give princes more time, but you're the second son, and your father isn't getting younger."

"If you're getting pressure, then why haven't you announced anything?" Aaron asked.

"The expectations for your future wife depend on you getting the crown," Guinevere said.

You're holding off for me?

Aaron turned to his father. "Since when do you put anyone's needs over Datten's?"

"Since your brother's death, I assumed you'd marry Elizabeth. I held off on another match to give Datten and Warren the chance to unite. Edward and I have been friends his entire life—it never even occurred to me he'd say no. Anyway, I'm not about to be told what to do with my son by some old men who have as little experience on the battlefield as you do. Edward has decided the princess decides who's worthy—so *be worthy*."

That won't be easy.

Aaron looked down, remembering the mocking smirk on Alex's face when he'd tried to charm her in the stable.

"Emmerich," Guinevere said, "go have an ale with Jerome. I'm sure he's done with the princess's guards, and I'd like a minute with our son."

Emmerich stood, kissed Guinevere on the cheek, and gave Aaron a commanding stare as he left. Aaron sat down beside his mother, holding his head in his hands and groaning.

"What's troubling you, darling? You must've assumed what we were planning when we sent you."

I'm not a simpleton.

"Of course I expected it. I agreed to go so if she was terrible, I could run."

"Aaron!" Guinevere smacked his leg.

"She's wonderful, Mother. Beautiful, as inquisitive as her father, brave, strong—everything we'd want. But emotionally broken too. She's apologized three times for Daniel, and she has nightmares. *Dreadful nightmares.* She buried her pain so deep that now she's struggling to control her magic. Michael told me that's why she hides her feelings so much."

"Datten survived a sorcerer coming into his powers; Warren will too. As for rushed marriages, that's how it's done with royalty. She is beautiful and strong but also a crown princess who will rule Warren one day. Suitors will come for her beauty, for Warren's wealth, and for the power they'll hope to wield through her."

Aaron rubbed the back of his neck and chuckled. "None of them will be good enough for her."

"You're right. She deserves a prince, but they're in short supply," Guinevere said. "I can tell you feel you aren't enough for her, but don't dismiss yourself. Edward is fond of Datten, but he adores you. I wouldn't put it past your godfather to deny Emmerich while stacking the deck in your favor." Guinevere narrowed her eyes at him. "What do *you* think of the princess?"

Why does this feel like a trap?

"She's unusual. Even dressed as a boy, she was beautiful. She has Edward's wit and takes after him in how she considers things. Michael warned me about her temper, but I can't fault her for that—she's protective of what she cares about." Aaron rubbed his shoulder and winced. "But despite everything, she's kind."

Guinevere smiled. "She sounds like that same wonderful little girl we couldn't keep you away from, and that's enough for me." Guinevere kissed Aaron's cheek and stood up. "Find something you both love and start there. Common ground leads to a strong friendship. Friendship and connection leads to wanting to be around someone. And wanting to be around someone, even when they aren't at their best, is an important part of love."

CHAPTER 9
ALEX

Alex's mouth watered. She followed the aroma of fresh bread, roasted fish, and garlic wafting down the hall. She'd refused an escort, wanting instead to find her own way to dinner, but ended up getting lost until her nose led her in the right direction.

Please don't be full.

Alex took a deep breath and peeked around the entrance, only to find the dining hall nearly empty. Edward sat at the center of the long head table on a stone platform at the far end. Emmerich and Guinevere were seated to his left. Two enormous tables ran the length of the hall in the main dining area. Near the Datten royals sat the Datten nobility: Merlock, Megesti, the Wafners, and Michael beside Stefan. The left table had General Nial, Lady Edith, and the other Warren knights.

Alex then realized there were two empty chairs to her father's right. *Where's Aaron?*

"Everything all right?" said a voice behind her.

Alex jumped back, hitting a suit of armor and sending it

crashing to the ground. Alex faced Aaron, her heart hammering in her chest. "It's dangerous to sneak up on me."

"Understood. Though you're the one lurking outside the dining hall where we're expected for dinner."

Aaron's hand slid along her back. He moved beside her to brace himself against the wall and peek into the hall. Her stomach fluttered at his touch.

"It appears we're late."

"I assumed there'd be more people." Alex tugged on her dress's skirt.

"There should be. Your father kept it smaller tonight."

"Did you have something to do with that?"

"Perhaps. I know how overwhelming the nobles can be. I thought we should ease you in."

"Was it your idea to combine your birthday with my welcome home celebration?"

Aaron smiled apologetically. "My mother insisted on throwing this party for you, so I may have suggested you're not used to being the center of attention and that a dual celebration might put you more at ease. If I was mistaken, I cou—"

"No! Please, *don't*."

"We should go inside. I'm not wild about fish, but it tastes better hot."

Aaron held his hand out to Alex. After glancing down at it and looking back up at Aaron, she accepted it, marveling as she did so. *How do you put me at ease so fast?*

Aaron smiled for a second before leading her into the dining room.

Alex gulped, knowing everyone's eyes were on her, but Aaron looped his arm through hers, squeezed, and then they were walking down the aisle. Edward was fidgeting so much Alex thought he might topple out of his chair, but his smile lit up the room.

When Alex spotted Michael, fresh and dressed in a crested shirt, she couldn't stop staring at him. A mischievous smile appeared on his face as he took in the sight of her in a dress and wearing a crown, and Alex shot him her warning glare. *Don't you dare laugh at me.* She felt a smile tug at her lips despite herself, but it died once she spotted Stefan. He was watching Aaron, not her, wearing a pinched expression she'd never seen him make before.

Are you upset I'm not staying away from Aaron? I can't very well avoid a prince as a princess. Or is it something else?

"Alexandria. Aaron. Welcome." Edward leaped up as they arrived at the head table.

Aaron bowed to his godfather, and Alex took it as a sign to curtsey. When she looked up, Guinevere was leaning forward, a close-lipped smile on her face.

Why are you staring?

Aaron's hand was still touching hers, and when she realized this, she jerked her hand away as if he had bitten her. Alex went to the seat closest to her father. Aaron pulled out the chair for her and smiled as he took the remaining seat beside her.

"Alexandria?" Aaron quizzed.

"I'm used to it after all these years," Alex replied. "It was my maternal grandmother's name. I asked to use it, and my father agreed."

A host of servants appeared with trays of food, which they placed on the table. The kitchen staff had piled vegetables she had never even seen into enormous bowls and carved a squash into the shape of a ship. It took two servants to lift the swordfish onto the table. They sliced it into fillets, letting them float in a creamy sauce.

There is so much food. How much do they waste with a meal like this? This table alone could have fed all of us at the camp for a week.

The camp!

"Father, we made promises to the lads left at the camp. Promises of gold and supplies."

"I know." Edward leaned down and patted her hand. "Aaron already gave me the list. I'll send Merlock, Stefan, and Jerome back with the supplies tomorrow. It was rather clever of Aaron."

"It was lazy. Real princes command respect. They don't use bribes." Emmerich snorted and shook his head before taking a swig of his ale. Alex narrowed her eyes at him, though Aaron didn't seem bothered.

A piece of the swordfish appeared on her plate. The older servant woman who placed it smiled at Alex and nodded.

"Thank you."

Everyone went silent.

Oh, no. "Did I do something wrong?"

Aaron grinned. "You are a Princess of Warren."

"Royalty do not thank servants, princess," Emmerich said. "We pay them. It's their job."

"Just because their lot in life put them here doesn't mean I have to treat them as less worthy."

"They are less worthy," Emmerich said, his eyes fixed on Alex.

"According to *you*." Alex regretted her tone when Edward tensed.

Emmerich lifted his chin and pushed his shoulders back as he stared at her.

Dare I talk back to a king? Especially that king. What would my father think?

"Ignore my father's griping," Aaron said, trying to defuse the tension at the table.

"He's my father's best friend," she replied, though her eyes didn't leave Emmerich's. "His opinion matters."

"Don't let the scolding of a drunk old man ruin your first meal at home. My father's always cranky about something."

Emmerich glared at Alex, unflinching, for several seconds before he finally looked away. She felt frozen in place by his stare. Now freed, she looked down at her plate and realized she couldn't eat a single bite.

"I'm tired, and it's been a long day. I'd like to go to bed," Alex said, touching her father's arm.

"Of course." Edward nodded, and Alex spotted the sad look on his face before it vanished. "I'll meet with the council tonight about your tutors."

"Thank you." Alex nodded to her father and stood up. She flinched as everyone in the room leaped to their feet. The sound made her throat go dry.

"Sir Stefan," Edward called, "would you escort my daughter back to her room?"

Stefan bowed to the king before moving to the doors. Alex lifted her head. *Don't trip on this ferflucsing skirt.* She stood tall and made her way down the aisle. When Stefan offered her his arm, she took it.

In the hallway, Alex relaxed. *How am I this exhausted? I didn't do anything.*

"You look lovely in your dress," Stefan said, nudging Alex with his elbow. Groaning, she tried to shove him, but he didn't budge. Giving up, Alex looked Stefan up and down.

"You clean up pretty well yourself. But why are you wearing a Datten uniform? Shouldn't you have a Warren uniform since we're in Warren?"

"I'm a Wafner. Through my father, I'm a knight of Datten. Your father has knighted me, but they don't have any new Warren uniforms in my size. So until they're made, I'll wear Datten. How was your tour with your father?"

"Wonderful. He's as kind as Aaron said. But I didn't realize I'd need so many tutors."

Stefan chuckled. "You'll keep Michael and me at least. Are you nervous about any lessons?"

"Magic, but more so the dancing and etiquette lessons—there's so much to remember with those. Why can't *I* just be the general?"

"What would General Nial do then?"

"I don't know. Deal with the suitors?"

"He'll already do that once they arrive. It's going to be a challenge keeping them all in line."

"Shouldn't that be your job as my guard?"

Stefan laughed as they walked into Alex's room.

CHAPTER 10
ALEX

When Alex woke from her nightmares for a second time, she knew she wouldn't be able to sleep anymore despite it still being dark out. She put on her green dress and tiptoed out of her room. A few doors down the hallway, she realized she'd gone the wrong way.

Alex glanced to make sure no one saw her turn around and then scurried toward the throne room. When she arrived, she pulled up short, confused—the entrance to the throne room was unguarded. *They don't guard the throne room at night?* For a moment, she debated with herself and then finally pushed open the door before she could lose her nerve.

Despite being deserted, the room was lit with hundreds of candles. An icy wind swept across her face, extinguishing some of the nearby candles as she moved along the side wall, looking at the paintings of the former kings and queens of Warren. She saw her father in many of them, but not one of them included anyone who resembled her.

No princesses? That's odd.

Her breath quickened as she inched closer to the thrones. Before long, a crushing pain engulfed her chest.

I can't do this.

Alex turned to flee and crashed into Aaron before falling backward. Aaron caught her arm just in time, and she slammed into his chest. Alex smelled pine and dew on him before she pushed him away.

"What are you doing here?" she asked.

"Following you."

"What? Why?"

"I couldn't sleep. I was heading to the library and spotted you. You looked lost, so I followed you to make sure you were okay. What are *you* doing here?"

"None of your concern." Alex dropped the skirt she'd been tugging on and ran from the throne room.

"I MISSED A FEW OF THE NAMES," Alex said.

Edward sat across from her at the table on the second floor of the library. Housing generations of royal and military journals and all of Warren's books on magic, it was only accessible to the royal family or by royal permission. Emmerich and Jerome sat below in the common library to give them privacy but could provide input if needed.

Edward smiled and went through the list of tutors again.

"You'll also need to grow your guard. For now, Emmerich and I have selected a couple of knights to assist Stefan and Michael; Kruft Rassgat is a cousin of Emmerich's, and Julius Bishop is the youngest son of General Bishop. Are there other skills or things you'd like to learn?"

"Will I learn about my mother? Or the methods of ruling used by the royals before us?"

"The kings' journals are all over here." Edward strolled past the shelf with the bust of the first king of Warren and pointed to the shelf furthest from the staircase. "Royal journals start with mine and work their way back to Warren's founding fifteen hundred years ago. Your mother's are most likely in storage. I'll have them brought out. In addition, Emmerich and I will answer questions you have."

"So how long do I have to learn a lifetime of princess knowledge?" Alex examined the list of tutors.

"You'll show off your impressive princess skills at your birthday, so focus on the names of the nobility, etiquette, and dancing. I'm *still* learning about our legal system as it's always changing. Same with military strategy, depending on the whims of Datten. I know you'll make me proud."

"So nine weeks." *I hope I don't let you down.* She kissed Edward on the cheek.

"No lessons today. Tonight, you just need to make it through the mourning ceremony."

Alex gulped. "The what?"

"It's Warren's opportunity to say goodbye to their former king—your grandfather. I know you aren't keen to attend, but it's tradition, and it won't last long. Then tomorrow you'll start your studies."

CHAPTER II

AARON

Aaron crumpled the message from Caleb and shoved it into his pocket. Word of Alexandria's meltdown and disastrous spell at the official mourning ceremony for the late King Arthur had already made it to Datten.

He had tried to warn everyone that it wasn't right to ask Alex to attend—but no one listened. It had all started according to plan until Alexandria got spooked and sent a rogue wave crashing over the pier. Footsteps brought him out of his thoughts as Jessica rounded the corner.

"Have you found her? Edith and I checked everywhere, but —" She paused, brow furrowed. "I don't want to have to tell His Royal Highness we lost her."

"You didn't *lose* her," Aaron replied. "Royals hide when they think everyone is judging them."

"I know that, but she isn't a normal royal. Did you have any idea that she was *that* powerful?"

Aaron shook his head even as he bit back a sheepish grin.

Jessica's eyes narrowed. "You're amused by this?"

He shrugged, giving in to the smile. *It was funny.*

"Aaron! That poor girl had a panic attack in front of her kingdom, which resulted in an explosion—somewhere—sending a massive wave over the barrier rocks and soaking half the citizens in attendance. The wave was so large the entire royal gallery was washed into the crowd. I've never seen your father so bewildered."

"My father looking like a drowned cat isn't something I'll soon forget."

Jessica glared at him, crossing her arms.

You are your father's daughter.

"I know she's embarrassed and scared. I saw—no, sensed—her fear at the celebration. That's why I brought her to stand with my mother, to help her. Now, I'm going to find her and offer my help. Very few people understand the pressure she's about to be put under, but I do."

"If you find her, please let Edith and me know she's okay. Edith worries."

"Of course."

Jessica nodded and walked down the hallway. A moment later, Aaron walked down the hall in the other direction but stopped. The hall was ice cold. Without thinking, he opened the library door to find Alex sitting on a couch with a book on her lap. Her head snapped up when he shut the door, and the fireplace roared to life.

"Are you—"

"Hiding?" Alex wouldn't make eye contact with him. Instead, she glanced behind him. Aaron turned around, but there was nothing there.

"I want to help you," Aaron said, sitting on the couch across from her.

"Our parents have procured me the best tutors in the land. What more could I need?"

"A friend, someone who understands what you're going

through," Aaron said. Alex wrinkled her nose at him. Aaron smiled, remembering the little girl who'd do the same any time she didn't like something. "You don't have to make *that* face. Having a friend with the same title as you can help take some pressure off."

"What face?" Alex sat up straight and stared at Aaron, wrinkling her nose again.

"*That* one." Aaron pointed at her. "You seem to forget we were together a lot as children, and you made that face as a girl too. It's obvious you aren't that little girl anymore, but some things don't change."

Alex clutched the book on her lap. "If I agree to this friendship, what exactly would you help me with?"

Aaron straightened up and tossed back his hair, giving her his most serious prince look. "Anything and everything. People think being a crown royal is glamorous, but in truth, it's boring. There are too many rules, not enough time to do things you enjoy, the clothes are uncomfortable, and everyone's waiting for you to mess up."

Alex tensed at this, and recognizing his mistake, Aaron reached for her hand.

She breathed deeply and dropped the book to take his hand. "I spent twelve years hiding. Crowds are hard."

"And the throne room—"

"Leave that alone if you actually want to be my friend." Her voice was curt and cold.

"All right. For tonight."

"Thank you."

"It's the least I can do after what you gave me today. I've never seen my father so confused and angry as when that wave knocked him on his rear."

Alex went pale. "That doesn't make me feel better!"

Aaron stood and bowed. "Apologies. I will strive to be a better friend of Her Highness."

"Do we have to do that?"

"What?"

"Use our titles."

"No," he said amiably. "What would you like me to call you?"

"In formal settings, Alexandria will do. In private, I would prefer it if, I mean, my friends all—"

Aaron felt a gentle breeze hit him as Alex glanced away again. He squeezed her hand, bringing her attention back to him. "Friends. Talk to me ... like you would with Michael."

She looked at him, and after a few seconds, she said, "I prefer Alex. The other names—they feel like someone else."

The sparkle in her eyes reminded him of that little girl who got him into so much trouble as a boy. Aaron's hands grew slick, and his stomach rumbled, making Alex look at him and giggle.

"Well then, *Alex,* I seem to need a snack. Would you like to sneak into the kitchen with me?"

Alex squeezed his hand. "Delighted, Your Highness."

Aaron kissed her hand. "You've always called me Aaron."

"Okay ... Aaron." Alex smiled as she looped her arm through his, and they strolled off toward the kitchen.

CHAPTER 12
ALEX

"Change of plans this morning, princess," Merlock said the next morning, "if you'll indulge us. I'll answer your questions, but I want to see where you are with your powers. So I'd like to go into the forest."

Alex nodded but paused upon seeing the knight dressed in a Warren uniform standing behind him.

"This is Sir Kruft Rassgat, King Emmerich's cousin. We've assigned him to your guard, and he'll accompany us to ensure your safety since Sirs Stefan and Michael are with the general," Megesti said.

"Thank you, Sir Kruft. I appreciate you coming along."

Sir Kruft nodded in reply, and Merlock turned to Alex. "Lessons begin now, so pay attention." He snapped his fingers while spinning his wrist, and they arrived in a clearing in the Dark Forest. Kruft went to sweep the area while Alex looked around in amazement. Despite its ominous name, the Dark Forest made Alex feel at peace; she could smell the trees and feel the soft ground under her boots.

"Is cracking that easy?" she asked. "I've only done it by accident."

"When you've done it enough times, it will be," Merlock said. "But it's challenging to learn since it comes naturally to most."

"I still can't do it, so don't get frustrated if it takes time," Megesti said.

Alex smiled at her uncle and cousin as the flowers in the clearing burst into bloom.

"Why do you look so young?" she asked. "My father looks so much older than both of you."

Merlock chuckled. "Not the first question I was expecting. I'm a hundred and eighteen, Megesti is sixty-seven. Since sorcerers live so long, we age differently once we hit eighteen. Children age normally, but once we mature, it takes seven years for us to age one year in appearance. That's why we look more like brothers than father and son."

"You'll appreciate it when you're older," Megesti said.

"Can you make trees grow?" Merlock asked.

Alex nodded but added, "I have to be elated and at peace, though, in order to do it. Why are there no portraits of princesses in the throne room?"

"There hasn't been one until you," Merlock said.

"How is that possible?" Alex was trying to focus, but the meadow was calling her—she realized she'd been growing flowers.

"You are the first Princess of Warren. The royal family has only had sons since Warren's founding, and the same holds true for Datten—after the first Prince of Warren married into the royal family. The story's so old it's legend, and no one remembers all the details."

"Please?"

Merlock looked at Megesti, who nodded, and then Merlock began to tell the tale. "Fifteen hundred years ago, three families —Arthur Warren, Patrick Nial, and George Veremund—founded Warren. The first queen was an outsider. Where she came from has been lost to history, but it's said she was a runaway who fled her homeland during a time of war. The legend goes that their strongest sorcerer cursed her for fleeing. After she arrived in Warren, she married Arthur Warren, and they had two sons. The youngest went and married the last Princess of Datten, forming the first alliance between Datten and Warren."

"First? You mean—"

"The peace between the kingdoms has broken down twice," Merlock interrupted, "resulting in short but *bloody* wars. The current peace has lasted over six hundred years."

King Emmerich seems angry with my father. What if I cause another war?

"So if the kings only have sons, how was I born?"

"Your mother," Merlock replied. "Sorcerers can determine the gender of their children, and for Victoria and me to pass our powers to our children, they needed to match our genders. Your mother needed a daughter as I needed a son."

"Daughters are born throughout Torian, from the Betruger to the southern kingdoms of Hessen, Beaten, Madras, Oreane, Fans, and Darren, but *never* to the Datten and Warren royal families. Until you. It seems unlikely that would have happened without magic at play," Megesti said.

Alex felt a lump in her throat as she wiped her dirty hands on her pants. "May I ask you about my mother?"

"Of course. She was my sister. After Megesti, she meant more to me than anyone or anything. She was a gifted and exceptional sorceress in terms of both power and skill."

"Did she ever struggle to control them?"

Megesti laughed, and Merlock grabbed her hands. "Every

sorcerer has mishaps when they're learning. For our line, it's an inconvenience; for others, it can be devastating."

"I burned down a tower once in Datten," Megesti said. "The castle used to have three. I think it looks better with two."

Merlock smiled. "I tried to heal someone's wart and ended up covering them in warts instead. And, yes, your mother had some terrible mishaps. The more powerful the sorcerer, the more troublesome they can be. She once set me on fire." Alex gasped, but Merlock waved her away. "My hair grew back fine. The point is this: I want to make it clear this happens to all sorcerers. What occurred at the ceremony was devastating for you, but you aren't alone."

"You're getting tutors to help you learn the ways of Warren, but *we* will educate you in the ways of magic," Megesti said.

For the first time since her mother's death, the giant hole in Alex's heart began to heal, but then a torrential downpour soaked them.

Merlock raised his eyes at her.

"Sorry."

"And with that, we're finished for today."

"You'll need time to change before your lesson with the queen, who, for the record, can trace her lineage back to the original Veremund family," Megesti said.

Merlock enveloped the three of them in a warm wind, drying them off before cracking them back to the library.

Sir Kruft escorted Alex to her room and then left for his rounds. Slipping inside, she found her ladies gone. Alex changed into her green dress while her mind wandered, processing all she'd learned about her magic and family that day. When she stepped back into the hallway, a sloshing sound caught her attention. Turning toward it, her eyes grew wide, and she giggled.

"Not a word," said Aaron.

∼

ALEX ARRIVED outside the dining hall to find Generals Wafner and Nial on guard. As she smiled at them, hurried footsteps echoed down the hall. Alex turned to see Aaron hurrying toward her.

"Sorry, I had to change."

Aaron offered his arm, and Alex accepted it, allowing him to lead her into the dining hall where Guinevere was waiting. She stood up with her arms wide and kissed them both on the cheek.

"You're as beautiful as your mother. I know you must be tired of hearing it, but your mother and I were dear friends, and I miss her."

"Thank you, Your Majesty."

Guinevere lowered her chin at Alex. "We talked about this."

"Thank you, Guinevere." Alex flushed and turned to Aaron for help.

"Should we sit?" Aaron asked.

Alex was about to sit but caught the look on Guinevere's face and stopped in time. A hand on her lower back sent shivers up her spine as Aaron whispered, "A princess doesn't sit on her own."

His teasing tone made her remember their kitchen heist the night before. Aaron pulled out her chair and bowed. Alex curtsied and allowed him to slide it beneath her. Guinevere poured the tea while Aaron sat beside Alex.

Aaron put his crown beside him and stole Alex's cup, taking a swig of her tea. Scowling, Guinevere poured Alex a fresh cup.

"Is it normal to remove your crown at the table? I'm never

sure what to do with mine." Alex looked from Aaron to his mother.

Aaron examined her carefully. "Most don't. I remove mine because it's large, and it slides off when I eat—so I started setting it beside me."

"Why don't you make a new crown?"

"It's special. May I?" Aaron asked as he held up his palms to Alex. She nodded, and so he took her crown and placed it beside his.

"They're identical!" Alex picked one up in each hand.

Guinevere said, "When Datten and Warren last called a truce, Warren carved a stunning dais for Datten. It's identical to the one in your throne room. Datten's finest goldsmith made matching crowns for the heirs of each kingdom. The hope was eventually they would come together when the kingdoms did, but there's never been a princess until you," she finished, sipping her tea.

Ever the gracious hostess, Guinevere spent an hour instructing Alex in all aspects of a royal tea from pouring the drinks, to place settings, to proper conversation topics.

"You're welcome to ask me anything now, and not just about the tea."

"I have too many questions."

"Then ask, dear."

"Why don't you adjust the crown so it fits better?"

Alex caught the look between Aaron and his mother.

"We would adjust it for a crown prince," Guinevere said, "but after Daniel died, Emmerich refused to change a thing."

"Sorrows of the spare who became the heir," Aaron said.

Guinevere sighed and glared at Aaron. She stood up, rubbing her neck. "I need to lie down for a while before dinner. Alexandria, I apologize and hope you'll excuse me."

Alex stood up, and Guinevere kissed her cheek.

"Mother, I'm sorry—" Aaron sprang up.

"It's fine, darling," she replied, kissing his cheek and holding out her hand. Aaron handed her his crown, and then she placed it on his head before leaving the hall.

"What was that?" Alex asked.

"Mother hates it when I call myself the spare. I take after her side and am her favorite. She's always believed in me, whereas my father thinks I have too much Warren in me."

"I meant the crown."

"*Oh*, that." Aaron flushed and faced Alex. "My mother believes no royal should ever put their own crown on their head."

"That's sweet. Who knew Datten's prince had a soft spot for his mother?"

"Few things spark my temper, but insult my mother and you'll meet my Datten side."

"Noted." Alex locked eyes with Aaron for a moment and then looked down.

Why does looking at you make me so nervous?

Aaron chuckled as if he'd read her thoughts and then crowned her before pouring them another cup of tea.

"So before we talk about how I ended up dripping in the hallway, I have a question. A serious one."

Alex nodded. "I have one too. You first."

Aaron set down his tea. "Even the most loyal of my father's knights slip up, so how did you keep the lads at the camp quiet for twelve years?"

"You found me," she replied evasively. *More than once, even if you haven't figured that out yet.*

"Megesti sensed your powers," Aaron said. "You two are family. I worry we would never have found you without him."

"I would've returned upon learning Arthur was dead or when I turned eighteen—that was the deal Stefan and I made."

She went quiet, thinking about Arthur and how horrible it must have been for her father. Aaron's hand squeezed hers, bringing her back.

"The lads had no reason for such loyalty. How'd you get them to stay quiet?"

Alex laughed. "I started out as a little sister, so they were protective—everyone except Graham, that is. He would've sold me out if Stefan hadn't threatened him. You've also heard what happens when I lose my temper, so when my powers manifested, a rumor started that I was Merlock's bastard child and that Stefan's father had murdered my mother and was after me. No one wanted him to come to the camp, so they kept quiet."

Aaron's mouth hung open. "That's mad."

"That's why it was a rumor."

"How did you survive?"

"The camp collects orphans. We're—we *were*—a family. As lads grow up and start their lives, they give back what they can to take care of the next group. Though Michael, Stefan, and I will make sure they never want for anything again."

"Did you rain on me?"

"Yes."

"Magical mishap?"

"Yes. I giggled because it made me remember another time I made you wet."

Aaron's eyes went wide as he began laughing. "You remember pushing me in the moat? You were three!"

Alex shrugged and smiled. "Daniel made me."

"That's what I get for being chivalrous when you cried about your lost boat. You and Daniel nearly died of laughter. Now your question, princess."

Alex swallowed hard. "How do I ask my father about what happened after my mother died?"

Aaron went pale as he stared at Alex. "You don't." Aaron glanced behind them, running his hand through his hair.

"But I need—"

"I'll tell you, but you must never ask another soul."

Alex nodded. *Never ask another soul? What did my father do?*

"I overheard Jerome say that when your father returned from the pier and found your mother, he went mad. You were missing for an entire day while Daniel brought you to Datten. Edward had the guards tearing the town, woods, and castle apart until Merlock came to Warren and told Edward that we had you and you were safe. Daniel hid you with the Wafners while Warren prepared to bury Victoria. Later, the Wafner house burned down, and we lost you."

My poor father. Alex nodded for Aaron to continue even as her tears fell.

"When you vanished, your father changed. He sent guards to scour the entire land, but nothing. As the first anniversary loomed, he ..." Aaron looked away, closing his eyes.

"He what?"

"He tried to kill himself." Aaron paused when Alex gasped but then pressed on. "My father somehow felt that something bad was going to happen, so he left for Warren. He's the one who found him. Merlock and Edward's physician fought all night to save him. After that, my father came up with a plan. Matthew stepped down so Randal could become general. Then Matthew began hunting your mother's killer and trying to find you. A year later, your grandfather became ill, and Edward became acting king. Then this year, they tried a fresh approach, sending Megesti, Jerome, and me to find you."

"He never gave up on me," Alex whispered.

Aaron rested a hand on Alex's arm until her eyes met his. "Not for a single minute."

They sat in silence, listening as rain fell outside.

"What do you have next?" Aaron finally asked, breaking the silence.

"Dancing."

Aaron held out his arm. "May I escort the beautiful princess to her dance lesson?"

"Please don't," Alex groaned, looking away.

"Don't compliment you?"

"Don't tease me about my failings as a princess. It's hard enough to feel like a disappointment without being reminded of it by someone who does the job perfectly."

Aaron threw his head back and laughed, the sound resounding through the entire hall before he brought his face so close to Alex's she barely breathed. "First, you *are* beautiful —even when you were dirty in the camp. And second, I fail at being a prince every day—my father can give you a list. No matter what other people believe, royalty are human, and you need to know you'll make mistakes. So when I compliment you, I mean it."

"I'll remember that."

CHAPTER 13

AARON

I *hate fish, but at least I'll get to talk to Alex.*

Aaron adjusted his tunic and stepped out of his room, but he paused when he heard a strange sound. He grew still, and a few moments later, he heard it again. Aaron crept into the main hallway that spanned the outer edge of Warren's castle until he came upon a narrower hall that led to smaller guest rooms. A door creaked open and then banged shut. Footsteps followed, and a moment later, Alex rounded the corner. Looking up, she screamed, and a wind sent Aaron stumbling backward into the main hallway.

"I'm sorry!" Alex exclaimed. She was playing with her skirt and looking around the hallway as she moved toward him. "Are you all right?"

"I'm fine."

Then Alex's entire body went rigid, and her eyes widened. Aaron realized she was staring at something over his shoulder —again. Aaron smiled and whipped around. *Caught you, Michael!* But there was nothing there. When he spun back, Alex was trembling, her arms locked across her chest.

"What's wrong?" He rushed to her side and began rubbing her shoulder, first to calm her but then to warm her. "You feel like ice."

"I'm fine."

Aaron stared at her. "We agreed to be friends, remember? Talk to me."

Alex sighed and pulled away. "I got lost, and the door stuck. Could you please escort me to the dining hall?"

Eyeing her, Aaron nodded. "On one condition. You tell me the whole truth."

Alex explained that she'd gotten lost snooping through some rooms after her dance instructor had quit. "I was trying to get back to the first floor when a door slammed behind me and I couldn't get it open. I panicked."

"Why do you look over my shoulder sometimes?"

Alex exhaled and looked away. "I thought I saw a ghost."

Aaron smiled. "I've spent countless nights wandering these halls, and I hate to disappoint you, but there are no ghosts. Secret passages, yes. But ghosts, no."

Alex shrugged. "I think you're wrong."

CHAPTER 14
ALEX

"Three!" Alex moaned, throwing her holey knitting on the couch. "In one day, I drove away the three best dance instructors in Warren."

"Your father will find more," Edith said.

"Why do I have to learn this?" Alex pointed at the mess of wool.

"Jessica and Her Majesty believe some ladylike activities will help quiet your mind and help with your nightmares."

"I'd rather just read." Alex crossed her arms and huffed.

"Hmm. I didn't think Warrens were *quitters*."

Alex whipped around to face Edith. She wore a small, mischievous smile as she tugged the knitting, unraveling it to roll back into a ball. Unflinching, she locked her sandy eyes on Alex, eyebrows raised.

"Thank you, Edith. You're free to turn in. I'd like to read a little before bed."

"If you insist," Edith said, slipping out the door to her own room.

Once Edith's door had closed, Alex headed to her bedroom,

kneeled down, and pulled her satchel from the hiding spot at the back of her wardrobe, dumping the contents onto her bed. Despite sifting through the pile, she couldn't find her worn copy of *The Iliad*. Instead, in its place was a pristine copy.

The only good thing that came from a war between mortals and sorcerers over two thousand years ago was their legends and stories being left behind.

Alex picked up the book, opened it to the first page, and found an inscription:

For my little brother,

I hope our adventures are as fantastical but less bloody. Try to stay out of trouble.

Love,

Daniel

Smiling, Alex traced the inscription and tried to remember when she'd left Aaron alone with her bag. *In the hut, when I went to collect water for his shoulder.* "Nosy prince," she said as she caught movement from the corner of her eye. "It's late, Daniel, and I'm tired. Could we do this tomorrow?"

Daniel grinned at her and pointed at the book she was holding.

"Go watch your brother." She waved dismissively, and he vanished.

Turning to shut her wardrobe, she spotted Aaron's cloak. That strange warm feeling in her stomach hit again, like when he'd wrapped his cloak around her at the camp while they were talking after her nightmare.

He's kind to everyone. A handsome, kind, perfect prince—stop thinking about him like that. He's my friend, nothing more.

This time of year, she'd fixate on things to distract her from thinking of her mother. *I won't sit here and think of Aaron all night. I'm going to read.* After putting on some clean sparring pants, she flung her empty satchel over her shoulder and put on Aaron's cloak.

When she left a few seconds later and found Sir Kruft standing guard, Alex gulped and huffed as he followed her to the library. Climbing the staircase, she passed the bust of the first king and soon found the royal journals. Leafing first through her father's journals then continuing farther back in history, she soon froze. *Grandfather's journals.* A chill washed over her as she contemplated the fact that these books contained the thoughts of the man who had wanted her dead and murdered her mother.

After glancing over her shoulder to make sure Sir Kruft was on the main floor, Alex picked up a journal and flipped through it. His handwriting was much neater than her father's. Alex knew she wouldn't like its contents, but she wasn't sleeping anyway, so she was prepared to be repulsed. Stuffing the first few journals into her satchel, she then heard footsteps. Her blood went cold, and an icy wind brushed past her as she looked around.

Silence.

Alex didn't trust her eyes or her instincts, so she sprinted back to her room.

Once on her bed, Alex bit her lip and tried to slow her breathing as she stared warily at the neat pile of journals, as though they might suddenly attack her.

I must be exhausted if books are scaring me. Just because my grandfather appeared at the ceremony and sent me into a panic doesn't mean these books will bring him here.

Tucking them under her mattress, she lay back on her pillow. Alex closed her eyes and waited for sleep while hoping the effort would prove fruitless, knowing what familiar tortured nightmares awaited her.

~

COOL SAND SHIFTED *beneath her bare feet as she waded into the waves. Alex could taste salt as the chilly sea air filled her lungs, and gulls cawed above as they soared past. Alex didn't recognize the beach but suspected she was somewhere north of Warren from the icy breeze coming off the water. Wrapping her arms around herself, she exhaled, staring out at the endless cerulean sea.*

The hairs on her neck stood up as she sensed she was being watched. Still holding herself, Alex spun around and spotted a man on the beach. His hair was obsidian black with a strange streak of gold running through it starting above his left eye. When his golden eyes locked with hers, she knew he could see through all her barriers, peering into her being and finding parts of her Alex didn't know existed. He was tall, and though he wore a dark orange robe that clasped shut at the front and draped over most of his body, his muscular legs told of his great strength.

He turned his head to look away for a moment, and Alex noticed two small marks on the base of his neck in the same spot as Merlock's. But while Merlock had a sun and infinity symbol—this man's neck had an ax and a crescent moon.

He turned back and stepped toward her, but Alex instinctively jumped back. The man looked hurt by her movement, but Alex felt power emanating from him—something dangerous. It beat like a drum in her ears, calling to her. Her breath sped up, and her palms became clammy as she stared at him, terror and excitement coursing through her veins. When his stare intensified, she felt exposed and nervous.

He held his hand out to her, and it drew Alex toward him with a force she didn't want to resist. Grasping for his hand, the cold sea swallowed her.

She tried to scream, but her lungs filled with icy sea water until a flash of orange light erupted around her.

CHAPTER 15

ALEX

Alex awoke in a panic, drenched in sweat and with Edith and Jessica hovering over her, trying to calm her down—Edith with soothing words and Jessica with a firm, steadying grip.

Such a Wafner.

"Did you know your mother had nightmares too?" Edith asked.

"No." Alex shook her head.

"My father told me about hers when I told him about your last one. He guarded both your parents. Sometimes the nightmares were so bad she'd get violent, and your father would have to restrain her. I'm sure he'd talk about it if you asked him."

"Thank you, Edith," Alex said, but her mind had wandered back to the journals hidden beneath her bed.

"You should go with Edith to the pier," said Jessica. "The fresh sea air would do you good, and the dress shop needs some final measurements. I'm sure there are lots of guards who'd be happy to escort you."

"Guards or a certain *prince*." Edith giggled.

"Why do you always giggle when you mention Prince Aaron?" Jessica asked.

"I can't help it. He's delightful to look at. With all that thick blond hair and those rippling muscles and that tight—"

"Edith!"

Edith turned back to Alex. "You agree with me, don't you?"

Alex stayed silent, but the heat on her cheeks betrayed her.

"Blush means yes," Edith said, sticking out her tongue at Jessica.

"I don't understand."

"Good. Less competition." Edith winked as she and Jessica left the room.

Curled in a tight ball, Alex tried to get back to sleep, but then her stomach rumbled, so she climbed out of bed, dressed, and left for the kitchen.

On her way, she paused at the small northeast stairs. She knew from her tour that those stairs led to the crypts. A frigid breeze raced up the stairs, and holding her breath, she took the first few steps down.

No. I can't.

Alex hurried back up the stairs but felt a pull before she even reached the top. Turning back around, she crept down a few more stairs—each step causing her pulse to gallop even faster. She'd reached the landing when a familiar face strode up the steps.

"Good morning, princess," Sir Kruft said.

"Hello, Kruft. It's nice to see you again," Alex said.

"The pleasure is mine, Your Highness." Kruft bowed to Alex and climbed the steps until he was one below her. Even on a lower stair, he towered over her. Almost her father's age, he had dedicated his life to protecting the royalty of Datten and Warren. Emmerich had handpicked him to be part of her guard, but something about him felt off. Stefan and Michael had teased her because all her other guards were her friends or young men she could control by batting her eyes or smiling. But Alex knew better than to doubt her gut; she had never doubted that Graham had been dangerous, and she'd been right.

"Are you lost?"

"I'm fine. Thank you," Alex said.

"It isn't safe for a young lady to wander the halls alone." Kruft moved up a step and stood next to her. Alex opened her mouth to reply, but a sense of dread washed over her, intimidated as she was by his size.

At that moment, footsteps echoed from further up the stairs.

"What are you doing here?" Stefan's voice sent a rush of relief through Alex as she spun around.

Alex recovered and explained about heading to the kitchen.

"Surprise, Alex is hungry," Stefan replied, rolling his eyes knowingly. "I've got her, Kruft."

The knight nodded and vanished up the stairs.

"What's wrong?" Stefan asked when he and Alex climbed up the stairs a short while later.

"I don't trust him."

"You can't dislike every knight that isn't Michael or me."

Alex pointed at Stefan. "I like *lots* of the knights. Julius is delightful. I just don't like Kruft. He makes me nervous—like Graham did."

Alex rubbed her eyes as Stefan slid his arm around her shoulder. "You're tired and adjusting takes time. Try not to judge anyone too harshly until you find your footing. Come on. I'll take you to the kitchen."

After talking the kitchen maids into sneaking her some

bread, Alex set off to find Merlock. She wandered for a while before she finally heard his voice in the throne room with the kings. Biting her lip and clenching her fists at her side, she marched up the aisle.

"Good morning, Father. Emmerich." She curtsied to them. "I'd like to steal Merlock, if I may. I was hoping to start my lessons early."

Edward beamed, and while Emmerich looked surprised, he nodded his assent. Merlock marched to her side. As soon as they reached the hallway, Alex said, "I want to know what those marks on your neck are and if you can stop dreams."

"Specific questions today, princess," Merlock said as they strode toward the courtyard. Upon their arrival, Merlock waved Sir Kruft over while speaking to Alex. "Up for another training lecture?"

Alex kept her misgivings about Kruft to herself and simply nodded. Merlock turned to her, and Alex tried to crack. She did the motion correctly, but they didn't go anywhere.

"Good try," Merlock said, smiling. The next instant, he snapped his fingers, and they were on the beach near the castle. Kruft found a large tree to lean against and observed. "All right, princess."

Alex moved to stand next to Merlock, and as she did so, he loosened his robe so he could lower his collar, giving Alex a better look at his two marks. Alex couldn't decipher whether they were birth marks or if someone had burned them into his skin.

As though knowing her thoughts, Merlock explained that the Forbidden Lands had ten sorcerer lines. Every full sorcerer came from one or two—they inherited one line from each parent, and if both parents were from the same line, they were stronger in that one line. Sorcerer parents could choose their child's gender and which line they would inherit. Once they came into their powers, the Head of the Generation confirmed their lines, and then the marks were burned onto the young sorcerer's skin to identify their lineage.

"Why doesn't Megesti have them?"

"Megesti was born in Datten, so he didn't receive his lineage marks. But if he had been given some, it would have been from the line of Merlin." Merlock explained that the line of Cassandra was the sun and granted the power of healing and premonition. The infinity symbol from the line of Merlin gave one a broader range of powers rather than a specific skill set.

Merlock pulled a small amount of water from the sea and placed it in a puddle before stepping back. "Try to move the puddle while we talk."

Alex nodded. "So what are the other lines? What's a head?"

"The head is a conversation for later," Merlock said. "For now, think of him as our king. The lines are Merlin, Cassandra, Mystics, Celtics, Salem, Ares, Hades, Poseidon, Tiere, and Mire. They control nature, the earth, the seas, the weather, and fire; read minds; and talk to animals as well as spark chaos, ignite peace, and crack people great distances. Why the sudden interest?" Merlock asked.

"Last night, I dreamed about a sorcerer unlike any I've encountered before. It was like he was made of power and could hurt me, and it scared me. I want to get rid of these dreams so I can sleep." All the while, Alex held her hands over the puddle, but nothing happened.

"Well, I can't banish them," Merlock began, "but I'll see if I have any spells that can help."

"I think I'd be less on edge if I could sleep. Everything is happening so fast—I'm worried I'll lose my temper or that I'll keep seeing things."

Merlock crossed the space between them and took her hands in his. "What are you seeing?"

Alex fidgeted. "I see *them*."

"Who?" Merlock asked, his eyes fixed on Alex's face.

"My mother, Daniel, my grandfather. Other dead royals."

Merlock examined Alex so closely she felt as if he were trying to count the freckles on her face.

"Megesti said you fell through the ice when you were young."

"Yes, but what does that have to do with seeing dead royals?"

"We have a few special sorcerers in our world. A Returned One is a sorcerer who died but has come back. They have a closer connection to the afterlife; they can see and even talk to the dead. You might also have powers from the Hades line. Their powers all relate to the dead. I'll need to check my books."

"And my grandfather?" Alex asked. "Is there a way to make him go away?"

"Only a powerful Hades sorcerer can influence the dead." Merlock put his hand on Alex's shoulder. "I know it won't ease the stress of seeing him, but he cannot hurt you. Ghosts cannot touch things or people."

Alex looked back to make sure Kruft was still out of earshot then swallowed the lump in her throat. "That's not true."

"What do you mean?"

"Daniel's touched me."

Merlock's eyes went wide, his mouth agape. "How often?"

"Countless times. It happens most often when I'm in danger," Alex said.

"I'll need to cut our lesson short so I can go back to my lab in Datten and consult my books," Merlock said. "I will let you know what I find about the spells. The puddle can wait."

Just ask him.

"One last thing. I'd like it if you called me Alexandria instead of 'princess' or 'Your Highness.'"

Merlock smiled and nodded. "I think your mother would like that."

CHAPTER 16
ALEX

"Alexandria, try not to fidget. It'll scar if I do it wrong," Jessica said. Seated on one couch in Alex's receiving room, Jessica was trying to clean the gash on Alex's bicep. "How *did* you dance into a candleholder during your lesson? They're very large and easy to avoid."

"I didn't dance into it," Alex replied, defensive. She paused then added sheepishly, "I fell." Jessica and Edith laughed. "What am I going to do? I'm managing everything—except dancing. And now, I'm more confused than ever."

"How many instructors have you chased away now?" Edith asked.

"Five," Alex said, groaning. "I'm never going to do this."

"Yes, you are," Edith said. She grabbed their cloaks off the edge of the couch and handed Alex hers.

"Go with Edith to the pier," Jessica said. "You wanted the dressmakers to give you more room in the shoulders, and you wanted time to look at the shops—it'll take your mind off things."

"I know. I want to, but I have lessons and can't fall behind on anything else."

"Michael is escorting me," Edith said.

"There's a bookshop," Jessica said. She picked up her needlework and raised her eyebrows at Alex. "Have fun."

"All right." Alex stood up but rejected Aaron's cloak. *It's so fancy they think it's mine. Well, now it is.*

Edith handed Alex her crown and headed into the hallway where her father waited. "They'll bring the coach to the courtyard. The king has business to attend to at the pier and will join us."

Alex smiled as they strolled to the front courtyard. A minute later, a massive carriage arrived, driven by one of the senior stable boys. The entire carriage was silver except for the doors, which were decorated with a glittering silver, green, and blue crest of Warren. It was the same carriage they had taken to the mourning ceremony. As the memory of the disaster flooded Alex's mind, a wind tore through the courtyard.

"Strange weather we're having," Edith said, squeezing Alex's arm.

The carriage door flew open, and Michael leaped out, dressed in his Warren-crested silver shirt with a blue tunic beneath it. He lowered the steps and held his hand out to Alex. Edith playfully pushed her forward, and as Alex accepted Michael's hand, she climbed into the carriage to join her father and Randal. She took her seat on the empty bench, rubbing the soft blue velvet that lined the cushion. Edith and Michael climbed in last.

Arriving at the pier a short while later, they left the carriage at the royal stable and strolled along the water. It was easier, Alex noted, to take things in without the crowds. Alex marveled at how beautiful the port was even without the mourning ceremony decorations. The massive ships tied to the piers were entrancing. As they walked, she breathed in the salty sea air but wrinkled her nose when the aroma of fish hit her. Alex felt at home here.

People milled about while workers unloaded supplies and wares for trading. Even if Alex hated her dresses, the women all looked beautiful in their gowns, and the men were fetching in their tunics—some of whom wore crests other than Datten and Warren. Alex noticed the little shops that lined the piers, selling everything from books to flowers. Alex could smell the flower shop from up the road.

"Do you have to attend to your business immediately?" Alex asked her father.

"It can wait until after your tour—since I wasn't able to give you one upon your arrival." Edward held his arm out to Alex and led her along the pier with Michael, Edith, and Randal a few steps behind.

"Something about the sea and the sound of the gulls calms me," Alex remarked.

"When you were little, you wanted to come to the pier every day, and your mother and I indulged you. The ships and people fascinated you. You loved to watch the cargo being removed. Before we left, we'd always visit the flower shop, and you always picked the same flower."

"Lilies."

"They were your favorite."

"They still are."

"Mine are hydrangeas—"

"But only the blue ones," Alex finished. "Blue is your favorite color."

Edward laughed. "Yours is green, and your mother's yellow. It always delighted her how our favorite colors made yours. Do you remember anything from here?"

"The ships, sounds, and smells all ... *feel* familiar, feel like home, but no, no specific memories."

"I see you're wearing your mother's necklace."

"It makes me feel close to her," Alex said. She clasped the jagged black stone. It looked rough but was smooth to the touch. Edward had gifted her the necklace when he'd told her about her tutors. It had been Victoria's favorite.

"She was wearing it the day we met. No matter how many I gifted her, she always wore that one." He came to a stop and fixed her with a serious look. "What can I do to help you settle in? I've heard you're having nightmares."

"They'll get better—they're just bad this time of year."

Edward raised his eyebrows.

"Fine, the swordfish you served on my first day here? I was too nervous to enjoy it, but I would love to have it again. And since I can't sleep, I'd like some new books."

"Fish and books? That's all it takes to make you happy?"

Alex nodded.

"Randal, have a swordfish sent to the castle for dinner tonight." The general nodded and crossed the street, heading to the open-air fish stall. "After your dress fitting, you may stop at the bookshop. Pick out anything you like."

"Thank you, Father."

Edward beamed when she said "Father."

They had stopped in front of a building at the far end of the port, one made from white stone instead of black and with larger windows than the rest of the buildings Alex had encountered. A wooden sign hung outside with *Wescott Barrister* carved into it. Edward told her to continue on with Edith and Michael and then kissed her cheek before ducking inside.

"Where to first?" Alex asked.

"Dress fitting!" Edith said.

Edith and Michael dragged Alex into the shop, but once

inside, the fitting went quickly. Alex tried on a few simpler gowns, and the seamstress figured out how to give her space to move her arms. Her celebration dress for the upcoming banquet was gold in honor of Aaron's birthday. To Alex's disdain, the skirt was fuller than any she'd ever worn, making it weigh more than she could have imagined. Worse, the neckline was lower and even exposed her shoulders. Alex couldn't get the dress off fast enough and left Edith in the shop to decide what gold lace to use for trim. She was so desperate to flee the tiny shop that she slammed right into a nobleman before tumbling onto the cobblestones. Looking up, ready to apologize, she was surprised to see the man smiling at her. His Warren tunic was colored like the general's except it featured an opulent letter *S* stitched on the top left. His golden hair sparkled in the sun while his sea-blue eyes stood out against his light bronze skin. He was incredibly handsome, and Alex's cheeks burned as he apologized and held his hand out to her.

"I'm so sorry. I should have been paying more attention to where I was going, milady."

"Thank you, but it was really my fault. I was fleeing the shop and should have paid more attention," Alex replied, accepting his hand and then brushing herself off once she had stood up.

"I'm Baron Cameron Strobel. And you are?"

"Alexandria." Alex curtsied. *Don't curtsy to barons.*

"Are you new to Warren? You look familiar, but I can't place it."

"I was born here then left—for some time. Now I'm home."

"I hope you stay. It'd be a shame for Warren to lose such a lovely and well-mannered lady."

"I'm much more than a pretty face, Baron Strobel."

"I believe you. Most Warren women have something

hidden behind their sweet smiles. And my friends call me Cameron."

Charmingly cocky. "How are you so sure I'm friendly after a minute of knowing me?"

"Lady Edith is in the shop you've just fled from. Her father would never allow her to associate with anyone *not* worth knowing."

Alex turned and saw Edith pointing at something on the counter. Michael was watching Alex and waved. She turned back to the baron. "How astute. What does your family do?"

"We raise horses for the royal guard."

Alex couldn't help but smile at the handsome nobleman. His demeanor put her at ease, and he knew a lot about horses. Alex turned as the shop door opened, and her friends came out. Edith smiled as she spotted them.

"Cameron, how's your mother?"

"She's well. I'll tell her you send your regards, Edith. I should be off. My father must be wondering where I am. It was a pleasure speaking with you, Lady Alexandria. I'd like to do it again."

"I believe my father would approve," Alex said.

"Ask for me at the castle if you wish to," Edith said. Cameron bowed and left.

"He *likes* you," Michael said, poking Alex's side.

Edith handed Alex her crown, which she'd forgotten in the dress shop, and they strolled down the pier to the bookshop for Alex and flower shop for Edith.

After Michael completed a preliminary sweep, he opened the door for her, and a bell jingled as Alex stepped inside. She'd never seen so many books crammed into such a small space. The older man behind the counter nodded but let her be. Alex ran her hands along the shelves and let herself wander the stacks picking books. Stefan had always limited her to one book when they went to town; it was all they could afford. Alex intended to make up for it.

When she was ready to pay, she realized she hadn't brought money. Just then, the doorbell jingled, and Aaron strode in. He smiled at her, introduced her to the owner, and asked him to send her books and invoice to the castle.

Once outside, Alex slapped Michael's shoulder. "Some guard."

Michael just grinned.

As they walked toward the flower shop to collect Edith, everyone they passed came over to visit with Aaron. Alex marveled at how he could speak so easily with everyone. When he turned to Alex, he caught her staring at him. "What is it?"

"How do you remember so many people?" Alex asked, awed.

"I've always been good with names."

"Do you know the people of Datten this well?"

"No. The Warren nobility knows who I am, but I try to only come to the pier dressed as a knight or with my cousin. He's well liked too, and the blond hair makes people assume I'm another Datten knight. People talk more freely with a knight than they would with a prince. But I like to hear how people feel about happenings in the kingdom. Give it time—soon everyone will know you too."

"That explains why no crown," Michael said. Alex became even more aware of the crown on her head in that moment as people looked at them.

"It suits you," Aaron whispered.

"Sometimes it feels ... heavy, if that makes any sense."

"It does to me."

Edith came bouncing out of the flower shop with three bouquets. She handed some roses to Michael and lilies to Alex.

"Michael, could you give these to Jessica?" Edith asked, winking at Alex. Michael almost dropped the flowers.

Arriving at the barrister, Aaron went inside to check on Edward. Alex leaned against the cold stone wall and observed the pier while they waited. Salty sea air mixed with fresh bread from the nearby bakery and fish from the fishmonger up the road. Several knights patrolled the pier, and Alex watched how effortlessly they conversed with the citizens before moving on to speak to the harbormaster. She grinned when the youngest knight left the group to scold some children climbing on the seawall to look at the water below. Workers hurried past the children and down the closest pier. Another ship had arrived, and everyone was rushing to unload the goods. Crates and barrels of various sizes came down the massive gangplank. The men moved with such precision and speed to empty the hold that Alex noticed when they suddenly struggled with a particularly heavy crate. The next thing she knew, the pier exploded, the blast blowing Alex's hair back and burning her eyes.

When she could open her eyes again, a giant hole marked where the men had been. Workers and knights charged onto the pier while Alex shouted at the children to get away as the fire rushed along the wooden dock, setting everything ablaze. The young knight grabbed the petrified children and pulled them away from the carnage. Bits of burning wood and ash rained down around Alex as she frantically searched for the harbormaster, but he and the men unloading the crate had vanished.

A second explosion shook the pier and sent the people around Alex into a panic. A man stumbled into Alex, almost knocking her over, but she stabilized herself.

Michael! Edith!

Alex spun around, searching for her friends, but they had disappeared into the surrounding chaos. Alarm bells rang out, sending Alex's attention back to the pier as more knights charged onto it. The fire had weakened it, and Alex watched, helpless, as the end broke off and began spinning into the sea. A massive wall of water rose out of the sea, and the fire flew from the pier toward it.

The next moment, a gale-force wind slammed Alex into the stone wall. Unable to move, all she could do was watch as her people ran from the burning pier. Black smoke filled the sky, choking her as she began shaking.

"Alexandria? Deep breath! You're all right."

Alex blinked at her father's voice, and when she opened her eyes, the pier was back to normal. The harbormaster was leaving the men to their work, and the older knights were calling the younger one over. As soon as he left, the children scrambled back up on the rocks. Alex trembled, and her breath burned in her throat.

She looked up at her father; she'd ended up on the ground. Edith was pale, clutching her flowers as she stood nearby with Aaron. Michael and Randal were at her feet, and when Edward nodded to Randal, they hoisted her up. Michael grabbed her bicep to steady her when Alex struggled to stand on her own. Edward picked up her discarded bouquet of lilies.

"I want to go back to the castle," she whispered.

AFTER RETURNING TO THE CASTLE, Alex wouldn't speak to anyone. The pier had shown her terrible images twice now, but at least her grandfather's ghost hadn't taunted her today as he had done at the mourning ceremony. In an effort to avoid thinking or speaking about the incident, Alex threw herself into her lessons, including hiding in the library with Megesti to memorize the names of Torian nobility.

After a day of reading, she begged Jerome and Stefan to give her an evening lesson. Stefan was unsure about the idea, but Jerome was thrilled. Alex changed and rushed outside. Jerome wanted to determine her endurance, so she and Stefan raced. Alex pushed herself to the absolute limit, but Stefan still won. He always won. Alex hoped pushing herself hard enough would let her sleep through the night since Merlock couldn't find a spell or potion to help. Once Jerome decided they had run enough, Alex lay on the ground and stared at the stars until Stefan came to escort her back to her room.

"Are you ready to talk about what happened at the pier today?" Stefan asked, leaning on the door frame. Alex was sitting on her couch, dressed for bed, working on the needlework Jessica was trying to teach her.

"What did Michael tell you?" Alex asked.

"That you had a vision."

"I'm fine, but I'm not going back to the pier soon."

Stefan squatted beside Alex and took her hands in his. "You know we're available—day or night—anytime you need us. I know you're busy with lessons, but don't forget that we're still family."

"Thank you." Alex went silent, her way of telling Stefan she wasn't ready to talk.

"Maybe tomorrow." Stefan looked at her work. "That looks good. I like the ship."

Alex gave him a dirty look and shoved him. "It's supposed to be a horse."

CHAPTER 17
ALEX

Early morning sunlight shone through the windows of the castle's outer wall, lighting up the hallway before her. As Alex glanced at the paintings on the wall, she realized these weren't the paintings by Megesti's room.

Lost again. Alex groaned and meandered down a series of smaller halls, trying to find someone who could point her in the right direction. Unlike the bustling first floor, the second floor—a veritable maze of smaller guest rooms, lush suites for visiting royals, stuffed storage rooms, and massive open spaces that overlooked the first floor—was as silent as a tomb. Alex grumbled as she rounded a corner and found another dead end, but as she turned to leave, a creaking sound startled her. Turning around, she noticed a lone door now stood open, so she walked into the room.

It was one of the nicer guest suites, with a large four-poster bed near the balcony overlooking the courtyard, a wardrobe on the opposite wall, and a small wooden table in the corner. In her previous explorations, Alex had deciphered that the size of the fireplace determined how luxurious the room was. Here the fireplace was as large as her own. Alex crossed the room and threw open a second door, which led to a simpler bedroom.

The space felt *wrong*. A rush of power flowed through her as she stepped toward the wardrobe. The hinges creaked as she opened it and found Warren clothing: nightshirts, tunics, undershirts, all hanging in a line. Alex ran her fingers along the first shirt and flinched. The fabric was the finest she'd ever felt and made Aaron's royal shirts feel like scratchy wool, but from the moment she touched it, fear engulfed her. Invisible hands ripped it from her grasp, opening the second wardrobe door in the process.

Alex gulped and reached for the wardrobe's small drawers with trembling hands. There were a few gold rings, some strange-looking coins, a journal, letters, bits of parchments—one of which was torn and had writing on it. Alex flipped through a few letters, but she recognized neither the names nor the handwriting. She returned her attention to the ripped parchment:

R. *Vinur,*

Follow the trail that leads to the mountains for three hours.
When you see the dead tree with the rock shaped like a fox, follow the small trail to the castle. The cost will be twenty gold coins, but success is guaranteed.

Alex turned the paper over, but the back was blank.
Such an odd thing to keep. Vinur? Aren't there Vinur knights?
She dropped it back in the drawer and dug through the others until she found an old, wrinkled, yellowed letter stuffed at the bottom. Alex instantly recognized her father's handwriting:

Your Royal Highness, King Arthur of Warren,

Father, I've arrived in Datten to prepare for the birth of the new prince. Emmerich sends his thanks for the gifts and agrees to your request for more guards to patrol the Ogre Mountains along our borders.

I have news. In my travels, I have met the noblewoman I intend to marry. She is part of Datten's court and well ranked. She will make an exceptional Princess of Warren. I know you hoped for me to wed a princess from one of the southern kingdoms, but Malota is about as sharp as a stone, and Roesia is insufferable.

Victoria is intelligent, beautiful, and has a kind heart. I believe my choice will please you, and I cannot wait to bring her home and make her my bride. I know you will accept her once we provide you with the next heir of Warren.

Your ever obedient son,

Edward

The air turned icy, and goosebumps ran up Alex's arms as her breath fogged. Shivering, she turned to see the monstrous face from her nightmares staring at her.

The rage on Arthur's face made her heart stop and her throat go dry. His hair, skin, and mouth were so similar to her father's it hurt. His brown eyes bore into her as she backed away from him, bumping into the wardrobe a moment later. Her scream stuck in her throat as he scowled and began circling her, never taking his eyes off her.

Run!

Alex pushed her trembling legs to move and rushed past the apparition. She heard the door slam behind her as she tore down the hall, her fright so great that she couldn't stop when she reached the main hallway. She collided with a suit of armor, sending pieces scattering down the corridor. The passage spun, and she fought to keep from vomiting. She then dropped to her knees, gasping for breath, and before things went dark, Alex heard hurried footsteps.

CHAPTER 18

ALEX

Alex spent the next week bouncing from lesson to lesson, hiding in her studies. Outside of training and getting dressed, she didn't see her friends. At night, she thought about the handsome baron she'd met, wondering if his touch would make her stomach flip the way it did whenever Aaron touched her. After chasing off another four dance instructors, she worried she'd never be able to manage a simple dance for her celebration without setting the room on fire.

One night, after waking from another gruesome nightmare, Alex donned her green dress and took her grandfather's journals to the library. Finally comfortable, Alex began reading the journals. After the first few entries, she checked to make sure it was the right set. It was clear Arthur had great love for his wife, Elizabeth Veremund. They had met at a celebration and married soon after, but they waited years to have a child. When Elizabeth died giving birth to Edward, Arthur's kindness died with her. Miraculously, Edward still became gentle and kind. Arthur blamed everyone—especially Merlock—for his wife's death, for failing to save her.

Alex needed more answers. She read journal after journal, trying to piece together why he had hated her mother so much. *Could it be because Merlock couldn't save my grandmother? My mother was the better healer, but she didn't or couldn't help?*

Alex soon found her mother's journals on the shelf, but they began when she became Princess of Warren, so there was nothing about where she had lived or what she did before meeting Edward.

Out of ideas, Alex went back to her grandfather's journals and lost herself in the words of a madman.

"What are you doing up?"

Alex jumped in her seat at the sound of Jessica's voice. She was wearing her nightgown with a blanket wrapped around her shoulders.

"I thought ladies didn't go around in nightgowns," Alex teased.

"What are you doing here? It's late."

"Research. I'm trying to figure out why my grandfather killed my mother."

"You might never get that answer. Sometimes people just do terrible things. I always wondered why someone would kill my family, but I've had to let that go."

Alex looked away.

"I know what you're going to say," Jessica continued. "Yes, someone hurt them to find you, but what kind of madman kills a woman and her children for not revealing the location of a child? That is what we'll never get the answer to—or the justice for."

Alex sighed as she looked up at Jessica. "Did you have a good time at dinner with Michael and Stefan?"

"Of course, they're always delightful company."

"Oh? Because Edith said you didn't talk to anyone besides Michael the entire meal."

"Edith needs to stop gossiping. That girl has one thing on her mind, and it isn't teaching you etiquette."

Alex giggled. "He's a good man, Jessica. Stefan and I approve, and I believe Jerome would too."

"When did you decide to start calling my father Jerome?"

"Since Jerome, Randal, and Matthew insisted my father make me do so. They were uncomfortable with my insistence that they call me Alexandria if I wouldn't use their first names too."

A bang made them look toward the wall, but nothing seemed out of place. Jessica narrowed her eyes at the wall before she turned back to Alex. "Since you seem unable to sleep, why don't you go practice dancing in the throne room? Maybe you'll find your footing."

"Couldn't hurt," Alex said. "Are you going to join me?"

"In my nightgown? *Certainly not.*"

Alex groaned at her research. Too lazy to bring it back to her room, she pushed it into a big, messy pile and placed it behind the bust of the founding king on the bookcase. She left the library and ambled into the throne room sometime later. Alex had expected the room to be empty, so finding Aaron lounging on her father's throne startled her.

"There you are!" Aaron exclaimed. "I thought you'd never make it."

Alex sighed in exasperation. "What does that mean?"

Aaron leaned forward. "I see you sneaking off every night. We agreed to be friends—I told you I get nightmares too. I'd hoped we could keep each other company, but you avoid me." Aaron strolled down the dais and held his hand out to her at the bottom. "We *both* witnessed the death of someone who meant the world to us. That leaves a scar, one very few people can understand."

"What do you want?" Alex ignored his hand. She turned her back to him but glanced over her shoulder.

"To help. I know why you come here at night when no one is around."

Alex's hands grew slick. "You don't know what you're talking about." She darted for the doors.

"It took me a year to get back on my horse," Aaron called after her. "To go into a stable without crying or running out."

Alex stopped. The cold wind she felt anytime she was near the thrones was swirling around them. She swallowed the lump in her throat and turned to him. Aaron ran his hand through his hair.

He only does that if he's nervous.

Alex trudged toward him, keeping her eyes averted. "How did you do it?" she asked.

"I went a little further each day, and then one day I realized nothing was going to happen. My brother's death was the odd event, so I didn't need to worry about the stables catching on fire every time I went inside. I realized I could go into a stable and be fine. I'd like to help you with this ... and your other problem." Aaron held his hand out again.

"What *other* problem?"

"Castle gossip says you can't keep a dance instructor."

Alex pursed her lips as she considered his outstretched hand.

Why do I trust you so easily?

His gaze set off that familiar tingle that started whenever he was close.

Do it.

Before she could change her mind, she took Aaron's hand and a bolt of electricity flew through her.

"I can help," Aaron said as he cradled her hand. Alex squeezed it so hard, she worried she'd break it, and her breaths came hard and quick as they walked across the hall. As they approached the thrones, an icy hand grasped her free one. Turning, she saw Daniel, who nodded at her. Alex stepped right up to the thrones, hanging onto the hands of *both* Datten princes. She wanted to flee, but the princes held her, and she looked down.

"Tell me what you see," Aaron whispered.

Tears soaked her cheeks as she gasped. "I see her body, the blood surrounding her." Her voice cracked, and she fought back the pain in her throat and lungs. "We were in the middle and ... she ran here to save me. She handed me to Megesti. I don't know where, but I was safe, hidden, and I watched him draw his sword and kill her. I saw her fall, heard her last breath, and saw the sparkle, the life, drain from her eyes. I see it in every nightmare."

Alex cried out and released the princes' hands before covering her face. Aaron pulled her to him, but immediately afterward, a second pair of icy arms encircled them, a pair only Alex could feel. Aaron held her tight while she rid herself of all the pain she carried. When she pulled back, Aaron tucked her hair behind her ear, and she let out a heavy sigh.

"Will you tell me yours?" she asked. *Let me in. Let me help you carry your burden.*

Alex rested her cheek on Aaron's chest to avoid looking at him. Calm filled her as she breathed in his rich pine scent. Megesti's words crossed her mind.

Aaron's simple. His eyes give him away every time. Look at his eyes if you want to know what or who he's thinking about.

Alex peeked and found Aaron's eyes fixed on her.

Daniel moved to Aaron's side, sending a chill through Alex.

When she shivered, Aaron tightened his grip on her. Daniel watched his brother, resting his hand on Aaron's shoulder.

"I remember talking my brother into taking me riding for my birthday that day," Aaron said. "When we got to the stables, a man appeared. I only remember his face—those gold eyes haunt my dreams. Daniel argued with him, then the man threatened to leave Datten heirless if Daniel didn't tell him where he hid you. He refused. The man dropped his lantern, setting the stable on fire. Daniel put me on his horse and sent it out, and then he attacked the man." Aaron paused. "He died for it."

Alex felt Aaron's heart pounding as he squeezed her in silence for a long while. When Alex eventually pulled away, she walked around the dais and said, "I still don't see how I got out."

A mischievous smile spread across Aaron's face. He walked to the painting of her parents' wedding, reached behind it, and pulled with both hands, revealing a secret passage. "I told you after your first tour of the castle I'd show you what your father left out—its secret passages. This one leads through the library, your room, my brother's room, and ends at my room. I knew you were coming here because I watched you reading your grandfather's journals and talking to Jessica. When you packed up, I ran here."

Alex narrowed her eyes, and all the candles flared up. "You were *watching* me?"

"No! I was trying to help you. Before you get any ideas about burning me for watching you read, let's solve your other problem." He ran his hand through his hair, and his posture suddenly changed.

Dancing with you is a terrible idea, dangerous even. But despite the reasons not to, Alex couldn't say no.

Aaron strolled into the middle of the hall. He stood with his left arm outstretched at shoulder height and his right curved down at hip height.

"What on earth are you doing?" Alex laughed. Daniel moved to the side of the room, watching his brother.

"My mother is from Warren. I would *never* place my hands on any maiden without her express permission. So take your position."

A snort escaped from Alex before she could stop it. Aaron smiled and wiggled his fingers to beckon her over. Alex sauntered toward Aaron to ensure he would remain in that ridiculous position for a little longer and give herself time to summon her courage.

It's just one dance. You'll mess it up in three steps and he'll leave.

As she reached him, she slid her hip into his grip at waist level and put her left hand on his shoulder, the other into his hand.

"Almost a perfect fit," Aaron said, sliding his hand around her waist and pulling her close. Shivers prickled up her spine, and butterflies fluttered in her stomach. Her heart beat so fast; she thought it might burst, yet she forced herself to look at his face, into those blue eyes. "Trust me?" He smirked playfully, tickling her back with his hand.

Answer him. Say something. She paused for a long minute before whispering, "Yes."

"Okay. *Attack.*"

"What?" She tried to pull away, but Aaron locked his grip, keeping her against him. The scent of pine and dew enveloped her, and her body temperature rose precipitously as he stared her down like they were sparring. For a moment, Alex felt Aaron's heart pound harder than even her own. Aaron was talking, but Alex couldn't focus. The feelings he was waking inside her were overwhelming.

"You step forward to attack, and I'll retreat," Alex finally heard Aaron say. Alex nodded.

The first few times, she bumped him or stepped on his foot, but he wouldn't release her. After a few minutes, they could predict their next movements. Aaron gave sparring orders, and Alex moved fluidly through the motions as he swept her across the room. Eventually, she stopped watching her feet and looked up to catch Aaron staring with a boyish grin. He winked before he released her, spun her, caught her, and dipped her— all as if they'd done it a thousand times before.

When he stood her back up, he released her and bowed. "Milady."

"Your Highness," Alex replied, curtsying. They were both out of breath, and Aaron's cheeks were red.

Are you blushing from our dance?

Over Aaron's shoulder, Alex saw Daniel bowing. He smirked as he disappeared a moment later, and her attention returned to Aaron.

"I can't believe it worked," she gushed. "I knew you'd have a plan, but I didn't believe I could pull it off."

"We'll keep practicing. I also heard a rumor you're curious about Datten. Is that true?"

"Yes."

"My father and the Wafners are going tomorrow. Would you like to come?"

Alex smoothed out her skirt, trying to hide her excitement. "Yes, I would like that."

"Good, because I already told them we're bringing you. We'll leave after you've finished with your defensive training. Now, shall I escort you back to your room? It's rather late."

Alex took his hand and intertwined their fingers. "Can you show me the secret passage?"

Aaron laughed heartily as he grabbed one torch from the wall and led her into the dark tunnel.

CHAPTER 19
ALEX

A lex dreaded every training session with Jerome because they always ended with her in the pond. But as a spring breeze blew her hair back and she stepped onto a log, she told herself today would be different.

Less than an hour before, she'd woken up after having slept well; it hadn't been a complete night of sleep, but for the first time in weeks, she felt rested. Proper sleep had made her over-confident in challenging the general—or perhaps it was the memory of Aaron's hand on her hip, their bodies pressed together. Even now, the image made her lose focus.

He's an amazing dancer.

"Your form's off," Jerome warned, snapping her back to her senses as she crept forward on the log.

"Your right hand is good," Stefan said from behind. "When you release, your left hand isn't gripping correctly."

As Alex arched her back and adjusted her footing, Jerome raised his eyebrows in the same way Stefan often did. "Remember our deal. *If* you beat me, we leave for Datten without the run," Jerome said.

After a few weeks with Jerome, Alex understood why Aaron was so quick on his feet. If he'd spent years training with Jerome, he would undoubtedly have encyclopedic knowledge of self-defense and fighting techniques. Jessica explained how Aaron had received intensive knight training at a much younger age than normal after Daniel's death. He had to protect himself. Alex swallowed, ready to face the inevitable. Her fingers locked on the staff, Alex shuffled along the fallen tree. Jerome waited for Alex in the center.

You can do this. Just don't fall.

After Alex reached Jerome, they nodded and tapped their staves.

Alex gripped her staff so hard her palms burned as she adjusted her stance on the log, but before she could plan her first move, Jerome lunged. Alex ducked just in time. Jerome was even taller than Stefan and knew how to use it to his advantage. Alex jabbed at him like she would with a sword, but Jerome batted the staff away easily. After repeated strikes, Alex's arms began burning. Counting his strikes in her head, Alex knew he'd come after her soon—he always struck her staff a dozen times before he went for *her*. She dodged the eleventh strike, but she knew the smirk on Jerome's face too well, and so she braced herself for what was to come.

This is going to hurt.

Jerome lunged, aiming for her shoulder. Alex dodged the first swing and barely deflected the second and third swings at her hip and shoulder, respectively. The fourth connected with the side of her knee, and the fifth ended it. Alex fell off the log before she felt the pain of the strike hit her calf.

The water was liquid ice. Alex's lungs froze as the murky pond water submerged her.

Kick. Air.

Her legs were heavy, and when she opened her eyes, a

massive wave the size of her castle slammed her into the muddy side of the pond walls. Pain engulfed her; bones snapped, ribs punctured her lungs, and the air left her as the dark water entombed her. A faint orange light appeared right before she blacked out.

"I'm so sorry, princess. I didn't think I hit you so hard."

Jerome's voice sounded strange—higher. When she looked at him, Alex recognized his expression from Stefan.

You're terrified.

"You didn't." Alex's throat was raw as if she'd been screaming.

"You had a vision, didn't you?"

Alex sat up. "A massive wave. It destroyed—" The words caught in her throat.

"What did it destroy?" Stefan asked.

"Me."

"WHAT DO YOU MEAN, 'they left already'?" The fireplaces roared to life around her, matching her tone.

"I'm sorry, Alexandria," said Edward, "but Jerome felt letting you go was a bad idea after your vision this morning. And ... I agree." Edward rose from his throne and came toward Alex, his tone and presence more regal than fatherly.

"Why do you let Datten order you around?" she complained. "If not Emmerich, Jerome. I'm a healing and premonition sorceress. Why did no one ask me what I thought about my vision?"

Edward sighed. Taking her hands in his, he squeezed them. "You are still sixteen, still my daughter, and I won't risk your health or safety, especially after Stefan pulled you out of that pond."

Alex groaned. *What if?* "May I at least ask Merlock to take me somewhere new to train? You trust him with me."

Edward narrowed his eyes. "Of course. But if I hear about the Princess of Warren being in Datten, there will be *severe* consequences."

Alex curtsied and left. She glanced around the hallway where General Matthew Bishop was waiting for her. His smile mirrored that of his son, Julius, as did his rich brown eyes, onyx hair, and warm umber skin.

"Matthew, have you seen Aaron this morning?"

"I believe he's in his room, Your Highness. Should I escort you?"

"Thank you, but I also need to find Merlock." Matthew looked her over. "Please don't be as overprotective as my father."

Matthew nodded and remained at the door. Alex ambled down the hall to avoid being conspicuous, but once she made it far enough, she sprinted for Aaron's room.

Before she even reached the door, it flew open. Aaron's mischievous grin surprised her. He was garbed like a Datten knight and held out her emerald pendant.

"Ready to see Datten, princess?"

"How—?"

"Secret passageways, remember?" Aaron interrupted, winking. "I expected your conversation with Edward to be exciting—more yelling. At first, I was disappointed when you didn't put up a fight, but then I understood what you were saying."

"How do we get Merlock to take us?"

"Leave Merlock to me." Aaron held his hand out, and Alex took it. The clamminess of his palm made her smile.

Soon they were in the library, ready for Merlock to take them to Datten. Aaron smiled when Merlock took their hands.

A crack sounded, and Alex found herself in a strange-looking room that smelled musty and spicy with a hint of campfire smoke. The main door was in the far left corner, and beside it, Merlock had filled the entire wall with floor-to-ceiling book-shelves. Alex ran her finger along the books' spines, briefly forgetting about her companions. Merlock's books had trained Megesti, and soon they would help her. Turning and looking beyond the large table Aaron and Merlock stood behind, she saw a monstrous fireplace in the farthest corner near a small table covered in pots. Along the wall to the right were many shelves covered with unusual jars. Alex loved seeing matching jars—nothing in their camp had ever matched.

"They were a gift from my grandfather," Aaron said, as though intuiting her thoughts.

"Great-grandfather," Merlock corrected. "Questions?"

"No," Alex said as she examined a jar. She shrieked when she tapped it and something moved.

"That's why I don't touch the jars anymore," Aaron said. "Ready for your tour?"

"Absolutely."

"When you're done, Your Highnesses, simply summon me."

Alex and Aaron nodded. Alex watched as Merlock went to grab a book.

This room is amazing. Maybe I should stay here and learn something.

Just then, Aaron's hand found hers and squeezed, and when she looked up, his piercing gaze made her breath hitch. Aaron opened the door and stuck his head out to look around before he pulled Alex into the hallway.

"That door across the hall leads into the king's suite and the one farther down into the queen's suite."

"Wait—your parents sleep apart?" Alex asked.

Aaron chuckled. "Of course. All the royalty in Torian do."

"Why?"

"Kings may be summoned at any time. Why should my mother be woken because your father needs to speak to mine in the middle of the night?"

Alex frowned, staring at the doors. *Why would you want to be away from the person you love? Did my parents sleep apart?*

"I'm not doing it," Alex said.

"Not doing what?"

Alex whipped around so fast her chestnut curls flew over her shoulder onto the front of her dress. "When I get married, I expect my husband to be at my side day *and* night. I'm going to be the ruling royal."

Aaron scoffed. "What if your husband disagrees with your decision?"

Her cheeks burned. "I'll have to convince him otherwise."

Aaron's eyes widened as he rubbed the back of his neck, and then he cleared his throat. "We should get you changed for your tour."

Alex followed Aaron, trying to take in everything. Her ancestors had decorated Warren's castle with beautiful art, stunning tapestries, and paintings from all over Torian. Datten, by comparison, was a sparsely decorated fortress. Aaron soon glanced down the next hallway, and when he surreptitiously reached back, Alex took his hand before he hurried them into a spiral tower.

As they climbed the stairs, Alex was drawn to the bedroom on the first landing. "Is this Daniel's room?"

Alex faced Aaron, and he nodded, tears welling in his eyes. "I'm sorry."

Aaron's hand slid across her lower back, and she let him lead her on. Aaron's room was on the top floor.

"Merlock and Megesti have the east tower. Daniel and I

had the west. Merlock and your mother put protection spells on them after an incident occurred with the third tower," Aaron said.

Alex giggled. "You mean when Megesti *burned it down* when he was learning to wield his gifts?"

Aaron shrugged playfully and leaned against the wall beside the stairs. The room was spotless and smelled like the woods. Alex looked around for a bit until she realized Aaron seemed lost in thought.

"What is it?"

"Nothing important."

"Tell me anyway," Alex said, squatting to pet his brown bear rug for a moment before moving on to examine his elaborate carved wardrobe.

"I just never thought—"

"So you admit you don't think?" Alex interrupted, eyebrows raised.

Aaron laughed. "No. I never thought *you'd* be here," he said, shooing her out of his wardrobe.

Alex slipped past him and went to his bookshelf across the room. "It's impressive—a bookshelf that curves along the wall."

"Merlock helped."

Alex flipped through a book before returning it to the bookshelf. After she walked her fingers across his crown table, tracing a worn circle on the wood, her gaze stopped on his bed. "Do you make your own bed?"

"What do you mean? It always looks like this." Aaron moved in close behind her. Alex could feel the heat coming off him.

Turning to look at him, she leaned down and ruffled his quilt without breaking eye contact. Aaron's nose pinched, and

Alex laughed. "Thought so. Uptight Datten men and your meticulously made beds. Stefan's the same."

"What about Michael?"

"Never."

"So—he's not from Datten then," Aaron said.

"Probably not," Alex said. She waited a long while before she asked, "Have you had many maidens in your room?"

"Some," Aaron replied without looking at her.

Alex didn't reply but looked down.

How many is some?

When she looked back, Aaron had placed some clothes on his bed.

"These are clean. We'll need you to look the part if we're going to have fun today."

He took her pendant out of his pocket and laid it on the shirt before heading to the stairs. Alex caught his arm.

"I need your help. Could you loosen my dress?"

Aaron's face flushed, but he nodded, and so Alex turned around. It took him a while to figure out how to loosen the corset.

"Is that enough?"

"It is. Thank you," Alex said.

"I'll wait for you outside Daniel's room," Aaron said as he hurried down the stairs.

Alex put on Aaron's clothes and scurried down the stairs, disguised by her pendant.

"They're huge. Maybe we should find you something else," Aaron said, looking her up and down.

"I'm used to loose clothes when I'm a boy. Besides, it isn't my clothes that give me away—it's the hair. To me, it's still here. I see it even if you don't, so if I play with my hair it looks ..." Alex smiled as she wiggled her fingers in the air.

"What are you doing?"

"Twirling my braid. *See.*"

Aaron laughed, and Alex smiled, waiting for the plan.

"The only part of you that doesn't change is those eyes. Do you know how intimidating your stare is?"

"I've been told that before. Michael always said it's the emerald color. In the camp, everyone had blue and brown eyes, so my green made them feel like the forest was watching them. Now *quit stalling*. I want to see Datten."

CHAPTER 20
AARON

Aaron carried a bucket as Edith allowed him into Alex's room.

"She's upstairs in her bedroom. We changed her into training clothes and braided her hair—but don't let her get sick in it," Edith ordered, holding open the hallway door. "Now, if you'll excuse me, I'm spending my night off at a family dinner."

"*If* she requires new clothing, summon me," Jessica said. "Otherwise you're the nursemaid tonight."

Aaron raised an eyebrow. *Nursemaid?*

"What? You expected to get away with this?"

Aaron explained how he'd planned to show Alex around Datten and bring her back. Somehow, they'd ended up at the Lion's Chest pub and run into the younger knights. He'd stepped away to get another chair, and the next thing he knew, Alex had downed multiple ales and was already drunk. Being caught by Jerome was just bad luck.

Jessica gave him Jerome's disappointed look. "The guards

will watch you like a hawk around Alex now, and she'll never open up to you unless you two are alone."

"I know that." *But I'm trying to let her have some fun too.*

"You don't. She feels out of place, and you understand what that feels like. Both your fathers were raised to be king; you weren't. She doesn't know how to handle what's expected of her. Now stop acting foolish and make her realize what she means to you. She won't believe Michael, Edith, or me. *You* need to convince her."

Feelings don't come easy for me. "I'm working on it. Speaking of feelings, have you told Michael about yours for him? He's terrified of your father *and* brother, so he won't start anything." Jessica scowled in response. "Does anyone know how you talk to me?" Aaron continued.

"No—it would be inappropriate for a lady's maid and a crown prince to speak so freely."

"But they know you're updating my mother on Alex?"

A smirk stretched across Jessica's lips. "Not with certainty. But you should know I'm giving Her Majesty information about both her goddaughter and her son."

"Treacherous Wafner," Aaron said.

"Spoiled brat. Rags are next to the fireplace," Jessica said curtly before leaving for her own room.

Aaron snatched the rags and went to check on Alex. Her bed was empty, and he found her curled up beneath a blanket, lying on the floor. Aaron set the rags and bucket down and slid along the stone floor to get to her.

"You don't need to sleep on the floor. That isn't part of the punishment," Aaron said, moving her hair off her face. She twitched at his touch, and her skin felt clammy.

"I know, but the stones are cold. They feel good."

"Would you like some water?"

"No."

"Bucket?"

"No. I have nothing left." Alex took Aaron's hand. "Just sit with me until I fall asleep. If I puke on myself, please don't tell anyone."

"Not a soul." Gently, he moved her head onto his thigh, and Alex nuzzled against him. He stroked her hair as his parents' scolding echoed in his mind. *I'm too upset to even look at you. You brought dishonor on yourself. You can't keep her safe on your own. What were you thinking? You put her life in danger.*

"Thank you for today," she said, her voice breathy, small. "I had fun ... with you."

Aaron smiled. "I'm glad. I'd love to show you more."

"Okay, but tell Daniel to leave me alone. He's teasing me about the alley."

Aaron froze. "What did you say about my brother?"

Her only reply was soft snoring. Aaron lightly nudged Alex's shoulder just to be sure, but she didn't move. Leaning back against her bed, his stomach tightened when her hand suddenly reached for his tunic. He brushed her hair from her face as he watched her sleep.

The next time we kiss, I don't want any outside influences. No ale for you, no teasing friends for me. Just you and me so I know it's real.

CHAPTER 21
ALEX

lex's head was pounding, and her stomach hurt more than that time the entire camp got food poisoning. Stefan dragged her out for a training session that ended with her in the pond after every strike. As the morning wore on, she felt guilty about lying to Merlock, so she took Michael to find him. When she realized where they were, Alex stopped.

"What are you doing?"

"I found something that day I knocked the armor over, where you and Aaron caught me hyperventilating on the floor. I want to get it while you're here with me."

"Why? Did you see a ghost?" Alex glared at him, but Michael pulled her down the hall. "What happened in Datten?"

I can't lie to you.

Alex swallowed. "We went to town to see if it would help my memories. We started at the old stables, and I remembered things, and we talked, but then we went for a drink and—" Alex closed her eyes and exhaled. She remembered everything:

the boisterous bar; stories from Aaron's friends Caleb, Hunter, and Lucas; the heat from Aaron's hands on her hips as he pulled her close; the smell of pine that followed him everywhere. Alex still felt Aaron's lips on hers.

He's a great kisser.

"And?" Michael asked.

"I don't remember," Alex lied.

"I feel bad for him."

"Why?"

"He's running both your miles today, and Emmerich has ordered every Datten knight to watch him anytime he's near you. They're furious he took you to Datten unchaperoned."

"They're upset because we were *alone*? What do they think happened?"

Michael listed the concerns the Datten knights had about their prince's behavior.

"Stefan and I see how Aaron looks at you. If Stefan had the chance, he'd make Aaron pay for it."

Alex's pulse sped up. "I find this insulting. I can handle myself around Aaron."

"I know, but Aaron cares about you, Alex. He struggles to say it—look at how his father treats his mother, but I see how he lights up when you enter the room. He's different."

"Sounds like you when Lady Jessica is around."

"We aren't talking about me."

"Now we are. Let's talk about you and my lady's maid, Michael. Stefan and I think you make a lovely couple." Alex snickered when Michael turned bright red.

"That doesn't change how Aaron looks at you."

Alex stopped, having found the room. She paused as she opened the door but then went right to the wardrobe. Inside, she pulled open the drawer, but it was empty.

Michael said, "This room feels—*wrong*."

"It was my grandfather's sick room," Alex replied. A stone beneath her foot shifted as she stepped back. Kneeling, Alex picked at the stone until it came up.

"What is that?" Michael crouched beside Alex.

Alex reached into the hole and pulled out a small journal as her breath fogged before her. Michael's eyes widened, and Alex could see his breath too.

"You feel that?" Alex asked.

Michael's face went ashen as he nodded. "What in the Forbidden Lands is that?"

"My grandfather." Without looking up, Alex knew he was beside them. "He doesn't like me in here. Get up and leave. I'll be right behind you."

Michael stood, but he didn't move. He gripped Alex's bicep and pulled her up. Heading to the door, he pushed Alex through it first. When he followed, the door slammed behind him. He dragged Alex back to the main hallway, shaking the entire way.

"How often does *that* happen?"

Alex avoided Michael's gaze and shrugged.

"Want me to put the journal in your room?"

Alex nodded.

"How many others can you sense?"

Alex frowned and shrugged again. "Several ... but he's the worst."

Though seeing my mother is harder.

They walked in silence until they found Julius Bishop and learned Merlock was in the garden. When they found him, Michael left for rounds.

Merlock's look of disappointment made Alex glance away. They made it ten steps on the garden path before she broke down.

"I'm sorry. I shouldn't have let Aaron lie. It won't happen

again." The plants near her yellowed and shriveled.

Merlock rested his hand on Alex's shoulder until she looked at him. "I'm disappointed you lied, but you're a young sorceress; you're going to make mistakes because you will insist on doing things your own way. *And,* like with Victoria, my job will be to pick you up when you fall or help you put the world back together when it crumbles around you. Your situation involves a Datten prince, so it'll require more effort."

Alex smiled, and the plants turned green again.

"Megesti said you were full of questions at your last lesson. Perhaps I could answer some."

"I want to know about blood oaths and why my grandfather hated my mother."

"A blood oath? What have you been reading?" Merlock narrowed his eyes at her.

"Where I learned of them doesn't matter." Alex's voice had more authority than usual.

Merlock's eyes widened briefly as they paused at the roses. "Very well. Blood oaths are taken between sorcerers when one might not hold up their end of the deal. Once made, it's almost impossible to break without dire consequences to the oath taker."

"Their blood?"

"Their *life.* Breaking a blood oath forfeits your life. There are lesser oaths we can swear; Megesti swore an oath to protect Aaron after Daniel died, so now if Aaron were in mortal danger, Megesti would be summoned to him. I took an oath to the royal family of Datten, which is why only they can summon me."

Alex ran her fingers along the rose bush. She smiled at the idea of Megesti having to go help Aaron even if he wouldn't want it. "If you took a blood oath, could you tell anyone?"

"It would depend on what the oath was for. If the oath

were to keep things a secret, then no. I can tell you I have taken a blood oath but not about what or why." He looked at her and added, "I am pretty confident Megesti has as well."

Alex exhaled. "I didn't realize he still can't talk about it. Megesti witnessed my mother's death; he brought me to Daniel."

"I've suspected he was there but never could confirm it," Merlock said. "I'll have to inform the kings of this. There have been rumors your grandfather didn't act alone, and Their Royal Highnesses will need to hear your side to develop a plan. I'll tell them, but the queen will insist they hold off on any action until after your party."

"Okay," Alex whispered as rain fell around them.

"You don't need to feel sad, Alexandria. If you don't wish to recount your story with words, you can use the pearl. After twelve years, your memories could be distorted."

"The pearl?" Alex turned to Merlock, and the rain vanished.

"Imagine a pearl the size of your clasped fists. If you hold it, it will make your memories real before you."

Made real. I can't see his face again.

Alex's eyes widened, and her heart began racing.

Merlock squeezed her shoulder. "Not flesh, merely a mist that shows a story. It's the same manner in which I see my premonitions. Megesti's premonitions are weak, so he speaks in riddles or phrases. In our lineage, the strongest are always the daughters. The line began with a sorceress named Cassandra; she was cursed by her gods to see the future, but no one believed her. It's a curse that occasionally appears in her daughters."

"Is that why I have nightmares?"

"Your mother's premonitions began as dreams for decades. Remember our discussion of the lines? We call the strongest in each line the titan of that line. We're the end of both our lines, so when your full powers arrive, you'll be the Titan of Cassandra."

Alex exhaled.

"As to your other question," Merlock continued, "I don't believe your mother did anything to incur your grandfather's wrath, but perhaps you can ask your father."

"Everyone keeps saying that." Alex pressed her lips together and kicked at the rocks on the path.

"Why haven't you? Your father's a good man. He's probably waiting for you to bring it up."

"I'm home for a month." *I feel guilty for wanting to know more about her when I've learned so little about him.*

Merlock smiled at Alex and leaned forward. "Alexandria, you'll have years to get to know your father. It surprises no one you're being curious about your mother. Now, was there anything else? I know Her Majesty said you were to be given no reprieve, but I can keep a secret."

"Thank you." Alex nodded and hurried back to the castle.

CHAPTER 22
ALEX

A lex slept a few hours before the nightmares ripped her from her slumber. This time they'd all combined to create a horrible image: her mother's death and then Alex drowning in a river of blood. She couldn't shake it— she flung her blankets off the bed and dropped her soaking wet nightdress on the floor. Unable to find her green dress, she went for her simplest blue one instead.

Just because my father loves blue that doesn't mean everything should be blue.

After she'd managed to get into it, she realized she wouldn't be able to tie it properly herself, but she did her best and then put on Aaron's cloak over it. Grabbing a torch, she went over to the painting and felt around its frame until she found the latch and pulled. It sprung open, and she climbed into the secret passage, closing the painting behind her.

Her mind wandered as she walked, remembering her morning rides with her father. Alex was enjoying getting to know him and hearing about her life when she was younger.

Arriving at the throne room, Alex crept out of the painting and found Aaron lounging on Edward's throne.

"Don't you have your own throne to sit on? Or is this how you make yourself at home in *my* castle?"

Aaron stood and walked toward her. "Why do you have my cloak on?" he asked with a hint of a smile.

"I can't reach the back of my dress, so I couldn't properly tie my corset."

Aaron chuckled. "Turn around and I'll try to fix it."

Alex unfastened the cloak and turned. Aaron's fingers danced across the fabric, sending shivers through her whole body. She flinched when he pulled the first few loops, but once he got the hang of it, Aaron managed the dress pretty quickly.

"I'm sure it's not as good as Lady Jessica would do it."

Alex turned and noticed Aaron's cheeks had flushed. She tried to give Aaron his cloak back, but he stopped her.

"Keep it. It looks better on you."

"Thank you."

Aaron held out his hand, and soon they were dancing. After a few minutes, Alex realized Aaron wasn't saying the steps out loud. She smiled with pride and wondered if he could feel her heart pounding.

With how tightly he's holding me, he must.

Alex took a deep breath to calm herself and tried to say something—anything—to break the tension.

"Why *always* this dance?"

"It's the traditional Warren Waltz—the one you are most likely to need at any banquet." He regarded her for a few seconds. "Are you ready for tomorrow?"

Alex nodded, trying to determine if the pounding she felt was from her heart or Aaron's. Datten flashed in her mind: the memories of strange but familiar streets, the feel of his lips. He'd held her tight and kissed her back, hadn't he?

But why did he pull away?

Even now, she wasn't sure. He acted like he wanted to kiss her again, but he'd acted like that in Datten too.

What am I supposed to do?

Alex tried to focus on the dance steps, but her feet had lost their rhythm, and she stepped on Aaron's foot.

"Sorry," she stammered.

Aaron raised an eyebrow. "Are you okay?"

"I'm fine. The party isn't for two days."

"Yes, but we might not have time to practice since the suitors will arrive tomorrow. There will be many—and most will be unworthy of you."

Alex batted her eyelashes. "Is that a compliment, Your Highness?"

In response, he dipped her low, their noses and foreheads nearly touching.

Aaron's eyes are his tell.

Slowly, he pulled her up, and she slipped back into place in his arms. Her skin was on fire, and she could still smell the woods on him. As his cheek grazed hers, she whispered into his ear.

"So many suitors, and yet here you are. Not *all* of them can be unworthy ..."

She pulled back enough to look at his eyes again. His breath mingled with hers.

Kiss him. Kiss him now!

Aaron narrowed his eyes. "I never said *I* was a suitor."

Alex's stomach dropped as a gust of wind knocked into Aaron, blowing his hair in all directions. She wrenched herself away from him, feeling droplets on her face as she stared at her feet, the thrones, the paintings on the wall—everywhere except for Aaron's face.

I don't understand. How is he not a suitor? What in the

Forbidden Lands has he been doing all this time? Don't rain in the hall. Just run.

Alex tried to force a smile, but a bitter laugh escaped as the raindrops started. "I should get back to my room, try to sleep a little before I need to work with Jerome. Thank you for your help. I won't bother you again." She turned and fled, knocking over three candleholders as she left.

"Alex. *Alex!* Wait."

But she couldn't—wouldn't—risk it. She heard it pour inside the throne room.

CHAPTER 23
ALEX

Kruft helped Alex onto Flash while Randal finished saddling Edward's steed. The sun hadn't yet risen over the Oreean Sea when they rode out of the stable. Once they'd left the castle grounds, Alex noticed Randal and Kruft pulling back.

"Are they staying back for me or for you?" Alex asked her father.

"Both. Even a king needs to be guarded."

Aaron's words weighed on her heart as she looked at Edward.

I lied to you for a prince who sees me as nothing.

Alex suppressed her pain, put on her proper royal face, and turned to her father. "I'm sorry I lied and disobeyed your orders about Datten. It was reckless and foolish, and I won't take such risks with my safety again."

"I'm glad to hear that." Edward fidgeted with his horse's reins before he spoke again. "I hear you've been asking people about your mother. I'm happy to answer any questions you have. It won't hurt my feelings. Your mother was astounding, and I miss her every day, but you deserve to know about her."

Alex nodded. "I miss her. I want to know everything, but I *need* to know why my grandfather hated her so much. It haunts me."

Edward patiently answered all of Alex's questions. He described meeting Victoria when she came to Warren to get the furniture for Aaron's nursery. She lived with Merlock and helped Guinevere while they waited for Aaron's birth. He told of how he fell in love on the ride to Datten, laughing that Warrens somehow always know when they find their perfect match. He even discussed the unpleasant parts, the fact that Victoria refused to marry him, but they carried on with their relationship for two years anyway. It took becoming pregnant with Alex for her to agree to marry Edward.

"So was it my mother's station, her powers, or my illegitimacy that made my grandfather hate us?"

"I believed Arthur would warm up to your mother—especially after she gave him an heir. But you were born a girl, and after centuries of only sons, it convinced my father your mother was behind it. He betrothed you to Daniel without telling me. We let it go because he was king; I didn't have a say, and we assumed if he was promising you to Datten, it was a good sign."

"Did you ever ask Emmerich about it?"

"No. I assumed we'd have a boy next, my father would get his proper heir, and it would all work out. But Victoria *knew* things, the same way you do. She told us you would be the only heir, which enraged my father. I doubted her, but four years later, you remained an only child."

"So it was *my* fault," Alex whispered, vision blurring.

Edward spun his gray steed and blocked Alex's path. His eyes locked onto hers. "Never utter those words again or even think them. Your grandfather was a horrible, violent, crazed man. He thought something was wrong with your mother, and, by extension, you—but there is nothing wrong with you. You are perfect."

Alex blushed. She'd always felt out of place, so knowing he thought she was perfect made her feel special.

If I'd stayed in Warren, would I still feel out of place? Being raised as a princess wouldn't erase what I am.

"Did Merlock tell you about Megesti? That he was there?"

"Yes. We suspected he knew more than he let on, but being aware of blood oaths, I never pushed. Asking a sorcerer to break a blood oath amounts to murder, and although it cost me time with you, I know now you were safe and loved."

"I was."

"We should head back. It's going to be a busy day." Edward took Alex's hand to kiss it. "*Never* be afraid to ask me about your mother, and let no one make you feel inferior, especially men like your grandfather, because one day you will rule them all."

Michael was waiting when Alex returned to her receiving room. Emmerich needed Jerome and Stefan for some Datten business, so they left training up to him. Alex was thankful to be away from Stefan's suspicious gaze, and after collecting supplies, they strolled to the archery range.

"I never said I was a suitor." Then why did you kiss me back?

Lost in thought, Alex didn't hear Michael until they were almost to the field.

"What is going on with you?"

Alex shoved him and snapped, "Why don't you leave me alone?" But the damage was done. She burst into tears, and after he hugged her, she told him everything, the Datten kiss, the dance, the *not a suitor*. "I won't go after someone who doesn't want me."

"I don't know why, but he *lied*. Alex, I see how he looks at you. The moment you walk into a room, his face lights up. He ignores everything if you're there."

Alex laughed. "I don't care what you think you saw. His words say otherwise."

"Aren't you at least willing to try? Isn't love worth some risk?"

"You fawn over Jessica but won't do anything about it. Stefan and Jerome would approve of you in a heartbeat if you asked."

"We aren't talking about *me*. You ran off to Datten with him, and now he's nothing? Feelings don't just vanish."

Alex bit her lip as she shook her head. "I won't survive another heartbreak; I've lost too much. If he lied, then he needs to fix that, though it's doubtful I'd even believe him."

Michael stared Alex down. "Coward!"

Alex shoved him away and stormed toward the archery field where she found Edith nocking an arrow. Alex stilled and watched Edith draw the string, line up the arrow, and release. With impressive speed, the arrow struck the target dead center. Just as Michael arrived, Alex saw Julius clapping from the other side of the range.

"That was amazing," Michael said.

Edith shrugged, and Julius laughed.

"You should see her when she's trying," Julius said. "This is the warm-up."

"I didn't know you two were friends," Alex said.

Julius raised his eyebrows at Edith, and she laughed, throwing her head back. It sent her braid from her shoulder down her back as she nocked another arrow and sent it flying.

"Randal was my father's second for years. All of us grew up together, but Edith has always been happier around my brothers than her sisters," Julius said, holding another quiver of arrows out to Edith. Alex watched in fascination as Edith let arrow after arrow fly. Speed and precision—just like her father with a sword.

Edith explained how Randal had always wanted a son, so when her mother couldn't have any more children, he had taught Edith the Nial secrets. The Nial family dynamics intrigued Alex almost as much as the stunning chest shield Edith wore.

"Julius or I can ask Aiden to make you one," Edith said when she caught Alex examining the shield. "Julius's middle brother married my oldest sister. I'm sure you've noticed that marriage connects most of Warren's noble families."

"Once you have the hang of it, you'll understand our political web much better," Julius said.

"Can you show me how you tied your string to get your arrow to go that far? I can't get my bow to do that," Alex said.

"Of course. Julius?"

Julius rolled his eyes and left to do her bidding.

"You missed breakfast," Jessica said, sitting across from Edith and Alex on the bench in the dining hall. Whenever the senior royals were absent, Alex preferred to eat at the lower tables.

"I had an early morning ride with my father followed by lessons with Michael. Then I had to change."

"I'm glad you aren't wearing that *old* green dress today," Jessica said. She smiled at the poufy blue dress Edith had selected for her.

"If you don't like me wearing the green dress, then you need to be in my room when I get back from defense training. And besides, it's the only one I can manage alone. Or you could allow me to wear sparring clothes all the time." Alex and Edith giggled while Jessica rolled her eyes.

As they ate their dried fish, nuts, and bread, Alex scanned the dining hall, curious. "Why are there so many more men around?"

"They're all here for you," Jessica said. "Suitors and people here to celebrate your return."

"They can't *all* be suitors," Alex said.

"But they are." Aaron appeared and stole some bread off her plate before squeezing in beside her, trapping her between him and Edith. Michael and Stefan appeared on the other side of the table and sat down beside Jessica. Alex tried to wiggle away from Aaron but couldn't. She swallowed hard to control her emotions.

"Ignore him," Michael said, helping her focus.

Alex recognized Michael's expression—he knew she was losing control and was trying to decide how much to interfere. Alex shook her head once, thankful Stefan was too busy filling his plate to notice. Aaron's leg brushed hers.

Why is he so close?

Alex exhaled and fake laughed as she took her bread back from Aaron and tossed it at Michael's forehead.

"How many of the people do you know?" Edith asked Aaron.

"In the hall right now? All of them."

"Prove it," Jessica said.

Aaron stole the rest of Alex's bread and pointed at the farthest table. He then named every man in the room, including title, occupation, family details, and some funny or interesting anecdote. Francis was a baron from Warren and a sore loser. Reilly was Alex's law tutor and the most boring man Aaron had ever met. Prince Rudolph was from the southern Oreane Kingdom, the youngest of five sons.

They were seafaring merchants too. Edith loved his silver hair.

"You missed the ones in the Warren crests," Jessica said.

Aaron nodded. "The blond is Lord Gabriel Schmitz, my mother's cousin. Good noble Warren stock there. Respects the Warren ways."

Alex elbowed Aaron hard enough to make him yelp. "Do *not* call my suitors stock, as if I'm some prized mare. I don't appreciate being compared to a farm animal."

Aaron grimaced and looked away before continuing. "The umber-skinned one with the big muscles is—"

"Julius Bishop," Stefan finished. "She knows General Bishop's son. He's one of her guards and stops by enough to gossip with Edith."

"She's not his type," Edith said.

"Oh?" Jessica asked.

"Julius prefers men," Alex said. "He'd be happier with Megesti."

"Who's that waving at us?" Jessica asked.

Aaron turned and beckoned the man over.

"Aaron, it's been too long!" The man smiled, looking at the group. "Who are your friends?"

"Baron Cameron Strobel, meet Lady Jessica Wafner and Sir Stefan Wafner, the children of Datten's general. Sir Michael of Warren. You know Edith, and this is Her Highness, Princess—"

"Alexandria," Cameron finished, staring at Alex. "You neglected to mention *that* title when we met at the pier."

"You never asked. Please join us. I insist," Alex said, motioning for him to sit across from Aaron. "Strobel—why do I recognize that name?"

Seeing Cameron near Aaron, she realized both had unruly golden blond hair and crushing blue eyes, but while Cameron's face was contemplative and his skin a light bronze color,

Aaron's skin was pale. At that moment, he was grinning mischievously.

Oh no.

"Strobel is my mother's maiden name," Aaron said. "She and Cameron's father are siblings. His mother is a Bishop—Matthew's baby sister. My parents have large extended families, but you'll notice I much prefer the Strobel side."

"That's because you wish you were a Strobel," Cameron said.

"Did you talk to His Royal Highness about your plans for the next year?" Edith asked.

"I did. He's delighted with my plans for the royal horses."

Alex looked at Aaron. "Is that where you got Thunder?"

"It is. Cameron picked him for my eighteenth birthday."

"Excellent choice. He's a magnificent horse," Alex said, and Cameron smiled at her.

"Would you care to go for a ride to our stables to visit the horses?"

Alex's eyes grew wide, and she looked at Jessica.

"It's fine," Jessica said, "so long as you have a chaperone."

Alex felt Aaron shift, but Stefan spoke. "Michael and I will chaperone."

"Take Sir Rassgat as well," Edith said. "You need at least one non-suitor guard."

"I am not a suitor. Ewww," Michael teased.

Alex exhaled, putting on a fake royal smile.

"We'll bring Kruft. The kingdom considers any unmarried man a suitor if he's between the ages of eighteen and thirty—regardless of their opinion of me." Alex said, smiling at Cameron as she rose from her seat. She glanced at Aaron. "Though I *do* think three chaperones is excessive. I can't see Guinevere's nephew being threatening. After all, he isn't from Datten."

Michael cleared his throat, giving Alex a look.

"We'll go prepare the horses," Stefan said, noticing the tension between Michael and Alex. They grabbed Kruft and left.

"We'll see you later, Aaron." Cameron said before bowing to Alex and holding out his arm to her the same way Aaron always did. Alex pushed away the thought that Aaron might never do that again and instead focused on Cameron; shyly, she took his arm. They were at the door before Alex stole a glance back. Jessica was shushing Edith, who was waving excitedly at Alex. Aaron stood beside them, fists clenched and pressed into the table, his face pinched.

Could Michael be right? But why did you lie?

CHAPTER 24
ALEX

"Randal, have you seen Edith?" Alex asked as she exited her receiving room. She'd returned from the Strobel estate and wanted to tell Edith about everything—especially that kiss.

"I believe she's looking for your crown. She's excited to hear about your visit to the Strobels." Randal's brown eyes sparkled. Alex stifled a giggle as she hurried off.

When she found Edith, a blond-haired, sickly pale man in a Datten-crested shirt was leaning on the wall beside her. Alex watched him slide his hand down Edith's bicep. Edith shook him off and stepped away, but he blocked her. Every instinct Stefan had drilled into Alex woke up.

"Edith—please come with me," Alex called out.

Edith and the man looked up. When he noticed Alex, his blue eyes sparkled.

"Well, hello, *gorgeous*. Where did you come from?" He sauntered toward Alex, looking her up and down at a languorous pace.

Bile rose from her stomach.

Go gorgeous *someone else.*

When Alex saw that Edith was trembling, she crossed her arms at the man and nodded for Edith to leave.

Kings and princes guard the princess, but I guard my ladies.

She moved into her fighting stance, sending the torches and fireplaces roaring to life, but the man was oblivious.

"Are you going to give me your name, or do you prefer 'gorgeous'?" he asked.

"My name isn't important." Alex stood tall and lifted her chin. "What matters is that in Warren, people have manners, and we expect guests to as well. Stay away from the ladies of this court."

"I'm from Datten. We're all about honor, beautiful, but what if I don't want to leave you alone?" He was steps from her, but she refused to back down.

"Your attire and arrogance tell me you aren't here to woo castle maidens. So why are you bothering us?"

"Just because I'm going to win the princess doesn't mean I can't have fun with you." He winked at Alex before running his knuckle along her shoulder. His pungent cologne made her want to vomit as he leered at her chest.

"You're the least honorable man I've *ever* met," Alex said. She smacked his hand away and turned to leave.

The man grabbed her forearm and yanked her back. He pulled her so close she could feel his warmth. The fireplaces crackled. Alex stilled her breathing as revulsion filled her.

Don't set your guest on fire.

He said, "You've got fire in you."

"You have *no* idea."

"Allow me to introduce myself. Earl Wesley Rassgat, successor to the King of Datten."

Aaron's not getting Emmerich's throne? Could that be why he isn't a suitor?

"Your title doesn't matter—keep your hands to yourself or there will be consequences." Alex wrenched her arm free.

"I'm not afraid of girls."

He reached for her again, but Alex slapped his hand away. "Touch me again and you'll lose that hand." She spun and dashed toward the doors.

"I'll find you at the party tomorrow," he called after her. "Afterward, I'll take you back to my suite. Show you what a real man is capable of. These Warren *boys* clearly can't handle you."

Alex found Edith with her back against the wall in the hall.

"Please don't tell my father. I don't want him to send me home. I love being here with you and Jessica. Don't tell Jessica either."

"Tell them what?" Alex winked and linked her arm around Edith's. "Though I think you need a refresher on some of your father's lessons. Care to join me in my receiving room for some awful knitting? I won't be appearing at dinner tonight if that pig is going to be there." Alex shuddered, remembering how it felt when he'd touched her.

$$\sim$$

"I'm sorry, Alex—I don't think it's salvageable, even by Jessica."

Alex groaned and threw the knitting on the couch across from them when Jessica's door slammed.

"Where were you this time?" Jessica demanded. Red-faced, she dropped Alex's crown on the table in front of her. "Do you have any idea how badly it reflects on your father that people arrived to meet you the day before your party and you can't attend dinner?"

"She was too busy kissing Cameron in the Strobel stable."

"Edith!" Alex exclaimed, elbowing Edith in her side.

"That's why you didn't come to dinner? I don't even know what to say to you anymore." Jessica scowled and dropped onto the couch across from Alex.

"I'm sorry I upset you," Alex said. "He invited me to stay for tea, and I did because Cameron's parents knew my mother. Once we were back, I felt ... drained. I couldn't bring myself to be regal."

"All right." Then Jessica turned and gasped, noticing Alex's knitting. Edith and Alex laughed until another door opened, and Stefan stormed in with Michael behind him.

"We have to talk," Stefan said.

"No. I refuse to have this conversation with you."

Alex rose and turned toward the stairs when Stefan grabbed her forearm. Still holding Alex's knitting, Jessica stood up, her eyes fixed on Stefan's hand. Michael shook his head at both ladies and motioned for them to come with him.

Coward.

Alex scowled as Michael and her ladies left.

"Don't think I don't hear what you say to people. Your flirting ... was inappropriate. You were out of line with Baron Strobel. And you let him *kiss* you." Stefan moved into Alex's space to stare her down, but Alex ripped her arm from him and shoved Stefan away as a fireplace crackled behind her.

"How I speak with *Cameron* is none of your business. If you're so worried about my flirtation, maybe you should have taught me about proper etiquette instead of making me run laps through the woods every day!"

"How was I supposed to know you'd have no common sense with men?"

"I'm not some naive girl, Stefan. I've spent most of my life around men. You do not get to stand there and tell me I'm behaving inappropriately when you can't even tell me what people expect of me."

"Alex, I didn't mean it like—"

"Liar! You're being an overbearing big brother. Except here —in *my* kingdom—that isn't your job anymore. You think Aaron's trouble because he's a spoiled prince—well, he made his lack of feelings for me perfectly clear, so stop worrying about him." Tears came as her voice rose in pitch. "As for the other Datten men I've met, the pigs in the barn seem like better suitors. So forgive me for enjoying myself with a man who's nice to me, who wants to get to know *me* and not pretend to because of my crown or what I can offer."

"What did you mean about Datten men?"

"Try doing your job of protecting me instead of lecturing me about how I talk to Cameron. Now get out."

"Alex—"

"I said get out! I don't want to look at you anymore."

Stefan hesitated but then left the room. Heading up to her bedroom, Alex tried to get some sleep. When sleep wouldn't come, Alex replayed the day. Cameron's smile, how sweet he'd been when he asked her about herself, the concern he'd expressed about her at the mourning ceremony, how expertly he'd gotten her guards away from them. And that kiss—there was no doubt he was interested in her.

After an hour, Alex gave up and crept to the library. Even though it was the middle of the night, Julius was outside her door. He nodded and followed as she went to the library; Julius took his place at the door while she slipped inside. On the second floor, she grabbed the bust, putting it on the table so she could gather her notes and grandfather's journals. Alex stopped, realizing the shelf they kept the bust on was narrower than the others. She reached behind the shelf and ran her hand along the wall. It wobbled and sounded hollow. Alex retrieved a fire poker from the first floor and stabbed the wood. The poker became lodged in the grain, and when Alex pulled it, part of the wall came off. Tucked behind it were three journals: one green, one black, and one gold.

Alex picked up the black one and examined the cover. The handwriting matched Arthur's. The date of the last entry was the night before her mother's death. She grabbed the gold one and opened it to find her mother's handwriting.

What is this?

Her mother had filled an entire journal with letters to her. Alex trembled as she ran her fingers over the pages. Outside, it poured rain.

Alex stuffed the first two into her satchel and squatted for the last book. Exhaling, she opened it. The handwriting was her mother's, but the date was 1470, exactly eighty years ago.

The journal Megesti had hinted at.

She placed it and her notes on her grandfather into the bag with the other journals. Prying the last bits of wood off the wall with the poker, she replaced the bust and tossed the wood into the fire. As she turned, Daniel's ghost was watching her.

Not another brother.

"Daniel, I'm not in the mood. Go away."

Daniel crossed his arms and glared.

"You disapprove of Cameron too? Well, I don't care because you're dead, and dead princes don't get a say. Though, if you were alive, I wouldn't be in this mess."

Daniel strutted up until he was inches from Alex's face. His eyes weren't angry like she had thought—they were sad. He pointed at the journals in her bag and the library shelves.

"I'm not flipping through journals so you can try to find something to show me how Aaron and I are meant to be. I tried, and I won't make a fool of myself when Aaron doesn't want me and Cameron does."

Daniel threw his hands in the air.

"I'm tired. I'm going to bed."

Daniel continued pointing at the journals. Frustrated, Alex grabbed one and threw it at him. He simply looked back at her.

"Go away or I'll burn them."

Daniel dropped his arms and vanished.

If Julius heard her one-sided argument, he made no mention of it as he followed Alex to her room.

Back at her door, she nodded to Julius, and he left to do his rounds. Instead of going into her room, however, Alex slipped down the small hall, climbed the spiral stairs, and arrived on the second floor. She wasn't sure where she was going until she was knocking at Aaron's room.

Daniel, did you do this?

The moment she realized what she was doing, Alex turned to leave, but the door opened.

Aaron wasn't wearing a shirt. Alex's eyes widened at his chiseled chest and simple sleeping pants. The wounds on his shoulder had scarred and made Alex feel sick. Aaron looked at her with raised brows and a surprised smile.

Alex's stomach dropped, and she backed away. "This was a mistake."

"Alex, wait—"

But she was already running down the stairs and didn't leave her bed for the rest of the night.

CHAPTER 25
AARON

*S*he was supposed to laugh or call me a liar. Instead, she believed me and bolted. Now she can't even look at me and won't let me explain. And then she went off with my perfect Warren cousin.

Frustrated, Aaron made his bed. Edward had a fantastic birthday planned for him, but Aaron couldn't stop thinking of the heartbreak on Alex's face when he'd claimed he wasn't a suitor.

So many of her childhood facial expressions made it to adulthood. The last time he saw that one was when he went back to Datten before everything happened. Edward promised her she'd see Aaron on his birthday, but they didn't. His mother's words came to mind.

Wanting to be around someone, even when they aren't at their best, is an important part of love.

"I hope you're right."

Everything chafed and pissed him off. Aaron changed clothes. Maybe pushing himself on a run would make him stop thinking of Alex for a few minutes.

The chilly morning air invigorated Aaron as he ran through the forest. No route, no plan. He simply needed to run until his lungs and legs burned. He relented only to get a drink. His heart hadn't even slowed when he heard twigs snapping followed by the lush forest withering.

"Alexandria, I thought you had control of your Celtic powers," Merlock said.

Michael said, "It's her foul mood from her screaming match with Stefan last night."

"Can we go back? Nothing is going to grow today," Alex said.

As the group left the woods and arrived at the river, Aaron chuckled at the looks on Merlock and Michael's faces. Alex's face was stoic and gave away nothing, but the speed at which every living plant around them died did.

"Aaron." Merlock bowed.

"Your Highness." Alex's voice was ice.

Michael whispered to Merlock, and he led Alex further into the woods. As soon as they vanished, Michael spun toward Aaron and shoved him. "Why did you do it?"

"I didn't mean it. She took it wrong."

"I know. I'm picking up the pieces because you broke her. Now fix this."

"Excuse me?"

Michael listed every amazing attribute about Alex that Aaron already knew and a few he hadn't known about.

She can't climb a tree that high, can she?

He took his scolding in silence until Michael mentioned Cameron.

"You hurt her enough to send her blindly to Cameron, and he isn't afraid to show her how he feels."

"What does that mean?"

"You're the only royal who *doesn't* know he kissed her. Jessica updated the queen but not you."

"What?"

No, no, no. Ferflucs, Cameron.

"They've bumped into each other several times already. Unlike you, he took his opportunity."

Aaron's hands clenched as he pictured Cameron kissing Alex.

She kissed me first.

"Then tell her how you feel. Or better yet, show her. To have a chance at fixing the hurt, you'll have to outlast the anger. The more you fight, the harder she'll push you away."

"*How* do I fix it?"

"If you can't figure that out, Stefan's right—you don't deserve her."

Michael left, following the trail of dead plants.

Aaron's hands ached from clenching into fists throughout the entire conversation.

Let me fix this, Alex. Don't give up on us.

Aaron groaned at the dead plants and followed them back to the castle, hoping they weren't a sign that things between him and Alex were over for good.

CHAPTER 26
ALEX

Stefan had to drag Alex from her bed because after her magic lesson, she had avoided everyone. Edith and Jessica chatted as they got her into her massive gown and fixed her hair. Alex's mind was a swirling tornado.

Cameron's kiss.

Aaron's dancing lessons and his comment.

Datten.

The mourning ceremony disaster.

All the things that might go wrong at the party.

Jessica pushed Alex's formal crown into her hands. It was twice the height of her usual one and decorated with rubies, sapphires, and obsidian stones. It belonged to her grandmother.

Michael's voice brought her back. "Someone looks nervous. Careful or you'll get wrinkles."

Alex half smiled.

"Tonight's different. I'm making up for twelve years—" Alex shook her head. "Twelve years for my father, presenting me to Torian and celebrating Aar—His Highness's birthday."

"Birthdays aren't special in Datten," Jessica said. She gathered their supplies and slapped Michael's arm for making faces at Alex.

"Ouch!"

"Leave her alone," Edith said.

"But teasing Alex is what I'm good at. If you're ready, I'll fetch your escort."

Alex's heart stopped.

Oh no, Aaron's escorting me. How could I have forgotten that?

"I need a minute."

Alex threw her crown on her bed as Michael, Jessica, and Edith disappeared down the stairs.

So many rules, expectations, and names of noble families. Who bows to me? How to address everyone. The suitors—so many suitors. And I can't even tell if suitors are interested in me.

She tried to calm her pounding heart, envisioning the halls filled with people. She'd watched them arrive for days.

All of them looking at me in this stupid, ugly, heavy dress that doesn't cover enough.

Alex couldn't breathe, so she threw open the balcony doors and rushed outside. Her knuckles turned white from clutching the balcony's stone railing so hard. Wind sent the training supplies in the courtyard flying as she sobbed.

Please don't rain.

"Alex?"

Alex spun around. She flushed as she pressed her back into the cold stone. Aaron was watching her.

The last person I want to see. You don't get to look at me like you are now after telling me you aren't a suitor.

Alex glanced over her shoulder, trying to summon the courage to berate him, but when she turned back, he was holding her crown.

"I'm sorry. I tried to knock." He gingerly stepped onto the balcony. "We have things to talk about, but those can wait."

"We have nothing to talk about, Your Highness. You've made yourself perfectly clear."

He paused and looked at her hard enough that Alex swallowed. "May I?" He held her crown out the way his mother did.

Alex nodded, and Aaron placed her crown on and wiped her tears from her cheeks. His touch made her shiver and sent heat to her belly.

Why can't you be easier to forget? Why do you have to have such an effect on me?

Somehow, his stare intensified. It was disarming. Alex broke the stalemate, looking at Aaron's clothes. Black shirt—longer than usual. Actual gold on the Datten crest. A fluffy cape and sword? Alex snickered.

Only Datten men would wear a sword to a celebration.

His golden blond hair sparkled even in the dim light, and his blue eyes seemed richer.

How do you always look so perfect when I feel like a mess? It's not fair.

"You look enchanting, Alex."

Alex stared at him, suspicious. He stared right back.

Dragons, Michael. What did you say to him?

I never said I was a suitor.

Pain and frustration fought against her pounding heart as his closeness and touch spurred on her desire for him. Her hand soon became hot, and when she realized she was gripping his bicep, feeling the muscles beneath, Aaron stiffened. Emboldened by this reaction, Alex leaned closer.

"Happy birthday, Your Highness."

Aaron shuddered as she spoke against his ear and neck, and he stared at her as she stepped back.

Why'd you shiver if you aren't interested in me?

"May I escort you to our party?" The arm he proffered trembled before Alex took it.

When they arrived at the hall, they waited to be announced.

Breathe.

Alex struggled to stay in control. The hall fell silent once they entered.

"Presenting the guests of honor, His Highness Prince Aaron Edward Johnathon Arthur, the Crown Prince of Datten, escorting Her Highness Princess Elizabeth Katrina Alexandria, the Crown Princess of Warren."

Alex's breath hitched as they entered. Aaron must have sensed it because he squeezed Alex's arm right when she wanted to run. Alex stepped forward, ignoring her pounding heart. Despite everything between them, Alex was thankful to have Aaron at her side. He led them to the thrones where their parents awaited them.

"Sweetheart." Guinevere kissed Aaron before embracing Alex.

"Your Majesty," Alex said. "You look beautiful."

"Beauty is for youth, Alexandria," Guinevere said.

"You do, though, dear," Emmerich said and kissed Guinevere's cheek.

Edward said, "You, my darling daughter, are a vision." Her father embraced her. "Now the ball may begin. I'll give the welcome address, and then you will start us off with a dance."

A wind rushed through the room as the words sunk in.

Dance first? Alone in front of everyone?

Aaron's hand gripped hers reassuringly.

Edward gave his welcome speech. He thanked everyone who had traveled far to be with them to celebrate Alex's return. Then he listed off Aaron's best traits and accomplishments before wishing him another amazing twenty years, noting he couldn't wait to see what his godson and daughter would achieve. Once finished, he toasted them, and the entire room cheered and drank. Alex gulped her wine. Guinevere then took Alex's glass and nudged her toward the center of the room. The crowd dispersed, leaving an open space.

Breathe!

Aaron held his hand out to her. Alex put on her royal face and stepped toward him, accepting his hand.

"You're my only hope to not set the room on fire," she whispered as the music began.

Aaron pulled her against him, and she nearly burst into flames. Even now, her heart pounded from Aaron's touch, not her fear.

"You'll be fine. Follow me like we practiced."

Alex looked at him.

"Every celebration starts with the Warren Waltz. Some traditions are too old to change," Aaron said. He held her tight enough against him that Alex could feel their hearts pounding in unison.

The instant the music started and Aaron stepped toward her, every pair of eyes in the room fixed on them. Aaron's hand locked Alex's hip tightly against him, keeping her in line with him every step he took. Alex tried to find someone to watch to distract herself, but the crowd obscured her father and friends.

Heat rushed to Alex's face and chest as Aaron's hand slid gracefully down to her lower back. Her heart ached at how natural it felt to have him touch her—hold her. As they moved through the dance, Alex soon realized the suitors were watching Aaron as much as her.

Do they see something I don't? Or do they just assume because our fathers are friends that Aaron will have an advantage?

She gulped.

Did they find out about Datten or Cameron? What if my father knows?

Aaron spun her briefly, giving Alex a momentary reprieve from his arms, but the instant he brought her back, Alex turned her head to avoid looking at him. She turned the wrong way. Aaron's lips grazed her cheek before his cheek pressed against hers.

Oh no, everyone can see me blushing.

Alex gasped and missed her step, but Aaron gripped her harder to him and saved her from falling. She closed her eyes to calm her hyperventilating and dug her fingers into Aaron's shoulder to keep herself going.

How many people saw me almost trip? Are they laughing? I can't do this. I'm going to lose control of my magic. I can't ruin this event too.

Aaron exhaled and whispered, "You're doing great. Ignore everyone. It's just you and me practicing in the spare hall. The only other people here are your ladies and your self-proclaimed brothers."

Alex whimpered and risked a glance at Aaron. His eyes sparkled in the candlelight, and he was only watching her. Not his feet, not the room, not the guests—only her.

You make it feel like I'm the only person in the world when you look at me like that, but then you say you aren't a suitor. You're infuriating.

Looking up, Alex caught sight of Jessica and Edith. She managed to focus on her ladies and gave herself over to Aaron, and he led her for the rest of the dance without issue. At the end, everyone clapped, and within a minute, the nobles and suitors swarmed Alex, eager to meet her.

Alex stole a glance at Aaron, her chest tightening when she saw him surrounded by beautiful noblewomen. As she attempted to smile at the men vying for her attention, she soon sensed she was being watched. When she glanced around the room, her eyes landed on Aaron, who was looking at her. Just as she smiled, a man came into view.

"That dress fits you especially beautifully, princess." The suitor smiled as Alex refocused on him. His gaze lingered on her neckline longer than she would have liked.

"Thank you, Lord ..." Alex couldn't remember.

"It's duke, princess." He slid his hand around her waist. Alex tried to slip away, but he caught her again. She fought hard against the instinctual urge to punch him. Her stomach clenched, and her palms glowed gold.

"There you are, princess. I wondered where you'd got off to." Another pair of arms pulled her away. "Duke Summerstock, I assume you have somewhere to be."

Alex looked up at the man, begging the light to leave her palms. His gold eyes were familiar. His skin was paler than hers, and he was less muscular than the suitors she had been meeting and dressed more practically. His clothes were designed for comfort and not to impress.

"Word of your beauty has been understated," he said.

"Thank you, Sir ...?"

"My name isn't important."

Alex glanced around for her guards. He'd given neither name nor title and had made no mention of accolades or accomplishments. After a tight-lipped smile, Alex felt her powers shift away. Her palms stopped glowing, but her heart thundered. Behind him, she saw the torches flickering.

"Are you enjoying your party?"

"I am," Alex said, taking a step back.

His attention diverted momentarily, so she moved another step away. When he turned back, he said, "Then I will leave you to it."

Before Alex could speak, the man vanished into the sea of

people. Alex gasped when a gentle hand touched her arm. Spinning around, she found Cameron smiling at her.

"Are you okay, Alexandria?"

"I am. Cameron, did you recognize that man?"

"Sorry, no. Would you like to dance?"

Alex looked down. "I'm not as good as Aaron made it appear."

"Don't worry." He leaned in close. "Aaron's dancing ability comes from my side of the family." He beamed when Alex let him lead her across the room.

Cameron's hands gripped her waist as he swept her across the dance floor. He hadn't exaggerated about his dancing ability—he was even better than Aaron. Despite Alex's inexperience, he successfully led her in a rendition of the Warren Waltz and another simple traditional dance. Alex laughed and forgot about the strange man, her fight with Stefan, and even Aaron's hurtful words. Cameron's mannerisms were so similar to Aaron's; he put her at ease, letting her enjoy herself.

"I'll grab us a drink," he said. "Wait here."

Alex nodded and smiled, watching Cameron head off. Once he left, she turned toward the crowd to look for her ladies and spotted Duke Summerstock stalking toward her. She looked for someone to save her, but she couldn't even find her guards— an odd, unsettling feat given that she could spot Stefan and Michael in the forest at night. Trying to move past a knight, she soon found herself face to face with Wesley Rassgat. He was trying to dress like his royal cousin, and the way the earl smirked was so similar to Aaron she gagged.

"Princess, the gold suits you. You were *made* for Datten." With inhuman speed, he grabbed her hand and kissed it. She shuddered with revulsion. "I seem to have quite the effect on you, Your Highness."

Alex pried him off her while he winked at his men. "The

effect you have on me, Earl Rassgat, isn't the one you're going for." Alex went to leave, but Wesley grabbed her arm and pulled her against him. Her powers stirred when his pungent cologne hit her.

Gross. I've had enough of men thinking they decide when they touch me.

Behind Wesley, the torches' flames doubled in size as Alex struggled to control her temper. His eyes narrowed at her before growing wide.

Recognize me now, do you?

"I warned you not to put your hands on me again." Alex shoved him away and slapped him so hard his head snapped to the side. When his guard grabbed her, Alex flipped him over the way Stefan had trained her. Everyone around them leaped back, silence spreading through the room as Wesley rubbed his face. Alex straightened her dress and crown then glared at Wesley.

Don't make this worse for yourself. Just leave me alone.

Wesley snarled. "Boar—guess you can't teach a peasant to be a lady."

Alex noticed Generals Nial and Wafner pushing through the crowd toward them. "I thought men from Datten were honorable. Only pigs touch women without permission."

"Better a pig than a whore. I bet you're like your mother!"

Alex saw spots as rage seized her. She made fists, and then all the candles, torches, and fireplaces tripled in size. Before she could reply, a blur of gold crossed the corner of her eye. In a blink, Wesley was on the ground with Aaron standing above him, his fist covered in the blood pouring from Wesley's nose. The hall went silent as a crypt. The air left the room as everyone stared at Datten's crown prince and potential successor. Alex was so stunned she couldn't even summon wind. Then Aaron's roar shattered the silence.

"If you *ever* speak ill of Alexandria or Victoria again, my father won't have to decide who gets his crown."

Alex couldn't take her eyes off Aaron standing above Wesley, his face stern and his fists shaking.

You defended me.

Alex strode toward Aaron, took a trembling hand in hers to make him look at her, and tried to speak. But nothing came out.

Thank you. I'm sorry. I don't know what to say.

Footsteps sounded as the generals arrived.

"Generals, remove the earl," said Aaron. "He's no longer welcome at my party."

Aaron's gaze had shifted from her to his father. Emmerich's body was a compilation of emotions: face red, hands in fists, brows furrowed. But his chin was up and his shoulders back as he considered his son as if seeing something in Aaron for the first time.

"Aaron. Library. NOW!" Guinevere said from beside them.

The generals took Wesley and his guard, dragging them from the room.

Guinevere turned to Edward and Emmerich. After one look from her, they hurried after her.

Thank him. Kiss him. Do something!

Aaron released Alex's hand, and before she could act, he'd left.

Alex tucked her hair behind her ear as all the eyes in the room watched the generals drag Wesley away. She gasped as a hand hit her lower back.

"Come on," Cameron said.

Grabbing her hand, he moved through the crowd of people toward the back exit. Michael nodded at her, and Cameron took them into the courtyard. Alex relaxed, breathing in the cool summer night air. Before she could speak, Cameron pulled her to him—his lips found hers.

What do I do? Where do I put my hands? He's a good kisser.

When he gripped her against him, Alex's hands rested on his chest. Goosebumps that had nothing to do with the cool night air appeared on her arms, and she kissed him back.

Too hot. Too much wine. Too much excitement. Should I even be kissing you? What about Aaron?

When Cameron pulled away, fixing her with an intense stare, Alex's head spun as she tried to catch her breath. Over his shoulder, she noticed a man sneaking around the entrance to her room.

Not more idiots.

"I'll be right back," she said. Lifting her gown, she stormed across the training grounds before proclaiming, "The royal suites are not for guests."

The man she had met earlier in the evening but who hadn't provided his name turned around, smirking. "You are the spitting image of your mother. My father will be pleased. Ready to come with me?"

Alex stilled when her magic stirred inside her. She held her arms out and backed away from him.

Stay back. Don't lose control.

"I don't know you."

"You don't remember me. I'm Lygari, son of Moorloc, and you are Alexandria, daughter of Victoria. We're special—oldest son of an oldest son and youngest daughter of a youngest daughter. We hold the power in our lines. Too bad about Megesti, but every family has a black sheep."

"We aren't family."

"Of course we are. But you, dear princess, you have a power I've never felt before. I know you can feel mine. And these mortals tried to hide you from us, as if they could hide the heart."

"You're lying."

Lygari laughed, shaking his head as he moved toward her. "Did no one ever tell you your mother had *two* brothers? Twins —unheard of. My father is the firstborn, so he inherited all the power. *I* should be the one with the power to bring down the world—but no, it's you. The heart is a silly half-mortal girl."

Calm down and breathe.

Her chest clenched tighter than when she fell through the ice as a child.

"Your mother warned my father you'd be powerful, made him give a blood oath that he'd teach you. You should've come to us after she died, but Datten stuck their nose where it didn't belong, so we punished them for it."

"Punished ... you're responsible for Daniel's death?" Horrified, Alex sprinted away, but when she glanced back, he'd vanished. A crack sounded, and he appeared, striking her in the face, the force sending her to the ground. Sitting up, Alex spotted Cameron running toward them.

"Allow me to remove the distraction." Lygari snapped his fingers, and Cameron vanished. He leaned down and held his hand out to Alex. "You must come willingly or Merlock can track you. He's not talented, but he can manage a tracking spell."

"You're wrong. I don't have special powers."

"You don't know what you are. You're not merely a princess of mortals but the princess of sorcerers. The power you *wield* decides our crown, not who births you. The first sorceress heart in generations. The power radiating from you is unreal, and you aren't even of age. If you reject our help, you'll destroy yourself."

When Alex slapped his hand away, Lygari snapped his

fingers again, sending a crack reverberating through the castle. Alex heard people screaming in the halls.

What is happening? I have to help them. How do I get away from you?

"I said you'd be trouble. *Witches* always are."

Alex swallowed hard and shuffled back.

No. Please! Not him. Kruft Rassgat appeared at Lygari's side. The shadow from her nightmare flashed in her mind. She'd thought her mother had glanced to the side so Alex could see her face one last time, but that wasn't true. She'd been looking at someone else. Looking at Kruft.

"You were there?"

I hate your family.

She tried to crawl away backward, but her feet wouldn't move. The two men came closer, and Alex closed her eyes, letting her fear overtake her.

Then the winds came.

CHAPTER 27
ΛARON

Aron had learned the hard way not to interrupt his parents when they were arguing. He examined the dried blood on his knuckles.

Even Edward won't save you.

Wesley and his man were under guard in their suites, and the generals stood inside the library, glancing at one another while the Datten royalty fought.

"What is wrong with your family?" Guinevere shouted. "Honor above all! Why is our goddaughter slapping your worthless successor at our son's birthday celebration? The son you don't think is worthy of your crown. At least Aaron knows what honor is!" Her face was red from shouting.

"Guinevere, it's complicated." Emmerich reached for her hands, but she slapped him away.

Aaron knew to be quiet when his mother was so angry she was shaking with rage, but a snort escaped.

"Are you amused?" she asked.

Aaron swallowed and looked down. "No."

"Good because I'm *extremely* disappointed in you."

Aaron's head snapped up. "You called me honorable."

"It's been years since you let your temper take control, but you start with Wesley at your birthday celebration."

"It wasn't a fight," Edward said, winking at Aaron. "If it were an actual fight, Wesley would have hit him back and not dropped like a stone."

"Jerome did not train Wesley," Guinevere said.

"He still enjoys starting fights his men need to finish," Jerome said.

"Why did Alexandria slap him?" Edward asked.

"I don't know." Aaron removed his cape and sunk into the couch. "She's avoiding me."

And she's upset with me.

"Then what made you punch him?" Guinevere asked, crossing her arms. "If you resorted to immediate violence, it must have been horrible."

Aaron sat up. "Bad enough that I won't repeat it."

"Tell us what he said, boy, or I will get it out of you," Emmerich growled.

"You'd have to catch me first. Care to try?"

But before Emmerich could reply, a crack reverberated through the room. Aaron jumped up.

"What was that?" Randal asked.

"Merlock!" Emmerich shouted. Almost immediately, Merlock and Megesti cracked into the room.

"Your Royal Highnesses, he's here," Merlock said, trembling; his face was ashen.

"Who?" Edward asked.

"My nephew," said Merlock in a strangled voice.

"You have a nephew?" Aaron asked. *But Victoria only had Alex. How is that—?*

Everyone jumped as the door flew open, revealing Michael and Stefan.

"Mercenaries are everywhere in the celebration halls," Stefan shouted. "Guards, knights, and even guests are fighting them, but they're huge! They make my father look like a boy."

Someone told me they heard a sorcerer murdered the Betruger king. What if that sorcerer is the nephew? Aaron spun to face them. "Where's Alex?"

"In the courtyard with Cameron," Michael said.

Aaron unsheathed his sword. "Stefan and Merlock, get Alex. Michael, Randal, and Jerome, come with me."

"Merlock, armor!" Edward shouted. Merlock snapped his fingers, covering Aaron and the knights with handcrafted Warren armor. Aaron's helmet appeared in his hand.

"Aaron, what are you doing?" Guinevere shouted. Merlock cracked away with Stefan.

Aaron tossed her his crown before putting on his helmet. "It's my celebration. The guests are my responsibility."

Jerome and Randal darted after Aaron toward the throne room. The celebration had morphed into complete pandemonium. Aaron spotted Datten knights fighting mercenaries to keep them from the noble guests. At the dais, Matthew and Julius were fighting more men. Every guard's armor was identical.

Keeping us hidden? Thank you, Merlock!

Stefan was right. Mismatched clothing, dissimilar weapons, exceptional height, and viciousness surrounded them.

"Michael, grab Julius and get Jessica and Edith to the Bishop estate. They'll be safe there. Randal, grab the Warren guards and get the women and guests out. Jerome, we'll distract the mercenaries with Datten knights so the others can escape."

Michael nodded and rushed toward Julius. Randal left to get Matthew and gather the Warren men.

A small crack sounded, and Cameron appeared.

No!

Aaron's heart stopped.

Alex! Stefan, you better have her.

Aaron grabbed Cameron. "Where's Alex?" he shouted over the thunderous clanging of swords on armor.

"I don't know. She ran off before this started."

"It's not safe. Go with Julius. Get Edith and Jessica out."

"Aaron, I can do more—"

"Not without armor, you can't. Get her ladies out. Alex will thank you."

Jerome grabbed a sword off a dead mercenary and handed it to Cameron, who nodded and ran after Julius and Michael. "Ready?" Jerome asked.

Aaron answered by charging into the fighting.

The mercenaries wore no armor as their skin was almost as strong as the guards' steel. Aaron and Jerome fought their way through a group of mercenaries to reach some of Datten's knights. Aaron glanced and saw Matthew leading a group of guests to the kitchen entrance.

Who's screaming?

Spinning, Aaron saw Jessica hit a mercenary with the bottom of a cast-iron candleholder before she pointed and shouted. Aaron turned in time to see the blade coming but ducked too late. The blow dented his helmet. He struck the mercenary with such vigor it knocked the man out. Pain radiated up Aaron's arm from the force of the strike. He looked back and saw Julius grab Edith while Cameron held open the secret passage for Jessica. Moments later, they vanished into the painting.

Good. She needs you both safe.

Matthew rushed to them. "Aaron, the royal guests are safe,

but some of the Datten and Warren nobility refused to vacate. They're helping the guards fight the mercenaries."

"I expect that from Datten, but Warren?" Jerome asked.

"Their princess gave them something to fight for. We fight until they surrender," Aaron ordered.

Another crack sounded, and every mercenary vanished.

How?

He removed his helmet to make sure he wasn't imagining it. Even the bodies had vanished.

"Aaron, you're bleeding," Jerome said.

CHAPTER 28
ALEX

Hurricane winds tore through the courtyard, scattering everything from flowers to barrels and supplies to weapons like a ship in a storm. Alex's hands burned from the power erupting out of her, and the wind sped up as she struggled to her feet. A training sword sliced Alex, leaving a deep gash as it flew past. Another hit Kruft, but he didn't notice.

Fear was overwhelming her when Lygari cracked, appearing beside her. Stefan's lessons rushed to her mind, and she punched him, knocking him backward. Squinting through the violent wind, Alex spotted Stefan and Merlock across the courtyard.

"Stefan!" Alex cried.

She covered her ears and tried to focus. Large arms suddenly grabbed her, and she fought against them until Stefan's voice hit her. "I've got you."

Alex opened her eyes and realized she was between Stefan and Merlock.

Merlock touched her shoulder, killing the wind. A moment

later, Lygari and Kruft charged across the courtyard toward them. Alex gripped Stefan's arm when balls of fire erupted from Lygari's hands. Stefan pushed Alex behind him as he switched to a fighting stance. Alex's breath hitched as she reached for Stefan's hand even though she knew he'd need it to fight Kruft. Stefan squeezed her hand in response.

"He was there, Stefan, when they murdered my mother."

Kruft helped kill my mother.

"Get her to safety. Send her to the kings," Stefan ordered. Releasing Alex's hand, he unsheathed his sword and charged at Lygari and Kruft.

"Stefan," Alex said as she tried to follow him, but her legs gave out. Another crack, and Alex's knees hit stone instead of grass. She looked up at the faces of her father, Emmerich, and Guinevere. "You knew!" she screamed at them. "You all knew."

CHAPTER 29
ALEX

Alex couldn't breathe. Pulling her knees to her chin, she gripped her head and tried to drown out the surrounding voices.

Kruft was there. He helped kill my mother, and I was alone with him.

Why didn't anyone tell me I have another uncle? Liars.

Why did he treat me like a child?

Don't set the room on fire.

Arguments surrounded her, overwhelming her senses, suffocating her heart.

"... Mercenaries ... gone." Jerome's voice cut through the noise, and her head snapped up.

Randal was talking now, but her eyes fell on Aaron, Stefan, and Michael. Their armor was in shambles. Scanning Aaron for injuries, she noted the blood on his hand was in fact Wesley's, but the blood on his face was his own—that was new. Michael's stance suggested he was favoring his left leg, and something had slashed clear through Stefan's armor, though he otherwise seemed fine.

Alex swallowed hard as Aaron's eyes locked onto hers. He moved toward her, his brows furrowed.

"I'm sorry," Alex said, shaking her head. She closed her eyes and put her forehead on her knees. When a hand touched her shoulder a moment later, her head snapped up, and she shouted, "No!"

As she screamed, a blast of wind burst forth from her, sending Edward flying back into the couch. Emmerich and Megesti moved back while Guinevere stared wide-eyed from her seat. Alex turned to look at Aaron.

Please don't be afraid of me.

"We're unharmed," Aaron said, moving closer, but Stefan brushed past him. King Emmerich grabbed his arm.

"She knows about your brother," Emmerich said to Merlock as he tried to hold Stefan back. "It's not going well."

"I don't care," Stefan said, pulling away from Emmerich. "Are you in pain?"

He dropped beside her on the floor and touched her left shoulder. Alex winced and instinctively looked at the injury.

Why is there blood? When did that happen?

"I'm here," Stefan said.

"Did you know?" she asked Stefan, her voice wavering.

"Know what?"

Merlock moved toward her.

"Stay away from me!" she screamed. "You all knew and said *nothing*!"

Her chest heaved with ragged breaths. She stared at the royals and sorcerers as the fireplace behind them erupted into flames.

No fire. Calming breaths.

"Elizabeth—" Edward began.

"How could you not tell me I have another uncle and cousin who are *clearly* more powerful than Merlock?"

"Dear," Guinevere said, crouching down by Alex, "we were going to tell you. We were just waiting for the right time."

Alex laughed.

Liars.

"It's not enough that I'm a princess who sets things on fire. Now I have to be the most powerful sorceress of a generation—and *no one* thought to tell me."

Emmerich scoffed. "I argued you should have been told the day you arrived. Your father disagreed."

Alex looked from Emmerich to her father and closed her eyes.

How is Emmerich the sane one?

"They were here for *you*?" Michael asked.

"What would they want with Alex?" Aaron asked.

Merlock sighed. "Lygari is my nephew. I suspect my brother agreed to train Alexandria when her powers became too powerful. We should have had years before that happened."

"The Betrugers' sorcerer. Is that him?" Aaron asked.

"Are there any other lost family members we need to know about?" Michael asked.

Megesti shook his head.

Alex felt sick. "I need some time." She stumbled as she rose to her feet, and when her father moved to help, she threw her hands up. "No one touches me. You all lied, told me my powers were normal, but *nothing* about me is normal."

Alex moved to leave but stopped when she came to Aaron. He stared at her, dumbfounded.

Please, not you too.

"Tell me you didn't know."

Aaron's hand was clammy when he took hers and squeezed it. "I had no idea, but I am sorry this is how you found out."

"Thank you." Alex hurried from the room.

CHAPTER 30
ALEX

Alex slammed her suite door so hard books fell off her shelves. She threw her crown and necklace on the floor with her shoes.

I need out of this dress.

Upstairs, Alex dropped to the stone floor in front of her wardrobe and reached under her bed until she felt the cold steel.

Thank you, Jerome and Stefan, for being paranoid enough to demand I keep a dagger in my room.

Alex stood, unsheathed the dagger, and reached around to cut the corset ribbons. She threw the dagger onto her bed and dropped her dress on the floor, kicking it away. Yanking open her wardrobe, she tossed everything out until she found her tattered clothes and boots from the camp. She dressed and then paused, looking at her mother's portrait.

"Why did you leave me to deal with this alone? You should have fought harder! Why couldn't we leave?"

Alex reached behind her mother's painting until she felt the latch open. When she reached for a torch beside the fireplace, it lit the moment she touched it. Looking for her cloak as she prepared to leave, she froze when her mother's ghost appeared. Alex gasped, surprise giving way to longing and sadness in the span of a moment, but then the fury returned.

"I hate you both—him for lying and you for dying."

Abandoning the cloak, Alex took her torch and climbed into the darkness. The tunnel opened into a supply shed close to the stables. Alex hurried through the shed but found Aaron waiting when she opened the door.

"Just let me go," Alex begged. "I can't control it. I don't want to hurt anyone."

Aaron blocked her path. "I'm sorry you learned the truth about your family this way. Edward shouldn't have kept it from you."

Aaron pressed his lips together. He tilted his head, struggling to look at her. Alex stepped forward and ran her thumb over the facial wound she'd noticed earlier, her skin emitting a faint yellow glow as she did so. "You're hurt."

"I'm fine," Aaron said. He took her hand in both of his.

"You got hurt fighting the mercenaries my cousin cracked in." Alex felt her stomach lurch.

I get everyone hurt.

She tried to move away, but he gently pulled her to him.

Aaron wiped away her tears. "You didn't ask him to—no guilt. Tell me what you need, and I'll do it—except I can't let you go running off alone in a kingdom whose terrain you haven't mastered yet."

"I need to clear my head. Think."

"Then *we* will go. Forget our parents' rules, the guards. Forget it all."

"They'll look for us."

"They will, but I know the perfect place to hide. When you're ready, we'll come back, and our fathers will still be arguing. But please don't make Edward worry for too long. No matter how angry you are at him, he's spent most of your life worrying about you."

Alex nodded, swallowing the pain she felt. Aaron took the torch from her, offering his hand. Alex took it, and they slipped out of the shed, creeping along the wall until they reached a strange-colored stone. Aaron pressed it with his shoulder, and the stones rumbled and slid aside. Alex gasped as a salty sea breeze rushed out.

That wasn't me.

Aaron glanced back, squeezing her hand, and she nodded. He closed the door and led her down the dark stairs and into another secret passage wider than any she had yet seen. Once they finished descending the stairs, Alex saw a dim light far away. They passed several other tunnels before reaching the end of the path, which ended in a steep drop-off. Aaron released her to set down the torch, but when Alex peeked over the edge to the sea below, his arms were suddenly wrapped around her waist.

She simultaneously shivered and burned within as his chin brushed her ear, and his stubble tickled her cheek. Alex closed her eyes and let Aaron hold her as she breathed in the salty sea air. As the waves lapped against the shore below, calm washed over her. The nearness of Aaron—his breath, his scent, his warmth—made her dizzy. Despite everything, he still affected her. They sat on the damp ground in silence, leaning against the wall of the tunnel, watching the moonlight dance across the waves. Aaron's hand rested on Alex's leg, and her mind became a blur as she took the moment in, trying to still her galloping heart. After what felt like an eternity, she was ready to talk.

"What do we do now?"

"You're the one hiding. You tell me."

Alex scoffed. "When I run off, I don't plan."

"Do you want to talk about everything?" Aaron asked.

Alex curled her legs under her, but Aaron's hand remained. "Was anyone hurt?"

"Michael hurt his ankle helping Cameron and Julius get your ladies out, but there were no serious injuries."

Alex gasped.

How could I not think of Jessica or Edith? What is wrong with me?

She fought back another wave of tears.

"Everyone keeps getting hurt around me."

"It'll take more than a few arrows, a handsome baron, or a throne room full of mercenaries to get rid of me."

Aaron leaned in, touching her cheek. Alex realized his breathing was off, and she trembled as he tilted her chin. Her lip throbbed, making her realize what he was looking at. Alex explained it had been Kruft, that he'd betrayed them.

"Can I ask you something?" he asked.

"Of course. We're friends." The words tasted like ash in her mouth.

Friends ... I want to be so much more to you.

"Do you have feelings for Cameron?"

She looked away toward the sea. "I don't want to talk about Cameron with you."

"Alex, your father gave you a gift—to pick the person you want to be with. I saw the way you looked at each other."

"How does Cameron look at me?" Alex snapped, turning to Aaron.

"Like I do. Like you're the most amazing person he's ever known. Like you're someone special, someone to be treasured."

Alex blinked, but he was still watching her face.

Kiss him. NO—this isn't the time for that even if I want to.

"What did I do?" Alex whispered. "You changed. In Datten, you—I thought—"

"Nothing. I didn't mean what I said the other night. I was teasing you, and I'm sorry."

"Does that mean you are a—?"

Aaron nodded. Alex tried to look at the sea and ignore Aaron, but too soon, she looked back at him. She was shivering now, and it had nothing to do with the chilly breeze coming from the sea.

"May I?" Aaron offered her his arm, and Alex snuggled against him. The warmth from his body soothed her, and touching him, she realized his heart was pounding as hard as hers.

"You don't know how truly amazing you are. Cameron sees it, and despite myself, I'm jealous anytime he's near you or touches you. It's easy for him."

Change the subject.

"What will our fathers be discussing right now?"

"Strategy. How to protect you from Lygari." Aaron went into detail about what each of their fathers would argue about. "They'll need to know everything that happened tonight. If you can't remember the details, they'll get the pearl. Did Merlock explain it to you?"

"A little. You hold it, and it shows memories?"

"Exactly. If you're nervous, I can go first," Aaron said.

Alex laughed. "I escape sorcerers, crazed kings, stand up to dishonorable potential kings, and flee from my guards at night, and you think I'm scared of a magic ball?"

Aaron laughed, and Alex felt his chest rumble against her.

"There is something I need to know," he said, "something I don't think you're going to want to talk about. It's important, and I need you to be honest with me."

"Okay." She tried desperately to keep her nervousness from escaping in her voice.

Is he going to kiss me?

"What did Wesley do that made you slap him?"

Aaron explained how he'd been trying to prove Wesley's dishonorable behavior for years, but no one would help in case he became king. Alex explained what had happened in the throne room, and Aaron listened with rapt attention.

"Now I'm even happier I punched him."

"Thank you for that," Alex said.

"I thought you'd be mad. You like to defend your own honor."

"I can handle most suitors just fine, though the Datten ones are challenging."

She turned and gulped when she saw how close Aaron's face was.

Just kiss me already. I'm not admitting anything first. Not with what you said dancing.

Aaron smiled and tucked her loose hair behind her ear. Alex felt her breath catch. "I have to go home tomorrow," he said.

"What? Why?"

"Do you want me to stay?" Aaron asked, grinning.

Alex couldn't figure out what he was getting at. "Why would you leave?"

Aaron explained the mourning ceremony Datten held for Daniel every year. Even in the moonlight, his eyes lit up when he talked about his brother, and it made her heart hurt.

I need to keep you here with me. But how?

She was so lost in thought she didn't realize Aaron had stopped talking.

"Alex?"

"What about a tournament?" she blurted. "We could hold

a tournament to honor your brother and help me find men for my guard."

Aaron's eyes grew wide as a smile spread across his face. "It's brilliant. A tournament is actually simple enough to plan, and it will remove those unworthy suitors."

And I'll add an extra event to stack the odds in your favor. "Would the kings approve?"

"They'll love it. We should go tell them."

"No." Alex rested her hand on Aaron's chest. "I have kings to scold but not yet."

"Now you're scolding my father. Nothing about you is normal." Aaron laughed.

"You're the only one who believes me."

Alex snuggled against Aaron and listened to the waves. As she nodded off, she felt a gentle kiss on her forehead.

"Please don't give up on me, Alex. It's always been you. I just need some time to figure things out."

CHAPTER 31
ALEX

The flames in the fireplace pulsed in time with Alex's heartbeat as she sat on the queen's throne—her throne. In a perfect world, it would have been her mother's. Alex sighed, shifted about, and tried to sit straight and proper, her head held high like Guinevere. With her trembling knees, fidgeting hands, and camp clothes, Alex knew she looked anything but regal.

I'm a mess.

The doors opened, and Michael and Stefan entered. Seeing Michael's limp and Stefan's bandaged arm, she leaped up and ran down the dais, throwing her arms around Michael hard enough to knock him over. Stefan caught them, and soon Alex embraced him as well, hugging him harder than she ever had before. They always protected her, but this time was different.

"You could have died," Alex said, sniffling.

"I'm fine," Michael said.

"We're all fine," Stefan said.

"We won't let anything happen to you. Not now, not ever," Michael said.

Alex's whimpers died down. "You wrecked your shirt," she said to Stefan when they let go.

"I promise to get a new one. We can't have the head of the princess's guard looking frumpy, can we?" he teased as he kissed the top of her head. His gaze moved to the doors as Aaron arrived.

"Behave," Alex said, pinching Stefan.

Aaron nodded and opened the doors to let the others in. Edward, Merlock, and Emmerich took their places in front of the thrones while Megesti and the knights stayed by the doors. Stefan and Michael remained at her left, Aaron on the right. Alex crossed her arms and held her chin high as she surveyed the men before her, knowing she had all the power for the first time in her life.

"Elizabeth, I'm so sorry," Edward stammered.

Torches roared to life.

"It's Alexandria. Princess Elizabeth died with my mother. You have Princess Alexandria, or you have an angry sorceress. I would caution you against letting my old name slip unless you want your castle set on fire."

"Enough childish antics, young lady," Emmerich said. "You're a crown princess, and you have a duty to your kingdom."

Aaron scoffed.

Alex took a few quick steps toward the royals and pointed accusingly. "And what of your duty to *me*? How am I supposed to take care of myself and my people if I don't even know what I am? I've always known I'm a princess. I've known I was a sorceress since I was nine. But no one bothered to tell me my gifts aren't ordinary—nothing about me is." Alex considered the pearl in Randal's hands. "I'll show you everything, but I have demands."

"All right," Edward said, unable to look at her.

I hope you know how disappointed my mother would be.

From the corner of her eye, Alex saw Daniel's ghost standing beside Aaron, nodding at her. Straightening up to her full height, Alex explained the decision she and Aaron had come to and with more authority than she would have thought herself capable of. "Warren needs a prince who possesses the strength and bravery Daniel exemplified. So make it known: if a man can't hold his own in this tournament, he won't sit on Warren's throne."

Edward swallowed and nodded.

Emmerich shot her a mischievous smile, reminiscent of the ones she'd see on Aaron's face. "What else?" he asked.

"Merlock will increase my magic lessons. Not history, not lineage, but proper instruction on how to use my powers. I can't control them, and I'm going to hurt someone."

"As you wish, Alexandria," Merlock replied as he bowed to her.

Randal came closer, and as he did, Alex peered more closely at the pearl. It seemed to glimmer with swirling mists.

"Now. Explain to me how this works and what exactly you need from me."

A SOFT FOG appeared around them, and everyone heard small children giggling. It was a few moments before the swirling mists formed into the faces of children playing in front of a stone wall. The Datten crest hung upon it.

"Shhh or he'll hear us," said a four-year-old Alex, looking around.

"He'll hear your talking or chewing," a seven-year-old Aaron replied.

"Found you." Daniel appeared behind her. "I knew you were

hiding down here." He tickled them until Alex was giggling so hard she couldn't breathe.

"Who took the cookies out of the kitchen?" came the voice of a cook from far off in the fog.

Daniel stuffed a cookie in his mouth, turned toward the cook, and mumbled, "I don't know."

Young Alex and Aaron erupted in laughter as the fog faded.

"Is it supposed to get hot?" Alex asked as she looked at the nobles when the fires in the room roared to life. She felt her power surge, and memories erupted out of her all at once.

Alex sat playing with her books and toys. Victoria and Daniel were arguing across the room.

"He's not coming?" Victoria asked, crumpling a letter with the Datten seal on it.

Daniel shook his head. "He doesn't believe it."

"The one time I actually need Datten to be violent. This choice will destroy both our kingdoms if we don't sacrifice everything now."

"I know. As long as Aaron is fine, I'll do it."

"He will be."

"Are you sure?"

She threw the letter in the fire. "If we do this correctly, Aaron will be the greatest king Datten will ever know."

Daniel nodded and climbed through the open painting.

Victoria closed it and said, "One more. Brother?"

An instant later, a man who looked identical to Merlock except for the gold eyes and beard cracked in. His fine cloak shone violet, but his face bore none of the softness Merlock's would.

"I don't care what you're trying to do. Pack your things, I'm taking you both. Now!" His threatening voice made young Alex tremble, but Victoria didn't even flinch.

"I didn't listen to you as a girl. Why would I now?"

"Because this time your life depends on it!"

"*Someone's life always depends on us, Moorloc. This is no different.*"

"*No different?*" His enraged gold eyes flashed violet. "*I see the pendant she's wearing. The moment your life ends, our mother's pendant will protect her, hide her from all of our kind until her awakening. She'd only have it if you were doing something foolish.*"

Victoria grabbed a dagger and calmly held her hand out to Moorloc. "Hand."

Moorloc groaned but obliged. Victoria cut his palm before reopening the wound on her own.

With their fingers interlaced, she whispered, "*Blood of my blood, blood of your blood. Moorloc son of Hermes, son of Merlin, I demand your oath that you will train my daughter when her powers become too much.*"

"*Too much? She's half mortal. She'll have minimal power, like Lygari.*"

"*She's the heart.*" *Victoria turned toward Alex and smiled.*

"*The heart,*" *Moorloc whispered.* "*That's impossible.*"

She turned to Moorloc. "*Don't argue with the daughter of Cassandra. My premonitions are correct. You're powerful. I know you can sense her gifts already because I can.*"

Moorloc looked at Alex and shook his head. Scoffing, he turned back to Victoria. "*The second most powerful sorcerer in our world in the body of a tiny half mortal girl. What am I swearing?*"

"*To teach her. Merlock has his own duty around her. Megesti too.*"

"*You should train her. We talk of the most powerful, but that's always been you. Cassandras teach their own.*"

"*That isn't a choice, Moorloc.*"

"*But—*"

"*No.*" *Victoria's emerald eyes flashed gold as she grabbed Moorloc's arm.* "*I've seen every possibility. The only way she survives to become the heart is if I'm dead.*"

"Victoria—" Moorloc began but stopped.

She stepped closer to her brother and caressed his cheek before kissing the other one. "Train her. Help her. Don't go after them. He has as much of a role to play in all this as you do."

Moorloc scowled. But then, lowering his head, he nodded before kissing the top of Victoria's head and cracked away without another word.

Stones began lighting up on the floor as a young Alex hopped past.

"No," Alex begged as the memory that still haunted her dreams played for everyone. At the end, both versions of her cried.

Alex's nightmare vanished, and Daniel's face appeared. Megesti's voice whispered an incantation, and a horse cantered off. General Wafner's face appeared and took Alex from Daniel.

"Hide her. Don't tell anyone where she is," Daniel ordered Jerome before turning to a young Stefan. "If anything happens, you take her and run. Don't stop. Tell no one who you are. If Arthur finds her, he'll kill her. When the time comes, Datten will come for her."

Black smoke filled the room, and the unmistakable crackle of flames echoed. Four-year-old Alex was fighting to get away from an eleven-year-old Stefan. They had been playing in the woods behind the Wafner house. Now, cinders from its flaming roof blew down on them as more of the structure collapsed. Stefan threw her over his shoulder and ran.

"Make it stop!" Alex begged.

Michael tried to take the pearl, but the moment he touched it, he cried out and more memories came.

The frozen Darren River appeared before them. Alex's delightful laughter echoed through the hall as she appeared on the ice, spinning in circles.

"Michael, hurry," Alex said. "Stefan told us to stay away from the river, so if we're caught, we'll be in trouble."

"If he told us not to play on the ice, there might be a reason for that?"

Alex teased, "Worrywart! Worrywart! Michael is a worrywart—"

In a second, the ice broke, and Alex disappeared.

"Alex!" Michael's panicked scream reverberated throughout the hall as he hurried to the spot where she'd fallen through. Michael scrambled to get onto the ice but slipped and fell. He groaned and struggled to his elbows as an older boy appeared. He had blond hair and looked to be in his late teens, and he ran across the ice, carrying a large rock without fear of falling in. Michael watched him run downstream and smash the rock into the frozen river. It broke through, making a much larger hole. He dropped to the ice, reached inside, and pulled Alex out.

She was turning blue. The boy lay her down, whispered into her ear, and pushed on her chest. After what felt like an eternity, Alex began coughing and spitting up water. The boy's eyes—blue like Aaron's—locked onto Michael's. Nodding, he vanished.

"Help! Stefan! Ian! Someone!" Michael threw his coat over Alex as Stefan and Ian came crashing through the woods.

"Dragon flames!" Ian screamed as they ran for Alex.

All at once, a flurry of childhood memories flew by. Michael lying about what happened on the ice. Alex gifting Stefan the ugly scarf she made. Michael scaring Alex in the bush. Her shoving him out of a tree before falling out herself. Alex setting bread on fire and another boy putting it out.

Stefan's training flashed by. At the beginning, Alex struck a surly-looking Graham in the leg with an arrow and threw a plant book at Stefan's head, barely missing him. But at the end, Alex stood blindfolded on a narrow log, holding a staff. She listened for Stefan and Michael, striking them both with an all too smug smile on her *lips. Aaron, facing Alex and Michael in the bush, flashed by, and everyone gasped as they watched Alex threaten and then shoot Aaron with her bow—twice.*

Aaron pulled Michael away from Alex, and the pearl flashed to earlier that night when they had fled from the group. Everyone stared at a red-faced Aaron when their drunken kiss in Datten flashed by.

Finally, Lygari and Kruft appeared. Merlock listened to their words.

At last, the pearl stopped glowing and allowed itself to fall from Alex's grasp. Alex dropped to her knees, exhausted, while the pearl rolled away. Michael caught her shoulders.

Across the hall, Megesti spoke in a deep, distorted voice wholly unlike his own. Everyone turned to face him and saw that his eyes had gone white as he spoke:

"*What is lost will be found, only to then lose itself again and again.*

The sea harbors the answers, but the blood reveals the truth.

Flames that don't burn will reveal a destined bond.

The wounds of the past are coming to take the future back.

His honor will be what rips them apart in the end.

Only the truly lost can save the lost.

The beast must be contained, or she'll meet her end.

A new blood oath will form from broken sons.

Your destiny is at hand, but you must fight it to win it."

"What in the Forbidden Lands was that?" Stefan asked. He'd reached Michael and was helping Alex to her feet.

"A Cassandra son premonition. They're rare," Merlock said.

"He had this same one when we started looking for Alex," Aaron said, picking up the pearl. "I'm sorry, but there's more."

"What do you mean?" Edward asked.

Aaron turned to face his father. "I'm sorry," he whispered and closed his eyes.

The fog spun quickly, forming into Daniel's face.

"Daniel, I want to go for a ride," a young Aaron could be heard saying.

"Okay, we'll go, but a quick one. Mother will be angry if we miss breakfast on your birthday." Daniel beamed at Aaron and took his small hand. They hurried down the stairs of the Datten castle to the stable.

Daniel was getting their saddles when Aaron asked, "Who's that man?"

Daniel turned, and his eyes grew wide. "Lygari? You're not welcome here. Leave."

"My father isn't a patient man," Lygari said. "Tell me where she is or Datten will find itself heirless." Lygari scowled, swinging the oil lamp in his hand.

"Don't threaten my brother." Daniel hoisted Aaron onto the horse and whispered to him to hold on tight.

"Tell me or you both die!" Lygari raised his chin at Daniel and dropped the lamp. The flames raced across the dry hay and stable wood.

"No!" Daniel slapped the horse hard, and it bucked and charged out of the burning stables.

Aaron looked back and screamed, "Daniel!" His brother charged Lygari with his sword drawn while the stable went up in flames. It went dark briefly, and then there was whimpering and crying. Megesti and Jerome's faces appeared.

"We've found him! Emmerich, he's alive!" Jerome yelled. The terror in his voice was something Alex had only heard once from Stefan.

Megesti scooped Aaron up, and he clung to him. "I'm here and always will be when you need me. I won't leave you."

The fog swirled away.

"The blond boy who saved Alex," Michael said.

"You mean the one you never told us about?" Stefan asked.

"That was Daniel. But he was dead. How did he save Alex?"

"How long has he been with you?" Aaron asked Alex.

She felt everyone's eyes on her. "As long as I can remember. There isn't a time where Daniel wasn't watching over me."

Merlock said, "Another oath."

"Is it true?" Alex asked, turning to Emmerich. "Did my mother ask you for help?"

Aaron reached for her, but she moved away from him.

"Alexandria, nothing is ever that simple," Emmerich said.

"This is! Did she ask for help? Yes or no?" Alex roared, her blood surging.

Traitor!

Edward moved to Alex, but Emmerich stepped ahead of him, placing his hand on his friend's shoulder. His footsteps echoed as he walked toward her, but Alex held her ground.

"You're furious. Get it out. Scream. Burn something. Do whatever you need to do to get this rage out of you."

"I don't need a cowardly old man to tell *me* how to manage my temper," Alex snapped.

"You want someone to pay? I'll pay. But keeping this rage inside will destroy you like it did your grandfather."

"*Never* compare me to him," she growled. "And I don't need you to let me punish you. I need the truth."

"She asked, but after consideration, I deemed the risk was unwarranted. I was wrong."

Alex stopped breathing.

You failed us. But I won't let a mountain of stubborn royal arrogance beat me.

Just as Aaron moved to comfort her, Alex slapped the King of Datten. The sound echoed through the halls. Jerome and Edward were at Emmerich's side before his cheek even finished turning red, but in the blink of an eye, Aaron leaped between them.

Emmerich raised his hands to calm everyone. "Alexandria, you didn't let me finish. My denying your mother is the biggest regret of my entire reign."

Alex crumpled to the ground, and Emmerich quickly kneeled before her as rain poured outside.

"You bear no guilt. *I* failed your parents, and the price I paid was to watch my two dearest friends lose their entire families while I lost my firstborn son. Now I know it should have been both. Daniel saved you and Aaron then made sure Stefan would protect you. Despite my failure as king, he somehow protects you in death."

Alex looked up at Emmerich, tears pouring from her eyes. He helped her up, and Aaron took her hands.

Aaron stared at her. "It's true then? Daniel's *stuck* to you?"

Daniel appeared next to Aaron and reached out for him as Alex nodded.

"After the tea—what you said—it scared me you'd think I was insane."

A deathly quiet fell across the room as everyone struggled to comprehend everything. Michael took Alex from Aaron, and she clung to him, avoiding looking at anyone, while Stefan flanked them. Before anyone could say a word, the room spun, and she dropped to her knees.

"It's the pearl," Merlock said as he hurried over. Michael and Stefan were already trying to help her up. "The first time is hard—"

Alex heard muffled voices as her breathing sped up so hard she couldn't keep up, and then it just stopped.

So tired.

The scent of earthy musk hit her, and she let herself drift off as Stefan carried her from the room.

CHAPTER 32
AARON

Aaron groaned and tossed back the blanket. Rising from bed, he kicked his pile of bloodied clothes aside. Last night, he'd been too tired and sore to find clean ones, so he'd gone to sleep naked. Still half dreaming, he heard a click and turned to the door.

"When I agreed to hold a tournament, you failed to mention *I'd* have to plan it. So you'd better know what to do since I don't."

Alex.

Alex slammed the door with her hip as she finished speaking. For a moment, they both froze, Alex's face flushing as red as Aaron's Datten shirts while she gawked at him. The next instant, Aaron scrambled to grab his pillow to cover himself.

It's too early for this. But if you're going to see me at least I'm in prime form.

"Alex." His voice broke the spell over her as she then dropped her packages and spun to face the fireplace.

What are those?

Aaron tossed aside the pillow and grabbed his cleanest pants off the floor.

"I'm so sorry!" Her voice cracked.

"You should knock."

"You should lock your door!"

Aaron reached for her arm, but Alex turned to flee and slammed face-first into the door.

"Are you okay?"

Alex buried her face in her hands and whimpered. "Yes."

Aaron slid his hands over hers and pulled them down.

"The lock's broken. Has been for years. Until recently, no one came to my room."

"Then get it fixed." Alex pressed her eyes shut.

"Look at me. I'm only a little inappropriate now."

Alex opened her eyes, making him smile. Her emerald eyes sparkled as they looked at him.

"See? Pants," he teased, shaking his leg at her.

But Alex flushed harder when she looked down.

Oh. Sorry.

He examined her forehead. "There might be a mark, but I can't tell—you might simply be blushing."

Alex pulled away. Everything Aaron did seemed to make her blushing worse. Aaron couldn't help but grin. Alex swallowed before she tilted her head back up to look at him, stopping at his shoulder.

"Does your shoulder still hurt?" Her fingers landed on his hip where the pitchfork marks were. Aaron felt heat rush to his core when she touched him. He exhaled, willing the blood to not head south.

Behave or you'll scare her off.

"There's another scar on the back of your shoulder."

"The circle with a line? It's been there since the fire. I like my scars. They make me look tough." Aaron's heart raced when he took in her scent. Alex always smelled like the sea air and royal gardens. Aaron leaned forward, rested his arm against the door beside her, and whispered, "You're staring at me awfully hard, princess. You might give a prince the wrong idea."

She trembled briefly before her eyes narrowed and her mouth opened. Ultimately, she said nothing and simply looked at him.

I need us to be okay again. Please be okay.

"What were you going to say?" He smiled at her.

Play with me.

"Didn't *anyone* teach you how to get dressed in a reasonable amount of time?" Alex's tone switched to teasing like she'd heard his thoughts. Her normal skin color returned as she exhaled sharply, straightened up, and raised her chin as if looking down at him despite his height advantage.

"Not all of us have someone to dress us." Aaron laughed, pulling back.

"At least I'm *capable* of putting on my own pants."

Good retort.

"So you only need help to take them off?"

Ferflucs! Did I just say that out loud? Please laugh! Don't bolt again!

Aaron realized he'd crossed that thin line between proper and risqué. He froze, wide-eyed, as an awkward silence filled the room.

Say something. Anything!

"Good thing I wear dresses now," she said after looking him up and down once more. Then she picked up the packages and handed them to Aaron.

"What are these?"

"Birthday presents. With all the avoiding and the commotion yesterday, I never gave them to you. You don't have to open them now. They're my thank-you, or sorry, or ... I don't know. I'll leave."

Don't leave—you're cute when you're nervous.

Aaron touched her hand.

"Stay. I want to open them with you. Sit?" He motioned to the chest at the end of his messy bed. "So you *were* avoiding me. I wondered."

"I couldn't face you. After your joke and Wesley." Aaron placed the gifts on the chest before he grabbed a shirt from his wardrobe. A moment later, she said, "How do you have so few clothes?"

"Princes need pants and shirts and a few royal accessories. Princesses need everything for every occasion. Plus, dresses are larger than tunics."

"Especially here." Alex wrinkled her nose.

Aaron smiled.

I love when you do that.

Aaron sat on the chest and pulled on his shirt. He watched as Alex examined his bookshelf.

I love the Alex I get when we're alone.

From the side, he watched her bite her lip, concentrating on the books. He recognized the one she held as he'd been gifted that plant book during his honor rite. Without it, Lucas or Hunter probably would have gotten him killed. Her fingers stopped when they hit her copy of *The Iliad*. Aaron cleared his throat, and Alex looked at him.

"What?"

"Nothing. I enjoy having you to myself. The real you, not the formal princess version. There has been an awful lot of competition for your attention the last few days. Plus, you were avoiding me. In the future, be honest when you're upset."

Alex reached for her book, but Aaron cleared his throat again. "It's mine now. I haven't finished reading your notes."

"Do we need to talk about me seeing Daniel?" she asked, changing the subject. "You seemed upset last night."

Aaron held her hands and pulled her down beside him. "We can talk in time. I wasn't upset but confused. I assumed he was gone, so knowing he's protecting you, I'm not sure how I feel about that. But I do like knowing he's watching over you."

Alex nodded and pushed the gifts toward him. When she turned, their knees touched, making Aaron feel hot all over. The larger package contained a Warren royal tunic, the shirt being black rather than the common blue. "Thank you. I thought these were only for relations of the king."

"Godson counts. Randal shouldn't tease you so much when you wear this one."

Inside the second package, Aaron found a copy of *Torian Legends*.

"It's my other favorite," Alex said, leaning over his shoulder as he opened it. "I didn't have a copy to bring back with me because I read the other one to death. I put some notes in it the way you did in your copy of *The Iliad* you left me when you stole mine." Alex's fingers brushed his as she pointed to the notes.

Aaron ran his finger across the beautifully written words and looked at her. "I love them. Thank you."

Alex smiled while Aaron exhaled to summon his courage.

Just say it. Your joke was much worse.

He pulled his tunic over his shirt. "You could have saved yourself the hard work of going to the pier and just given me a kiss."

"I don't gift kisses. They have to be earned." Alex stood, adjusting her green dress.

"How *exactly* are they earned?" Aaron stepped toward her.

"Through bravery and winning at the tournament. I read

it's tradition, so you'd better be as good at jousting as people say you are."

Alex moved toward the door, but Aaron touched her hand, making her turn back. He leaned down to her, making her arch backward slightly. "I've never lost a jousting match," he said. There was a pause, both of them searching each other's eyes, and then he added, "I was also exceptionally brave yesterday, fighting off the mercenaries."

"You're right," Alex replied, but before Aaron could respond, Alex kissed him on the cheek and raced out of the room.

AARON STARED at the library door. He'd hunted for Alex after she kissed him, but she'd vanished. Julius and Gabriel were debating archery targets, but Cameron was watching him. He always knew when Cameron watched him.

Back off, Cameron—I'm not going to back down.

Aaron picked the best books to help Alex while trying to ignore his cousin's stare.

The door opened, and Alex arrived with Michael.

"Where do we start?" Alex sat on the couch across from Aaron while Michael went to join the archery conversation with Julius and Gabriel. Aaron handed her a book from his stack. She took it just as Cameron dropped beside her. Aaron noticed Cameron's hand graze Alex's thigh as he took the book from her.

"This one's boring. Give her the green one," Cameron said. Aaron turned over the green book; realizing Cameron was right, he handed it to Alex.

For the next hour, she listened as they explained the different parts of a tournament and how it worked. Aaron took the lead explaining Datten rules, Julius and Cameron explaining Warren's.

"Your father must have a copy of jousting traditions of Warren. I'll find it," Cameron said as he rose and walked off.

Alex had shifted to the end of the couch by this time, and Aaron watched as she examined the bear rug on the floor.

"What are you doing?" He leaned over the couch to get closer to her.

"Deciding on a name. If the bear is here forever, he should have a name."

Aaron whispered, "His name is Hercules. I've named all of them."

Alex looked up and smiled the way she did when they were alone.

"The usual three events?" Julius asked, ruining their moment.

"No. We're having four events," said Alex. "Archery, jousting, swords, and a secret challenge of my design. I was late because I was briefing the generals."

"Secret challenge?" Cameron asked, returning with the book. He handed it to Alex, sitting next to her again.

"Yes. But it's with the generals and Michael. No suitors can help." Alex's eyes darted to Aaron's. When he winked at her, she blushed, looking away.

"Datten or Warren rules?" Gabriel asked.

"I assume Datten's are harder?" Alex asked.

"Warren allows for younger and citizen participants, so they're indeed less stringent," Julius explained.

"Could we do both?" Alex asked. She stood up with the Warren book in her hand.

You stand like your father, princess. I'll tell you that later.

Channeling her father's diplomacy, she explained her plan. It was unheard of, and the men loved it.

"It celebrates both kingdoms. We both honor Prince Daniel while celebrating the princess's birthday," Cameron said, smiling.

"Does everyone know when my birthday is?" Alex asked.

"Only anyone who's been in Warren in June. Your father celebrated it every year you were missing," Aaron said.

"I think we're almost done," Julius said. "Gabriel and I should head off to rounds. If you need us, princess, talk with General Nial or my father. They'll know where we are."

Alex nodded as they left. Then she said, "Cameron, would you stay for dinner?"

Alex smiled at him, making him stand taller. Jealousy hit Aaron like a lance to the chest.

Don't give him that smile. That's my smile.

"I wish I could, but my father has council tonight, so if I don't return home, my mother will have to eat alone." Cameron sounded disappointed.

Good. Go back to your horses.

"Would you walk with me to the stables?" Cameron asked. "I can check on Flash."

"Such an attentive equerry. However did my father get so lucky?"

Aaron's stomach dropped as Alex accepted Cameron's arm. She hadn't flinched or hesitated—not like she did with him.

In the hallway, Matthew was waiting.

"Do I require a chaperone, general? I'll be escorting Cameron to check on Flash before he heads home."

"Yes, princess," Matthew replied before following them.

"I'll see you tomorrow, Aaron," Cameron shouted.

"I'll see you at dinner. Save me some bread," Alex said as she gripped Cameron's arm.

Aaron watched them go, a pain gnawing at his insides as Alex turned to look up at Cameron.

210

They do make a lovely couple. Maybe he is the best match for her. Maybe he'd make her happy.

But then he remembered her lips when she kissed him in Datten.

It wasn't just the ale. Something is there. I saw it when she looked at me in the tunnel and before she kissed me this morning.

Aaron groaned and returned to the tournament plans in an attempt to take his mind off Cameron being with Alex.

CHAPTER 33
ALEX

"Thank you for checking on Flash," Alex said as she leaned against a support beam, watching Cameron inspect Flash's leg.

"Of course. Tending to the royal horses is my job."

"Is that the *only* reason you came?"

Cameron stood up. Alex noticed how his biceps barely fit in his crested shirt as he strode toward her, wiping his dirty hands on his pants. Cameron glanced at the general, who was talking to Gregory, the royal stable master, and the next thing Alex knew, Cameron had gripped her hips and kissed her. Heat flooded Alex's body as Cameron's lips touched hers. Her hands gripped his tunic, feeling the powerful muscles beneath as he pulled her close.

"You don't need to have *any* doubts about my feelings for you, Alexandria," Cameron said when they broke apart.

"Even after last night?"

Cameron cupped her cheek, caressing it with his thumb. "A little wind doesn't scare me."

Thank you for making that clear.

A loud cough from Matthew made Cameron step back.

"Will I see you tomorrow?" Alex asked.

"Of course. I could even give you a jousting lesson—my father and I train Warren's knights for jousting."

Alex looked at Matthew, who nodded, and she did the same upon returning her gaze to Cameron.

"Wonderful. I'll set up a time once they finish the field."

"I look forward to it," Alex replied as Cameron kissed her hand and headed toward the guest stables.

"Well done, princess. Your mannerisms and poise would have impressed Lady Jessica," Matthew said.

Back in the castle, Edward was hovering around the doorway to her room.

Alex asked, "Were you waiting for me?"

"It's a father's job, especially where it involves noblemen."

Alex exhaled and forced herself to look at her father. "I don't want to stay angry with you. Could we go for a morning ride tomorrow?"

"Of course. I'm happy to explain myself to you tonight," Edward said, a hopeful look on his face.

"No. Riding calms me. Your best chance for me to listen is when I'm on Flash. Besides, I'm supposed to give Prince Jesse a tour later, and I have my first proper lesson with Merlock tonight."

"A morning ride it will be. You may summon me as soon as you rise."

It was then that Alex became aware that Daniel, Stefan, and Aaron stood behind her father. Daniel shook his head at Alex then tried to ruffle Aaron's hair.

Silly ghost.

"Have you gotten anywhere with the tournament?" Edward asked.

"We have." Aaron walked over and filled Edward in on

their plans. The event would run over three days with Warren rules in the mornings and Datten in the afternoons.

"Emmerich is thrilled," Edward said, winking at Alex. "He loves tournaments."

"I'm also following traditional prizes," Alex said.

"What does that mean?" Stefan asked.

"A kiss from a princess," Edward said, staring at Aaron. "So it will be a large tournament."

"The plan is to weed out the unworthy suitors," Aaron said.

"Then I'll have the guards assemble the tournament grounds," Edward said. "They'll need a day. Maybe two."

"I'll let Aaron fill you in further," Alex said. "I'm already late for my magic lesson."

Alex found Merlock waiting for her on the couches in the library. He pointed to the shelf. "Have you read any of your mother's journals?"

Alex shook her head.

Merlock looked stern. "Tonight, I expect you to read about why we left our home. I'll ask you tomorrow. For now, we'll test you. Change into your sparring clothes and meet me in the courtyard in ten minutes. We won't be doing the gentle little tests we were doing before."

From the courtyard, they cracked onto an unfamiliar rocky beach. A sea breeze whipped Alex's hair around. Alex rubbed her arms to ward off the cold and immediately wished she'd brought her cloak. Merlock moved so they stood side by side on the larger rocks. The late afternoon sun reflected off the eerily calm Oreean Sea, colorful rays showering them and the beach.

Merlock explained how they would test if Alex's Poseidon and Salem were equal. If her mother's prediction was correct, this odd pairing would confirm it.

"Show me what you can do," Merlock said, staring at Alex.

"Show you? We've been working for weeks, and I still don't know how my powers work or how to control them. How am I supposed to show you?" Alex asked, throwing her arms up.

"They're connected to your emotions, so tell me something that makes you sad or scared."

Alex described the nightmares that tore her from her sleep every night. When she finished, Merlock pointed behind her.

Alex spun around to see towering waves colliding, each one large enough to sink the massive ships in Warren's port. Dark clouds rumbled and sent lightning into the already treacherous water.

"I did that?"

Merlock flicked his wrist, and a small fire appeared on the rocks before them, the flames snaking upward. "Enlighten me about the day Prince Aaron and my son found you."

Alex told of the day's events, of the terror she'd felt knowing she was being hunted, and of how she and Michael had found Aaron and she'd shot him before she knew who he was. As she spoke, the sea grew rougher. But when she spoke of Stefan arriving, shouting at her in front of the camp, and about Graham and Michael getting into a fistfight, her temper roared to life, making her blood rise and turning the tiny flames into a raging fire. The flames flickered so high they split and floated away before vanishing into the sky.

"Can you create fire, or can you only work with what's there?"

"I've made it before, but I don't know how I did it."

"I've seen you grow plants. Have you ever cracked? Thought of something or someone and ended up somewhere else?"

Alex paused. "Maybe once or twice while I was in the woods."

Merlock paced, deep in thought. "Your powers are beyond your mother's."

"You're going to teach me, right? Testing isn't helping."

"Figuring out how will take some time, and I'll only be able to take you so far. For now, focus on trying to move this puddle." Merlock waved his hand, dousing the fire, and brought a small puddle of water from the sea, placing it in front of Alex.

Alex exhaled and willed it to move, but nothing happened. She whispered but, again, nothing. Finally, Alex lost her temper and yelled at it. The puddle exploded, covering her with mud. Alex looked at Merlock, who was kind enough not to laugh.

"Now you know yelling won't work."

"Can we go home? I feel like a failure."

"You aren't a failure. You're young and already have more power than a sorcerer decades older. It'll take time, but you'll learn to wield your gifts without your emotions dictating them."

Merlock snapped his fingers, returning them to the library where Stefan was waiting.

"Welcome ... back." He bit his lip to keep from laughing. Alex hugged Stefan before he could get away, covering him in mud too. She strolled to her room with Stefan grumbling and trailing behind her.

Alex needed two baths to wash all the mud out of her hair. Jessica spent most of that time reminding her that if she'd allow her to help, it wouldn't take so long. After leaving the bathing suite, Alex found Jessica waiting for her, arms crossed. "You're going to be late."

"No, I'm not," Alex said, rushing to the stairs. Her dripping hair made them slippery when she hurried up to get dressed. Alex slipped on the fourth last step when she was heading down and would have fallen if Michael hadn't been there to catch her. He'd dressed in his formal Warren knight shirt from the mourning ceremony.

Who's this date for? You or me, Michael?

"I'm not late," she said, turning her back to Jessica. Alex gasped as Jessica tightened her corset straps.

"Not so tight, Lady Jessica," Michael said. "I'd prefer Alex didn't pass out giving Prince Jesse his tour."

"You look handsome tonight, Sir Michael," Jessica said.

"Thank you, Lady Jessica. You do too," Michael replied.

Alex and Edith exchanged a look as Edith rushed to brush Alex's hair.

"Edith! I'd like to keep some hair please."

"If you were earlier, I wouldn't have to rush so much. Or maybe if you let me come—"

"Absolutely not," Jessica said.

"Fine." Edith finished Alex's hair as Jessica stepped beside Michael, handing him Alex's crown.

"Thank you, Sir Michael." Jessica smiled as he placed the crown on Alex's head.

CHAPTER 34
AARON

"Are you speaking to me yet?" Megesti asked.

Aaron looked up from his work and noticed the dark circles under Megesti's eyes and his disheveled appearance.

"You two need to make peace already. I'm done being your go-between. Forgive him—now," Jessica said.

Aaron dropped his pencil and slid his papers into a Warren tournament book and closed it, looking at his friends. "Forgiven."

"Thank you. I'm too tired for this," Jessica sighed. "Do you have any idea how much work it is to keep Alex in line?"

"She's almost as much a prince as you are," Megesti said.

Aaron laughed. "I love that about her."

"Tell her that. With *those* words," Jessica said. "How do you keep saying the wrong thing? You protected her from mercenaries, but you can't kiss her?"

"She's overwhelmed, but I think this whole tournament is a ploy to keep me here."

"That's something," Jessica said.

"I kissed her after she was asleep when we fled. I wanted to before but lost my nerve."

"Why? You've never been this awkward," Jessica said.

Aaron hid his face in his hands. "She's not mine."

Daniel's face filled Aaron's mind.

"She looks at you differently than the others," Megesti said.

"Edward gave her the opportunity to choose. She wants to choose you. I know she does," Jessica said.

"It doesn't matter," Aaron snapped, glaring at them both. "She isn't *mine*—she never was."

Jessica and Megesti exchanged glances.

"Aaron, Daniel's dead. Even if she sees him, he has no claim on her," Jessica said.

"*I'm* the reason he was in the stable. *I'm* why he's dead. If I win Alex, I'm benefiting from his death after having caused it. It's sick."

"There's more to their betrothal," Megesti said.

"What do you know?" Jessica asked.

"My father has always said it made no sense that Emmerich picked Daniel over you," Megesti said. "Daniel was twelve years older than Alexandria. Even if she married young, he'd have been twenty-seven. Datten requires the crown prince to marry before turning twenty-three."

"It wouldn't have worked. But then why arrange it?" Jessica asked.

"My father and Arthur arranged this betrothal without talking to Edward. My father does what he wants, but taking Edward's daughter from him without his consent? He wouldn't do that."

They discussed what the pearl had shown and tried to think of how to best navigate the other suitors, specifically Cameron. Jessica noted that Alex's birthday gifts were promising, considering she'd bought them without Jessica or Edith knowing.

"But Cameron did offer to give her a jousting lesson. I wish we would have thought of that first," Jessica added.

"He's going to teach her jousting. When?" Aaron asked.

"We don't know yet. The fields need to be completed first," Jessica said. "Aaron—I know you're honorable, but you're going to need to kiss her."

"And be another pushy Datten male."

"You aren't Wesley," Megesti said.

"I *know* she wants you to," Jessica said, getting up and straightening her dress.

"How do you know?"

"Because nothing makes her more flustered than when Edith asks if you kissed her yet." Jessica stood and left the room.

Aaron sighed, and Megesti stood up.

"Get some sleep. You're going to need your energy for wooing the princess tomorrow."

Aaron watched him go then looked at the tournament books around him. Grabbing the one on Warren's sword rules, he moved to the painting that would take him past Alex's room on the way to his.

CHAPTER 35
ALEX

I'm done with men thinking they can touch me. Emmerich made it clear it's my choice, and I intend to use it.

Alex knew she'd get an earful once Jessica learned her tour ended—abruptly—when she pushed the Crown Prince of Darren off the pier and left while the knights fished him out. Alex breathed easier when she returned to find Jessica wasn't there. Edith had listened to the news while helping Alex out of her dress, and after Alex slipped into her silk nightgown, they stayed up a while longer talking about Michael and Jessica. However, Edith soon began to yawn.

"I'm off to bed. Do you need anything before I go?" Edith asked.

"I'm fine, thank you," Alex said. Climbing the stairs, Alex curled up in her bed with her mother's journal from the library. She growled at the fire, and it leaped higher, casting a glow across her bed bright enough for reading.

Spring 1469

Our journey to the mortal world was less an adventure and more of a fleeing for our lives. Even once we were on the ship, I couldn't believe we'd managed it.

Merlock and I had the same dream—a nightmare, really. I neglected to tell him I'd been having the same terrible dream for weeks. My brothers didn't need more reasons to fight and blame each other for my situation. But after learning Merlock had the dream too, I knew we had to leave. If we stayed, it would have ended badly for both my brothers.

Secretly, Merlock and I said our goodbyes. I even stole the white pearl to guarantee no one would ever know she helped us. I can't say who in case this should ever fall into the wrong hands, but she was a dear friend who sacrificed so much to get us to safety.

After the farewells, we came home and packed the family books, clothes, and valuables. Moorloc walked in on us filling a trunk with Mother's journals. He was furious and argued with us well into the night, but he couldn't sway us, even if his temper rivaled our father's. Merlock and I had traded most of our valuables for three tickets on that cursed boat, and Merlock swore we'd leave with or without him.

I begged Moorloc to not make me choose between my brothers, and he relented, agreeing to come with us just as I told Merlock he would. My oldest brother is always predictable. Father said the oldest son was heartless and got all the power, but no other firstborn son had to say no to me. Logically, he knew it was better to risk fleeing our home than losing our lives. If he had the Cassandra gifts Merlock and I do, he'd have known the truth. Fleeing or not, we couldn't stop what would happen to me, but at least this way, my daughter, you would survive.

What I never told my brothers was that I had two dreams. I had the same violent end dream Merlock did, and it might have been enough for me to side with him about leaving. But the truth of why I left lies in the other dream I had. I dreamed of the daughter I would have if I went to the human world. The only way I'd have you, Alexandria—my greatest joy—is if I left my home and married a prince of Torian.

Alex mentally repeated the words *my greatest joy* until she fell asleep. When she woke earlier than usual, Alex let her ladies sleep and dressed in simple fighting clothes and braided her hair before heading out to ride with her father and both Warren generals. Alex allowed Matthew to help her onto Flash, and they rode south toward the forest. Alex kept looking back at the generals following them. Edward spoke up, sensing her unease.

"They're my guards, Alexandria. I wish you'd stop hiding from yours."

"Old habits," Alex shrugged.

"Did you often hide from Stefan and Michael in the woods?"

"I had more freedom with Stefan then, but that's because Michael and I were inseparable. I hid from other boys at the camp. One boy, Graham, hated me."

"How could anyone hate you?"

Edward asked about the pearl visions of the camp. Alex told him how Michael had become her best friend, how she shot Graham, and how his nastiness led to their massive fist-fight, which took Michael, Oliver, and Stefan to separate them.

"Your fighting spirit must come from your mother because you didn't get that from me," Edward said, laughing.

That's how I remember it, how it echoed in my dreams.

"You've become proficient with a bow now," Edward

continued. "I'll ask Emmerich if Caleb is coming for the tournament. Perhaps he could give you a few extra lessons while he's here."

Alex remembered the look on Caleb's face in the Datten bar when she confessed she hadn't heard of him.

This could be fun. I wonder how long it would take him to figure things out.

Alex asked about the ties of Warren's nobility to the crown. Edward listed some of them, including his mother, Elizabeth Veremund, and a Bishop and Nial many generations back. Alex had remembered their names from her history and law studies, and Edward mentioned she'd impressed her law tutor with her quick learning.

"We might select you to be a judge someday," he said, and Alex smiled to see how proud this made him.

"What else have my tutors told you?"

"Randal says your etiquette lessons aren't going as well as they'd like."

"As Jessica likes, you mean. My manners are coming along just fine, but she's obsessed with me learning all these ladylike skills. I'm going to be a ruling queen one day! When am I ever going to need to know how to knit?"

Edward burst into laughter. "I've seen your work. No one will *ever* ask you to knit or sew anything."

Alex laughed too. "The sad part is what you've seen is the work Edith tried to fix. Mine's actually worse!"

Edward explained the goal was for her to have an activity that would allow her to relax. Alex thought for a moment before suggesting reading or gardening.

"Gardening sounds perfect. I'll suggest it to Jessica," Edward said, but a heaviness came over Alex's chest.

What about Wesley?

"Did you send Wesley home?" Alex asked, picking at the threads of the blanket beneath Flash's saddle.

"No. Emmerich believes it was a misunderstanding. Wesley entered the tournament, so I'll let him compete for Emmerich's sake. After that, he'll be back in Datten even if Matthew and Randal have to drag him there. Aaron and Guinevere were livid, but no one at the celebration would confirm Aaron's claims."

"No one would confirm he called my mother a whore? Or said I was like her?"

"He said what?" Edward roared as he stopped his horse. Alex's heart stopped as a massive wind struck them. Ice ran down her back as she stared at her father.

He looks like Arthur, like the monster in my dreams. The same eyebrows and lips. He looks like his father like I look like my mother. Breathe. Arthur's dead. He can't hurt you.

"You said Aaron told you," Alex whispered, her body trembling.

Edward's face softened, and he took her hand. "Aaron told us he spoke *ill* of your mother, but he wouldn't repeat the words. Now I know why. Datten ... is traditional. We conceived you before we got married, and to *some* Dattenites, that reflected negatively on your mother, though I've never heard anyone refer to her in such a brazen manner as that."

"Father ..." Alex began but lost her words.

Edward stayed quiet for some time then exhaled. "I'm so sorry, Alexandria—for Wesley, for not telling you about Moorloc, and for not being better at this. You're always tired, and you barely eat. I thought I was saving you pain by keeping you in the dark while you adjusted. Now I know I made things worse."

"I forgive you, but I need you to be honest with me even when it's hard."

"Honesty I can give you. In the future, I'll let you decide what you can and cannot handle as long as you tell me when things become too much."

Alex nodded then asked about the attack. Edward explained how Emmerich wanted to go to war, which didn't surprise Alex. Edward said it was because of Aaron's injury, as any royal blood spilled meant war for Datten.

Aaron's face flashed across Alex's mind. She remembered touching his cut and watching it heal.

I felt such guilt and shame for people getting hurt, but Aaron wouldn't let me. He held me and let me run, even made me bring him so I'd be safe. Was that just two nights ago?

"You look lost in thought."

Alex shook her head and sighed. "Why do you let Emmerich make all the decisions? You're allies. Shouldn't you be a team?"

Or does he not play nice?

"Emmerich has been king since he was thirteen, decades longer than me. I'm still learning, and I learn best by watching others."

"So you let him dictate what we do?"

"I take his suggestions into account," Edward corrected. "Datten's suggestions sound like orders, but Emmerich is more complicated than people would believe."

"I wouldn't have believed you a week ago, but now, knowing he knew about my mother, I don't know."

"Emmerich has a reason for everything he does even if he doesn't tell me what it is. He's been my confidant my whole life. You're going to need to find people like that—people whose opinion you trust."

"Like Stefan and Michael?"

"Yes, they would be ideal. You already trust them. Michael

is kind and cleverer than he's given credit for, and Stefan is a true Wafner. His honor is so ingrained in him he'd never let you become unscrupulous."

"Michael is observant, if a little skittish and clumsy. But you are correct about Stefan. He's principled and has always tried to keep me honest."

Edward raised his brows and grinned then brought up her suitors, noting that the nobility were placing bets. Most assumed it would come down to Aaron, Cameron, or a southern prince, while Guinevere was sure it would be Aaron or Cameron. Alex confessed that Prince Jesse and a few others were indeed out of the running.

"And you?" Alex asked.

"I have no opinion. It's your choice."

"But I *want* to know what you think. Honesty, Your Royal Highness."

"Cameron would give you the tie to the Datten royal family without the hassle of marrying a crown prince. He also is a nice young man with an exceptional reputation, and he is well liked throughout Torian. Aaron would make Datten happy, but he'd be happy letting someone else deal with Datten and staying in his mother's kingdom. Either as godson of the king or something more."

Alex laughed. "So you do have a favorite."

"How could I not? He's my godson, but he also brought you back to me. How do you feel about him?"

Alex turned crimson. "Aaron's complicated. He's easy to be around but confusing at the same time. I'm never sure where I stand with him."

"Oh?"

"Anytime I think he's interested in me, he does something that shows he isn't."

I never said I was a suitor.

Alex went back to picking at Flash's blanket.

"Despite his Strobel blood, Aaron's never been great at talking about things. The only people he spoke to for a year after Daniel died were Megesti, Jerome, and me. Like you, he guards himself. I think you two could heal each other."

Alex tucked her hair behind her ear.

Then he should kiss me already so I'd know.

"Why isn't Aaron the automatic heir? Shouldn't the son of the king get the throne?" Alex asked.

Edward explained how Datten's kings were violent and iron willed. Daniel took after Emmerich, but Aaron after the Strobels. His kind, humble, and thoughtful nature made Emmerich believe Aaron wouldn't be able to control the armies and old families and that he'd get killed trying to do so.

Edward said, "He's been working hard to prove to his father he's worthy of being King of Datten."

"What does he need to do?"

"Finding you helped. It showed he could take on an impossible task and not give up."

Alex stopped Flash and gazed downward. "Would winning my hand get him his crown?"

Is he only pretending to like me so he can be king? Is his crown worth more to him than me?

Edward reached over and grabbed her hand, squeezing it. "Alexandria, I know what you're thinking. I've known Aaron his entire life, and he doesn't have it in him to lie about his true feelings—not for Datten and not for his crown. He can smile and say he loves our fish when I *know* he hates it, but he's too honorable and too much of a Strobel to hurt someone like that. Whatever feelings he has for you, they're genuine."

Alex wasn't sure if she believed him and stayed quiet the rest of the way home.

ALEX HURRIED DOWN THE HALLWAY, hoping a few stragglers would be in the dining hall so some food might remain. To her disappointment, the hall was empty.

"Late night?"

Alex spun around, coming face to face with Aaron. "Early morning."

Aaron held out a loaf of bread. "Figured you'd be hungry, and I need you to approve the tournament setup."

Alex took the bread and Aaron's hand without a thought. Guarded by General Nial, they ambled over to the tournament grounds. The royal seating area was a large wooden platform with multiple thrones affixed to it. Staircases flanked both sides, and a beautiful blue carpet led to the thrones. Above their heads sat a roof that sparkled like silver, and the railing that would separate them from the field was carved with sea dragons. Behind the thrones were rows of benches. Aaron's fingers interlaced with Alex's as he led her up the stairs so they could get the full view from on top.

"I don't remember this being here when I arrived," Alex said, leaning on the railing and noticing that Randal had moved to the end of the jousting area.

"It wasn't. They built it yesterday. Tournament setups happen fast."

Alex turned to find Aaron sitting on the largest throne. He began explaining about the thrones' origins and who sat where, but Alex soon stopped listening, the conversation with her father swirling with the thoughts already filling her head.

Aaron's never been the best at talking about things.

Aaron or Cameron?

I never said I was a suitor.

A little wind won't scare me off.

I just need some time.

Will my magic scare them both off?

The jousting area was larger than she had expected. Just then, a hand tickled the small of her back.

"Jousting's my favorite."

"Horses and hitting people with giant sticks. Did your uncle teach you?" Alex asked, tickling Aaron back. His eyes lit up when she finished tickling him. Aaron leaned on the railing next to her and stared at the grassy jousting field as he explained how his uncle Bernhard had taught him, Daniel, and Cameron jousting.

I wonder what Cameron's going to teach me.

Then he explained how after Daniel died, he and Cameron became close and were still each other's training partners.

What if I ruin that too?

Trying to avoid having to look at Aaron, Alex soon spotted Randal again as he wandered farther off. "Is it normal our guard's not watching us?"

"No. Someone must have asked him to give us space," Aaron said.

"My father says it's Emmerich. He's trying to give you an advantage, which seems unfair," she said, playfully elbowing him. He grinned, pushing her back. When she stopped, they were a few inches apart. Alex's body tingled when Aaron smiled at her.

Just kiss me already.

"With how many suitors there are, I'll take any advantage I can get. But don't worry." Alex felt Aaron's lips brush her neck as he whispered in her ear. "Most of them will prove unworthy. Even those who finish the stipulated three parts of your tournament."

Aaron's arms slipped on either side of her as he braced

himself against the railing. Alex swallowed hard as their noses touched. Aaron closed his eyes and leaned toward her.

Finally!

Alex placed her hand on his chest to lean into him when a loud crack sounded behind her.

CHAPTER 36
ALEX

Alex walked into her room to find Edith and Jessica arguing. She forgot Aaron once she realized her ladies were listing betrothal rules Alex hadn't heard of. After a minute, she surmised Jerome intended to marry Jessica to Caleb Reinhart, Datten's finest archer. Caleb was the same man she'd drank with when she visited Datten with Aaron.

"Jessica, you can't. You don't love him, and the one you do is waiting for you," Alex said.

"I'm a daughter of Datten. It's my duty to marry whomever my father chooses, so don't lecture me about love."

"Excuse me?"

"The *entire kingdom* sees how you look at Aaron and how he looks at you, but every time he tries to get close, you push him away."

"This isn't about me and Aaron," Alex said.

"You claim to be an expert in following your heart, but you push the man you love aside."

"Jessica," Edith said.

"That isn't fair," Alex said.

"Life's not fair, Your Highness."

"You don't know what's happened between me and Aaron," Alex said. Her lip quivered as she remembered the kiss in Datten.

"By all means, enlighten us," Jessica snapped.

"I'm not doing this." The fireplace roared to life, and a sudden downpour thundered outside.

"You're a coward. You're going to marry the first nobleman who kisses you and calls you special. You could have a prince— a prince who'd give everything up for you."

"I'm not a coward!" Alex snapped. "When we were in Datten, *I* kissed *him*—he pushed me away. After his birthday, I kissed him on the cheek, and he did nothing! Worst of all, when he was teaching me to dance, he told me he wasn't a suitor. So forgive me if I expect him to prove his feelings."

Edith reached for Alex, but she pulled away.

"Cameron's pursuing me because he has feelings for me. He's nice, and I know he wants me because he tells me. I'm not willing to let Aaron break my heart again. You of all people should know how it hurts to have someone you love ripped from you."

Jessica's face was ashen. Her stoic composure crumbled as she moved toward Alex.

"We didn't know," Edith whispered.

"That doesn't change things. I'd like to be alone. You're both dismissed."

"Alex—"

"I said you're dismissed. *Don't* make me order you."

Without waiting, Alex lifted her skirts and stalked off to her bedroom. Once there, Alex screamed into her pillow until her voice went hoarse.

I'm going to bury myself in my studies.

She grabbed her mother's journal and read. In it, she learned about the other pearls. Her father's white one told of the past, and the others—one clear and one black—told the future and present. She learned about spells that could protect entire kingdoms, spells used to transfer one's power to another sorcerer, and the titans' ability to manipulate power development on their own.

There were also different sorcerers, such as a Returned One, like her. A Usurper was born every two or three generations and could take and use powers from sorcerers around them. Only one Usurper could exist at a time, and they always came from a small group of specific old families. She learned the first signs of a head or heart were having powers from more than just the two lines the parents gave the child or exceptional levels of power. The head was always ruthless—which is why they'd won the fight for power every generation.

Lovely.

Alex read all afternoon, skipping lunch. Often, her mother referred to specific magic books, but Merlock had never mentioned them. Alex looked up and saw her mother watching her. Victoria pointed down, and Alex picked up the journal sitting on her bed. Her mother nodded. Alex started flipping through the pages until her mother pointed to one.

"What is—?" Alex looked up, but Victoria vanished.

Blinking, she paused for a moment before returning to the diary.

The Verlassen Castle

You know where we were all born and how we arrived in the mortal lands but not where I lived all those years after arriving in Torian before I met your father. I spent them in the Verlassen Castle, my sanctuary. Now it's yours.

Since the castle was decaying when I discovered it, I used magic to repair it. When you find it, the castle will be crumbling as it was all those years ago. But it is marvelous.

It hides in the Dark Forest in a valley near the Ogre Mountains. There I have hidden all the secrets you seek and some you haven't even thought of that will reveal themselves at the appropriate time. This home will be the start of your future, but be careful: there are others who want these secrets, and not all of our kind are as pure of heart as you are.

Alex slammed the book shut harder than she had meant to and heard a thunk. Looking around, she realized a small bundle of paper had slipped out of it. Alex picked it up, and, unfolding it, she found a map wrapped around a shining white stone. Alex grabbed her training clothes, slipped the stone in her pants pocket, and ran for the receiving room, screaming for Edith to undo her dress. When Edith had untied the ribbon, Alex ripped the dress over her head, sending her crown flying. Redressed in seconds, she ran from the room.

Edward was in the throne room with a few members of his council when Alex burst in after getting past both generals.

"I have to find my mother's castle!" Alex shouted, gasping as she rushed to her father. "I found a map to where my mother lived before she married you. She says all the answers are there. How many guards do I have to take? I need to go tonight."

"Alexandria, I don't think it's the best idea right now. Merlock, Jerome, Emmerich, and Aaron are all in Datten picking their tournament entrants."

Why are you speaking to me like I'm a child?

The torches grew as she raised her eyebrows.

I don't need Datten's help. I can take care of myself.

"General Bishop or General Nial? Whom do I take? Sir

Stefan and Sir Michael will escort me, but you'll expect me to bring at least one senior guard."

"I'm sorry, princess, we agree with your father," Randal said, arriving behind her. "It's too dangerous without Jerome and Merlock. We haven't assessed the risk Lygari poses yet."

Traitor. Edith would go.

Alex stared at her father. "Please."

"Is she always this forceful?" one of the council members asked.

Edward exhaled. "Alexandria, this isn't a no—it's not tonight. When Emmerich and Jerome return, we'll come up with a plan."

"Excellent suggestion, Your Royal Highness," Cameron's father said.

Alex nodded and allowed Randal to lead her from the hall.

No one in the kitchen dared look at Alex as the fires erupted simultaneously when she stepped inside for some carrots. She stormed to the stables, every fireplace and torch she passed erupting in flames, and outside, the grass beneath her feet died with each step. Inside the stable, she found Flash and Thunder next to each other and soon began feeding them. Moments later, however, she heard a clink behind her. Alex whipped around to find Stefan with staves and wooden swords in his hands.

"Randal and Jessica told me what happened. I suspected you'd need to burn off some frustration. We can talk, we can spar, or we can do both."

"Spar."

Stefan nodded and slid his arm around Alex's shoulder. Together, they left the stable for the knights' workout area.

"Should we talk about your fight with Jessica?"

"Later. I'd rather not set you on fire."

ALEX WOKE up crying so hard she couldn't breathe, fragments of the nightmare lingering, overwhelming her. Images of burning wooden structures, swords clanging, and a swirling vortex of debris clouded her vision. She covered her mouth to silence her cries, and then got her legs tangled in the blanket, and she slammed onto the hard stone floor, taking the blanket with her and sending Victoria's journal flying across the room. Alex untangled herself and inspected her bruises. Her right palm was ripped open, and her knee throbbed. Crawling to the journal, Alex pulled it to her, leaving a bloody palm imprint on the page, and she spotted the spell.

Summoning the Dead

I could talk to my mother.

Alex crawled to her wardrobe and reached underneath. She grabbed her dagger, tossing it on her bed. Dressed in her training clothes, she wiped the drying blood on her pants and fastened the dagger to her belt before grabbing the journal. Reaching behind the painting, she felt it give, and then, removing a torch from the wall, she peered into the dark passage. Breathing to calm her nerves, she shouted, "Light!" and the torch lit up.

Once inside, she pulled the painting shut. Pausing for a moment, she looked in her room as if through a window, and panic seized her.

This is how I watched when she died.

Right would lead to the library and the three halls,

including the throne room and the main floor. Left would take her to Aaron and Daniel's rooms and keep her on the second floor. Aaron would still be in Datten picking the tournament knights, so Alex turned left and ended up in Daniel's room, which was like Aaron's but more luxurious.

Aaron's room must be a knight's room. This is a royal guest room.

Looking around, Alex ran her fingers along the dusty quilt. The crest stitching was perfect, as if no one had ever used it.

"Why do we keep this?" Alex asked as she walked to the wardrobe. Inside were several old Warren- and Datten-crested shirts; their style wasn't quite right. Alex moved toward the door but then paused at the bookshelf; it was almost identical to hers.

With one last look, Alex crept into the deserted hallway and hurried past the paintings and tapestries, passing several hallways until she found the one she was looking for. Seconds later, she was about to knock on Megesti's door when it suddenly opened.

"I need your help," she blurted.

Before he could reply, she grabbed his arm and pulled him into the hallway. Then she handed him the journal already open to the page with the spell.

"Do you have any idea how dangerous this is?" he asked, incredulous. "I've only heard of spells like this. We could bring the wrong person ... or worse."

"We have to try. I'm getting stronger, and I couldn't live with myself if I hurt someone. I keep reading about family books. My mother hid them for a reason—maybe to keep them from Moorloc. They can help me. I see the dead often, but they don't talk to me. If we summon them, they'll be able to. Please."

Alex grabbed his arm, begging him. Megesti stared at her, pursing his lips.

"Fine." Megesti grabbed her hand and pulled her down the hallway to an empty guest room. "It won't last long, though. I'm not that powerful, and your powers are erratic."

He twirled his wrist, and the room lit up. It looked like Aaron's minus any of the personal touches: a bed with a Warren quilt and a fireplace that was now crackling. Standing before the flames were her mother and Daniel.

"They're already here." Alex unsheathed her dagger and held her hand out to Megesti.

"I hate blood spells."

He took the dagger and cut his palm along the old scar, and then he did the same on Alex's. Alex grunted as she copied Megesti's motions and squeezed a fist. Their blood dripped to the floor as they chanted the spell from Victoria's journal. For a while, nothing happened. Then a freezing wind tore through the room followed by an explosion that sent the furniture crashing against the walls, snapping two of the bedposts. Alex shrieked. Victoria stepped toward them with Daniel at her side.

"Daniel?" Megesti asked.

"Mother!" Alex gasped.

The apparitions looked at each other and then turned to Alex and Megesti. "You look beautiful, dear. So powerful already; your great-grandfather would be proud."

Tears fell from Alex at the sound of her mother's voice.

"You summoned us, princess. You better ask your questions before your spell wears off," Daniel said. "But tell my little brother I'm watching over him too."

"Is that where you go when you aren't watching me?"

"Always. I watch over both of you," Daniel said. "Though you've always been a lot more troublesome than he is."

"The books," Megesti blurted out. "Where are our ancestral journals?"

Victoria was about to answer when the door burst open and Merlock stormed in. "What in high Hades did you two do?"

"Do *not* speak to my daughter like that," Victoria scolded. Merlock froze, looking at his sister. Victoria turned her attention back to Alex. "I've hidden the books in my castle. You'll need a blood spell and two of our line to find them." Her hand grazed Alex's face. It felt like a winter wind kissing her cheek.

"What do I do? Can I learn to control them? Will Moorloc help me? Or are there others?"

"No! Never go to the Forbidden Lands!" Victoria grabbed Alex's shoulders. Alex's chest clenched at the cold and the force of her mother's words, much like when she'd fallen through the ice. "They would know what you are immediately. You're the strongest of our line but nowhere near ready to face what lies there."

Edward threw open the door. "Merlock, what is going on?" He froze at the sight of Victoria.

"Hello, Edward. Take care of our daughter."

Daniel nodded. "Megesti, you were right. It was always him. Princess, *never* give up on my brother. If you do, Datten will fall."

Alex turned to Megesti, who looked as confused as she felt. Victoria kissed Edward's cheek as Merlock picked up the journal, and when he closed it, Victoria and Daniel vanished.

"Bring her back!" Edward shouted.

"She's still here," Alex said.

Merlock scowled at Alex and Megesti. "What were you two thinking? Megesti, you know what happens if a blood spell goes wrong!"

"I'm not sure you should speak to my daughter like that," Edward said.

"I'm not scolding the princess, Your Royal Highness. I'm scolding sorcerers for practicing dangerous magic without taking *precautions*. The risks that come with this sort of spell are monumental. They could have summoned Arthur, became possessed, or drawn attention from the Forbidden Lands."

"Why are the Forbidden Lands so dangerous?" Alex asked.

"Because that's where all the other sorcerers live," Merlock replied.

"Well, why can't we get help from *them*?" Alex asked.

"Did you hear nothing your mother said? Why perform this spell if you won't listen to her? Sorcerers who are powerful enough to help you would see how young and vulnerable you are—you wouldn't stand a chance."

"I am not a child!" Every nearby torch and fireplace sprang to life.

Merlock raised his brows. "But you *are* inexperienced. Sorcerers live a long time. To us, you are a child."

"Wait. How long?"

"The oldest of us makes it past three hundred," Megesti replied.

Alex's mouth dropped open.

I don't want to lose anyone else.

"Alexandria." Edward reached for her, but Alex pushed past him and ran from the room.

Centuries without them!

Alex raced down the stairs and into the courtyard.

Just get away. Don't set anything on fir—

Her thoughts were interrupted when she ran straight into Michael. The moon reflected off the silver tunic of his knight uniform; he was on duty.

"Alex? Are you hurt?" He grabbed her shoulders, looked her over, and held up her cut palm.

"No." She pulled her hand away, making a fist.

"Then what?"

"*Hundreds.* I'm going to outlive everyone I love by hundreds of years."

CHAPTER 37

AARON

It took until well past midnight for Emmerich to stop drinking long enough to pick the knights that would represent Datten at the tournament. Aaron needed to get to Warren, so after all the choices were made, Aaron hurried to the lab to find Merlock. When he turned down the final hallway, his mother's door opened.

"Mother, why are you up? Is everything all right?"

Guinevere tied her robe as she stared at Aaron. She always seemed older to him when her hair was down, the white in her hair more visible.

"I'm fine, dear. What are you doing here?"

"I want Merlock to send me back to Warren."

"In the middle of the night?" Guinevere raised her eyebrows. "What's the hurry? Perhaps there's a princess you want to get back to?"

"You know perfectly well, thanks to your little spy."

"Jessica relates what she hears from Alexandria—and what I've heard is concerning. She's busy with lessons and Cameron.

She has no time for anyone else, and now ... but I shouldn't gossip."

"Mother, tell me."

"Before we left, they had a terrible fight. Alexandria threw her ladies out of her room, and only an hour ago, Merlock left in a rage and hasn't returned."

"What was the fight about?"

"Jessica wouldn't say, but I'm worried about Alexandria. I remember what it was like to go from being a Lady of Warren to Queen of Datten overnight. It was overwhelming, and she's gone from peasant to princess to powerful sorceress in two months."

"Her birthday will only bring more powers."

"Talk to her. Make sure she's all right."

"I'll try."

"Merlock. I summon you as Queen of Datten."

A crack sounded in the hallway, and a scowling Merlock stood before them. "Your Majesty. What may I do for you?"

"Could you bring Aaron to Warren?"

"Of course. Perhaps you can talk some sense into Megesti and Alexandria."

"What did they do?" Aaron asked.

Merlock groaned. "They summoned the dead."

Aaron looked toward his mother, whose mouth hung open.

"The *dead*?" Guinevere asked.

"My niece wanted to speak to her mother."

"She is very persuasive," Aaron said, laughing.

"Well, you'd know, wouldn't you?" Guinevere kissed Aaron's cheek and went back to her room.

"Now I have a furious king, a weakened young sorceress, and a sorcerer who should know better than to listen to a seventeen-year-old girl." Merlock sighed, cracking them back to Warren.

CHAPTER 38
ALEX

Alex awoke to Edith nudging her shoulder. Outside, it was still dark. "Merlock and our fathers are waiting for you. They say it's time to practice your magic. Should I get Jessica to help?"

Alex could hear the hope in Edith's voice. "No."

Alex dragged herself out of bed and struggled into her training clothes while Edith braided her hair. In the receiving room, Edith handed Alex her cloak, and Merlock cracked them to the usual beach. Alex went to the shore and watched the waves lap at her feet while the others built a large fire. As she gazed at the sea, her thoughts swirled.

Why won't Jessica fight for Michael?

When will you stop treating me like a little girl, Father?

I miss you, Mother.

Why can't Aaron just tell me how he feels? I'd accept it if he just told me to my face. Why doesn't he want me back?

As the seconds passed, massive storm clouds rumbled over the sea, and the waves grew larger.

"We're ready for you," Randal said, touching her shoulder.

Alex turned, finding a raging fire before her. She crossed the cool sand until she stood before it.

"Put it out—*any way* you want," Merlock said.

Alex swallowed as the chest-high flames danced, lighting up the surrounding area. Wiping her clammy palms on her pants, Alex closed her eyes and allowed herself a deep, calming breath. She pictured her mother.

I'm sorry for what I said when I was angry. I love you and just want to make you proud.

When she opened her eyes, power coursed through her, and soon a small stream of water slithered up the beach toward the fire. When the stream hit it, the flames fizzled, but the water was no match. She tried to grow the stream but couldn't. Alex pushed herself; her chest tightened, and her throat felt like ash as she tried again and again, desperate to extinguish the fire. Edward came beside her. The reflection of the fire in his silver tunic looked like blood.

"You're tired. I think you've tried enough today," Edward said.

"I can do this. I have to do this." Tears fell down her cheek.

I've caused enough death and can't be responsible for any more pain or be this helpless again. I'm tired of feeling weak and need something to just work.

"Alexandria," Edward said, touching her shoulder.

"No!" she snapped, wrenching away from Edward. As she did so, both the stream and fire exploded, and although Merlock and Randal were far enough away, the blast hurled Edward and Alex across the beach. Air left Alex's lungs as she slammed into the sand, and amid the chaos, she felt Daniel's icy hands leave her back as he looked down at her before vanishing. The next moment, Alex screamed as her shoulder began burning. Debris from the fire had struck her, and then

Randal slammed into her, trying to extinguish the fire spreading down her arm.

Edward had taken the brunt of the blast protecting her, and his entire chest was ablaze. Alex gagged at the smell of burning cloth and flesh, and Merlock doused him with water while Randal kept Alex from interfering. Merlock's face went ashen when he cracked them back to the castle as the sun was rising.

Arriving in Edward's room, Randal took charge. "Merlock, fetch the doctor."

Merlock cracked, leaving them to get Edward into bed.

Alex whimpered as rain fell around them. "I'm so sorry."

Edward touched her cheek. "I'll be fine."

Minutes after Edward was in bed, Merlock arrived with the doctor. The crack rang louder than usual from Merlock's panic.

"Princess, this is work for the healers," the doctor said, rushing to Edward.

"Check my daughter first," Edward ordered despite his considerable discomfort.

"I'm fine." Alex squeezed her father's hand.

"For me?" Edward asked.

Alex sighed, rubbing her father's uninjured shoulder as she stood up. When she removed Aaron's ruined cloak, the gold lining crumbled into a charred heap and reminded her of the flames. Alex loosened her shirt and slipped her arm out, exposing her shoulder and neck for the doctor.

"Not even a scratch," the doctor said.

"How is that possible?" Edward asked. "I saw the flames on her."

Merlock narrowed his eyes at Alex. "Show us the hand you cut last night."

Alex held out her perfect palms.

"Is that how you healed from falling through the ice?" Merlock asked.

Alex nodded. "I've always healed *unnervingly quickly,* as Stefan says, and Daniel protects me. Today, he caught me after the blast."

The royal doctor looked at Alex before turning to Edward. "Her arm didn't need stitches after the fight. She's the same as her mother, isn't she?"

Edward nodded.

"You're fortunate, princess. I have been your father's doctor his whole life. Your mother had a genuine gift for healing herself and others. I hope you inherited both of her gifts." The doctor put his hand on Alex's shoulder. "Your father will be fine. He'll need rest and some herbs. You'll only need to delay your tournament by one day."

The doctor patted Alex's shoulder and turned to Edward. "You—rest. Take today and tomorrow off. Then you'll be able to get through the tournament without too much pain."

Edward nodded. Then he said, "As for you, young lady, *you* have a jousting lesson. The young baron has been patient, considering how much of your time his cousin monopolizes."

Alex grabbed his hand. "I can't leave—I set you on fire."

"Things happen in war every day. That isn't a reason to stop living," Edward said, smiling wearily at Alex.

She groaned. "Fine." Alex kissed her father's cheek and left to meet Cameron. He was in the library reading a book about Betruger horses. When he saw her, his face lit up.

"I heard what happened. Obviously, we can reschedule."

"My father insists he's fine and would like us to carry on. So I'm all yours." Alex gasped and blushed, realizing what she said as General Nial snorted behind her.

Cameron proffered his arm to her. "Then we're off to the stables."

"FLASH IS MY HORSE. Why can't I use him?" Alex asked, rubbing Flash's face. Thunder was in the next stall and stomped his hoof when Alex didn't pet him too.

"We breed coursers for speed, not jousting. It wouldn't be safe for you or for Flash. I'll use my horse, Sparta, and we'll see which horse works best for you." Cameron walked down the stable, looking over the horses. "Jousting can scare horses, so they need the right temperament, and you need to be good enough with horses to control one with that level of bravery."

Alex stopped listening and leaned against Flash's stall. He pushed Alex with his muzzle, and she quickly realized he was pushing her to Thunder.

"I thought you didn't like him," Alex teased, but Flash stomped his hoof, and she laughed. "Cameron, I'm taking Thunder. Flash insists." Alex grabbed Thunder by the bridle, and he came over and rubbed his head against her.

"You can't take Thunder. He's wild and doesn't listen to anyone except—" Cameron froze, wide-eyed.

"He likes me. Karl, could you fetch my saddle?" Alex smiled when the stable boy returned with it.

"I'm brave enough if you are, but don't say I didn't warn you when he throws you," Cameron said, casting a nervous glance at Thunder.

Cameron and Alex led the horses to the jousting fields where a stable boy had left Alex's armor. After helping her into it, Cameron let her get a feel for the lance on solid ground. He stood behind her, adjusting her form while explaining the finer details and how it would differ once she was on the horse. Her heart slammed in her chest as he firmly moved her body around into position. When Cameron stepped back, Alex

249

smirked at the sight of his red face as he brought Thunder to her.

Blushing are you, baron?

Alex looked at Thunder and paused, realizing how heavy her armor was.

"Do you need help?" Cameron whispered in her ear.

"Yes, please," Alex replied.

Cameron helped her up, and once she was balancing the lance, he mounted his horse and let Alex try to hit his shield. Alex loved it, even if jousting required more skill than she expected, and her arms felt like water in no time. She broke a few lances and even knocked a shield from Cameron's hand, though she suspected he let her. Thunder behaved the entire time, and after they finished, Cameron steadied Thunder so Alex could dismount.

Once she had removed her armor, Alex grabbed Thunder's reins. "That was fun. Thank you," Alex said before she kissed Cameron. He grabbed her waist to keep her close, and she bumped into Thunder's leg.

"I had fun too." He leaned down, and Alex closed her eyes as Cameron's lips touched hers. His kiss was firmer, and muscular hands gripped Alex's hips, pulling her against his body. She grabbed Cameron's arm to steady herself and felt his tongue slip into her mouth and tickle hers. Before Alex could process what was happening or respond, Thunder moved. Alex lost her balance, and they both ended up sprawled in the mud, laughing.

When she looked up, Thunder was gone. Alex turned to tell Cameron, but he was looking at someone else.

CHAPTER 39
AARON

aron had spent hours keeping Edward company while Alex was off with Cameron, and when he'd finally come down to take Thunder out, he'd caught Cameron kissing her.

I know he's kissed her already—but I don't need to see it.

Now, standing in front of Thunder's empty stall, he realized the horse he'd seen wandering off had been Thunder. Edward had insisted Alex go despite that morning's incident. But once she had, he'd summoned Aaron to sit with him. They had discussed the issues at the pier and how to help the farmers in the smaller towns as well as the tournament plans.

Leave me sitting in the sick room wondering what my ferflucsing cousin is doing with her.

Thunder's whinny reached Aaron from the path that led to the stable. As it grew louder, he spotted Cameron leading Sparta and Thunder back to their stalls. It didn't matter that Cameron was the only person he trusted to tend to Thunder when he was away. Just then, nothing mattered.

"What in the *Forbidden Lands* are you doing with my horse?"

Cameron turned to look Aaron up and down. "Returning him to the stable. Would you rather I let him wander the grounds?"

"I'd rather you never took him at all. You should leave things alone," Aaron said as he wrenched the reins from Cameron's hands.

"He was mine first, so I have more claim than you do," Cameron retorted calmly.

"Maybe you should keep your hands and other parts to yourself," Aaron snapped.

Cameron smirked and walked up to Aaron. "You're distressed because for the first time in your life, *that crown* doesn't give you the advantage. You have to compete just like the rest of us."

"Stay away from my horse."

"But who will keep him company when you're *so* busy?"

"Don't you have a job?"

"I do—but my father thinks I should be at the royal stables, providing hands-on support for the princess."

"Flash is fine."

"But you're not the expert. Whom will she believe?"

"If I find out your hands have been anywhere on her—"

"Oh, you mean we *aren't* talking about horses?" A feral smirk spread across Cameron's face. "Lucky for me, I don't have that Datten honor hanging on me at all times. Plus, my experience with women is better than yours."

"It's your *experience* that makes me anxious."

"Lucky for me, King Edward lets Alex decide who's worthy of her time, and so far, I'm at the top of that list. Well, that or she just really enjoys kissing me."

If you hurt her, I'll—

"But don't worry about my hands," Cameron continued, raising them for effect. "I always let her touch me first. My mother raised a gentleman."

Is Jessica right? Does Alex still think I'm not a suitor? No, she wanted to kiss me yesterday. The way she looked at me. How she touched me. Cameron's wrong. If I'd kissed her, would she still have let him kiss her?

Cameron stepped forward, tossing the other horse's reins at Aaron. "Thanks for putting the horses away, cousin. I wouldn't want to be late for lunch. I know Alex will be looking for me and will be disappointed if I'm not there. Can't have her thinking I've lost interest ... like *some* people."

CHAPTER 40
ALEX

Alex couldn't stop laughing at the mess on her clothes. Jessica and Edith rushed into her receiving room, and when Michael and Stefan tried to come in, her ladies chased them out.

"You're a disaster!" Jessica said, wrinkling her nose.

"What happened to jousting?" Edith asked.

"We jousted. I just ended up in the mud."

"At least tell us if he kissed you," Edith begged when Alex came out of the bathing room. Jessica sat on the couch frowning, trying to fix Alex's knitting. Alex ignored her and faced Edith.

What do I tell you? What's proper to tell you?

Alex smiled as her cheeks heated.

"He did!" Edith exclaimed.

"You let him kiss you—again?" Jessica dropped her needles.

"How else am I supposed to decide if a man is right for me? Unlike you, I'm not willing to find out after I'm married that he's a terrible kisser."

"You don't need to kiss every man who tries." Jessica scowled.

"It's not as if he was my first kiss."

"Who was?" Edith asked.

Alex shared the details of her first kiss with Thomas from the camp and then added, "Obviously, Lady Prudish has never kissed anyone, but have you?"

Edith reached over Alex and pushed Jessica playfully. "Jessica is saving her first kiss for a worthy man. She's found him now but won't kiss him because she's worried about disappointing her father. I, on the other hand, have kissed *far too many* in my quest for my perfect man. Most weren't great."

"How many is too many?" Jessica asked.

"However many is too many for you to want to tell your father," Edith said, winking at Alex.

Alex leaned closer to Edith. "Have any ever put their tongue in your mouth?"

"Ewww," Jessica said.

"I didn't ask for your opinion," Alex snapped and turned back to Edith. "Well?"

"A few. They were the best kissers. Men can do *amazing* things with their tongues," Edith said.

"We should get you changed for lunch," Jessica said.

"We won't need your help, Jessica. You may go for lunch. Perhaps Caleb has arrived." Alex said, marching upstairs without waiting for Jessica's reply.

"That was cruel," Edith said.

Both stopped at the top step. On Alex's bed was a large blue box wrapped with a silver ribbon.

"Maybe it's an early birthday gift," Edith said.

Alex opened the box to find three dresses in the same style as her favorite green dress—one red, one gold, and the last Warren blue.

255

"Could your father have ordered them?"

"No." Alex ran her hand along the red dress, and another royal's face came to mind. Alex bit her lower lip. "I think we should save these for the tournament. I'd like the red one for jousting. Today I'd like the blue one."

"You in blue?"

"I know," Alex said. "I want to visit my father."

She allowed Edith to put her hair up in an elaborate twisted braid, leaving half of her long locks flowing down her back.

Stefan and Michael arrived to escort them. Edith and Michael headed to lunch while Stefan escorted Alex to her father's room.

"You look guilty. Whatever it is, you'll feel better if you tell me."

"I'm losing control, Stefan. First, I screamed at Jessica and then a fire. I'm so angry. I thought I'd mastered keeping my powers in check, but with my birthday so close, I feel myself slipping. What if I—?" Alex broke off.

Stefan pulled her down a small side hall that led to the knights' rooms. "You'll get there. After the tournament, Merlock can increase your lessons. You're expecting too much of yourself."

"That's your fault," Alex said, pushing him.

"So how are things with Cameron?"

"Why?"

"The general stopped by, and I was told to keep a closer eye on the young baron when he's around you. He's on Randal's list."

Alex rolled her eyes. "Kissing me shouldn't put him on any list."

Stefan smirked. "Well, maybe your *suitor* list. But watching him won't hurt."

"While we're on suitors ... Michael and Jessica."

"Aren't you mad at my sister?"

"Yes, but not enough to risk her and Michael. I have a plan."

"You always do." Stefan laughed as they turned down the hall toward Edward's room.

Alex found her father in bed arguing with Merlock and the doctor about how long he needed to rest. His eyes lit up when he saw Alex. "How was jousting?"

"Harder than I expected, though I'm sure Randal filled you in." Alex glanced at the general as she walked to her father's bedside.

Edward squeezed her hand. "If you run out of activities, Aaron or your ladies can walk you through the tournament procedure. It sounds simple, but it helps to be prepared just in case."

"Yes, Father." Alex said as she touched his shoulder and kissed his cheek.

"Come along, Alexandria," Merlock said. "Your father needs to rest, and it's lunch."

When she arrived at the dining hall, Alex peeked inside and spotted Cameron at a table glancing back at the door.

Miss me already?

Then she spotted her father's empty chair at the head table, which brought a lump to her throat and a pain in her stomach.

Maybe I could skip lunch?

Her stomach rumbled, reminding her she'd already missed breakfast. Straightening her dress, Alex stepped inside, and everyone watched her walk to the head table. Arriving, she curtsied to the King and Queen of Datten, and Guinevere beckoned her over.

"Careful," Guinevere whispered. "Aaron is in a foul mood. Something about his horse."

"I appreciate the warning, but I can handle him," Alex said, winking.

"Don't worry about your father, Alexandria. He's in expert hands," Emmerich said.

Alex swallowed and walked to her side of the table. When she glanced around the room, Cameron was staring at her. She smiled before turning back to the table. Aaron had pulled her chair out.

"Thank you," Alex said, sitting down.

Instantly, her plate was full of food. Alex took a bite of her fish and turned to Aaron to apologize about Thunder when the commotion began. They leaped to their feet, and Aaron pushed Alex behind him as something shattered. Alex saw two men throwing punches across a table—one was Gabriel Schmitz, and the other looked like Wesley.

Jerome and Matthew broke up the fracas. The usually kind Matthew Alex knew had been replaced by the stern and terrifying General Bishop. He spun and faced the head table.

"I apologize for the interruption. We will handle these men. Please carry on with your meal."

Guinevere stared at Emmerich. "That's all right, Matthew, we're coming."

Emmerich stood and held his arm out to Guinevere. They followed the generals dragging the knights out.

"It would appear all my relatives have lost their minds," Aaron said. "First Wesley and now Gabriel and Lutiger."

Alex didn't laugh. "Gabriel's your mother's cousin. Lutiger?"

"Wesley's cousin and Kruft's nephew. Cameron can't take his eyes off you. Should we talk about your jousting lesson this morning?"

"It was fine. Cameron is an effective instructor. I even knocked his shield from his hand," Alex replied. Aaron said nothing, and as Alex watched him swallowing hard, she grinned mischievously. "You look nervous, Your Highness. Are you afraid of me with a bow and a lance now?" When Aaron still didn't speak, Alex looked down at her food and sighed, her smile gone. "I'm sorry about Thunder getting out. It's my fault —I should have been more careful."

"I don't care about my horse. I want to know what happened after the lesson."

Alex peeked at Aaron. There was an edge to his tone.

"What do you—?"

"Did you kiss him?"

Alex's breath hitched. It felt as if the entire hall could hear them and was watching.

You're asking this here? Now?

She swallowed hard and answered. "I did. It wasn't the first time Cameron kissed me. But why do you care? Are you trying to decide whether you're a suitor today?"

"If I were, would that make a difference?"

Ice trickled down Alex's spine.

Yes. I wouldn't kiss anyone else again if you admitted you want me.

"Do you mean stop kissing him? No. Cameron's nice. You said it yourself. He's good Warren *stock*. The sort of man I'm supposed to court. Kissing him helps me figure things out."

"So you're planning to run around kissing random men?"

Alex choked on her food and took a swig of ale.

"*That's* inappropriate." Her voice was a hiss. "I'm not kissing random men. I kissed one suitor who's my godmother's nephew. I'm not Jessica. It wasn't my first."

Aaron's face softened. "You remember?"

"I remember kissing Thomas at the camp. I was thirteen."

"No, your first *ever* kiss was with me."

Alex felt hot. When she looked down, his leg was touching hers.

"We were visiting you about a month before you disappeared. I picked you a bouquet from the royal garden, and when I gave them to you, you kissed me."

"I don't remember that."

Aaron flushed. "I do. Afterward, I told my brother that when I was older, I would fight him for you. I didn't quite understand how betrothals worked." Aaron said as he nudged Alex's leg with his, making her shiver. Alex gazed into Aaron's sparkling blue eyes and felt her heart beat faster.

The entire room can hear it. Too much. I'm feeling too much. Don't look at Cameron.

Alex's control over her magic started to slip.

Suddenly, Michael appeared in front of the table. "Stefan told me you wanted to check the archery fields."

"Yes." Alex stood up so fast she knocked her chair over. Aaron stood and reached for her hand as Alex tried to control her breathing. "I have to go. Michael, let's go."

Alex brushed past Aaron and ran from the room, leaving Michael shouting for her to slow down. Neither of them spoke as they walked to the archery field. Alex was finally breathing normally again when they arrived. Michael handed her the bow he'd brought, and, moving beside her with a quiver full of arrows, he held them while she adjusted her stance.

"I hope it isn't too windy for the tournament," Alex said.

"You could help if it is."

They stood in comfortable silence while Alex nocked an arrow and sent it sailing to the target.

"Who's winning: Cameron or Aaron? This morning I'd have said Cameron, but that intense conversation between you and Aaron caught *everyone's* attention."

Alex aimed her next arrow. "Who knows what happened with Cameron today?"

"Every knight and guard—it's our job to keep you safe, after all. We're forbidden to leave you alone with him."

"How is Stefan actually handling it?"

"Not well." Michael chuckled. "Cameron had better pray he never runs into Stefan alone. After twelve years protecting you, these suitors are stressing him."

"Him and me both."

"Who kissed whom?" Michael's voice was kind and curious.

"We already talked about Cameron," Alex said, wrinkling her nose.

"I meant Aaron."

All right, we'll do this once.

"I kissed him—in Datten. But we haven't managed another." She handed Michael her bow and walked to retrieve her arrows.

Michael held his hand up to block the sun. "A little rusty. We should practice more. So does Cameron make your stomach flip?"

Alex let the question hang in the air as she finished retrieving her arrows and returned to where Michael stood. "Maybe. We've only kissed a few times, so comparing that to a drunken kiss with Aaron and Thomas before isn't much to go on."

"Whoever makes you feel ... more is who you should go for."

"What if they don't feel it back?"

"Tell Aaron how you feel. He made a mistake, so now you're scared. Do it anyway."

"Or you could focus on Cameron," Stefan said as he came up behind them.

"Ignore him. A Datten knight voting against his prince? Dishonorable."

Stefan and Michael debated the pros and cons of Alex kissing Aaron until she snapped. "Have you kissed Lady Jessica yet? You're a princess's guard and proven in battle. You're a fine match."

"I would never presume to kiss a lady without her approval," Michael said.

"How about with my approval?" Alex asked.

"My sister won't kiss you first," Stefan said. "That's why we entered you into the tournament."

"You did what?" Michael asked.

"Stefan signed you up for the tournament. Don't worry, it's only swords, archery, and strategy," Alex said as she nocked her bow and drew back.

"But I'm supposed to help you with strategy."

"Stefan will do it."

"I've only entered swords, and since I'm already captain of the princess's guard, I have nothing to prove," Stefan said.

"I thought we were co-captains."

"No," Stefan said, and then he turned to Alex. "When are you going to forgive my sister?"

"When she stops acting like you and starts acting like she's on my side." Alex lowered her bow and looked at Stefan and Michael. Alex explained her suspicions that Aaron and Jessica were friends and she was feeding information to the queen. "You know how I am. I've forgiven her—but she said hurtful things, and I need time. For now, please talk to your father."

"I already did. He won't make any plans for the time being. Like Edward, he wants her to be happy, and he approves of the suggested suitor."

"What suitor? Jerome is considering suitors for Jessica?" Michael asked, panicking.

"You! We told my father to consider you! That's why we entered you in the tournament!" Stefan said.

Alex giggled.

"Are you ready to talk about what upset you the other night?" Stefan asked.

Alex groaned but nocked her bow and aimed again. "Which part? The part where we have to follow a weird old map to find my mother's castle to get her sorcerer journals or the part where I'm going to live to be three hundred and every single person I love will die centuries before me?" Alex released the arrow, and it sailed to the right, missing the target.

"You need practice," Stefan said.

"I need to not shoot when I'm upset. We can't solve my lifespan, but will you help me find the journals?"

"Of course," Michael said.

"Thank you for asking for once," Stefan said. "And you won't be alone. You'll have Megesti, or you can keep having babies with Cameron until you get a sorcerer child."

"She's not having babies with Cameron."

"Obviously—they have to get married first."

Time to change topics.

"Stefan, when you signed Michael up for the archery contest, did you see a Dean Ilith?"

"Yes. Do you know him?"

"He's my *champion*." Alex sauntered off to grab her arrows.

"You have a champion?" both men exclaimed in unison.

Alex refused to answer questions about her champion as they headed back. Michael was panicking about the tournament, so Stefan tried to reassure him. Alex spent the afternoon with the generals, finalizing her secret portion of the tournament. Word had spread that Alex required suitors to take part in her component, but all they knew was that it involved the library. For the sake of secrecy, they met in Edward's room.

Edith and Jessica brought them all dinner, but Alex refused to acknowledge Jessica. After a few hours, Alex was happy with all their preparations.

"I think it's brilliant, Alexandria," Matthew said.

"Testing their intelligence will ensure I find a match who will keep my mind as sharp as the Wafners keep my fighting skills," Alex said. "Why are these books different?"

"They're Datten's copies," Jerome said. "I thought we should leave the books in the Warren library undisturbed so as not to tip off the men about what to review. I revealed your plans to Merlock, and he retrieved these for us to plan with. I will now give them to His Highness," Jerome said.

"Isn't it unfair to provide Prince Aaron with all the books we used?" Matthew asked.

Jerome smiled. "It would be unfair if we gave him *only* the books we used. I intend to give him some books we used, many we didn't, and several I know he hates."

Alex laughed.

Jerome gathered an armful of books and bade them all a good night.

Alex nodded to the generals and strode to her father's room. The doctor informed her he was asleep, so she kissed him on the cheek and went back to her room. The knights were starting their evening rotation, so there was a lot going on. Pausing at her door, she thought of what Michael had said.

Maybe it's time to be honest with him. No more being a coward.

Alex padded upstairs, speaking words of encouragement to herself the entire way. Arriving at Aaron's door, she knocked and then opened the door, but Aaron wasn't there. Disappointed, she slunk back to her room. Everyone was already asleep, and her footsteps quietly echoed on the stone floor as she walked through the receiving room and made her way upstairs. When she stepped into her bedroom, she swallowed her scream.

Standing up from the edge of her bed was Aaron.

Alex's heart stopped as she stared at him. There were always interruptions whenever they were together, but now he was here, in her room—alone.

"Aaron—I ..."

Before she could finish, Aaron bolted across the room to her. Alex's stomach lurched as he slid his arm around her waist and pulled her against him. She thought back to the alley in Datten where she'd drunkenly stolen their first kiss, and then she slid her arms up his chest, feeling his heart hammering. Her throat went dry, and a tingling sensation flooded her body. The same electric feeling every touch from Aaron gave her swelled through her, but there was a new feeling too. Tingles erupted through her entire body, setting off an almost painful pressure between her thighs. Aaron looked down at her, and Alex felt she could stare into his eyes all day as long as he was touching her.

CHAPTER 41
ALEX

"**N**o running. Not this time. Never again," Aaron whispered, pressing his forehead to hers.

Alex bit her lower lip and gripped his shirt. *Say something. Tell him how you feel. Tell him to kiss you. Speak!*

"I—Aaron—" Trembling, she couldn't get the words out. Aaron tilted her chin up and then kissed her.

An explosion of sensations erupted within her. His lips were softer than Cameron's, and the emotions he awoke in her were like lightning in her chest. Alex slid her hands around his neck, pulling herself closer to him. Aaron followed her lead, gripping her tighter. Every part of her body demanded to be touching him.

Aaron pulled away from her, but the feel of his lips stayed on hers. "Is this okay?" He rested his forehead against hers again.

Her heart was pounding so hard she worried it would break.

Don't stop. You're mine.

Her mind flooded with feelings—thoughts—and Aaron. She couldn't form words.

Kiss me again. Never stop.

"Alex?"

He's scared.

Alex struggled further for a moment but then found her words. "Enough honor. Just kiss me." She slid her hands along his shirt, feeling the muscles beneath.

"I had to know."

"Know what?"

Aaron tightened his grip on her, and Alex moaned. Her emotions became overwhelming as a turbulent wind opened her balcony doors. Aaron smelled like the forest in the morning, like her camp—like home, and his kiss was passionate and demanding, as if he was claiming her.

"I needed to know what it would feel like to kiss you," Aaron said when they broke off. "Know if I affect you as much as you affect me."

She shivered, and Aaron gripped her harder. Her skin burned any place his fingers caressed her. Every time she regained control, his touch stripped it from her again. No one had ever taken control of her so easily.

"Who was your first kiss?" Alex asked.

"You were."

"Not when you were seven."

"Anyone between that kiss and today doesn't matter." Aaron replied, gazing at her so intensely that Alex wondered if he could see her soul.

"I can't think when you look at me like that."

Aaron beamed. "I don't know why I waited so long to kiss you."

"Honor above all?" Alex asked, and Aaron nodded.

At this, Alex grabbed his shirt and pulled him to her, slipping her hands behind his neck as he grasped her hips. At first, Aaron didn't move as she pressed her lips to his, but then his steadfastness broke as he pushed her against the wall and kissed her more passionately than Alex dreamed was possible. Her hands wound into his hair, and a small gasp left her mouth as she felt his body heat engulf her. When she caught her breath, he moved to kiss her neck and nibble her ear. A moan escaped her, and Aaron kissed her neck with increased passion.

"Alex, are you upstairs?"

At the sound of Stefan's voice, Alex buried her face in Aaron's chest, and a breeze hit them. When she opened her eyes, they were in Aaron's bedroom.

"Did you bring us here?" he asked.

"I-I didn't mean to. I panicked, and my powers solved it. It's very rare that I crack," she stammered, releasing Aaron.

"As much as I want to keep kissing you, Stefan might summon the guard if he can't find you."

"He would."

Aaron cupped her cheeks and kissed her again. "I know you're going to compare."

Alex looked up at him. *What does that mean?*

"You've agreed to kiss the tournament winners and will have to kiss other suitors. I'll try not to be jealous."

"I forgot about the other suitors," Alex said, gripping Aaron's arm. *This is hard.* "I just ... I needed to kiss you."

"I hope it was what you wanted," Aaron said.

"You're an excellent kisser, Your Highness."

"Can we be alone tomorrow?"

"If you kiss me again and promise never to change your mind about being my suitor again."

"Never again." Aaron tilted her face up to him, pressing his lips against hers before he whispered, "I'll make it up to you by proving I'm the most worthy suitor. If you'll let me, I promise to kiss you until there's no breath left in us."

Alex moaned.

I'd let you kiss me until the end of time.

"Now, go back to your room because if I kiss you again, I won't be able to stop." Aaron opened his bedroom door and peeked out. "All clear."

Alex straightened her dress before she gripped his shirt, kissing him one last time. "Goodnight, Your Highness." She lingered before pulling away, savoring his closeness, and then she reluctantly headed back to her room.

ALEX BOUNCED up the stairs and peeked around the corner. Aaron was in a chair beside Edward's bed, gesticulating wildly with his arms and making her father laugh. Alex could see the years of friendship they'd developed.

And as Alex watched them—they suddenly changed.

Edward became an old man, and a pair of boys appeared, much younger versions of Aaron but with her emerald eyes. One small blond boy sat on the bed beside Edward while his identical twin held Aaron's hand. Aaron and his boyish looks had been replaced by a more rugged version of himself. The boys then turned to Alex and smiled in unison.

Alex blinked, and they vanished. Just her father's and Aaron's laughter remained.

"Are you telling him about the railing?" Alex asked.

"I was. Sit. I'll grab another chair," Aaron said as he rose and hurried off.

"Did he kiss you? Is that how you ended up in the grass?" Edward asked, making zero effort to hide the hope in his tone.

"No, he did not kiss me on the jousting field."

I need to talk to him before I tell you. I don't know the rules.

"Pity. I thought he'd have kissed you by now, especially since ... never mind," Edward said, waving his hand.

Alex rubbed her father's arm and smiled. "Honesty, Father."

"He gave me a list of issues with the stables that Cameron has to finish before jousting. He's going to be occupied the entire day, leaving only Aaron to keep you company."

A banging echoed up the stairs as Aaron arrived with another chair.

Aaron dropped the chair next to Alex's and sat down to continue the story, telling Edward how Randal shouted at the guards to fix the broken railing. A wave of heat swept through Alex as she further observed Aaron with her father, making her uncomfortable all over. She looked down and, seeing Aaron's leg pressed against hers, swallowed hard.

"Alexandria, don't look so upset. This is no more your fault than a young horse bolting after being spooked. You did what Merlock instructed, and it went wrong. You're a Warren: brush yourself off, learn from this, and keep going."

Aaron's hand found hers, and Alex looked down.

"Now I want your predictions on who's going to win the tournament events. The council members are placing bets, and I want inside information."

"Caleb archery, and me jousting. I'm not sure about swords," Aaron said.

"My champion will win archery," Alex said, making both men look at her.

"When did you get a champion?" Edward asked.

"I have a lot of free time."

"Which you spend watching men?" Aaron asked. His mischievous grin told her he was teasing, but she blushed all the same.

"Who's this champion?" Edward asked. "Do I need the guards to watch him too?"

"I thought the guards watched *me*?" Alex asked.

"Your guards watch you, but I have generals watching Cameron and Aaron when they're with you," Edward corrected. "Or have you *forgotten* that little adventure to Datten?"

Aaron sunk lower into his chair.

"But something's different between you two today ... while you finish preparing the tournament, I'll order the generals to leave you be. Aaron, I'm trusting you with my daughter. Wesley and Kruft taught me not to take any chances."

Alex stood and kissed her father. A gentle warmth soon spread through her as Aaron's hand slid down her back. Alex moved toward the stairs a few moments later but stopped when she realized Aaron wasn't behind her. When she turned around, her father was whispering to Aaron, a stern expression on his face.

When they reached the middle floor, Alex grabbed Aaron's arm.

"What did he say to you?"

"This." Aaron pressed her against the stone wall and kissed her fervidly. The juxtaposition of his warm body pressing hers into the cold stone made her head spin, and arousal roared through her as Aaron pulled away. Winking, he scampered down the stairs. Alex hurried after him, but when she found him, he was with Randal.

"Randal, you're on protection duty this morning. I have to help in the stables but will replace you after lunch."

Randal smiled at Alex.

Could he know?

"Where are we off to, princess?"

"My room. I have to speak with Jessica and Edith," Alex

replied, struggling to calm her breathing. She arrived to find Jessica sitting on the couch and working on her needlework. She asked, "Where's Edith?"

"Fetching us breakfast with Julius. With so many strangers, we are all supposed to be escorted everywhere. Hopefully, you'll abide by that."

Alex looked at Jessica and sighed. "I'm done being angry, and I'm sorry for what I said. I don't have many friends I can talk to."

Jessica set down her needlework. "I'm sorry too. I shouldn't have said anything about your suitors."

"You have every right."

"No, Alexandria, I don—"

"*I* say you do. You're my friend. I need you to speak your mind."

"Even if it's hard to hear?"

"Especially then. You can ask Stefan. I only fight people I know won't leave," Alex said as she sat down across from Jessica.

"I shouldn't have spoken about Aaron."

"You're friends, and you want to help."

"He told you that?" Jessica's eyes widened.

"No." Alex smirked as someone knocked.

Michael entered with a pitcher of water and some mugs and held the door for Edith. She carried a tray of bread, hard cheese, and smoked meat, setting it on the table by Jessica and Alex.

"Are you two playing nice?" Edith asked.

"Yes," Michael said. "I know the expression on Alex's face. It means she's trying hard to be on her best behavior."

Alex growled at Michael, making Edith laugh so hard she snorted.

CHAPTER 42
AARON

Aaron read the same sentence for the tenth time, but it was no use. His mind wandered off to replay the day's events again.

Aaron had to resist the urge to fight Cameron the entire time he helped in the stable. They'd always been close, but now, knowing Cameron had kissed Alex, Aaron wanted him gone. He couldn't stop thinking about Alex for even a minute. It took every ounce of willpower not to kiss her every time he saw her. Just sitting with her at Edward's side had been a new torture, and Alex didn't say a word about what happened.

Maybe she's scared I'll change my mind after my ridiculous joke.

"Aaron?" Her voice broke into his loud mind and brought him back. "We've been alone for almost an hour. Why haven't you kissed me?"

Aaron chuckled. "I'm supposed to protect you from eager suitors."

"Well—know that I want *your* attention very much."

Those emerald eyes will be the death of me.

Throwing caution to the wind, Aaron grabbed and kissed her. Alex gripped his arm tight the entire time she kissed him back, giving Aaron the sensation of being on fire. When they came up for air, he pushed their books away and pulled Alex against him on the library couch.

How do you always smell so good?

"Should we talk about last night? When or who to te—"

Alex's lips interrupted his question, and an adrenaline rush coursed through him like when he won a jousting match. Her smooth lips stoked a fire inside him he'd never felt before. She slipped her legs under herself and pushed harder into Aaron, her hands tangling in his hair. Intense heat rushed through him at Alex's urgent touch and the pressure of her body rubbing against his as she kissed him. Aaron kissed her back, aware of the pressure building in his pants and how her kisses threatened to push him over the edge. At that moment, Alex stopped and looked down. Aaron shifted, trying to hide his obvious desire for her, but it was too late. He gazed at her and watched as her cheeks turned pink.

This is what you do to me. I'll never get enough of you.

Aaron slipped his hand into her hair and pulled her face to his, pressing their lips together. Alex moaned as Aaron gently bit her lower lip. He smiled, feeling her grip his tunic with shaking hands. A whimper escaped her when he released her lips long enough to let her catch her breath.

"Too much?" Aaron desperately wanted to touch more of her, but he needed to be sure she wanted it too. Alex's chest heaved as she tried to catch her breath.

"Not enough." She gazed at him lasciviously as she gripped his chest.

Aaron lost all self-control when she grazed his erection.

Enough. Come here! He gripped her hips and pulled her onto his lap.

Thank goodness you're wearing pants. I need that extra barrier between us or I would behave dishonorably right now.

Alex caressed his face urgently as she kissed him. Desire burned within him as her breasts pressed against him through her tunic, and she moaned when he ran his hands down her butt and squeezed.

Just then, someone cleared their throat, and Alex practically fell off the couch trying to slip beside Aaron.

"From not even kissing to this in one day. You do everything at breakneck speed, don't you?" Jessica slammed the door and strolled toward them.

"Was that comment aimed at me or you?" Alex asked Aaron.

He asked Jessica, "Did you tell her?"

"She figured it out," Jessica replied. "You have a true Warren there, Aaron."

"You each knew a secret that I only told the other one. It was obvious," Alex said.

Alex's cheeks were red as Jessica aimed the icy Wafner gaze at them. Aaron looped his arm around Alex, holding her close while she buried her sunset-red cheeks in his shoulder, mortified.

"It's official then?"

"Official?" Alex asked.

"*This*," Jessica said, thrusting an arm out at them. "This isn't something I've caught either of you doing before, so I assume your parents know."

"Not yet," Aaron said. Alex's face dropped, but Aaron quickly kissed her.

"There's the matter of Cameron," Alex said. "I'd like to avoid hurting him."

Jessica sucked her breath. "I forgot about him. There's also your father."

"My father wants me to choose Aaron."

"This morning he told me I had to kiss you already," Aaron said.

"Emmerich," Jessica continued, clarifying, "will be the problem."

Aaron explained that Emmerich would have them betrothed or even married within the day. When Aaron tried to get Jessica to leave, she just laughed.

"I'll take you annoyed at me over things getting out of hand. Some things you can't take back, Aaron."

Aaron sighed.

You're right.

He escorted them back to Alex's room then returned to his room to read alone. Aaron skipped dinner and stayed in his room, reviewing the military books Jerome had left for him, starting with the ones he hated.

I still think he left these for me on purpose.

As the evening became night, Aaron's thoughts wandered back to Alex. He was wondering what his mother would think when he heard a soft knocking. He opened his door to find the hallway empty. As he closed it, he saw the painting on the far wall open, revealing Alex.

He rushed to her, and she threw her arms around his neck, kissing him. "Jessica's watching me like a hawk, so I don't have long. I just wanted to wish you good luck tomorrow from me and my father."

"How is he?"

"Healed—the doctor said I did it, but I don't know how."

"Did you tell him about us?"

Alex looked down. "No. I was afraid. What happens when we tell people?"

"Until we complete a betrothal, they'll keep us apart."

"That makes it hard to get to know you. I know the boy, but

I want to know the man." Alex twisted her shirt in her hands and looked up at him. Her hands slid up his chest, sending a shiver down his spine.

"And there's Cameron."

"What about him?" Alex asked, pulling away.

Aaron grabbed her hands to keep them against his chest. "Are you going to keep seeing him?"

"I don't know. No one prepared me for multiple suitors."

They should have; you're always forgetting how special you are.

"I can't answer for you, but the idea of him kissing you bothers me."

"Getting a little territorial?" Alex smirked playfully, and then Aaron pushed her against the wall, making her smile grow.

"Yes—there is *some* Datten in me." Aaron growled before he kissed her as she pulled him close again. "If I'm yours, I don't want you seeing anyone else."

Alex touched his cheek. "We'll tell them after the tournament. I'll try to avoid Cameron that long, but you better win. I'm a crown princess, and I expect a champion."

She kissed him then as his fingers grazed the hot skin exposed by her tunic, which had shifted from the force of her kissing him. He felt his control slipping again as she pressed herself against him.

I just want to rip your shirt off and throw you on my bed and—

Aaron suddenly pushed her away, grabbing onto his last bit of self-control. "Go."

Alex pouted, and he suspected his words hurt her.

Horses. Hunting. Alex with a bow. Ugh. Stefan. Jerome. Stefan. Better.

"I want you to stay, but I can't control myself with you," he explained.

"Aaron—"

"No. Jessica was right." Aaron opened the painting and kissed her. Closing it behind her, Aaron exhaled to get control of himself.

CHAPTER 43
ALEX

Alex was up before the sun, but this time it was from excitement, not nightmares. Michael was waiting in her receiving room when she came bounding down in her nightdress.

"I'll summon your ladies," he said.

Jessica and Edith came in to dress her and fix her hair into an elaborate braid.

"You seem different today," Edith said, tying up the corset on Alex's new blue dress.

"Have you picked a new favorite for the tournament, or have you developed a preference for a *suitor*?" Jessica smirked at Alex.

That was all it took. One thought of Aaron's lips on hers, his hands on her body, and Alex's entire face went red as her breath hitched.

"There is one," Edith said. "I was only busy for one night! Who is it? Is it Cameron? A prince? Not Jesse. Aaron? It's Cameron, isn't it? Tell us!"

A sly smile spread across Alex's lips. "I can't be late for breakfast."

"Nothing? You're telling us nothing?" Edith pouted.

Alex grabbed her crown and fled, cursing Jessica under her breath.

Alex had never seen so many people in the dining hall before. She stepped away from the doors to the hall to catch her breath as her heart pounded.

You can do this. They won't hurt you.

"Morning, Princess Alexandria," Julius said.

"Good morning, Sir Bishop." Alex nodded to him.

"If you're nervous, I'd be happy to escort you."

Alex accepted his arm, and they made their way into the hall. The boisterous sound of all the competitors chatting and eating died the moment Alex entered the room. As she sauntered toward the table, the men rose, and when she looked to the royals, they also stood. When Alex and Julius arrived, the knight released her and bowed to the royals.

"Good morning, Father. Your Royal Highnesses." Alex curtsied to her father and the Datten royals.

"Princess. Are you excited about your first tournament?" Emmerich asked.

"I am—but *nervous* too. I'm not sure what to expect." Alex hurried around the table and kissed her father's cheek. Once Aaron pulled out her chair, the men all sat, and Alex allowed Aaron to tuck her chair for her.

"Thank you." Alex smiled at Aaron and turned to her father. "I'm glad you're doing better."

"Not better—healed. The doctor doesn't know how," Edward said, winking. "Your dress is stunning. I love the color."

"Thank you." Alex turned back to Aaron, trying to avoid looking at him for too long. "Good morning, Your Highness."

"Princess."

Food before her, Alex caught Aaron staring. Thanking the kind woman who had served her, Alex lost her concentration when Aaron's hand brushed her knee. Her body warmed instantly, and her breath caught in her throat.

"Your father is right," Aaron whispered. "You look enchanting. New dress?"

"It is. A set of three arrived in my room the other day. No one knows where they came from." Alex stared at Aaron.

"No note?"

"No, but I've figured out where they came from."

"Oh?"

Alex placed her hand on his knee and ran it up his thigh, making Aaron drop his bread and sit straighter. She leaned toward him. "The Datten colors gave you away."

Aaron recovered and smiled. "They're for your birthday. I thought you'd want them early."

"I love them." Alex picked up her fork again. "Are you ready for today?"

"I am. I'm not great with a bow, but I learned Torian history and military strategy from Jerome. So, based on the books Jerome left me, I suspect I'll do well with your test. Any advice?"

"Inhale before you pull the bowstring; it'll help you focus. I'm impressed you're competing in all four events considering I stipulated suitors only had to compete in three."

"I have things to make up for and won't risk doing less." He rubbed his leg against hers. "Wish me luck?"

"You don't need it. But good luck."

General Nial appeared at the back of the room and nodded at the kings.

"It's time," Edward said to Alex. The excitement in his voice was so genuine Alex couldn't help but smile. He rose, and the room quieted. "Archers, you have one hour to get to the field and register. We will disqualify anyone not on the field when the bells ring. You're excused."

Alex watched as every man at the lower tables stood to leave. Edith and Michael nodded so slightly Alex hoped no one else noticed.

"General Nial will escort you out when you are ready, Alexandria. We're expected to be there to welcome the competitors when they arrive."

In mere minutes, the hall was almost empty. "Aren't you going to rush off?" Alex asked as Aaron stole the last piece of cheese from her plate.

"No, my father and godfather are the judges."

"Oh? What happened to not doing less?"

"I *mean*, my father puts my name down first on every tournament. He had a royal tunic made for me years ago. It'll be waiting in my room already. So at every tournament, I'm participant number one."

"I still think you should get ready. I'd hate for you to be disqualified. It *would hurt* your chances with the princess."

The room had emptied, and when Alex rose to leave, Aaron jumped up and grabbed her. "I was waiting for everyone else to leave so I could do this." He kissed her so fast she didn't have time to breathe. It felt like her lungs would explode, but she gripped his shirt and kissed him back, pressing as much of herself against him as she could. By the time he pulled away, Alex's legs felt like water. Aaron held her until she composed herself. Aaron then kissed her hand and made to leave, but Alex stopped him. She gave him a hideously embroidered green handkerchief and hurried out of the dining hall, turning back only to wink at him.

Jessica was waiting for her in the hallway, and they headed to the courtyard to meet the general. When they arrived at the tournament field, they found Edward seated on the largest throne at the center of the royal stands, Emmerich and Guinevere on his left. To his right were three smaller thrones.

"Why three?" Alex asked.

"After Aaron decided to compete in all the events, I suggested Edith and Jessica sit beside you. They can help you keep track of the suitors since they each know their respective kingdom's knights and nobility. Though where Edith is, I can't say. I'm surprised; she loves tournaments."

"Thank you, Randal. I'm sure Edith is around," Alex said.

The general nodded and stood beside the stairs while Alex and Jessica took their seats. Once settled, Randal moved to the edge of the field where the other generals were talking to some older Datten knights.

Bells rang from the castle, announcing the start of the tournament. Before them stood a field of men with numbers pinned to their chests. Edward rose to welcome everyone, thanking them for traveling so far and reminding all in attendance that the tournament was to both honor Daniel's memory and welcome home Warren's princess. He spoke of Alex's upcoming birthday and how they would use this tournament to add to her guard and to gauge the skills of the men vying for her hand. When he added that Alex intended to present a kiss to each winner, the men roared with excitement. Alex's face nearly burst into flames. Jessica patted her leg and smiled.

"We'll begin with archery, and after lunch, the new strategy component developed by the Princess of Warren herself will take place. She expects all suitors to comprehend military planning. I think she's been spending too much time with the Datten royals." The Warren men laughed, and Datten men cheered at Edward's jest. "Now, let the tournament begin, and make Torian proud!"

The men let out a deafening cheer as a Datten knight shouted numbers to set up the groups.

"Who's that?" Alex asked Jessica.

"Sir Avery Reinhart—Caleb's father. He's a high-ranking knight in Datten and is the general of the archers."

"I thought your father was the general."

"He is. But when there is no war, my father is the head of the swordsmen and castle knights. Sir Reinhart handles the archers."

Alex turned to her father. "Do Randal and Matthew have different duties?"

"No. General Nial handles all our men with General Bishop as his second. If we need additional help, we have Datten."

"Where's Caleb?"

"Number fifty-eight," Jessica said. "Best archer in Torian—and he *never* lets you forget it. Aaron discovered him watching a tournament. Aaron doesn't compete in archery or sword fighting at regular tournaments."

"Why?"

"He thinks swords are violent," Edward explained. "And he's never been great with a bow, though not for lack of trying."

"Do you see your champion?" Jessica asked.

"Dean Ilith is over there by Michael. Now shush!"

The archers arrived before the royals and bowed. Emmerich clapped at all the Datten crests before them, and the sheer number amazed Alex. She barely recognized any of them. However, she noticed Dean standing beside Michael, his short blond hair glistening in the morning sun. Alex stole the list from Jessica and examined it while the archers divided into groups of ten. She knew Aaron was number one but groaned at number five.

"You knew I'd already agreed to Wesley taking part to earn back some of his lost honor," Edward said.

Alex groaned louder and slouched. "If he becomes king, I'll have him assassinated once I'm queen," she whispered to Jessica.

"I'll help," Jessica replied, and Alex giggled.

The first group was firing at their targets. Those who hit the bull's eye with all three arrows would move on to the next round where they would shoot at twice the distance. Almost everyone in the first group moved on. The groups that followed were more varied in skill, and anywhere between one and six archers advanced.

Alex had expected Jessica to provide a rundown on each suitor, but she didn't. She was too busy watching Michael, Julius, and Dean move on. Cameron was disqualified in the first round but perked up when he caught Alex's eye. She waved weakly and glanced away.

"Do something about him," Jessica said.

"I will, but I don't know how."

In the second round, only the archers with a perfect score would move on to the last round. This eliminated most of the men, including Prince Aaron and Prince Rudolph, but Prince Jesse of Darren went through along with Dean Ilith and Michael.

With a dozen archers remaining, they moved the targets twice as far for the last round. Alex held her breath to calm her nerves as they fired their arrows, but her heart raced all the same. No one could tell who the winner would be from so far away, so once the archers finished shooting, they gathered in front of the royal stands while Generals Nial and Reinhart marched to the targets. Like Alex, everyone on the grounds waited with bated breath for the final tallies.

When Edward nodded to Alex, she took the prize bags from

Jessica and slipped down the stairs to wait with Michael and Aaron as General Nial handed Edward the winners. The general returned to his place beside Alex. Looking up at him, Alex exhaled, and something tickled her elbow. Her head snapped to the side. She found Aaron smiling at her, and with that, all her fears melted away.

"I'm sorry," Alex whispered to Aaron, returning her gaze to the archers.

"For what?"

"I suspect I'm about to get us both into a *lot* of trouble with your father."

"For you, I'd face all the kings of Torian."

Heat trickled to Alex's cheeks as Aaron's elbow grazed hers.

"Congratulations to all our competitors this morning," Edward announced. "After I announce the winners, we'll be serving lunch in the halls, and at two o'clock, we'll be back here for the princess's competition. If you're late, you're disqualified. Now for the archery winners. Our third-place archer comes from Datten, Sir Lucas Oakes."

Alex recognized Lucas from the bar in Datten. His tousled blond hair moved in the breeze as he took his place before the royals.

"Only one point separated our first- and second-place archers. Second place goes to the princess's champion, Dean Ilith of Kirsh, and our top archer is none other than Sir Caleb Reinhart of Datten. How many wins is that now, Caleb?" Edward asked.

"Eighteen," Caleb replied, making his way through the crowd to stand before the royals.

Dean Ilith moved through the crowd, an emerald pendant glistening on his tunic. Alex hadn't realized how much smaller Dean was until Caleb and Lucas joined him.

Alex turned to Aaron, clutching the prize bags to her. "Trust me?"

Aaron nodded and followed her.

"Congratulations, Lucas," Alex said as she handed him his prize.

It's just a quick little kiss.

Placing her hand on his shoulder, she kissed his cheek, sending the crowd into an excited roar.

Alex moved to Dean and stopped. He breathed rapidly but nodded to Alex. She glanced at Aaron for a moment and exhaled. Alex kissed Dean's cheek and spun to face the royals.

"I have a confession to make. I lied about my champion. Dean isn't from Kirsh."

"Where is he from?" Edward asked after a brief pause.

"*She* is from Warren," Alex said.

Aaron snorted as Emmerich's face became as red as a Datten tunic. His penetrating stare reminded Alex of her grandfather's and sent ice through her, but Aaron started stroking the small of her back and quickly restored her courage. Alex forced her shoulders back and held her hand out to Dean, who removed the pendant and placed it in her hand. Soft green fog swirled around Dean from his head to his feet.

It's strange to be on this side of the spell.

The blond hair vanished, leaving a raven braid in its place, and once the green fog evaporated, Edith remained standing between the two men.

Her mother's pendant safely in her hand, Alex glanced at Randal before turning back to the kings. "Our second-place winner is still my champion—Lady Edith Nial of Warren."

"Women aren't allowed in tournaments!" Emmerich roared, jumping to his feet.

"*My* tournament—*my* rules," Alex said, staring down her godfather.

"We didn't actually make a rule preventing women from competing," Aaron said. "So if Edith placed on her own ability, she deserves the prize."

Aaron took the prize bag from Alex and, turning to Edith, bowed and kissed her cheek before handing her the gold. Alex glanced at the generals. Jerome and Avery's faces wore hard frowns, but Randal's smile was a mile wide as he stared at Edith.

"You better train harder, Caleb," Aaron said. "You almost lost to a Warren lady."

"Daughters of generals aren't normal girls," Caleb said.

"Very true," Alex said as she handed Caleb the last prize bag. As Caleb leaned down for his kiss, she whispered, "Keep away from Lady Jessica or you'll get to find out if I breathe fire."

Caleb gazed at her emerald eyes before stepping back. He looked from her to Aaron and back again, eyes wide.

Recognize me from the Datten bar now, don't you?

"I still owe you for those ales," Aaron said as he held his arm out to Alex.

"And I should thank you for all the insights into your crown prince."

Caleb grimaced as Alex and Aaron turned to the royals. She curtsied, and Aaron bowed. Next, the champions bowed to the royals, and when Aaron and Alex turned to the spectators, everyone applauded. Participants and spectators soon made their way to the castle for lunch, but Aaron remained with Alex as Randal approached them.

"Princess, I'll be helping you set up. Though if you prefer to eat with your father, we could ask some servants."

"Thank you, Randal, but I want to approve everything."

"Of course." Randal nodded to Aaron. "Impressive display, Your Highness. I didn't realize you were such a skilled archer. What other talents have you been hiding?"

He's an amazing kisser.

Aaron asked, "You entered Edith and are leaving me to deal with our fathers?"

"I'm sure I'll hear about it later," Alex said.

"You should have asked Edward. He'd have let her compete if Randal agreed," Aaron whispered before leaving to have lunch.

"Aaron's right. Emmerich would've protested, but Edward would've gone against him. Next time, ask," Randal said.

"Would you have let her compete?" Alex asked as they headed to the library.

"If it made Edith happy, absolutely."

CHAPTER 44
ALEX

When the time came, Alex followed the generals back to the field. It felt odd being surrounded by the three most intimidating men in Torian.

"Are you nervous?" Randal asked.

"A little."

"Pick one person and focus on them. It helps when addressing such a large group," Jerome said.

The participants cleared a path as they arrived at the royal stand. Alex held her chin up as she ascended the stage steps. A breeze blew by as the generals gathered closer around her.

"Welcome suitors, knights, and citizens." Alex tried hard to at least look confident. She closed her eyes and exhaled, willing her winds to stop. When she opened her eyes, she found Aaron's face. He nodded, and she took another deep breath and spoke.

"This tournament will test your skills in both the physical acts of war *and* in military planning. As future Queen of Warren, I will need to lead armies, and my husband will too. So I have devised a strategy competition. I present to you the trials. The three generals and I have four military excursions from Torian, each of which involves a unique set of kingdoms that we consider to be unsuccessful. We'll each explain our military failure and will pick the winner of our own trial and, from those, determine a champion. You will decide how many to solve and write plans to persuade a council, a job any competent king must be able to do."

The men began chatting, so Alex waited for them to quiet down. When they didn't, Jerome bellowed, "Her Highness is not done!"

This silenced the crowd almost instantly.

"Thank you, General Wafner. I will begin with the case of Prince Victor of Datten and the diversion of the Darren River by the Betruger."

"But he succeeded," Emmerich shouted. "The river remained as it is."

Alex looked at Emmerich. "Succeeded how? He returned with twelve percent of his men and escalated the war with the Betruger. You are still fighting them today. Perhaps there was a better way."

"You mean a Warren way." Emmerich crossed his arms, and Guinevere shushed him.

"Naturally—I am the Crown Princess of Warren. The Warren way is my way." Alex looked back at the men. "Whether or not you think Prince Victor was successful, persuade us."

General Nial held his hand out to Alex and helped her down. She found Aaron amid the crowd again and smiled.

All right, my clever prince. This is your chance to prove to everyone you've got military prowess despite your gentle nature.

After they explained all the cases, Edward rose. "You will find parchment and quills in the spare hall along with most of our military books. The rest are in the library. You have until eight o'clock tonight to finish, after which you will need to bring your written battle plans to the generals before you. Those submitting to the princess's challenge will bring them to her head guard, Sir Stefan Wafner. Good luck."

Edward clapped, and the men scattered toward the castle.

"Why only require them to complete one? I know six hours isn't a long time, but aren't you testing them?" Edith asked.

"The choice is part of the test. Those who do more than required of them will have an advantage over those who don't," Alex said.

"A king cannot take the easy way," Randal said.

"Someone with exceptional military planning could solve two, maybe three, in that time. War doesn't offer the luxury of time," Jerome said. Jessica came over and hugged him.

Emmerich joined the group. "Alexandria?"

"Yes, Your Royal Highness?"

"When you've finished, I'd like to see the plans submitted by Wesley and Aaron."

Alex smirked as Edward replied, "Hoping to use my daughter's test to glean some insight into their military ability?"

"The test is brilliant. If the answers will help determine who's worthy of your hand, I think they could be insightful in terms of choosing a King of Datten too."

"I'd be happy to pass them to you," Alex said.

"What now?" Edith asked.

"They'll all be working on their plans for a while," Jessica said.

Just then, Merlock and Megesti appeared. "Alexandria has a lesson with us," Megesti said.

"Could I change first?" Alex asked.

"Of course." Merlock snapped his fingers, and the next instant, the group was in her receiving room.

ALEX ARRIVED BACK in the courtyard cold, wet, and frustrated. They'd gone into the Ogre Mountains where Merlock had asked her to summon water from around her. In chilly, dry mountains, the task had proved impossible, and instead, Alex had rained and then hailed on them.

Merlock left her in the courtyard so he and Megesti could head off from there. Alex hurried into the side entrance by the royal guest suites, trying to avoid dripping everywhere as she made her way back to her room to change.

"Alex, wait!"

Alex spun around. "Cameron. What are you doing here?"

He hurried to catch her, and once he had, he reached for her, but Alex threw her arms up. "I'm soaked."

"I don't mind." Cameron grabbed her, scooping her up to give her a kiss. "Is everything okay?" he asked, releasing her.

"Yes! I'm just tired and wet, and I'm already late to meet the generals and should change before I go. Can we talk tomorrow?"

"Of course." Cameron held Alex's waist and pulled her against him. Alex felt nothing, not even the slightest spark, but when Cameron moved his mouth toward hers, she felt her magic start to slip.

"There you are, princess," said Michael. "The generals have been waiting for an hour." He glared at Cameron, giving his best Stefan impression. "Baron Strobel."

"Sir Michael," Cameron replied, his hands leaving Alex's waist. He bowed to Michael and pecked Alex on the cheek before heading down the hallway.

Alex turned to hurry down the hallway, but Michael grabbed her arm. "Alex—"

"It's fine, Michael."

"You need to let him down easily. He's a nice man."

Alex turned. "How do you—? Jessica." She clenched her jaw.

"She was excited and needed to tell someone, and you know I can keep my mouth shut. Right now, you need to get changed and see the generals."

"Are they angry I'm late?"

"No. They aren't even in the library yet."

Alex's mouth dropped open. "When did you learn to lie?"

"It's a required skill in castle life. My opinion may not matter, but I prefer you with Aaron."

Alex smiled. "It matters to me, and I also prefer me with Aaron. I like what he brings out in me."

ALEX WRUNG her hair as she entered the library to meet the generals.

"How many cases did we get?" Alex asked.

"We have one hundred and seven suitors, and we got two hundred and thirty replies," Randal said.

"So some people did two. That's good," Alex said.

"After reviewing our own cases and discussing them when we arrived here, a dozen did three, and one did all of them," Matthew said.

"In six hours? Those have to be terrible. Let's start with them." Alex reached across the table and grabbed her stack of cases. The first was exceptional. It detailed a brilliant plan for how to improve the mission while acknowledging that allowing the river to be diverted would have been catastrophic to Datten and the southern kingdoms. Alex set it down and looked at the generals.

"How are yours? This one ... was excellent," Alex said, shocked.

"Same," Jerome said.

"If they're all like this, we're going to have a challenge on our hands," Matthew said.

"They aren't, though. There are some good ones, but this one," Randal said, holding up the paper, "is by far the best. One suitor did them all and did them brilliantly."

He can't be that good.

"Who knows military history that well?" Alex asked.

Jerome raised his eyebrows. "A prince."

Matthew asked, "You think a prince wrote all these?"

"No, Matthew. I *know*—that's Aaron's handwriting."

"Aaron? The prince who's against war?" Randal asked.

"When he was ten, we started studies in military strategy, and he argued that all the kings of Datten were foolish for risking their men on useless missions. He declared he'd never go to war once he became king, so I instructed him to read every military book and king's journal in the Datten library. Then I left to guard Emmerich during trade negotiations with the southern kingdoms. When we returned, months later, I assumed he'd have abandoned the project, but there was a stack of essays waiting for me in my quarters. Each one detailed the mistakes made by a particular King of Datten—in every war—going back as far as our records did. He not only read every single battle in Datten history but also the books for the opposing sides and the journals of their kings and generals. He then, in each case, developed a plan that would have ended the battle sooner and with fewer lives lost on both sides for every war."

Alex, Randal, and Matthew stared at Jerome.

"Daniel inherited Emmerich's bravery, but Aaron inherited his military strategy. I taught them both, and Daniel wouldn't hold a candle to Aaron's foresight and planning. The Prince of Datten may not believe in war, but he knows how to win one."

Alex shrugged. "Those who fail to learn their history will repeat it. We have our winner—now we need to rank everyone else."

It took them hours to rank the papers. Some were awful— Alex cackled when Matthew discovered his worst paper was Wesley's. Once finished, Randal escorted Alex back to her room, and she stood before the empty fireplace, closed her eyes, exhaled, clenched her fists in frustration, and focused. The force of the fire erupting to life sent immense heat across her legs.

You can visit him but just for a minute.

After changing into her nightgown, Alex picked up a torch and lit it from the fire. She crossed the room, pulled open the painting, and strode barefoot down the path until she reached and slipped into Aaron's bedroom. His fire was dying, so Alex glared at it, sending the flames back up. Aaron lay sprawled across his massive bed. Alex leaned over to kiss him, but before her lips touched his, powerful hands snatched her and flipped her onto the bed. She squealed as he pinned her wrists on either side of her head.

"I thought you could handle yourself," Aaron said.

"I didn't want to wake you."

"I was having the most wonderful dream." Aaron kissed down her neck toward her collarbone but paused as he hit the neckline of her nightgown.

"About what?"

"This." Aaron's lips covered Alex's as his tongue slipped into her mouth. Desperate to touch him, Alex wriggled in his grip, but he held her in place. Her body burned anywhere Aaron touched her. She moaned, and Aaron released her wrists before moving to her breast, caressing and massaging her nipple with his thumb. Alex wove her hands into Aaron's hair and kissed him, wanting him more than she ever had before.

After they had kissed as much as their exhaustion allowed, Alex lay her head on Aaron's shoulder, letting him run his hand along her back, lulling her to sleep.

Alex found herself back in her grandfather's sick room.

"You think because the man you let between your legs is a prince or you're in love with him, it'll save you from becoming a whore? It won't. You're exactly like your mother. A disgusting disgrace to my crown. Even marrying Datten won't change that. You'll only betray him."

Alex bolted upright, her chest burning as she choked on her screams. Aaron's hands were on her face in seconds, and then he brought her back to their world when he slid his hands down her arms to calm her. Alex felt drained from the vision. She watched Aaron's face and smiled.

He's right. I am in love with you.

"We should get you back to your room," Aaron said, and Alex nodded reluctantly.

Aaron left her in her bedroom, but Alex knew she wouldn't be able to sleep, so she crept downstairs. It only took seconds for Stefan to answer. With one look at her face, he sat on the couch in her receiving room and held his arm out. Alex curled up against him, and they talked about her dreams, her fear of failing her lessons, confusion about suitors, everything except her realization about Aaron. They talked until Alex fell asleep on Stefan's shoulder.

"Alexandria."

Alex stirred and opened her eyes to see Jessica.

"Time to get up."

Where's my bed?

As the room came into focus, a familiar musky smell hit her. She sat up. "Sorry, Stefan."

Stefan got up and grimaced, rubbing his stiff leg, but he leaned over and kissed the top of Alex's head. "It's fine. Knights don't have swords until this afternoon, and Randal's watching you this morning."

Alex yawned as Stefan trudged back to his room and collapsed onto his bed.

CHAPTER 45
ALEX

The second day was swords—Warren first followed by Datten. Dressed in her new gold gown, Alex squeezed between the knights to get to the stands. When she spotted Cameron, she changed direction only to smack into a knight.

"Gabriel."

"Do you need help to get to the stands?" he asked.

"Please," Alex said. "I never realized how short I was."

"Datten and Warren grow tall men."

Once at the stand, Alex paused, kissed Gabriel's cheek, and climbed the back stairs of the royal stands. When she took her place, Alex noticed only one seat beside her. A figure wearing gold caught her eye as he maneuvered through the knights.

How is that so easy for you?

Aaron arrived at the stand, pulled himself up, and slipped over the railing. He reached behind his seat and brought out Alex's crown.

"Thank you, Lady Jessica," Aaron said before crowning Alex. He sat on his throne and leaned toward Alex.

"What did you say to Gabriel? I noticed you two disappeared behind the stands."

"I thought you weren't the jealous type." She stared straight ahead, trying to avoid drawing attention to them.

"I'm not. I do, *however*, find it unfair how little the generals watch the knights around you while they scrutinize every move I make. And you still rely on Michael and Stefan despite other options."

Alex put her hand on Aaron's knee, trying not to smirk. "You *are* jealous."

Aaron glanced at her and shrugged. "Jealous of what? I'm a crown prince—they're knights."

Alex squeezed his knee and leaned toward Aaron. "I don't like this side of you. I prefer the humble Aaron. That's the man who's winning my heart, whose room I sneak to. Not the vain prince who wants to be better than everyone. *Him* I want nothing to do with."

Aaron looked down at her hand and took it, interlocking their fingers. "Sorry."

"I won't marry any man who tries to make me give up Michael or Stefan."

A smile filled Aaron's face. "Marry?"

Did I say that out loud?

Alex swallowed and tried to pull away, but Aaron squeezed her hand.

Edward and Emmerich arrived, making the crowd split. Emmerich climbed the stands to his seat while Edward faced the competitors. He announced the morning was for squires, young knights, and any people who wanted to take part. The afternoon was for full knights and any would-be suitors of the proper position to take part in a Datten tournament.

Alex leaned toward Aaron. "Is Wesley in the Warren portion of the contest?"

Squinting in the sunlight, she looked closer—it *was* Wesley. Aaron's hand moved to Alex's thigh, sending a tingle through her as he leaned to look past her.

"He is, and my father isn't pleased."

"He must have realized he didn't stand a chance with me."

"Who's your choice for Datten?" Aaron asked.

"As king—*you*, even if it complicates what's developing between us," Alex said.

Uh-oh. I didn't mean it like that. Why do I keep saying the wrong thing?

Aaron leaned over to Alex so his breath tickled her ear. "So there's an 'us' now?"

"I hope so, unless you have a habit of pulling maidens into your bed." Alex's cheeks burned as she avoided Aaron's stare.

"Only had one in my bed. Only want that one."

Alex turned to watch the first men take their positions on the field. Aaron's hand remained on her leg. Once the fighting began, Alex's blush vanished. The skill shown by the younger knights and normal men was impressive. Warren rounds had time limits and included shields. They paired the men up, and the winner moved on to be paired up again until the champion emerged.

Wesley did well, coming out as champion. Laurie Von Essen, a merchant from Oreane, took second place, and Henry Vinur, a stable boy from Warren, took third. As the men lined up, Edward narrowed his eyes at Wesley and leaned toward Alex and Aaron. "I want you to announce the strategy winners too. I don't trust Wesley with you, Alexandria. Aaron, escort her."

Edward and Aaron exchanged a look. Alex sighed and stood up. Edward straightened her crown and handed her and her ladies the prize bags. Aaron leaped down the stairs and held his hand out. Alex accepted it, and she strolled down the stands followed by her ladies. Alex noticed smug satisfaction on Guinevere's face as she watched Aaron help her.

"I'll begin with the strategy contest," Alex said. "After many hours of reading, I must say that you all have impressed us. There were amazing suggestions, but in the end, there were three exceptional strategists with one clear winner. Third place goes to Sir Julius Bishop of Warren." The Warren citizens erupted as General Bishop pushed his youngest forward to stand before the royals.

"Second place goes to Prince Jesse of Darren for his unique take on the battle of Datten and the southern kingdoms. Our clear winner submitted a plan for all four cases." Alex glanced at Emmerich, whose mouth hung agape as he leaned forward on the railing. Alex shrugged at him and carried on.

"We *all* selected his paper as the top choice for our military operation, making Crown Prince Aaron of Datten the clear winner." The Datten citizens erupted in roars so loud Alex cringed while she waited for them to quiet down. Aaron straightened his tunic and joined Julius and Jesse.

Edward and Guinevere grinned and clapped for Aaron while Emmerich stared wide-eyed. Edith gave Alex her two bags, and she congratulated Julius and Henry for their third-place wins. Henry turned red from Alex's kiss. Jessica's bags went to the second-place winners, Laurie and Prince Jesse. Like Julius, they accepted their kisses without embarrassment. Alex handed Aaron his prize of gold, and he tossed it to the squires. Smirking, he leaned down, and Alex kissed him quickly. The Datten citizens booed so loudly she blushed. Aaron glared at them until they silenced then leaned down again. This time Alex kissed his cheek properly, and the crowd roared so loudly that Alex felt the ground tremble.

Then Alex put on a fake smile and handed Wesley his prize. *Smile. Aaron's right here. He won't let Wesley do anything.*

When she went to kiss his cheek, he turned and kissed her on the mouth. Stefan's training took over immediately, and she punched him in the face, knocking him on his backside. Chaos erupted around her as Warren's knights and competitors charged Wesley. Alex turned to her father, but he was thundering down the stand with Generals Wafner and Nial. Aaron pulled her away from Wesley.

Emmerich arrived beside them and told Aaron to get ready for his sword event. Alex felt him hesitate before he released her, but eventually he marched off, leaving her with his father. Alex watched General Wafner drag Wesley away.

"What'll happen to him?" Alex asked Emmerich as they went back to the stands.

"He's being sent home. I've had enough of his nonsense."

"What does this mean for his chances of getting the throne?"

Emmerich paused and narrowed his eyes. "I don't know yet."

Alex grimaced. "With all due respect, shouldn't you? If he's brave enough to assault *me* in front of you, what is he capable of when no one's watching?"

Emmerich paused at the base of the stands and turned to Alex.

"Get me Aaron's essays. He's always been passive. I can't let someone who can't defend Datten or lead my armies take my throne, *but* if he understands our military history as well as you say, maybe he can lead through knowledge rather than experience. Just to know he'll take the role seriously is more than I ever expected."

Emmerich motioned for Alex to take her seat. An extra throne had appeared again beside Aaron's, and her ladies were waiting.

"I can't believe he kissed you!" Edith said.

Alex looked at Jessica. "Aren't you going to scold me?"

"I'm a Wafner. He dishonored himself, the Rassgats, *and* Datten when he kissed you. You put him in his place. Well done."

Edith and Alex laughed until Edward arrived.

"I'm so sorry, Alexandria," Edward said. "After the ball, I assumed Aaron's presence would make Wesley behave. General Wafner and Merlock are taking him home. He won't be back in Warren again."

"He may return after I'm married," Alex said. "Then we'll let the Prince of Warren set him straight."

"Well said, dear," Guinevere said.

Edward squeezed Alex's hand.

"It's not your fault," Alex said, squeezing back.

Randal returned to the field wearing a scowl Alex had never seen before.

"That's bad," Edith said. "I haven't seen him this angry since Matthew brought my sister Abigail home after he found her in bed with his son Aiden."

"What?" Jessica asked, trying to cover her wide open mouth.

"The wedding was lovely, and my niece is adorable, but we thought my father would have a heart attack that night."

"That explains why the generals watch Aaron so much. They missed it with their own children, and I'm confident your sister is better behaved than I am," Alex said.

Edith nodded at Alex. "She is. So *stop* sneaking around with suitors."

Randal began shouting names, drawing their attention back to the field. For the Datten portion, there were no time limits, and the first round had no shields. Alex searched for knights she knew, spotting Julius, Cameron, Aaron, Michael, and Stefan. When she caught Michael's eye, she waved encouragingly before he lowered his helmet.

No amount of warnings could have prepared Alex for the violence that Datten sword fighting entailed. The thunderous sounds of sword on sword made Alex's teeth chatter. Within minutes, Alex had to cover her ears. The first round ended brutally with a knight being carried off the field to Merlock and the doctors.

Alex clutched her father's hand. "Does that happen often?"

"Some Datten families have long-standing rivalries. We try to avoid pairing them, but it's difficult to keep track of who's fighting with whom."

"In Datten, someone is always fighting someone," Jessica said.

"Who decides the next round's pairings?" Alex asked.

Before anyone could reply, General Nial suddenly shouted, "Our gracious host, His Royal Highness King Edward of Warren!"

"Today, it's me." Edward squeezed Alex's hand and headed to the field. "Men, you all fought so bravely. You overwhelmed my daughter with your vigor and passion, so let's make sure this round is as exciting!"

Edward then shouted out that round's pairings, and the men moved toward their new opponents. Once finished, he returned to his seat.

Emmerich laughed. "Using your daughter to make them fight. I never thought I'd see the day."

Edward smirked at Emmerich as he sat down and took Alex's hand, kissing it.

"Do you think they'll be as violent as before?" Alex asked Jessica.

"After that—there'll be blood," Jessica said.

A second later that became clear as the clangs of swords

and armor became deafening. Alex flinched at how brutal the men of Datten were and wondered how they weren't all deaf after years of fighting. Her breath stopped any time a knight had to be removed to see the doctor. Despite her wild upbringing, Alex wasn't sure she could stomach swords.

"Are you okay?" Jessica asked.

"Yes," Alex squeaked. She tried to focus on her ladies and not on the violence before them.

"Pick one person and watch them," her father said. "Try … Aaron."

Alex squeezed her father's hand and peeked at the field. Stefan and Aaron were winning their matches, and Edward had been right—focusing on them helped. Once the second round was over, Edward went down to regroup the men once again. Michael was out after the third round; Aaron was defeated in the fourth. Edward sent Aaron to sit with Alex once he was out of his armor while he remained below to watch the last few rounds. Wesley's guard and cousin, Lutiger, ended up in third, and the final pairing was Stefan and Prince Rudolph of Oreane.

Aaron leaned over to Alex. "Prince Rudolph is the youngest of five sons—he'd need to be good at defending himself."

The last round was merciless. Alex struggled to watch Stefan and Prince Rudolph battle it out. Alex recoiled as Rudolph struck Stefan so hard he nearly lost his footing. She turned away as Jessica grabbed her hand and locked their fingers together while Aaron squeezed her knee.

"Stefan's strong," he said. "He'll be fine."

"I don't know why it's bothering me."

I hope the jousting won't be so bad.

Alex glanced at Aaron as everyone leaped to their feet and roared. Alex grabbed the rail, searching. Stefan's sword lay on the ground, but he stood before Prince Rudolph in one piece. Relief flooded her.

Alex joined her father on the field where they rewarded the three winners with prizes of gold. Lutiger apologized for Wesley's behavior before she kissed him.

Maybe not all Rassgats are terrible.

Stefan bent down so Alex could kiss him, and Prince Rudolph insisted on kissing her hand before receiving his, and then he asked for a tour of their lovely gardens. As they left, Alex noticed another prince roll his eyes.

After her boring walk with Prince Rudolph, Alex waited for Stefan to finish getting dressed in his room so he could escort her to the mid-tournament banquet. He took so long that Alex sent their friends off.

"Why are you taking forever?"

Stefan then came out and grabbed her hands. "Pick Cameron."

"What?"

"I know you're seeing Aaron. Forget him and *pick* Cameron."

"Michael or Jessica?" Alex asked, pulling her hands back.

"You deserve better. Cameron may not be a prince, but he's the better man."

"Stefan—"

"No. I see everything—I'm not blind. I even know about the library."

Alex gulped. "Stefan, it isn't what you think."

Stefan glared at her. "So my sister *didn't* catch you on his lap in the library with his hands all over you?"

Alex slunk back, feeling her hands go slick and the fire grow hot.

"From that guilty look, it's worse. Care to explain where you were last night when I checked on you?"

Alex couldn't breathe. Her dress was too tight.

"Everything he's done proves his dishonor—and before you tell me nothing happened, it doesn't matter. If anyone had caught you, he'd have ruined you," Stefan said.

"Stop."

"Aaron is more Datten than people see. He just hides it well. He's a disgrace. If you marry him, you'll end up being heart-broken over and over again. I didn't teach you to be strong so some dishonorable prince could swoop in, trick you into bed, and make you a queen with her head down and her mouth shut."

"You know I can't keep my mouth shut."

"Then maybe you should ask Cameron what his aunt was like before she married Emmerich. Because she had a fire in her too, and he smothered it."

"Aaron isn't like that."

"Did you already forget how he toyed with you? Made you fall for him and then told you he had no interest in you? That is, until *Cameron* showed interest."

Alex swallowed hard. Stefan was giving voice to every doubt she held inside.

I didn't imagine it.

She clenched her hands, and the spikes on her crown pricked her fingers. Stefan took it from her and placed it on her head.

"Twelve years I've been protecting you. I won't protect you from him. I refuse to pick up the pieces every time he breaks you because he will break you. If you pick Aaron, I won't be your guard anymore."

"You can't mean that."

"I do."

"No. The captain of my guard—a Wafner. You—you have a duty!"

"Being a Wafner will get me a job in any of the other kingdoms."

"Stefan—please." Alex's voice broke.

"No. Two months with him, and the girl *I* helped raise disappeared. Just another silly princess, falling for the useless prince who promises you everything until he takes what he wants and leaves."

Alex fought back tears as a knock sounded on her door. Stefan answered it, revealing Cameron.

"Baron Strobel, I trust you'll bring her to the hall," Stefan said, and without another word, he slammed her door.

Cameron rushed to Alex. Tears fell as thunder resounded through the room, and it poured outside. Before Alex could say a word, Cameron cupped her face and kissed her. Distracted by Stefan's words, Alex kissed Cameron back, but there was nothing to it. She didn't even notice the painting on her wall slip quietly back into place.

"Cameron, I can't—" Alex pulled away.

"It's Aaron, isn't it?" he asked, frowning.

Alex looked away and nodded.

I don't know how to do this.

"Every time. He strolls in with that crown and wins. Friends, tournaments, *maidens*."

"Maidens?"

Cameron scoffed. "You thought you were the first maiden he took from me?"

"No. You're lying."

Cameron smirked as he closed the distance between them.

"Are you that naive? You believed you were the first. That you were special. That—"

Alex fled into the hallway, accidentally knocking a suit of armor to the floor and startling some guests. Ignoring them, she rushed toward the hall, fighting to control the powers stirring inside her.

Once she reached the banquet, Alex put on a fake smile but couldn't focus.

Is Aaron really lying? How did I miss it? How am I so bad at this? Breathe. Please don't start a fire.

She needed to talk to someone but didn't know who.

As soon as she spotted Aaron, she rushed toward him.

I'll ask him—even if he might deny it.

But when he looked at her, she stopped. He locked eyes with her in an icy stare. Alex slowed her pace. "Aaron?"

"Elizabeth." He nodded, but his voice was rough with none of his usual playfulness.

Why are you using that name?

Alex moved to take his hand, but Aaron stepped back. "Why are you being cold?"

"I don't like being lied to, Your Highness."

Bile rose in her throat at the harshness of his tone. "I didn't lie to you," she whispered.

Stepping forward, he stared down at her. "We had an understanding that you would end things with Cameron, but I found you kissing him. That's after leaving my bed to seek comfort from Stefan. I know who you're picking in his ultimatum."

Alex went numb. "You saw that?" Her voice was small and weak.

"I was heading to your room to surprise you. What a surprise." His voice was sharp and short. "If you'll excuse me, princess, I have people to greet. People who I *want* to see."

As Aaron walked away, Alex's heart broke at the same time her anger burst out.

He won't even let me explain! How can I fix it if he won't talk to me? He said no more running ... that I could trust him. I believed him.

Her dress was too tight, the room too small, and her powers too much. Alex gasped and fled toward the courtyard. She needed fresh air, and she needed to be outside. When the crisp, chilly night air hit her, Alex broke into sobs while hail pelted her and the fire pit to the side exploded to life.

I can't do this. It's too much. I'm going to just explode.

"Alexandria?"

Alex gasped and turned around to see Guinevere standing with her arms out. "You look like you need your mother. I'm sorry she isn't here, but I can be a stand-in this once."

Alex rushed to hug her godmother. Guinevere stood in the hail and held Alex until her cries quieted and the weather abated.

"Tell me that tense conversation with my son didn't cause all these tears."

"Not all of them."

"But some?" Guinevere asked.

Alex nodded.

"So he's your preferred suitor?"

Alex nodded again.

"I wish your mother was here. I remember being your age. Everything is hard. You feel everything too much, but you have a title and powers on top of it. I know I'm not her, but I'm here if you need someone."

"Thank you."

"Let Aaron calm down. He has a temper and feels things much deeper than most. When he's hurt, he lashes out to protect himself, but he comes around. Don't let him push you away."

Alex sighed. "Could you tell my father I went to bed?"

"Of course." Guinevere said as she released her and strode back to the party.

Once inside her room, Alex escaped the giant poufy dress and put on her riding clothes. She avoided her door and snuck through Michael and Stefan's room to slip into the small hallway. Alex looked at the spiral stairs that led to Aaron's room and soon found herself outside his door. She stared at the door, chewing on the inside of her cheek.

Try to talk to him or leave him alone?

In the distance, the town's bells rang. She counted out as they hit twelve.

"Happy birthday to me," she whispered, and her eyes filled with tears.

Not on my birthday. I can't take that today.

Alex heard footsteps coming from the hallway, and she flew down the stairs, hitting the main floor so hard she stumbled. When she tried to catch herself, Alex slammed into King Emmerich so hard she fell backward.

Emmerich caught her and looked down at her. Alex tried to smile but wasn't fast enough. The change in his eyes told her he'd seen the pain on her face.

"Come with me."

Alex took Emmerich's arm, letting him lead her to her father's room and then one door further. The door was identical to her father's. "Your mother's suite. It belonged to your parents, but after your mother died, your father moved out and left this room untouched. I think it's time *you* claimed it."

Emmerich bowed and left without another word.

CHAPTER 46
ALEX

A lex's footsteps echoed on the stones, sending the torches and fireplace to life. The layout of her mother's room was the mirror image of her father's. She'd covered every free surface in bookcases, each shelf bowing under the weight of their books, a thick layer of dust covering everything. Alex walked to the door that joined the rooms, but the handle wouldn't turn.

My father locked away my mother's memory. Will Aaron just forget about me? Lock away everything he felt for me?

Alex hiccupped and walked to the dusty fireplace mantel and let her pain swallow her as she watched the flames. An icy wind caressed her cheek, but when she spun around, she was alone. A pair of forest-green reading chairs and a matching couch made a circle in the middle of the room. Alex remembered her parents reading together the same way she and Aaron had in the library. She ran her hand along the chairs' delicate fabric and sat down to take in the room. Nearby was the ornately decorated chest that had appeared in her pearl memories.

This is where she spoke to Daniel and Moorloc. Where we were before the throne room. Before she—

Alex slipped down to the dirty rug and faced the chest. Tears streamed down her cheeks as her shaky hands reached for it, knowing what awaited her. The lid's squeak broke the silence along with Alex's heart.

Inside was her lost childhood. There were dolls, wooden blocks, and other small toys—everything she had lost when her grandfather ripped her mother from her, her home, her life. Alex picked up the black-haired, acorn-brown doll in the green dress and clutched her to her chest. "I missed you, Birch."

The torches in the room dimmed as the ones on the stairs lit up. Alex stood and followed them to her mother's dressing room. The table with her jewels was untouched except for one clean circle in front of a pair of large crowns. Alex traced the circle, realizing it was the former home of the more formal crown on her head. She removed the crown from her head, setting it back in place with the others. Moving to the wardrobe, the doors slid open, and Alex ran her hand along her mother's silk gowns, most of which matched her favorite green dress.

They still look new and smell familiar, like spring sunshine.

Alex took them out to admire them one at a time. As she walked to the mirror with a yellow dress, Alex glanced at the portraits. There was one of her as a baby and another of her father as a young man. When she stepped before the mirror, Alex dropped the dress and gasped—her emerald eyes had gone black.

Icy wind hit her again as she shut her eyes, shaking her head; opening them, she saw green staring back at her.

Alex grabbed the dress and doll and climbed the stairs to her mother's bedroom, her feet thumping on the stones. The four-poster bed was exquisite. A pair of carved sea serpents snaked their way up each column, and someone had draped green linen above the dragons' heads. The quilt sparkled as if it had been stitched with silver. But like everything else, the bed was dusty, forgotten, the air stale as a tomb.

Alex spotted the balcony doors, and after she placed the dress and doll on the bed, she pulled the doors' latch. A warm breeze took the doors from her grasp and filled the room with fresh summer air. When Alex stepped out and looked into the courtyard, she spotted Michael kissing Jessica.

So he finally found his courage.

Retreating inside she picked up the doll, lay on her mother's bed, and cried. She wept for the mother she didn't get to know, the boy she loved who had hurt her again, the brother who'd betrayed her, and all the good people who had lost their lives for her. When she had nothing left, Alex fell into an exhausted sleep.

ALEX WOKE TO SHOUTING. She slipped off the bed and walked to the door that connected to the king's suite, putting her ear against it.

"What do you mean you can't find the princess? *Again*? She disappears on the eve of her birthday? Randal, I don't want excuses. Find her. And if she's with a suitor, I don't care who he is, he won't make it to the tournament today!" Edward shouted.

"Emmerich, you look too calm. What do you know?" Guinevere demanded.

Alex heard a rumbling laugh identical to Aaron's and then a gentle tap on the door. She turned her latch and stepped aside to let the door open inward. Standing at the threshold was Emmerich.

"Good morning, Alexandria. Happy birthday."

Her father shoved Emmerich aside, throwing his arms around her. Alex could feel his immense sigh of relief.

"I'll tell Randal this isn't a repeat of Abigail," Guinevere said.

"You were here this whole time?" Edward asked, looking around the room before pausing at the disheveled bed and picking up the doll. Alex nodded as she held her hand out.

"I should have moved you to your mother's rooms a long time ago. I'm sorry. Happy birthday, Elizabeth." Alex arched her brow at him, and he sighed. "Give me this one day. Your name is in honor of *my* mother, and she is innocent in your anger."

Alex nodded and, taking her doll, hugged her father. "All right."

"Emmerich, would you?"

"I'll get the participants to the field and ask someone to send some maids to set up this room," Emmerich said.

Guinevere then ordered *both* kings out, stating she'd help Alex. In ten minutes, Guinevere dressed Alex in a flowing red Datten dress, had her hair pinned like her mother always wore it, and had picked one of her mother's crowns.

"Put it on any way, dear. Your mother enchanted all the larger crowns to not come off unless you lift it off."

"Honestly?" Alex tilted her head to the side and observed her crown staying in place with a wide-mouthed smile.

"Very handy," Guinevere said.

Alex smiled.

I always miss my mother today. Thank you for staying with me in her stead.

As Alex and Guinevere left and entered the hallway, several maids were waiting to freshen things up. Alex gave them one request: leave her toy chest.

King Emmerich and General Bishop were waiting for them across the hall. Matthew bowed and took the queen to the field.

"We'll be along in a minute," said Emmerich, and he held his arm out to Alex. "When are you planning to leave for your mother's castle?" he asked.

"When are you returning to Datten?"

Emmerich chuckled. "You are your father's daughter as much as your mother's, and don't ever let anyone tell you otherwise. Guinevere and I will be on the road with our men by lunch tomorrow. I have a kingdom to run." He paused. "But ... Aaron will remain here."

"Why?" Alex asked, trying to sound aloof.

"He asked to stay."

"You should ask again. There was an incident yesterday, and he was very clear he couldn't leave fast enough. Add that to whatever will come today or after—since I'm of age—whatever that means. I'm sure all the suitors will run once they see what a mess I'm turning out to be."

Emmerich stopped walking and forced Alex to look at him. "My son sought me out this morning. Dragged me out of bed before dawn, demanding to stay behind. Something about needing to make things right with a young lady."

"Oh." Alex couldn't look at Emmerich, so she tugged on her mother's necklace safely around her neck.

"Forget Aaron for a minute. I know everyone thinks I want Datten and Warren joined at any cost—but the truth is more complicated. When you were born, I asked Arthur to betroth you to Aaron. He's our second son, and you were a crown princess. I already knew then Aaron was like his mother. Did you know he could ride a horse and read at three? Ridiculous."

"What happened?"

"Arthur. He planned to betroth you to the furthest away

kingdom he could. I wouldn't let him do that to Edward and Victoria, so I gave him the one thing he couldn't turn down."

"Daniel."

They walked on in silence.

"You should tell them the truth. My father deserves to hear what you did—from you. Aaron ... he needs to hear the truth. He has more demons around his brother's death than you realize."

"Oh, and who told you that?"

"Daniel," Alex said.

"Speaking of my sons, you wouldn't know with whom Aaron's so determined to make amends, would you?"

"Certainly not." Alex looked away to steady her breathing.

"Know this. Guinevere and I couldn't ask for a better goddaughter, and we would love to have you in Datten for a *proper* visit any time for however long you'd like. Datten already survived one young sorcerer, and all we lost was a useless tower. We can handle another."

He leaned down and kissed Alex's head in front of her crown the same way her father did then made a funny face.

"Careful, someone could put their eye out on your crown."

Alex laughed. It was her first genuine laugh since this complete mess began. Her mother's crown was ostentatious with so many jewels, but Guinevere had insisted it was "just a small crown."

As they reached the field, they could hear Edward announcing the Warren jousting rules. As soon as he spotted Alex, he stopped talking midsentence. A sea of faces turned to her, and murmurs spread through the crowd. Emmerich squeezed Alex's arm as the crowd parted.

"Deep breaths, princess."

The red dress Guinevere had chosen was simpler than anything the ladies were wearing, but every woman in attendance was in blue. The gold belt accentuated Alex's slim waist, and the trim made her features pop. But the red set off her emerald eyes like no other color could. Emmerich escorted her to Edward, and she curtsied to him. When she rose, he had tears in his eyes.

"I know," she said and kissed his cheek. He finished addressing the crowd while she stood beside him. Emmerich went to the stand and took Alex's seat between Aaron and Edward, giving Aaron a long, hard stare before sitting.

Edward took her hand, and they strode up the stairs. Alex sat beside Guinevere, who looked pleased with herself. Everyone kept looking at Alex and whispering. Alex knew they were marveling at how much she looked like her mother, but the attention made her shift in her seat and keep adjusting her skirt. Guinevere grabbed her hand to ease her anxiety, and they turned their attention to the match.

Alex could feel familiar eyes on her. Aaron, Cameron, and Stefan—all watching her, waiting for the least bit of acknowledgment. But Alex sat stoic and gave none.

CHAPTER 47
ALEX

The proper match would have to wait until the squires and citizens finished. The morning air, heavy with excitement, was filled with the smell of straw. Merlock, Stefan, and the generals stood across the field and watched the proceedings. How the young boys could stay on their horses and handle themselves, especially with shields and lances, impressed Alex. She watched them like a hawk, trying to see who had genuine talent.

The Warren round finished peacefully, and Alex went down to provide prizes and kisses to the winners. The first two worked in the Strobel stables; third prize went to one of the royal stable boys. Alex then turned to the royal stands as the younger knights scattered. Swallowing, she looked up, expecting Aaron to be watching, but he'd vanished. All the knights had disappeared, getting ready for their jousting match. A heavy silence filled the royal stand as Alex took her usual seat with her ladies, waiting for the competitors to be split up. Datten's joust had the fewest participants—only royalty, high nobility, and the strongest knights were brave enough for it.

"Remind me, what's different about Datten jousting?" Alex asked Jessica as the jousters lined up for instructions from Randal. In such a small group, Alex recognized Aaron's crest immediately. The Strobel and Bishop crests were also easy to spot. Alex's breath caught, but Jessica grabbed her hand.

"We know everything," she whispered. "After you fled, we forced Aaron, Stefan, and Cameron to talk."

"Well, I spotted you and Michael from my balcony."

Jessica's cheeks flushed.

"Explain the differences in Datten jousting," Alex asked again.

Jessica sighed. "The lances are all made of hickory or maple. They require more force to break, so the field is longer to allow more speed. Armor must meet the minimum Datten standards of thickness and coverage, and the men had to sign a death waiver."

"A what?" Alex and Edith asked in unison.

"A death waiver," Jessica repeated calmly. "It absolves the tournament and kings of any guilt in deaths since participation is voluntary."

What if he gets hurt and I never get the chance to apologize?

Alex swallowed hard and felt the rock in her stomach grow. "Is that why Merlock is here?"

"It is," Edward said.

"How many men are in the experts' group today?" Edith asked.

"Only twenty-four. It's the most dangerous. That's why there's so much glory in it," Edward said. "It was Emmerich's and my favorite in our youth."

A few of the Datten nobility Alex didn't remember went first, fighting for leadership. Compared to what Alex had heard during the Warren round and her own lesson with Cameron, this was unforgettable. The sound of the lance striking the shield reverberated like thunder, and a breaking lance sounded like the crack of lightning: powerful and too close for comfort. As chunks of wood flew into the stands, royals and citizens alike cheered with gusto while Alex fought the urge to be sick.

As the matches went on, Alex felt dizzy. The air felt heavy —like it did before a storm. Alex could swear she smelled blood and burning wood, but there were no fires anywhere, so she tried to push it out of her mind and focus on the event.

Prince Jesse, Prince Rudolph, Cameron, and Sirs Julius and Gabriel won their matches with ease. They knocked a few men off their horses, but none of them were seriously hurt. The only injury came when Wesley's brother Perry had to be carried off the field because the force of him hitting the ground knocked him unconscious. Alex wanted to leave. She didn't want Stefan near them, and her panic was getting worse, but then a horse she recognized made her sit up. Thunder arrived on the field, led by two squires. Aaron followed behind with his formal Datten armor and his Warren shield. He wore his helmet with the visor up and waved to the stands as he entered the field. His eyes locked on Alex for a moment before he mounted Thunder.

Please don't get hurt!

Duke Summerstock stood beside his horse and bowed. Aaron nodded in reply.

"He's going to put Charles in his place," Jessica said.

"What do you mean?" Alex asked.

"Charles behaves like Wesley. And like Wesley, no one would speak up. Aaron has been trying to stop him for years but couldn't. Until today, they've never faced each other."

Alex asked. "Is he as good as I've heard?"

"Better," Edward said. "Aaron has always excelled at

jousting without having to work at it. He's been doing it as long as he could ride. It's a Strobel talent."

Alex looked up to see the horses take off, and with one flick of his lance, Aaron struck the duke square in the chest and sent him flying. He held up his intact lance, sending the crowd into a roar.

How is it still in one piece?

The first round took them down to twelve. They competed in pairs until there were six left. Since Aaron was the reigning champion, the remaining five would compete against him. He took out Henry Vinur and the other two men from Datten with minimal effort, leaving him with Prince Rudolph and Cameron.

The prince mounted his horse and rode to the middle of the field to greet Aaron. They exchanged some words, and both looked at Alex before they nodded and took their places.

Prince Rudolph looked nervous as he pulled his visor down. Alex remembered his kiss in the garden yesterday before she'd slapped him.

Did Aaron find out about that?

Alex's stomach lurched, and she bit her cheek so hard she drew blood, but she couldn't look away. It was her honor Aaron was defending even if no one knew it. A wind tore through the field, scattering hay everywhere as they set up for the charge. Jessica's hand touched Alex's; in return, she squeezed so hard she expected Jessica to complain. But she didn't.

This time, both the lances found their marks, but neither fell, so they set up again. The second set was the same. Each round became more tense as the crowd held its breath, waiting for the inevitable fall. After another charge, Alex noticed Aaron's shield move. The squires had missed it. The fear that had been trickling through her became a torrent. Alex leaped to her feet and ran down the stairs just as Aaron and Rudolph were preparing to charge again.

"STOP!" Emmerich's voice boomed over the crowd's noise.

Alex marched over to Aaron and looked up at him.

"Alex, what—?"

"Your shield." Alex pointed at it.

Twisting his arm, Aaron's eyes grew large, seeing what Alex had noticed from the platform. He held his arm out to her. Alex tightened the straps that had come free and turned to leave without a word.

Say something. Anything, you coward!

Alex spun to face him and saw that he was still watching her. "Good luck."

She strutted back to her seat, making the crowd roar with excitement. Once she was seated, Edward announced the match could resume.

"You spotted a loose shield from here?" Emmerich asked.

"I'm well trained in defensive weapons and armor."

"And she stares at Aaron enough when he's training that she should know how his shield fits him," Edith said a little too loudly.

Alex turned to Edith, eyes wide, lips pursed.

"What? You do!"

Jessica rolled her eyes at them both.

Alex turned her attention back to the field and watched as Aaron gripped his shield closer and dropped his lance. With that charge, he took out the prince.

Only one left.

Cameron arrived on the field with his horse. Alex's chest tightened as she looked back and forth. Every cruel word from the night before came back.

Maidens. You thought you were special? I don't like being lied to, princess.

Alex twisted her skirt in her fist.

Stefan, Cameron, Aaron. How could three men who claim to care about me be so cruel?

Aaron and Cameron nodded and mounted their horses. Soon Alex was so focused on the match that she forgot about the dread spreading through her, but it quickly returned when, after another three rounds, Aaron's shield crashed to the ground. Her heart lurched, and she squeezed Jessica's hand as Aaron and Cameron lined up for another round. Time slowed down. The dirt and dust from the horses' hooves flew up while bits of straw floated by. As Thunder pounded down the track toward Cameron, Alex stopped breathing. She knew. With each pounding hoof, she felt it in her bones.

Aaron would go down.

Alex was already flying down the stairs when the crack of both lances simultaneously shattering resonated through the field. Aaron flew from Thunder followed by echoes of metal hitting the ground. Alex rushed to the field and dropped to his side in seconds, even before his squires and Cameron could get there. Bile burned her throat as her shaking hands removed his helmet.

Aaron groaned.

"I forgot how much that hur—"

He stopped when he opened his eyes and found her staring at him.

Without thinking, Alex touched his chest. A gold light left her hand and penetrated his armor. Tears welled in her eyes as she closed them and felt for damage. Her power took over, and a sharp pain hit her chest, like when she'd fallen out of a tree with Michael. As it faded, she opened her eyes and saw the gold light leave Aaron and return to her. He took her hands in his, holding her in place.

"Thank you."

Alex pulled away, scanning the crowd that had gathered. Cameron, the squires, the doctor, and Randal were all staring at her. Alex shook as she rose, and Randal grabbed her biceps to steady her. Alex pushed her shoulders back and walked to her father to collect the prizes. The royals gawked at her, but Alex avoided eye contact. She just held her hands out to her father.

"Alexandria?" Edward asked.

"No," she said, thrusting her hand out again, refusing to look at him. The weight of the bags hit her hand, and she spun to the victors. Cameron and Randal pulled Aaron to his feet, and then they watched her. Alex forced her feet to move toward them but stopped when she felt a sharp pain in her head. She dropped the bags as an alarm went off inside her. A rush of pine-scented wind hit her, and the tournament field vanished. Alex recognized the smell of the Dark Forest.

"Hello, cousin." Lygari stood up from the tree he was leaning on. "Have a tiff with the handsome prince?" He clucked his tongue. "Datten men."

"Send me back," Alex demanded, rushing toward Lygari, but he cracked further away.

"Not until they've done their job. My father is still rancorous that Emmerich never helped your mother, so ending his line seems like a fitting punishment."

"How is that a fitting punishment? Our line didn't *end* when my mother died!"

"I know. That's why Emmerich will remain alive. To suffer."

"Please, don't hurt them. I'll do anything!"

"Anything?" A deep voice rumbled behind her. Alex turned and found herself face to face with the man from her memory —he was almost identical to Merlock except his eyes were gold, and he had a beard. "What if I agreed to leave Datten alone *if* you came with us?"

"No."

"You can't have it both ways. Consider my offer, little *harbinger*. You'd save the boy you love from death, and you could safely learn how to use those blossoming powers. I'll give you some time." Moorloc grabbed her forearm, and her body went cold. Time stopped.

Then wind hit her face as shouting filled her ears.

Alex found herself at the far edge of the training field, facing a chaotic battle scene. As time caught up, she recognized people. Randal, her father, and Emmerich were fighting a group of leather-clad men while Jerome, Aaron, and Cameron were with some Datten knights holding back another group. She couldn't find Julius, Stefan, or Michael. Breathing deeply, she smelled it—fire. Both sets of stands were in flames as people struggled to get out. Megesti pulled her to him.

"Where did you go?"

"Moorloc and Lygari. This is their doing. They're after Aaron and Guinevere."

"What?"

"Stop the fires."

"I can't control that much water. You have to."

"I don't know how," Alex said.

"I believe in you. Focus. Stop the fire from spreading."

Alex exhaled and reached deep inside her for a calmness she had never felt. She dug deeper until something stopped her. She pushed against it with everything she had, and it felt as if a dam broke. Power flooded through her, and her hands glowed gold. Staring at the fire, Alex willed it to stop growing —and it did. She tried to make it smaller but couldn't.

"Good start. Come on."

Megesti grabbed Alex's hand and hurried them toward the

fire, but as they got closer, a massive cloaked figure leaped through the flames, landing before them. Kruft Rassgat smirked as he stared at Alex. Without hesitating, Alex dove and grabbed the end of a nearby broken lance.

"Alex, run!" Megesti shouted, summoning his flames.

"No, get help!" Alex swung the lance at Kruft's groin.

Kruft grabbed the lance with both hands and ripped it from Alex's hands. Stalking closer to her, he growled, "You'll come with me eventually, so save me the trouble."

Megesti moved to attack, but Kruft laughed and struck him with the lance, knocking him unconscious before Kruft dove for Alex. She dodged and nearly got away, but he grabbed her dress, dragging her back. Alex kicked and scratched him, trying to make him release her, but he wrapped his hand tighter around her skirt, pulling her right up to him.

"You'd be pretty if you knew your place and weren't such a *witch*," Kruft spat.

She spotted Stefan and Michael edging up behind Kruft, so Alex fought with all her might, scratching his face, biting his arm, and kicking him in the groin.

"Little witch," Kruft roared as he let go only to backhand her across the face. The metallic tang of blood filled her mouth as she slammed into the ground. The next moment, a broken lance swung through the air and shattered on Kruft's shoulder. His face went feral, but he ignored Michael, lunging for Alex instead when Stefan jumped between them, sword drawn.

"The younger Wafner," Kruft said. "Your father couldn't best me, so why would I fear you?"

"Stefan!" Alex shouted.

"Deal with the fire. We'll deal with him." The tone in Stefan's voice left no room for discussion.

Alex staggered to her feet, spitting out her mouthful of blood as she tried to run toward the stands again. She weaved around the knights and mercenaries, struggling to stop the flames as she focused on the stands. She moved her attention away from the field before her and back to the flames. The instant she did, someone ran into her, and she fell to the ground.

Alex looked up to see a sword punch through the mercenary's chest, splattering blood on her. Alex cried out when the blade retracted and he fell with a dull thud, but she swallowed her terror and scrambled backward as screams came from the stands. The fire roared larger.

Ferflucs. My focus slipped again.

Arms pulled her off the ground, and she slammed her fists into Datten armor.

"Alex—" Aaron's voice dissolved her fear.

"Keep everyone away from me so I can stop the fire."

"Of course."

As Alex thrust her still glowing hands over her head, she whispered a plea and closed her eyes. When she opened them, power engulfed her, and her winds appeared, slamming into the mercenaries as they fought to hold their ground. Then a roar sounded as a torrential spiral of water rose from the Oreean Sea. The water rushed toward them through the air like a raging river and slammed into the burning stands, dousing the flames.

Drained, Alex faltered—but Aaron caught her. His touch broke her spell, dropping the floating river of water on everyone beneath it. Alex flinched, and Aaron gripped her tighter.

"You okay?" he asked.

"Yes ... here," she said without thinking.

Aaron stared at her. "Alex, I—"

"Not the time, you two!" Michael shouted as he and Matthew fought their way toward them.

Stefan was still fighting Kruft across the field when something caught Kruft's eye. Stefan took advantage of the distraction and slashed him across the face.

Mercenaries were everywhere. Aaron was helping Alex to her feet when she heard a scream. She spun to see Jessica and Edith across the field fighting a pair of mercenaries beside one stand.

"Matthew! Michael!" Aaron screamed. "Get Jessica and Edith."

"What about the princess?" Matthew asked.

"We have her," Jerome shouted, appearing beside Alex. Aaron's hand moved to his sword.

They'll take too long.

Alex ran and grabbed a broken lance. Adjusting it in her hand, she threw it like a javelin, striking one of the mercenaries in the thigh, sending him to the ground screaming in agony.

"Nice throw," Michael shouted. Edith and Jessica attacked the other man until Michael and Matthew arrived.

Alex grabbed another piece of a lance. She turned back to Aaron, who was smiling in awe.

"What?" she asked.

Aaron pulled her to him, and she placed her hand on his armor. "Can I talk you into going with my mother and your ladies?"

"No. This is my home. I defend it." She kissed him, and Aaron grabbed her hand.

"Merlock!" Aaron shouted.

Merlock arrived beside them. "Alexandria, let's go."

"No. Take my mother and Alex's ladies to the Nial estates. We're going to help the others."

"If you insist." Merlock snapped his fingers, replacing Alex's dress with her training clothes and armor.

"Thank you," Alex said.

Merlock cracked the three noblewomen away while Aaron and Alex ran toward the spectator stage where Julius was helping people get off. Alex climbed through a small opening into the seating area and tried to remove the large beam that was still trapping people.

Aaron shouted, "Michael! Stefan! She's with Julius. You three help her get those people out. Jerome with me. We'll help my father and Edward."

CHAPTER 48

ALEX

Alex was so focused on pushing against the charred beam with Julius that when it fell, Alex went with it. Stefan arrived to catch her at the last second. As he stood her up, Alex watched the surrounding fighting. Suddenly, her skin began to prickle as static crackled through the air.

No.

A crack erupted, and the mercenaries vanished, leaving Moorloc standing before the kings with a sour expression. Lygari stood behind him. Both wore long violet-colored cloaks made from the best material. The style was fancier than anything Merlock ever wore. The collar came up below their ears, and on the front, an infinity symbol—the mark of the line of Merlin—glowed in darker purple. Merlock moved, but Moorloc's hand shot out. Invisible hands grabbed Megesti and Merlock, slamming them to their knees before Moorloc.

"Is *that* how you greet the titan of your line?" Lygari shook his head.

"Ungrateful spares. Perhaps it's time I remind you both

how to show me the proper respect." Moorloc lowered his hand, making their foreheads touch the ground. "Better. Titaness! Time's up." Moorloc snapped, and Alex shrieked as a vise grip locked onto her wrists, pulling her toward Moorloc. Julius tried to hold her, but the magic knocked him over. Aaron rushed to her but was thrown back too.

Alex stopped in front of Moorloc. She took one step to the side, placing herself between him and Aaron.

"You don't actually expect *me* to bow, do you?"

You can do this.

She stood taller and scowled at him.

Moorloc strolled until he was directly in front of her, staring down at her. "You carry an *exceptional* amount of power for a half-breed. Still, I suspect you'd bow to me if I threatened the Datten whelp." Moorloc snapped his fingers, and Alex shrieked as Aaron dropped to the ground, invisible hands squeezing his neck. He struggled to grip what wasn't there.

"Stop!" Alex cried. "Don't hurt him. I'll do it."

The hands then released Aaron, who rolled over and gasped for breath. Alex knew Moorloc had confirmed her weakness.

I'll do anything, just don't hurt Aaron.

"A reminder, Alexandria, of who is in control. But I'll play nice—you are, after all, a titan in your own right."

Moorloc clapped, and Alex's armor vanished, replaced by an outfit identical to Moorloc's except hers shimmered gold with the Cassandra line mark on it. The pants and top were gold, but the cloak was ostentatious. It reached the ground, and the collar came off her neck several inches. Around her waist, the jeweled gold belt reflected sunlight in such a way that she appeared to glow.

I look ridiculous.

"Being the last true daughter of Cassandra, you're the Titan of Cassandra—even if you're a child."

Alex lunged for her uncle, but he grabbed her wrist, holding it up as she snarled.

"Temper, temper. Seems you have several weaknesses, my little prophetess."

Out of the corner of her eye, she saw Aaron stagger to his feet.

"Release her, Moorloc. For Victoria," Edward begged.

Moorloc's eyes flashed violet, and he released Alex to growl at Edward. "Do not speak my sister's name! *You*—who allowed your mongrel of a father to end her life. But I will thank you because this suitor nonsense has made understanding my lovely niece simpler." Moorloc turned back to Alex. The skin where he'd held her was red and burned. She cradled it and stepped back.

"The weak give power and control to the strong. I know your weaknesses, Alexandria—better than you do. I've been watching you."

Alex shuddered, thinking of every time she'd felt watched since she arrived at the castle. Terrified to look at her father or Aaron, she looked down, trying to crack them away.

Look up! Don't let him see your fear!

"There's your Datten whelp. The one you gave so many firsts. The boy you sneak off to in the middle of the night and have inappropriate dreams about. I won't go into detail lest we shame everyone with your indelicate thoughts. Mortals are such prudes."

Aaron was forced to his knees beside Megesti by invisible hands. Alex felt her throat dry and swallowed. She tried to go to Aaron, but the hands squeezed her biceps, locking her in place too. She trembled so badly her teeth chattered.

"You have *Michael*, who serves no purpose beyond that of

court jester." Moorloc turned to Michael. "It was her mother's intuition that made her save you despite finding you covered in blood. Nature doesn't gift mortals in that regard, especially Edward's line." Moorloc waved his hands, and Michael dropped beside Aaron.

"Last and least, you have your lout, Stefan. Does anyone know what he said about your precious prince? Or about the rage and betrayal you *still* feel that he'd abandon you for loving the wrong boy?" Moorloc waved his hand, dropping Stefan next to Michael in this line of people who mattered to Alex. All of them grunted and strained, struggling to break free of the magical hold on them.

"I would have added that baron yesterday, but you've abandoned him for his royal cousin. Adolescent love is fickle, or perhaps it's all those midnight visits to the prince's bedroom."

Alex held her breath as Moorloc walked over to Aaron and studied him. "Judging by the whelp's rage, he's well aware of what the lout said. Datten men are rather possessive of what they *believe* to be theirs. It would displease your mother to hear this."

Hot rage bled into Alex.

Threatening my loved ones and implying you know my mother's wishes? Enough.

Straightening, her voice returned. "Please, go on. Try to embarrass me. My father told me to find the man who would accept me—my flaws, strengths, terrible princess skills, *everything*. I'm not afraid of you. I'm as much my father's daughter as I am my mother's. Warren runs through my blood. So you can belittle the kisses I've accepted from suitors—say anything you want, but my father and my people will stand with me."

Alex unfastened the hideous cloak and threw it on the ground before her uncle, leaving her in only the gold pants and undershirt. Moorloc grabbed her chin, and Alex could smell his foul breath.

"You've accepted more than kisses. I wanted you to follow in your mother's footsteps but not this way. She threw every-thing away—helped their ancestors stay in Datten, helped the unfortunate, married that simpleton prince—so she could have you. Now behave yourself or I'll do something you won't like," Moorloc warned, releasing her.

"If you lay a finger on any of them, the day I have my full powers, I will rain down a fury on you no one could imagine."

"You are your mother's daughter! Victoria would bite when provoked. But you found your well today, and there's no turning back." Moorloc moved in front of Alex. "Still I warned you. So let's see if you can handle all your powers."

"*Moorloc, no!*" Merlock shouted, but Moorloc grabbed her chin, forcing her to look up at him. "As the head of your family, I command all your powers to come forth. As the summer solstice arrives in the next week, I order your gifts to be revealed before the sun sets on the winter solstice."

Alex felt heat spread through her as Moorloc's hand glowed violet.

"You're already stronger than Merlock can handle. I give you a week before you come *begging* for my help."

When he released her, the light burned worse than any fire she'd ever been near, and as it faded, the warmth remained, as if a missing part of her was now filled. Then she crumpled to the ground.

CHAPTER 49

AARON

Aaron tried to quiet the terror drumming through him as he walked toward Edward's room. Alex was asleep and would be guarded by Stefan and her ladies until the tournament banquet. Aaron sighed.

Another ruined birthday.

Alex had drained herself after healing Aaron and dousing the fire, so she needed sleep in order to restore her magic. Merlock couldn't say for how long, and neither could he speculate as to the full effects Moorloc's spell would have on her.

Megesti had explained that heads of a family could influence developing powers for young sorcerers. It was crucial in lines with unpredictable and violent powers, like Salem and Ares, to protect young sorcerers if their powers manifested too fast. His own powers had taken fifteen years to come in, and he had still done damage in Datten.

Victoria was powerful, and Alex takes after her mother. It's going to be a rough year for her and Warren, but I don't care. My mind's made up.

Aaron slowed near Edward's room. *Last night, she didn't*

defend me to Stefan, but today, she stared down the most powerful sorcerer we've come across to keep me safe. Cameron and his ferflucsing kiss. She ended things with him, and I broke her heart. Cameron spewed lies. Stefan betrayed her, and I abandoned her.

Aaron felt sick. Today, when he'd fallen, she'd run to him. It didn't matter that he'd hurt her—she healed him, fought beside him, trusted him to protect her while trying to save both their peoples, and then stood between him and Moorloc. Whatever the result, Aaron would do this right. He nodded to Generals Wafner and Bishop before knocking, but he didn't wait for an invitation to enter.

Edward and Emmerich were drinking. As they turned their attention toward the door, Edward's lip curled while Emmerich glared at Aaron and huffed.

"I have a matter to discuss with you," Aaron said, cutting off Emmerich's protests. He swallowed his fears, stood tall, and looked down at his father.

You can do this. They both want this. The only thing I have to fear is her refusal.

"You're always welcome to speak freely, Aaron," Edward said, motioning for Aaron to join them.

"I want permission to ask Alex for her hand." The words flew out of Aaron, and he wasn't sure they heard them. Aaron took a seat.

"What Moorloc said is true?" Edward asked.

"You're in love with her?" his father asked, leaning on the table and staring at Aaron.

"Yes," Aaron said. The weight of his father's words hit him. He'd suspected it since they first danced but wouldn't acknowledge it. "She's unlike anyone I've ever met. It's exhilarating. I can't stay away from her and don't want to."

Edward laughed. "I knew it."

"She is remarkable," Emmerich said. "I watched her throw a broken lance to protect her ladies. And you gave her armor?"

"I had to," Edward said. "She'd never tolerate being left behi—"

"But more importantly," Aaron interrupted, "I believe she feels the same about me."

"Why ask my permission?" said Edward. "I've given full control over the decision to her."

"*What* I am complicates things. As Crown Prince of Datten, I can't propose without my king's approval, especially if I end up keeping my crown. Even if the choice is hers, you're my godfather—I don't feel right proposing without your approval."

Emmerich and Edward stared at each other.

"The choice of whether to accept is my daughter's, but you were *my* choice for her since the day she was born."

"As king, you have my approval—and my blessing as your father. In fact, I have something for you." Emmerich grinned as he left the room.

Aaron took a breath and exhaled forcefully.

Edward poured Aaron a glass of ale. "I don't know what he's up to. Unless he's yelling about something, your father is a man of few words."

"Are we still going to have the banquet for her birthday?" Aaron asked, accepting the ale.

"I think it's important. She won't need to stay long, but after today, we have to celebrate not only her but also what we have now that she's back."

Aaron nodded.

"Exactly ... how much of what Moorloc said is true?" Edward asked, raising his brow.

Aaron avoided Edward's eyes and took a large gulp of his ale. "We've been alone in my room but not in the context implied. Stefan wants her to choose Cameron. I saw Cameron kiss her but didn't hear the lies he told after."

"Is keeping Cameron away why you want to propose? Or did something happen on one of those nighttime visits that requires a proposal?"

"I love her. I want to be at her side. Though I will admit I can't stomach the idea of anyone else kissing her."

"Then there's something you need to decide, Aaron—before you ask her. Can you live with Stefan as her guard after what he said? He won't leave her because he loves her as much as he loves Jessica. You may not like him, but there's no one who'd protect her as ferociously as you two will."

Aaron groaned, knowing Edward was right. Alex wouldn't let Stefan leave, but the idea of having Stefan behind them for the rest of their lives made his stomach turn.

Before Aaron could reply, Emmerich strode in. He placed a small gold box in front of Aaron and returned to his ale. Aaron opened the box.

Great-grandmother's ring!

He picked it up and turned to his father.

"How did you—?"

"Your mother did. Now, clean yourself up. You fought bravely, but your victory is all over you. If you expect to win your princess, you'll need to change."

"Our princess, you mean," Aaron said, staring at the treasured Datten heirloom.

"No—*your* princess. I told no one, but when we came to Warren after Alexandria was born, I intended to betroth you to her." Emmerich then proceeded to tell Edward and Aaron everything he had told Alex. Aaron sat in stunned silence for several moments.

"I always planned to shift the betrothal to you once Arthur died," Emmerich continued, "but after Daniel's death, I didn't need to. I've come to learn you're struggling with loving the woman intended for your brother. I didn't believe them, but after your confession, know this—contract or not, she was never Daniel's."

"Since she could walk, she only ever wanted you," Edward said.

Emmerich nodded to Edward, and they clinked glasses in silent understanding. Aaron finished his ale, trying to drown his frustration.

All this time, all this guilt, and over nothing!

Aaron closed the box and thought of Alex. In the end, it didn't matter as long as she said yes. Bowing to the kings, he left to go change, clutching the little gold box.

CHAPTER 50
ALEX

E verything hurts.

At first, Alex couldn't remember why, but slowly things came back to her. She heard Aaron's voice.

Elizabeth.

The name she hated, and the one he knew would hurt her. His face at the party when he'd said he wouldn't tolerate being lied to. It all made her chest hurt, but then rage filled her.

Stefan betrayed me. How much of his brotherly love was lying?

Alex threw aside her quilt, realizing she was still in Moorloc's gold pants and shirt. She stripped and threw them into the fireplace as a fire erupted, turning them to ash. Late day sunlight flooded the room from the balcony. Her birthday celebration would start soon. On the second floor, she found her sparring clothes in the wardrobe and put them on. Then she asked Edith to summon Randal. Randal arrived with Michael, and she explained her plans.

"Tonight?" Michael asked.

"Shouldn't you rest more first?" Randal asked.

"No," Alex said. She stood tall and stared hard at them. "I

need those books. I can feel it starting. We leave now, and we leave Stefan and Aaron behind. I struggle to control my powers when I'm this upset, and I can't be around either of them right now. We'll bring Megesti, Julius, and whatever men you deem necessary, Randal. But the worst risk is from me. We'll leave with no one knowing."

"You want us to lie to the king?" Jessica asked.

"Not *lie*," Randal corrected. "It'll take time for the royals to realize Alexandria should be there, and by then, it'll be too dark to follow."

Jessica and Edith nodded. They slipped into their rooms to dress for the party to keep up appearances. Randal went to gather the others while Michael and Alex snuck out to the stables. Once there, Michael sent Gregory off so they could prepare the horses.

Julius, Megesti, and Gabriel arrived with bags, and Randal followed. The sun was nearly gone by the time they left Warren. Megesti held Alex's hand, whispering an incantation to light their way on such a cloudy night—Alex had the power, Megesti the knowledge. Together, they succeeded on their third try. Megesti rode beside Alex, allowing Michael and Randal to take the front while Julius and Gabriel had the back.

"Thank you, Randal, for allowing so few men."

"Your father expected us to leave in a few days. Everything was ready, and we had royal approval, though we could only gather enough provisions to give us two, maybe three days. If we don't find the castle, we'll have to head back."

"I understand." Alex pulled her cloak tight against the damp night air and turned to Megesti. "Will two days be enough?"

"Depends on how large the castle is and how good your mother was at hiding things. You have the map and the stone?"

Alex handed the stone to Megesti. After rubbing it between his palms, he whispered an incantation, and the stone glowed.

"What did you—?"

"The closer we get, the more it'll glow. The spell brings lost things together. We'll try it with the journal when we arrive."

"If you can do that, *why* are we always hunting for my crown?"

"I'd need Aaron's crown to find yours. Plus, he enjoys watching you hunt for it."

Alex groaned when her mind returned to Aaron.

Should I have told him? Let him come with me? He stayed with me during the battle. Was it out of duty? Did he do it for my father? Or did he want to apologize? After this, he'll go home and never speak to me again.

"You okay?" Michael had ridden up beside her.

"Of course. I'm focusing on where to go."

She stuck her tongue out as she returned to the map.

Alex noticed Megesti watching her. "He'll come for you," he said.

"I don't know wha—"

"When Aaron finds out you're gone, he'll come. I don't know everything that happened, but I know *him*, and he loves you."

Alex turned sharply to him. "How can he? He doesn't know me."

But a flutter of hope rose in her chest. She didn't realize how badly she wanted him to come until Megesti said he would.

"Aaron can read people," said Megesti. "It's why he doesn't resort to violence. But he's never demonstrated the kind of determination he does when he fights for and defends you."

The group rode through the night, changing directions any time the stone dimmed or glowed brighter. At sunrise, they stopped at a clearing beside a stream to water the horses. While Flash drank his fill, Alex noticed the stone was glowing brighter. She glanced upstream into the woods. The trees were thick from the June weather, but in the distance, white towers glimmered in the morning sun.

"Michael! Megesti!"

As soon as Randal got his bearings, everyone mounted up with Alex and Randal in the lead.

An hour later, a foggy path appeared. The entire forest had gone as still as the castle crypts, and the only sound was the horses' hooves and their own heartbeats. The air smelled of decay, and the fog chilled them to the bone. The stone in Alex's hand now had a milky glow about it. The castle was closer to Warren than Alex had ever imagined. As they continued, the path became more overgrown. General Nial flanked Alex as she focused hard to send plants back to seeds. Arriving on the grounds, she halted so the others could catch up.

Before them stood a crumbling white stone building. It was neither as large nor as grand as Warren, but Alex saw beauty in it. There were four tall square towers, a massive wooden gate in need of repairs, and a protective wall; intricate details were carved into the stone. Alex stared in awe as General Nial walked over and held Flash's reins so Alex could dismount. Megesti and Michael arrived next.

"Head in, Your Highness. We'll let the others catch up then follow you in," Randal said.

Megesti took Alex's hand, and together they crossed the bridge to the gates. After pausing at the threshold to take in the sight, Alex exhaled and stepped through the broken gate. The castle's interior wasn't as decrepit as the exterior. A small courtyard with doors on either side led to the castle spires, and a large doorway stood straight ahead. Entering through the main door, they crossed a hallway into a large hall that reminded Alex of Warren's throne room. Victoria had lined the walls with paintings of mysterious people, but at the end was a portrait of her mother as a girl with her brothers. Merlock and Victoria smiled; Moorloc's expression was dour. The family resemblance was obvious, excepting the eyes. Merlock and her mother's were emerald while Moorloc's were gold. The next portraits showed Merlock with a young Megesti, and then Moorloc with a young Lygari. Alex noticed a portrait of a beautiful woman. She had acorn-brown skin, black hair, green eyes, and a simple green dress. On her head sat a wreath of flowers and vines. Alex and Megesti were drawn to her.

"There is something eerily familiar about her," Megesti said.

She looks like my doll.

Alex felt watched as a draft hit them. Michael, Julius, and Gabriel had joined them, and they looked around in awe.

"If you wish, Alexandria," Randal began, "Megesti, yourself, and I can look around on this floor and send the others to the second story."

"Keep Michael with her," Megesti said. "I'll be able to sense the books we are looking for with Julius and Gabriel."

The knights followed Megesti toward a tower as Alex headed through the room into a crumbling hallway. Moss covered the walls, and a tree was growing through the wall from the courtyard. A branch as thick as Alex's chest had broken into the hall, and Alex pulled her cloak closer as she inched around the tree into the next room—the library.

It's beautiful.

"We can leave you here while we finish, princess," Randal said.

I couldn't read all these if I had a century.

Her pulse quickened, and she broke out in a cold sweat.

Breathe. No fire. Not here.

346

The entire room somehow lit up despite a lack of fireplaces or torches. In the center of the room was an old table where she left her small satchel. Two benches sat beside it with a third one on the floor, broken and surrounded by several large rocks. Alex looked up—they'd fallen from the ceiling. She carefully made her way to the ceiling-high bookshelves. Scanning, she found books on Datten, Warren, Betruger, the Forbidden Lands, the six southern kingdoms, and countless distant lands Alex had never heard of. She examined the Forbidden Lands books. There were books on lineages, history, geography, and culture. Frustrated, Alex leaned against the shelf.

What's that? How can a bookshelf feel wrong?

Alex moved toward the shelf when Michael appeared.

"Lunch is ready."

"In a minute."

"No." His tone was curt. "You need to eat. Merlock said it's required until you get your strength back."

Alex looked back at the bookshelf when Michael gently elbowed her, making her stomach growl. Laughing, they went to lunch. They'd discovered the castle was square-shaped with the main hall in the center. On one side was a smaller dining hall, and on the other was a tiny courtyard. Over lunch, Randal explained that the four towers in the corners were lookouts. In the basement was a small kitchen and a few storage rooms. The second floor was a maze of hallways that Julius suspected moved. All except one led to guest rooms, and that odd hallway led to the staircase to the roof, which featured an elaborate garden. It was all Megesti talked about. He explained to Alex how, even overgrown, it had more plant varieties than their garden in Datten.

After lunch, Randal assigned tasks, leaving Alex to handle the library, Megesti the roof garden, Michael to select bedrooms, and the rest to examine and record the structural issues found.

Back in the library, Alex looked up. Seeing no ladder around, she decided to scale the bookcases. Alex was halfway up when she thought she heard her name. She ignored it and started pulling books off the shelf and rejecting them when she heard a yelp.

"You're going to fall," Michael said.

"Nice Stefan tone, except I already have an overprotective brother."

"Alex—"

"I'm fine. It's like climbing a tree."

"That doesn't help. I know how many trees you've fallen out of."

Alex smirked. "You fell out of eight—I only fell out of three." She grabbed the next book.

"How will I explain you breaking your neck?"

She dropped the book and almost hit him again.

"Please don't hit me."

A mischievous smile spread across her face. "If I wanted to hit you, I would have. Catch this one and start a pile on the table."

Michael stood below her in silence, catching the books she dropped.

"Alex, I know you aren't ready for this, but we know what happened with Aaron. We worried when Edith and I couldn't find you, so Aaron told us what he said and saw. Jessica went straight for Stefan while Aaron and I threatened Cameron. I wanted to strangle all three of them."

He knew. When he fell jousting, he knew I chose him, and now I left him behind.

Alex swallowed hard and dropped another book. Michael caught it and stayed near her. She slipped twice but didn't fall, and after a few minutes, Alex gave him the look that told him to go away, and he moved toward the door.

"Thank you for telling me," Alex said without looking at him.

Alex turned back to the books as Michael's footsteps vanished. She spent the next few hours flipping through and cursing at books with no luck. Alex growled in frustration before an unnatural breeze came through the library.

Magic.

She froze and spotted the strange bookcase. It still felt wrong.

"Hello, princess." Ice rushed down Alex's spine when Aaron's voice hit her.

"Your Highness." Her voice was so quiet she didn't know if he heard.

She glanced down. The lions sparkled on his royal tunic, but he wore a red shirt instead of the usual gold, and he'd left his crown behind.

"Can you come down, please? I need to talk to you."

Alex felt her lunch try to come back up. She exhaled and began climbing down but couldn't stop trembling and slipped. Alex yelped and grabbed the shelf at the last second, only for the one below her foot to break, sending her plummeting. She braced for a hard landing, but it never came. Even then she was surprised as she expected the icy feeling of Daniel's ghostly intervention to be the reason she hadn't hit the ground, but instead, warmth flooded her. When she opened her eyes, Aaron stared at her, and her cheeks flushed as he set her down. Gently, he caressed her cheek; but she pulled away and started organizing the books she'd dropped.

I held up my end, but you didn't.

Aaron took her hand and entwined their fingers. "Alex, can you please look at me?"

Alex pictured his face at the party and shook her head to clear the memory. Ripping her hand from his, she returned to her books. "Where are the others? Emmerich never lets you go anywhere alone."

"Stefan, General Bishop, and a group of knights are on their way. I tricked them. I took Thunder out, and when they rode after me, I had Merlock send me here."

Alex turned to Aaron. "I thought he couldn't find the castle."

"He can't. He found Megesti. Randal left Matthew a copy of your map."

"Merlock can track us?"

"Only Megesti. Something about a stronger blood connection."

Alex trembled as Aaron ran his hand along her back. She turned away.

"Please look at me, Alex."

"I can't. I still see your face. You looked like you hated me."

Aaron sighed. "I'm sorry. I was angry and spiteful, and I should have let you speak, should have *trusted* you the way you do me. You let me protect you in the battle. I gave you my word, and I ... I broke it."

Breathe. Listen to him before you set him on fire.

Alex's lips quivered as Aaron's hand left her back.

"I can't leave things like this with you," he said. "We need to clear the air."

Her heart was pounding so hard she couldn't think. She could feel Aaron standing behind her, but he gave her space. "Okay," she said.

Clear the air how? You know the truth. She closed her eyes and tried to calm herself.

"Cameron kissed *you*, didn't he?"

"Yes."

"Did it change anything about how you feel about me?"

"No. Kissing Cameron was nothing like kissing you. It was how I imagine kissing Michael would feel."

"I know what Stefan said."

Her stomach lurched, but she didn't move.

"I told you in your room—no running. Not this time, never again. I meant it. Who are you picking?"

"I don't want to *pick*—I need to convince him to change his mind."

"All right. I'm sorry and will repeat how I'm an idiot. You made your feelings perfectly clear yesterday."

"I did?" Alex peeked at Aaron's face.

"You were terrified when I was jousting—then healed me when I fell, trusted me to protect you, refused to abandon our people, and fought by my side. You were amazing. That lance throw ..." Aaron let the words hang in the air as he moved closer.

"But what you—"

"I was an idiot. Would you like to hear it again?"

Alex couldn't help but smile.

Once more wouldn't hurt.

"I was wrong. When you vanished, it terrified me. Then I learned everything you heard from Stefan and Cameron. Alex, if you refuse to forgive me for this, fine. I can respect that, but Cameron *lied*—about everything. There's never been anyone else."

"But in Datten, you said—"

"I exaggerated. The only women ever in my room were my mother, our maids, and you."

Alex spun to face him and slid her arms around his neck. She kissed him, and he pulled her close. Electricity roared through her as Aaron kissed her back.

Tears rolled down her cheeks. "I was so scared when you

flew from Thunder and jumped into the fighting at the tournament. And then Moorloc—I thought he'd hurt you."

"*You* were scared? You're incredible. I was terrified he'd hurt you, but I had to keep reminding myself you don't need saving."

Alex crept her hand down Aaron's chest, gripping his shirt. His heart was pounding as hard as hers. She pulled him to her.

Slow breaths. Say it. You can't hold this in.

"I ended things with Cameron, and you changed your mind."

"It's unforgivable."

"I forgive you anyway."

"Why?"

Because a Warren knows.

Alex gripped Aaron's hips and pulled him against her as tightly as she could. Aaron shifted, pinning her between him and the bookcase behind them. He moved slowly, giving her the chance to pull away, but when she didn't, he kissed below her ear, placing kisses down her neck. When he hit a little dip in her neck, Alex moaned as a tingling spread between her legs.

You get too much satisfaction when you hear that sound.

She pressed her legs together, but the look he gave her made it clear he was well aware of what he was doing to her.

"I'll do anything to make it up to you because I can't imagine a day without you in it."

Alex exhaled. "I'm willing to let you try to make it up to me."

Aaron returned to kissing Alex's neck, making her whole body tingle. Alex's breath became raspy and uneven, so she could barely say his name. When he looked at her, Alex gripped the front of his tunic and kissed him.

"Alex, do you need any help with—Your Highness?"

Aaron and Alex leaped apart.

"Julius." Aaron took Alex's hand, interlocking their fingers.

"Alexandria, did you feel that breeze?" Megesti's voice beat him to the library.

Aaron waved at Megesti.

"Beating the guards?" he asked, and Aaron smiled mischievously in reply. Megesti's eyes widened at Aaron's hand and went to Alex's face. "I told you he'd come. I'm glad to see you two worked things out. "

"We have," Alex said.

"Well then. I'm going to steal your charming prince. I need help in your mother's garden, and he's the only other person here who's been in a sorcerer's garden."

"So long as you give him back. Could you send Michael to help me sort through these books?"

"Don't fall," Aaron said, kissing her. When he pulled his lips from hers, he winked and left with Megesti. Alex couldn't stop smiling.

Julius raised his eyebrows. "Thank you. I won the guard bet."

Alex smirked. "Even after Cameron?"

"Of course. My father gave up keeping you apart when you were little. He said that kind of bond doesn't break. Look at Abigail and my brother."

THE OTHER KNIGHTS arrived in time for dinner. Michael assigned everyone sleeping quarters while Aaron and Gabriel tended to the horses. General Bishop went over the list of things that would need repairing while Megesti searched the library. Alex and Stefan started cleaning the garden on the roof, Alex especially enjoying smelling the musty dirt and taking in the strange-looking flowers.

"Are you ever going to speak to me again?" Stefan asked after an hour of silence.

"You're the one abandoning me. Michael will need a co-captain once you're gone. I'm considering Julius. Thoughts on your replacement?" Alex asked, crossing her arms.

You may have taught me too well, Wafner.

Stefan grabbed her hand. "I'm not going anywhere," Stefan said.

Alex felt her shoulders relax as she sighed with relief.

"And I'm sorry."

"What?" Alex shook her head and stared, agape.

"I never should've said those things—*or* spoken to you like that."

"I *expect* honesty from you, but, Stefan, you were cruel, like you wanted to hurt me."

"No. I wanted to hurt him, never you. I spent twelve years protecting you, but since he's arrived, I've failed more than our entire time in the woods."

"Stefan ..." A familiar wind blew around them.

"You've been in his bed. You can't deny it. I went looking for you two nights ago, and you weren't in your bedroom, but after a nightmare, you sought me out."

Alex tugged her necklace while her stomach churned. The herbs in the garden boxes around her withered.

"The touches, the glances—I see them. Jessica caught you two in the library. Michael nearly punched him after he told you he wasn't a suitor, and he took you to Datten."

"You're being cruel again. Are you my guard or not?"

He sighed so hard Alex felt it. "No matter who you end up with—I will be there to protect you and keep him in line, especially if it's Aaron."

"It's my choice, not a contract forced on me."

"Not anymore—he's taken liberties with you. Now he has to marry you."

"It's still my decision. But you're stuck with me. We both know your father and sister would never let you go to the southern kingdoms. It's Datten or Warren for you."

"I know, but after seeing what he does to you, I hate him," Stefan said.

Alex's head snapped up. "You hate him? That's your opinion of *your* crown prince?"

"You wanted honesty. He thinks too much when he should react. You're going to have to handle everything on your own."

"Did you see him at the tournament?"

"It's easy to react when you have experienced men behind you, correcting you. It's different when the decision is yours."

Stefan held his arms out to her. Alex rushed toward him and let his arms swallow her.

After everything we've been through, I can't do this without you. I sleep better just knowing you're there.

Around them, the garden burst into bloom, and Alex felt Stefan sigh.

"He'll grow into his title. Emmerich hasn't given him the opportunities to prove himself."

Alex pushed Stefan backward. "But don't forget, I spent twelve years with you too."

Stefan frowned. "He's not good enough for you."

"What?" Alex laughed.

"No one will ever be good enough for you," Stefan said as he kissed her forehead. Then he tilted his head.

"What?"

"You're in love with him, aren't you?" Stefan narrowed his eyes.

"My father warned me that the Warren family always

knows. For my father, it took one ride to Datten, and for my grandfather, it was a dance at a celebration."

"Are you two done yet?"

Alex and Stefan turned and saw Michael's head poking around the doorway.

Alex looked around. The plants had now tripled in size. "Not even close," she said.

Michael laughed and came out. "At the risk of admitting to eavesdropping, you know you're stuck with both of us forever, right?" He pushed Stefan away and hugged Alex. "No matter who you marry. But I like you with Aaron."

"I'm not going anywhere. Warren is my home," Alex said.

Stefan scoffed, and Alex threw dirt at both of them. A few minutes later, Megesti and Aaron came up to find them having a dirt fight in the garden.

"What is going on here?" Megesti asked, glaring. Aaron stood beside him, holding back his laughter. Alex and Michael exchanged a glance before they threw dirt at Aaron, bringing him into their war. Megesti rolled his eyes and moved aside, waiting for them to tire themselves out.

CHAPTER 51
AARON

Aaron brushed the dirt out of his hair. Alex, Stefan, and Michael had left to hunt for the books, leaving Aaron and Megesti in the garden to sort out the wooden garden boxes that were scattered across the roof. Aaron recognized several of the wafting smells, but not all; there were several plants he'd never seen before, including one with blue leaves.

"So what am I doing?"

"You tell me. I don't know what you're doing," Megesti said.

"I thought I was here to help you with the plants."

"The plants can wait. I want to know what in the *Forbidden Lands* you're doing kissing the Crown Princess of Warren in front of her guards and cousin."

"Proving to Alex that my feelings are genuine and that I won't hide them. I love her."

Megesti's eyes bulged. "*You* told someone you love them?"

"I haven't told her yet."

"Oh."

"Don't make that face. You know I'm not great at telling someone how I feel, but she's different."

"So what are you going to do?"

"Figure out how to tell her. The only thing holding me back is my cowardice."

Megesti wrinkled his nose. "What aren't you saying?"

Aaron pulled out the gold box. "She ended things with Cameron. I'm going to ask her to choose me."

"That's not because of what Moorloc said?" Megesti's hands shook as he began ripping plants out of the garden boxes.

"No, you know me. Given the choice between Datten or Alex, it's Alex. I'd give up my crown for her." His heart slowed to almost nothing as Megesti stared, wide-eyed, his mouth agape.

"You'd give up being king?"

"If I marry Alex, I'll be King of Warren. I don't need to be king of two kingdoms. That's what everyone else wants. But Datten was Daniel's, and Warren was mine. My father admitted the truth. It was always me. So all that guilt for nothing."

"Aaron—we don't know what Moorloc did to her. Her powers could be uncontrollable."

"I don't care. I love her and *will* stay at her side to face whatever that spell brings."

Megesti dropped the plants. "You can't give up your crown. Not even for Alex."

"Why?" Aaron sat on the closest plant box and looked at his friend.

"When Alex and I summoned the dead, Daniel gave us a message for you. He warned Alex not to give up on you or Datten would fall."

"What?" Aaron's stomach dropped.

"I'm not trying to scare you, only to clarify that you two fit together in more ways than we realize. More deeply."

"I like who I am with her. The man I become *for* her? He's worthy of her."

"Somehow she brings out the Datten in you." Megesti laughed, shaking his head.

"You say that like it's a bad thing. Everyone else complains I don't have enough Datten in me."

Megesti was silent for a while. "I want you both to be happy. But there are things you must know if you intend to propose to a sorceress. You jest that she isn't a normal princess, but she isn't a normal *girl* either."

"What does that mean?"

"Sorcerers age more slowly, so puberty takes longer. She'll look exactly as she does today when you're fifty. She'll also remain as—um—"

"Loving? Brave? Wild?"

"Lascivious."

Wait—are we having a sex talk?

Aaron burst into laughter. "Are we really having this conversation?"

"It's either that or you have it with my father."

"I prefer you. Please carry on."

CHAPTER 52

ALEX

Alex and Michael spent the rest of the afternoon going through every book in the library. The other guards scoured the castle, looking for books. Megesti tried the location spell using her mother's journal, but Victoria had written it just for Alex, and it wasn't part of the set they were searching for. When Gabriel eventually summoned them to dinner, Alex sent Michael ahead, promising to follow. Alone, she studied the strange bookcase that continued to bother her. The smell of pine brought her back to reality as heat flooded her. Alex moaned and turned to kiss Aaron.

"What are you doing?" he asked.

"This bookcase feels wrong, and I don't know why."

"It's a door."

Alex raised her eyebrows. "How—?"

"We have three of them in Datten. One is between my parents' bedrooms. It's so if anyone got into the castle, they wouldn't get from one to the other. Watch." Aaron grabbed books on the fourth shelf until Alex heard a click. He gripped the side of the case and pulled it back.

"Come see," he said, holding his hand out to Alex.

The moment Aaron's clammy hand pulled her through the door, Alex gasped.

My mother's bedroom.

To her left was a portrait of her mother in the green dress Alex loved so much, her hair as wild as Alex's. It depicted her as her true self. No other portrait looked as much like Alex. The portrait separated a huge four-poster bed and a large elaborately carved wardrobe while the other side of the room had a small bookcase, a desk, and a fireplace that sprang to life as they entered. Large chunks of ceiling covered this floor too.

Her room. Everything here she picked, touched.

Alex heard a faint click as the door closed. On this side, it was a normal door. Alex examined the bookcase but found no journals. She touched the books lovingly. Aaron watched her.

"What?" she asked.

"I love seeing you happy."

"It's my mother's room. Not the stuffy royal suite she got when she married my father but the one she made for herself." Alex's voice cracked.

Aaron wrapped his arms around her, pulling her to him. Alex nuzzled against him and sighed as she felt her heart swell as she stood in her mother's room with the man she loved.

How can I explain what you mean to me?

"Aaron—" Alex struggled to summon her courage.

"Alex? Where are you? You're missing dinner, and Randal is blaming me—*again*—for your vanishing." Stefan's voice sounded distant despite the library being just beyond the door.

"Come on," Aaron said. "Can't give him another reason to hate me. Will you meet me here after everyone's gone to bed? I have a surprise for you."

Aaron kissed her and took her through the second, smaller door leading to the hallway.

AT BEDTIME, Alex's heart was bursting with love. Despite her worry that they wouldn't find anything before their provisions ran out, she was grateful to have at least worked things out with Stefan. After everyone went to bed, Alex went to explore her mother's room alone before Aaron arrived. She slunk down the hall, listening to the castle's strange noises, and slipped into the library without being seen.

Alex spent the next few hours exploring the bedroom. After a while, she settled on the floor before the fireplace, reading a ledger that detailed the people her mother had helped heal with her rooftop garden.

A calmness overcame her, and Alex turned to see Aaron.

He smiled. "I wasn't sure you'd come."

"Why?" Alex closed the ledger as Aaron came over, her stomach fluttering as she tried to still her fidgeting.

"It's been a long day, and I thought you might feel tired." Aaron held his hands out, pulling her up.

I'm never too tired for you.

"I'm fine, truly. I talked with Stefan and Michael," Alex said.

"Oh?" He cleared his throat.

"They're both staying regardless of whom I pick. I can't imagine my life without them. They're the closest I have to siblings."

Aaron let out a hearty laugh. "I'm glad you made up with them. I prefer happy Alex. She's less of a fire risk."

Aaron took her book, placed it on the desk, and pulled a leaf out of her hair. When Alex took the leaf from him, she realized his hand was trembling.

"They ground me," she said. "Whatever my uncle did to

me, I can feel it. The power—it cascades through me. Feels like there are squalls raging inside me. Keeping myself in check is exhausting and terrifying."

Aaron tilted Alex's chin up. "I'm not worried about your *brothers* or scared of your powers. We'll face them together."

"What if I can't get control of them? I already hurt my father. What if I hurt you—?"

Aaron's kiss cut her off, sending electric sparks through Alex's entire body as she pulled him closer.

How do you do that? You make me want you more with every touch, every kiss.

"What if you give up everything, push everyone away because you're scared, and then you master your powers?"

I can't lose you. If I hurt you, I'd hate myself.

"I'd give up everything to keep the people I love safe."

"Who's on that list?"

Alex's arms slid down to Aaron's waist.

You.

"Lots of people." Alex stilled for a moment, searching Aaron's eyes.

"Alex."

"I mean it. I couldn't live with myself if I hurt anyone who didn't deserve it—"

"So lighting Wesley on fire would be fine. Good to know." Aaron pressed his forehead against hers, trapping Alex's laughter between them. "You're clever, strong, feisty, and beautiful. You're everything a kingdom could ever want in a princess, though you need to work on names of nobility, and your dancing needs improvement."

Alex shook her head. "I won't dance with anyone but you." At this, Aaron's lips brushed her ear, sending tingles through her body and quickening her breaths.

He whispered, "Royal courting demands you dance with other suitors, so until you choose, you'll have to adjust to the idea of being with someone who isn't me. On the dance floor, of course."

"*No.* No more pretending." Alex's voice was so soft, so ragged, it was barely audible. She swallowed so hard it hurt.

Exhaling slowly, Alex pulled Aaron to her. He kissed her, pressing her back against the wall behind them, knocking books off the nearby shelf. Opening her mouth, she felt Aaron's tongue slip across hers. The kiss deepened until the heat of his body made her gasp for air.

"What are we not pretending anymore?" he asked.

You. Me. What we are.

Aaron nuzzled his nose against Alex's and moved his kisses from her mouth to her ear and then her neck. Alex moaned, her breaths deepening as her fingers gripped his back.

"You didn't answer me."

Her knees went weak. Aaron smelled like the dew and moss from the garden fight.

How do I say this? What do I say? Why you just—

Her brain stopped working when his mouth found hers. After a few more seconds of frenzied kissing, she steeled herself long enough to push Aaron away. For a second, he looked worried, but she knew she had to do this now.

Speak words.

"I can't think when you do that. If you want a proper answer with words, stop until we're done talking."

"You want me to do that again?" Aaron grinned.

Alex swallowed. "I don't want you to stop. I want you to do it every night for the rest of my life."

Aaron's eyes widened, and he gazed at her. Alex's heart pounded as she stared at Aaron. Hours seemed to pass while she waited for him to reply. Then he took her hands in his and he dropped to one knee.

"Then marry me. Not because our parents want it or our kingdoms want it or because I'm a prince and you're a princess. *Choose me* because I love you, and I promise I'll do everything I can to make you as happy as your father made your mother."

He held out a tiny gold box, and inside sat a gold ring with a large ruby in the center.

"Aaron—"

"I know it's fast, but royal betrothals can last years before the couple actually marries. If you need time, take it. But you're who I'm *supposed* to be with. I loved the girl, I'm in love with the woman, and I can't wait to love the sorceress you'll be."

Aaron took the ring and held it out to her.

You knew too.

"There's no one else," Alex whispered. "Not since that night you helped me face the throne room. No one makes me feel half the things you do."

Aaron slipped the ring onto her finger. Alex sniffled and wrapped her arms around his neck, letting him lift her up in his embrace. She ran her hands up the back of his shirt, and the moment he set her down, she ripped his shirt over his head. Aaron's smile was feral as he slid his hands around her backside to pull her to him. She examined the muscles on his chest. She'd always wanted to touch them but hadn't dared before. His skin felt on fire, and she slowly traced the small scars on his shoulder from her arrows.

"Claiming me the day I found you? I was suspicious when I was the one in our party who got shot."

"Nonsense." Alex tugged on the waist of Aaron's pants before pushing him toward the bed. "I claimed you when we were children. I always said you were *mine*."

Alex studied his face for a moment.

You're so handsome it hurts.

Then something in her shifted. She kissed him as his hands roamed across her body, and then she pushed him onto the bed. Alex moved between his legs and rested her hands on his thighs. She gripped the soft fabric of his pants and watched him take her in until she moved her knees and straddled Aaron.

Aaron pushed himself up as she gripped his shoulders. Closing her eyes, she kissed him again, and he gripped her tunic and back forcefully, moving them back but keeping her on top of him. Alex's chest tightened, and there was a throbbing between her legs.

Please don't stop.

Moans left Alex as Aaron's hands moved to her backside and hips, both pushing her down and encouraging her to grind against him. Even through their clothes, Alex could feel everything. She couldn't stop touching him; she needed to feel every part of him. Her arms wrapped around his neck. His skin was hot to the touch, and everywhere he touched Alex, her skin burned. When he pulled his lips off hers, she whimpered until he brought his lips to her neck. Alex's breath quickened, and she arched her back.

More. Please, more. I'll give you everything, just don't stop touching me.

Aaron's kisses and caresses made Alex lose all sense. Her breasts ached to be touched as a pleasure she'd never known flooded her.

"Please, more," Alex panted.

Aaron obeyed. His hand slid up her shirt, tickling her for a moment. All of her felt too sensitive.

Too much and not enough.

When Aaron caressed her breast, the feel of his hand on her

sensitive nipple was too much, and when Aaron bit and kissed that spot on her neck, she thought she would explode.

"Aaron—" She was begging him.

"I love you," Aaron whispered.

I love you.

Alex let her body take over and quickened her pace on Aaron's lap. His grip on her hardened as she rode him with extraordinary vigor.

Too much. Too hot. I can't.

Her breath hitched as a wave of pleasure washed through her, making her cry out as she dug her nails into Aaron's back. Aaron grunted into her ear as his entire body shuddered beneath her.

Alex felt a rush of wind. Her mother's room vanished, and it became cold and dark. Aaron's hands pulled her tighter.

"Aaron?"

"Are you okay?" he asked, helping her to her feet and pressing her close. He'd gone from passion to protection in seconds.

"I'm okay." She clung to him, terrified of losing him in the pitch dark, but then she lost her footing and slammed into a wall. Around them, torches roared to life.

"Impressive."

"It wasn't me."

Aaron pulled her back, and she froze. In front of them was a large wooden door with torches on either side.

"Do you hear that?" Alex asked.

"Hear what?"

"Whispers."

Calling me.

Alex reached her hand out and touched the wood of the door.

"We should wait until we have the generals and Megesti."

Aaron slid his hand into hers and led her away from the door. "I think I see some stairs at the end of this hallway."

Aaron took a torch from the wall—another appeared in place.

"Your mother's doing?" Aaron asked.

Alex squeezed Aaron's hand, and they crept toward the light. It was coming from the top of a spiral stair. Aaron went ahead as they made their way up the stairs. They both stopped when they reached the top, finding themselves behind a painting looking into a room.

"It's the hall," Alex said. "We're in a secret passage, like in Warren."

Aaron felt around the wall. There was a click; the painting swung forward, and he jumped through the opening with Alex.

"Your Highnesses?" Matthew moved from the main entrance and gaped at them and the open painting. He frowned, looking at Aaron's bare chest.

"Matthew, I need Megesti. I think we found the books," Alex said, ignoring the looks exchanged between Aaron and her father's general.

Fifteen minutes later, Megesti, Randal, Michael, and Stefan gathered in the hall. Aaron got his shirt back before the others arrived, but both Randal and Stefan eyed him suspiciously, making Alex suspect Matthew spoke to them. Alex was so desperate to get back to the door that Aaron struggled to keep her in the hall until everyone was ready to investigate.

"How *did you* find this place?" Stefan asked.

"We found my mother's bedroom through a secret door in the library. We were exploring it, and I got emotional—and ended up cracking us to the door. You know I can't control when I crack."

Stefan glared at Aaron. "Emotional?"

Alex thrust her hand out to Stefan. "My mother said it would require a blood spell. I need your dagger."

Stefan sighed but obliged. Without another word, Alex grabbed Megesti and dragged him through the painting and down the stairs to the door. By the time the others arrived, she'd already cut her palm. Making a fist, she let her blood drip on the floor. A chilly wind circled, and the click of a lock echoed. Alex tried the door, but nothing happened. Megesti grabbed the dagger from her and followed suit. When his blood hit the floor, another click echoed, and the massive wooden door swung inward.

Alex grabbed the torch, but brawny arms pulled her back. Expecting Aaron, she spun around and found herself face to face with Randal.

"I go in first, Alexandria. If you follow me, I'll expect one of your guards or your betrothed to remain at your side. Otherwise, you follow at the back."

"Betrothed?" Stefan's voice became high-pitched.

Aaron slipped his hand into Alex's and twisted her ringed hand at Stefan. "You're stuck with me."

Stefan's face went slack as Alex pulled their hands down again.

Please, not right now.

Randal went in first followed by Stefan and Megesti. Michael let Aaron and Alex go next, and he came with Matthew. When they reached the end of the narrow hallway, both Alex and Megesti gasped. They were in the most intricate lab any of them had ever seen. Victoria had lined the entire back wall with bookcases, and in the center sat a massive table, intricately carved from a wood Alex couldn't identify, with three simple stools on one side. Once Randal entered, a fireplace roared to life. The other walls were covered with shelves filled with jars of powder, flowers, herbs, and all manner of unexpected animal parts and oddities. There was a bag of healing supplies similar to the one Alex had treasured at the camp, a few tins, a long dead plant, a dagger, and a small doll. The dagger seemed to pull Alex to it, and when she unsheathed it, the red blade glinted in the firelight.

My grandfather's sword had a red blade. Why is it red?

Alex slipped it back in the sheath, replaced the dagger, and turned her attention to the books.

"Are they whispering?" Megesti asked her.

Aaron joined Alex and Megesti near the books. They each pulled a book from different parts of the shelves. Aaron opened his, but when he held it up, the book was blank. Megesti's was full of words, and when Alex opened hers, she gasped.

The Journal of Alexandria, Daughter of Cassandra yr. 1301.

"It's our grandmother's journal. My namesake."

"Why is mine blank?" Aaron asked. The others all grabbed books, but theirs were also blank.

"They're protected," Megesti said. "Only those with the blood of the line can read them. The same as the door."

Alex took the book from Aaron. When she opened it, the pages had words. She flipped to the front page. *The Legacy of Merlin the Great.* She held it up to Megesti.

"Merlin wrote that book!"

"We've found the books we are looking for." Alex's hand went to her mouth as she looked at them all. After a few deep breaths, she ran her fingers along their spines, tears coming to her eyes.

I can do this. I can learn to control this tornado of power raging through me.

Everyone jumped when a loud bang sounded from above. With a glance, the generals sprang into action.

"Alexandria, stay with Matthew, Aaron, and Megesti," Randal ordered. "The rest of you, come with me."

Aaron grabbed the general. "I am more than capable of helping."

The general spun and glared at Aaron the way he'd look down at a spoiled child. "I apologize, *Your Highness*. I assumed you'd follow Datten tradition and protect your betrothed. Stefan, remain with the princess."

Aaron stepped back and took Alex's hand. "No, I'll stay with Alex."

Randal nodded, and they hurried up the stairs to investigate.

A louder bang came from upstairs followed by shouting. Matthew went rigid, and Alex grabbed onto Aaron as thuds echoed through the lab. Her heart pounded as Aaron wrapped his arm around her to stop her trembling. A crack sounded beside them as Lygari appeared.

"Congratulations, cousin. Since you have tied yourself to the prince, you'll want to accept my father's offer for training."

"Never," Aaron said, stepping between Alex and Lygari.

"I wasn't talking to you, whelp."

"I'm not going anywhere."

"It's only a matter of time before you hurt someone *else* with your blossoming powers." A sneer spread across his face followed by a hard laugh.

Lygari made a move, and Aaron lunged after him, but then a crack echoed, and Lygari appeared behind Alex and grabbed her arm, cracking them away.

"Let me go!"

Alex wrenched away from Lygari and fell to the stone floor. Moorloc and Kruft were fighting her guards. Moorloc stood in the middle of the hall. His arms were raised, and he had guards pinned up on the wall across from him.

No, no, no!

Alex could hear them gasping for breath. Scrambling to her feet, Alex threw herself against Moorloc, breaking the spell and sending her men crumpling to the ground. Moorloc spun around, his eyes flashing violet.

"You don't scare me. I'm all you have left of my mother," Alex said, staring defiantly at him. Footsteps grew louder behind her until the sound of the painting slamming shut silenced them.

"Alex, look out!" Michael shouted.

Burning pain tore through her shoulder. Alex shrieked and spun to find Kruft holding a bloody dagger. He struck her with his free hand, and Alex fell to the ground.

"If you touch her again, I'll kill you, you dishonorable brute." The painting flew open, and Aaron raced toward Alex, but Moorloc threw him back with a flick of his wrist.

Alex's temper roared to life, overpowering her as fireplaces erupted in flames. She rose from the floor, and with the blood running down her arm, she raised both arms—and the winds came.

Never before had her weather been so violent. It threw everyone except the sorcerers against a wall, and the debris on the floor took flight, whirling around the hall at treacherous speeds.

"Someone's in a mood!" Lygari laughed.

The wind quickened when Alex bared her teeth and stared down her uncle and cousin. Her temper boiled over as the wind and debris formed a vortex in the center of the room, engulfing the sorcerers. Alex could hear shouts but not their words.

"You call this control, princess?" Moorloc asked.

With Moorloc's taunt, Alex lost what little control was left. She screamed, and her powers exploded out of her. Alex then dropped to her knees and retched, and when the vortex halted, it catapulted the debris throughout the room.

Lygari grabbed Kruft, and they cracked away.

Moorloc stood in front of Alex, clucking his tongue as he looked at her. "Your mother would be so disappointed. So much pain and destruction because of your arrogance."

No. No. No!

Time slowed as Alex looked around. Debris had hit everyone. Some were bleeding, others had black eyes or bruises already forming. Alex had to blink to focus on people's faces. All she could see were the wounds, the bruises, the scattered debris.

Aaron was kneeling on the ground, and Alex watched a red stain grow as it soaked his silver shirt where his hand pressed into his stomach. He was arguing with Megesti to help Matthew with Stefan.

Then time returned to normal speed.

"Stefan!" Alex shrieked, seeing the torch embedded in his chest. Blood poured from the wound and coated his lips. Alex staggered to her feet when Moorloc grabbed her injured arm.

"Come with me and I'll make sure he doesn't die."

Don't scream.

Alex ignored the searing pain, wrenched her arm from Moorloc, and snarled at him. "Never!"

"They'll die without my help."

Alex felt a fire burn in her as a rage she'd never felt awakened.

Moorloc stared at her. Wide-eyed terror filled his face as he stepped back. "As you wish."

Alex rushed to help put pressure on Stefan's wound.

"Merlock!" Aaron screamed.

"Good luck, brother," Moorloc cackled and cracked away.

"What happened?" Merlock asked, rushing to Aaron.

"Stefan first."

"No, Aaron. I can see how badly he's hurt. Let me see you."

Aaron stood up, letting Merlock examine his wound. Alex cried and felt nauseated at having caused his injury, but there was no anger on Aaron's face, only love. Alex went to him, and he grabbed her hand.

"It's deep, Your Highness. We need the doctors. I'll get you to Datten, and Edward's physician will assist me with Stefan. The rest of you will need to ride back."

"Heal Alex first," Aaron said.

"No. I don't need it. I'll be fine by the time we arrive in Warren." Alex squeezed Aaron's hands.

"Books?" Stefan choked on the blood in his throat.

The books! Please, no!

Alex leaped over some debris and sprinted toward the painting that her tornado had ripped from the wall, descending the stairs so fast she tripped at the bottom. She sucked her breath as her palms and knees slammed into the hard stone. When she forced herself up, she ran so hard the torches couldn't ignite fast enough to light her way.

When she arrived in the lab, her heart shattered. She dropped to her knees in front of the empty bookcase and sobbed.

It was all for nothing. It's my fault. I brought them here. If they die, it's all my fault!

"I'm sorry, Alex," Michael said. He squatted beside her and rubbed her back.

"I'm also sorry, Alexandria, but we need to leave," Randal said. "Your father will panic after he sees Stefan and Prince Aaron arriving so injured."

"Can I have a minute, Randal? I don't want them knowing it was for nothing yet." Her entire body convulsed as the pain and terror swallowed her.

Randal patted her back. "Michael will wait for you at the top of the stairs. I'll prepare the horses."

After they left, Alex exhaled to compose herself. She took one last glance around her mother's lab, grabbed the dagger she'd found earlier, and swallowed.

"Moorloc ... I summon you."

CHAPTER 53
ALEX

Alex collected all the books and ledgers in her mother's room to bring back. The group rode hard in heavy silence through the dark night, arriving in Warren as the sun was rising over the glistening sea. After the horrors they'd endured that night, the morning looked beautiful, and it filled Alex with rage.

Edward was waiting on the path. After one look at Alex, he dismounted and ran toward her. In seconds, Alex was off Flash and engulfed by Edward's arms. She felt his body heave as he sobbed. She let herself cry with him.

"Tell me they're all right." Alex said once their sobs quieted. Everyone except Randal had continued on to the castle.

"They're alive, and that's all we can ask for right now. Are *you* all right?"

Alex shook her head. "It's my fault. I caused this. I was so excited I found my mother's home, her world. I wasn't careful."

"You cannot blame yourself for Moorloc's actions."

"They got hurt because of *me*. Stefan is my guard, and Aaron was there because he came after me."

"Did you accept his apology?"

"He proposed and then put himself in danger to protect me. I can't be responsible for Datten losing him too." Sobs burst out of her as Edward squeezed her. Alex buried her face in his shirt.

"Have you accepted him?"

Alex nodded. "But now I worry I'll only be a danger to him."

Edward chuckled. "If you knew half the trouble Aaron got himself into, you wouldn't worry. He loves you, and nothing will keep him from you. It's how Datten men are."

"I don't want to leave you ... or Warren." Alex's voice trembled.

"You won't because I won't let them take you."

Alex focused on her father. "You knew I'd choose him."

"I suspected," he replied as they mounted their horses and rode to the castle. "After you were betrothed to Daniel, your mother told me with certainty you would marry into Datten but not by Daniel. Only recently did I realize she was right."

"Then why give me the choice? Was it to give you power over Emmerich?"

"While I enjoy having power over Datten for a change, I gave you the choice because you deserved the chance to choose for love and not have Aaron forced on you. I hoped your mother was right, but you could've picked another, and I would have lived with Emmerich being furious with me for that." He sighed and shook his head. "I just got you back, and I don't relish the thought of you leaving."

"We both know Aaron loves Warren. He'll stay as long as possible," Alex said.

They arrived at the courtyard, and several stable boys were waiting to take their horses.

"Randal will take Stefan's place as your head guard for the time being while my doctor sees to his injuries," Edward said.

"Who'll guard you?"

"Matthew. I'd rather the general with three daughters watch you."

"Your Highness," Randal said. "You should have the doctor check your shoulder."

Alex reminded Randal of the gifts she had inherited from her mother and assured her father she was fine. Then she demanded to see her men before she'd rest.

Edward nodded to Randal. "I'll take her. Aaron is in Datten at the moment explaining things to his parents and being seen by their doctor. Stefan is in my room."

Tension, pain, and disappointment hit her as soon as she opened the door. The doctor was stitching up the gash on Julius's arm while Michael held him still. Alex took Julius's hand, and he gave her a weak smile. When she spotted General Bishop in the corner, her face flushed.

"Don't be ashamed, princess," Matthew said. "We've gotten worse injuries from royal decisions."

"I can't help feeling responsible," Alex said.

"It's good you feel responsible for your men," Edward said. "But you didn't mean to get them hurt, so you shouldn't feel guilty about that. Each of them would give up their life for you. Your powers are a force of nature. So until you learn to manage them, you do your best. That's all we ask."

Michael and Julius nodded, but Alex sighed and looked down.

If I knew how to use my healing powers, no one would ever suffer for me. This is what my uncle should be teaching me.

Once the doctor finished with Julius's stitches, Alex crept

next door to Stefan's room. Warren knight rooms were identical: a gigantic bed, a fireplace, a simple wardrobe, and, in the furthest corner, a dummy wearing their armor. The bedroom belonged to General Nial, but Edward had Stefan put here.

Jessica sat in a chair beside Stefan's bed, holding his hand and watching over him. Alex couldn't bring herself to look at either Wafner; instead, she focused on the back of Jessica's chair. It was one of the reading chairs from the royal suites. A second one sat empty beside her.

Alex squeezed Jessica's shoulder. "How is he?"

"Merlock and the doctor got all the broken torch pieces out. But the wound is deep, and he lost so much blood. Merlock worries the torch hit his lung or caused internal bleeding or an infection. He tried a few different healing spells. Now Stefan is in a magical sleep to help with the pain."

"Where's your father? He should be here."

"Merlock and Aaron are in Datten to retrieve him. Aaron refused to let anyone else deliver *this* news. He's worried about his parents' reaction."

"May I join you until your father arrives?"

Jessica looked up at Alex with teary, red eyes. "Thank you. Edith sat with me but she needed rest."

"You need rest too. I give you my word I won't leave his side until your father arrives."

"I'll stay with them," Michael said from the doorway.

"You'll both stay?" Jessica asked. "All right. You're his family too. I'll rest ... but just for a little."

Michael rushed to her side as Jessica stood up. The love between them was so obvious.

Is that what Aaron and I look like?

Jessica finished examining Michael's black eye and brushed a bit of dirt off his uniform. She kissed his cheek and left. Michael pushed the second chair next to the first and sat.

Alex forced herself to look at Stefan, swallowing hard at the sight.

Why is there still blood on your neck and shoulders? Couldn't they wash you?

The doctor had wrapped his chest in layers of bandages, but the blood was already seeping through, and his skin was pale. Alex turned to the doorway. "I need some warm water and rags."

When Matthew returned with the basin, Michael held it for her while Alex washed the remaining blood off. Then she sat in Jessica's chair and held Stefan's hand. Michael put his arm around her, and they sat in silence, holding vigil over Stefan until Alex fell asleep on Michael's shoulder.

A HAND NUDGED HER. When her eyes popped open, she saw blue eyes staring at her.

"I'm going to bring you to your bed," Aaron said.

Alex struggled against his arms. "No. I promised Jessica—"

"I'm here." Jerome squatted beside her. "Thank you for staying—and cleaning him properly."

"He's done it for me."

"You go rest. We'll be here," Michael said.

Alex looked from Jerome to Stefan. Her heart hurt to leave him.

Aaron rubbed her back. "He'd want you to rest. There isn't anything you can do here for him right now. You need to get your strength back. Eat or sleep?"

Alex's stomach rumbled. "Eat."

Aaron found her hand, and, squeezing it, they slipped out of the room.

"I can't face anyone," she said.

"Go to my room. I'll bring the food there."

Alex held onto his hand as he tried to leave.

Aaron turned back and kissed her cheek. "I'm all right."

Alex made her way to Aaron's room and left the door ajar. Alex saw her old copy of *The Iliad* on the bookshelf. She picked it up and sat on Aaron's bed.

It's all my fault. How long before he changes his mind? Until he realizes I'm not worth the trouble?

"You can't have that back."

Aaron came into the room with a tray of bread, cheese, and smoked meat, kicking the door shut behind him. Alex scurried off the bed and took the tray from him.

"I can carry a tray, Alex."

She ignored him and placed the tray on the chest at the end of the bed and turned around. "Show me."

"Alex—"

"I need to see it. I know you don't want to hurt me, but I need to know what I did to you. To remember the next time I lose my temper."

Aaron kissed her before he pulled his shirt off, and Alex looked him over.

Chest fine. Arms fine. Abdomen—

Alex counted the stitches from his hip bone through his belly button.

Thirty-one. Thirty-one stitches from a wound that gutted you.

Bile rose from her stomach. Alex pulled away, but Aaron stopped her. He held her so gently Alex whimpered. Even after everything, he was always gentle with her.

"Look at me," he said, and Alex complied. "I love you. I don't care what happened today. You're going to use those books to gain control of everything, and then you'll be able to heal everyone."

Alex burst into tears and pulled away.

"What did I say?"

"Moorloc took the books! When we went back, they'd vanished. It was all for *nothing*."

Aaron's face fell, but he recovered in a blink. He moved to her and tilted her chin up. "I still don't care. You're amazing, and *we* will figure this all out, but not this second. Right now, you need food and rest, so afterward we can tell the world you're going to marry me."

Alex laughed. "You still want to marry me after my vortex skewered you?"

"More than before, but I do think you should change."

Alex glanced down and realized she hadn't even changed since meeting Aaron in her mother's room.

That feels forever ago.

Aaron pressed his lips to hers and slid his arms around her waist, pulling her against him. Alex felt the familiar heat rise in her core as she thought of his touches from the day before.

"We eat so you can rest," Aaron said, his giant smile spanning his entire face.

"I agreed to marry you, impaled you, and you expect me to sleep?"

"I want you to change so I can *burn* that shirt. Then eat something. It's been a rough day, but we have each other, and everything else can wait."

Alex clutched her necklace as Aaron walked to his wardrobe. He held out a clean shirt to her, facing away, but Alex lowered his hand.

Enough of that. If I'm yours and you're mine, I'm done being shy.

Alex held her hands over her head and stared at him. Aaron swallowed as he untied the top, grasped the hem of her shirt and dragged it over her head, careful not to pull her hair. Aaron remained facing her, and they stood in silence until Aaron cupped her cheeks and kissed her. Afterward, he held his red Datten shirt over Alex's head, allowing her to slip into it. He threw her bloody one into the fire, and they watched it turn to ash.

"Sorry it's big."

Alex sniffed his shirt.

Pine and dew. Home.

"It's perfect. And you're right. We'll eat. The rest can wait."

As they ate their breakfast, Alex felt the weight of the previous night build on her. Aaron was staring at her. "It's hitting you, isn't it?"

Alex nodded, trying to hold back the emotions that seemed determined to free themselves.

He moved their food out of the way and pulled her to him. "What do you need?"

She could only manage a whimper.

Aaron lay down on the bed, and she nestled against the uninjured side of his chest. He wrapped his arms around her, kissed her head, and ran his fingers down her back. Soothed by his affectionate touches, Alex was soon asleep.

Edith and Michael's voices sounded far away.

"This is a recent development."

"I *told* you," Michael said.

"Well, I would be more concerned if it weren't for the giant ring on her finger."

"Datten does like to show off, doesn't it?"

"Why are you talking so much?" Alex asked. She snuggled her pillow only to realize it wasn't a pillow.

"Because you're in *my* room, not yours," Aaron said. He kissed her forehead.

Alex bolted upright. "How long have I been asleep?"

"Hours. It's almost dinner," Edith said. She looked at Alex's hand, which somehow remained on Aaron even as she bolted awake.

"You needed it," Michael said.

"How's Stefan?"

"The same," Edith said. "The doctor said it'll take a few days to see any sort of improvement. Right now, *the same* is all we should hope for. I'm here to get you cleaned up for dinner."

"Who cares about food with all this going on?"

"Your father. He's requested you both join him for a private meal. Something about putting your heads together to get Datten to loosen their grip on a certain ... *prince*," Edith said.

Randal's voice came from the door. "Your father intends to keep you in Warren, which means ensuring Prince Aaron remains here. Jerome sent me to ensure His Highness allows the doctor and Merlock to examine his wound. Apparently, you have a habit of refusing to allow anyone to see to your injuries. Since you are betrothed to the Princess of Warren, I won't tolerate that."

Aaron looked horrified. "I thought Jerome was bad," he said.

Alex kissed his cheek. "Do it for me?"

Aaron frowned but nodded. He kissed her back and followed Randal, letting Alex go with Michael and Jessica to her room.

CHAPTER 54
ALEX

Dinner was in the spare hall. Alex tried to act normal, but as usual, being beside Aaron made her feel out of sorts. Aaron's hand rested on her leg, and she could hardly stand it.

God, your lips are so soft, and they taste amazing. And you always smell wonderful, like the woods at dawn. All I want to do is get you alone and rip your shirt off and let you rip my dress off me and have me.

"Alexandria?"

Alex startled and realized her father was talking to her. She blushed. "Sorry, I was just thinking."

Edward discussed what they should ask Datten for in the betrothal contract. They added some extra demands they could compromise on in order to ensure they'd get what they absolutely wanted, which was Alex and Aaron both staying in Warren. They refused to be separated, which Edward agreed with. They decided Datten would receive the first wedding ceremony as the way to get Guinevere on their side. One last request Alex made was that she and Aaron would have full control over which future child ruled which kingdom.

Aaron and Edward exchanged looks then turned to Alex. "You know something?" Edward said. "I recognize that look. Your mother had the same look."

"Warrens know," Alex said, taking a bite of venison.

"Aaron?"

Aaron smiled at Alex and turned to Edward. "I'm going to marry your daughter. I have everything I want. All I *need* is for you to sign the betrothal with my father so she can't change her mind."

Alex caressed Aaron's cheek and kissed him. Then she gasped, realizing she'd kissed Aaron in front of her father. Blushing, she turned to Edward. His eyes were soft, and his smile was almost as large as the day she'd returned home.

"You're going to have to stop blushing whenever you kiss me," Aaron chided. Alex rolled her eyes.

"Now the only thing left to decide is how to bring Datten up to speed," Edward said.

"I want my parents to hear the news from me. Last night, they woke to the news of Stefan and my injuries."

"Do they know how you got injured?" Alex asked.

"They know the truth. A spell went wrong when Lygari and Moorloc were trying to abduct you. They know it was your spell, but they also know it went wrong because Kruft stabbed you. No one blames you."

"All right," said Edward. "Aaron, you'll head to Datten tonight. I'll go tomorrow after you return. Don't tell your father about our plans. I'd like him to spend the night being excited and celebrating Datten and Warren uniting before I go in with demands."

They finished their dinner, and Aaron offered to walk Alex back to her room before he left for Datten.

"Do you have to leave?"

"If I don't go now, my parents will be asleep, and I'll have to stay until the morning."

Alex pulled Aaron down a small side hall. "Or you could go in the morning and spend the night with me."

"Have some plans for me, princess?" Aaron kissed her, making her knees weak.

"Would they keep you here?"

"I'll leave for one night, and then I'm yours every night."

Alex sighed and made a pouty face.

"You made that same face when we were little. Who would have thought twelve years later that little princess would become my bride?"

"Please hurry back."

Aaron laughed and kissed her before leaving to summon Merlock.

Alex breathed deeply to regain her composure. She grabbed her satchel with her mother's books from her room and added Stefan's favorite books to it. When she arrived in Stefan's room, the fire roared, making her feel hot and bathing him in an eerie red light.

At least he's got some color back.

Alex took the hot water off the fire and rolled up her dress sleeves. Jerome held him up for her, and she replaced his blood-soaked bandages with new ones. Alex was one of the few people the doctor would allow to assist, hoping it would help Stefan heal.

If I knew how to heal you, I would. I'm so sorry, Stefan.

Michael joined her in the room, letting Jerome get some sleep. Alex looked at Michael with tears in her eyes. He nodded, and she climbed into the bed beside Stefan. She snuggled up to him like she had when she was younger and scared. Michael sat in the chair beside her and rubbed her back until she fell asleep next to Stefan, Michael still reading to him about battle plans.

CHAPTER 55
ALEX

Alex awoke to Edith shaking her shoulder. She slid off the bed, leaving Stefan under Jessica's vigilant eyes, and went to her room with Randal.

"Why isn't he waking up?" Alex asked.

"Merlock's spell. He won't wake until he's healed or can handle the pain. Merlock healed Aaron first because Stefan insisted, but then he was too weak to fully heal Stefan," Randal explained.

"Stefan did that?"

"He did," Edith replied.

Alex sighed and got ready for the day. She and Edith talked for a long while as they strolled through the gardens until Alex realized she'd forgotten about the way she'd left things with Cameron. Edith explained Aaron had been to see his uncle before going after her, and Edward had informed the council of the betrothal. Alex told Edith about the kiss she'd witnessed between Jessica and Michael. Edith was so ecstatic she made Alex tell the story three times.

Afterward, they went to join Edith's older sisters, Abigail

and Diana, for tea. As they neared the spare hall, Edith touched Alex's arm. "Did anyone tell you what this tea is about?"

"Yes. My father said your sisters will help me learn what Aaron expects of me after we're married." Edith's sisters both had husbands already.

"And do you know what that entails?" Edith asked as they opened the doors.

"No, but how bad can it be?"

"You could have warned me about Warren's tradition!"

"Which tradition?" Aaron's eyes widened.

Alex had been sitting on the bed trying to find books to read to Stefan when Aaron entered. "Explaining wedding night expectations to newly betrothed noblewomen?"

An impish smile spread across his face, and she threw a pillow at him—hard.

"Exactly," she said. "During my tea, they explained in *great detail* what happens when—" Her cheeks burned.

"Oh." Aaron crossed the room and sat beside her. He caressed her knee and kissed her. "Are you afraid of ... that?"

A shiver ran through Alex as she remembered what Edith's sisters had said. *Maybe if we got it over with.* "Of course not."

Aaron raised his eyebrows. Staring back, Alex pushed the books off the bed and gripped Aaron's face, kissing him before she pulled him into the bed with her.

Lost in each other, they didn't hear the door.

Alex sat in the ornate chair at Stefan's side, looking him over for signs of healing. A tattered military book rested on her lap.

Wake up!

Aaron watched her from his chair on the other side of Stefan's bed.

"I love seeing you wear my great-grandmother's ring—my mother told me she removed it the day you were born. And remind me to send Edith's sisters a nice present."

"That's not funny," Alex said. Opening the book, she flipped to a certain chapter.

"*Datten Battle Strategies*?" Aaron raised his eyebrows.

"Pay attention. You'll learn something," Alex said. "Chapter twelve. 'Dealing with Stubborn Princes.'"

Aaron was at her side in seconds. "It doesn't say that!" He looked over Alex's shoulder. "'Dealing with Stubborn Royals.'"

"Close enough." Alex smirked, and Aaron kissed her, snatching the book from her.

"Oh, a Balthild Wafner book. He likes this?"

"Stefan's tastes in books have always leaned toward military matters." Alex held her hand out, and Aaron gave back her book.

"Do I need to watch you two even *more closely*?" Michael asked from the doorway.

"Not *anymore*." Aaron sat back down and smiled.

"It's official now?"

"Signed by both kings and everything," Aaron replied. His smile turned into a self-satisfied smirk. "For better or worse, the Princess of Warren belongs to me."

Alex lifted her eyes from the book and stared at Aaron. She waved her hand, and his entire mug of ale dumped itself onto his lap. Michael and Alex burst into laughter.

"Someone's getting better with control," Edith said.

"I deserved it," Aaron said. "Since you have company, I'll go change and check on our horses." He kissed Alex's cheek and headed out.

"I'm here for details and not about the ring," Edith said, winking at Alex.

"You heard about Edward catching them half-naked in Aaron's bed with their hands down each other's pants too?" Michael asked, and Edith nodded with an eager look on her face.

"Does *everyone* know about that?" Alex asked.

"Yes," Michael said.

"Your father's yelling ... carries," Edith said.

Alex tried not to die of embarrassment. She told Edith enough that Michael soon became uncomfortable and fled. They admired the ring and worked out the schedule for watching Stefan the next day. When Jerome arrived, Edith left for bed. Alex wanted to stay, but he insisted she rest. Alex gave him Stefan's favorite book and let him know where she'd left off. She'd redressed Stefan's wound and noticed the swelling was going down.

Alex arrived in her bedroom and dropped her dress on the floor, picking out a nightgown. She braided her hair as she trudged up to her bed where Aaron was waiting dressed only in sleeping pants.

"Didn't you hear my father's order? None of *this* in my bedroom?" she said.

"No expectations. You looked tired, and I know how much you struggle to sleep alone. And while my bed smells of flowers and sea air thanks to how much time you've spent in it recently, nothing compares to the real thing." Aaron dropped his legs off the side and pulled Alex onto his lap.

"Thank you." Alex leaned her head against Aaron's collarbone, and he wrapped his arms around her, locking her into place. She'd forgotten how strong Aaron was as he moved them to her pillows despite his injury. Alex traced the scar on his shoulder and avoided the side with the wound. "Does your stomach hurt? After this afternoon?" Alex asked.

"A little. But I'd endure the stitches all over again to be with you."

"You mean between my legs," Alex teased, and Aaron choked, making Alex giggle. "You'll have to get used to that. I won't be keeping my thoughts to myself any longer."

"What changed?"

"You're mine, and I'm yours. I won't be a silent Datten queen—that means I have to be honest with you." Alex looked down at Aaron's chest and sighed. Her heart hurt looking at him.

Aaron moved his hand to her cheek. "I know you're keeping something from me."

Alex's back arched, and her eyes widened.

"After how I behaved, I understand. When you're ready to talk—I'll be ready to listen." Aaron pulled her close, and she smelled the woods on him. It calmed her as she snuggled into him.

The premonition dream started as soon as Alex's eyes closed.

Gone were the fragments of a single event. Alex watched multiple events unfold simultaneously. Then each event split into multiple visions. It quickly became frightening and overwhelming. She watched the castle tornado explode, injuring Stefan and Aaron. Datten and Warren's armies stood on a field engulfed in fog and fire. Jessica screamed, and Alex spun to see her holding a bleeding Michael. Merlock and Megesti appeared beside her—followed by Lygari and Moorloc. Her mother's ghost appeared dressed in the Titan of Cassandra robe. More possibilities swirled and flew by.

"Merlock, your oath is near." Victoria held her hand out to Alex, and when they touched, everything stopped. Victoria stared at Alex, and behind her mother, a single vision moved. Alex and all those she

loved stood across from each other on opposite sides of a battlefield. "People you love will die on this battlefield."

Alex stepped back as the vision split into all the distinct possibilities.

"Remember, you're my daughter and possess my gifts and curse. You must harness the peace in you or you will lose everything, including yourself."

Victoria vanished, and the visions all moved.

Alex couldn't think as the images swirled around her. A man she didn't recognize held a red blade and sat on his horse beside Aaron. His skin was dark, but not like her father's, and his eyes were purple. Dressed for battle, Alex realized there was a third army—Datten and Warren were fighting Moorloc's mercenaries.

Ships burned at the Warren port. Castles crumbled. Aaron held a bloody sword, a monstrous expression on his face. Megesti's eyes flashed violet. A three-headed dog. A tidal wave swallowing Alex, and so many more visions she couldn't focus on them fast enough.

Then she saw an image of her with Aaron and walked to it. They were dancing at a wedding—he was older with gray hair. A bride who looked identical to Alex was dancing with a young man with familiar fire-red hair. This was the only vision without fire, rivers of blood, and endless death.

Alex looked at Merlock and Megesti, watching the same dream she had. Beside it was the worst one. Aaron and Alex faced each other. Aaron told her he loved her. Alex's eyes flashed black, and she stabbed Aaron. The visions vanished, and Alex screamed.

Alex couldn't breathe. The air became blood in her lungs. Hot and thick, it stuck to her insides as she gasped and fought the powerful arms that surrounded her. Panic coursed through her veins. The arms weren't Stefan's, and the room wasn't hers. Alex fought harder when a voice broke through the fog of terror.

"Alex. You're safe."

Strong arms pinned hers down, and before Alex could react, Aaron's lips were on hers, and everything came back. His body pressed against hers, pushing away the terror, and his woodsy smell calmed her breathing. Alex deepened their kiss.

Aaron. My friend, my love, my future husband. Mine. I'm safe.

She opened her eyes and looked up at Aaron as he kissed her forehead and released her.

A crack erupted, and they turned to see Merlock standing at the foot of Alex's bed with Megesti just behind. Merlock shook his head and demanded, "What in Hades did you do?"

Alex locked eyes with her uncle but said nothing.

Aaron said, "Don't speak to the future Queen of Datten like that."

"Stay out of this, Aaron," Megesti said, trembling.

"Go away," Alex said with a snarl.

"How did you bring us into your vision? We saw everything," Merlock said.

"Get out!" Alex snapped.

"Wait!" Aaron ran his hand down her back lovingly. "Does this have anything to do with what you needed to tell me?"

"I don't know. Maybe? I have no idea how I pulled them into my vision."

Aaron grabbed Alex's hands. "Then we'll try to figure it out together."

Alex sighed and nodded. "Merlock, please meet us in the library in half an hour. We need to figure out this vision."

"And come up with a plan for getting back those books," Aaron said, standing up.

Alex gave him a small, weak smile. Merlock nodded and cracked himself away with Megesti.

"What if we can't?" Alex asked.

"Failure isn't an option."

Alex couldn't help but laugh at that. "And yet everyone

rants about what a pacifist you are. How are we going to get my books back from my psychotic uncle?"

Aaron pulled Alex close. "War. I'll do *whatever* it takes to get them back. Until you, I've had nothing worth going to war for."

Aaron stared at Alex with such intensity it made her entire body heat, her heart quicken, and her throat go dry all at once. Aaron cupped her cheek and kissed her gently.

"Get dressed. I have people to shock by declaring war on your uncle."

CHAPTER 56
ΛARON

"Y ou? *You* want to declare war on Moorloc?" Randal asked, rubbing his temple as he shifted his gaze from Edward to Jerome and then back to Aaron across the table.

"Yes." Aaron refused the seat Edward offered him, choosing to stand in Datten form. Aaron could feel the true Prince of Datten emerging from inside of him.

"You don't believe in war," Edward replied.

"In most cases I still don't, but my betrothal with Alex changed things. Moorloc stole the books she needs to gain control of her powers. I'm going to get them back." He squeezed Alex's shoulders as she sat at the table in front of him.

"Merlock, what happens if we don't get the books?" Edward asked.

Alex's trembling hand squeezed Aaron's. When he looked up, he realized Merlock was sweating. Merlock told them the danger everyone would be in if Alex couldn't master her powers. "Our best case would be that she goes mad."

Randal was on his feet, slamming his hands on the table.

"Her choices cannot be to go mad or die in an accident. There has to be another!" He turned to Aaron. "We need your father. Warren cannot make these decisions without him."

"I agree with Randal. We need Emmerich," Edward said.

"No." Aaron squeezed Alex again. "You have Datten's crown prince and the general."

"Aaron, this isn't the battle to cut your teeth on. Alexandria's life may hang in the balance," Jerome said. Aaron recognized that face—the one Jerome wore whenever he went against his king's suggestion. Jerome was a patient man but would push if he needed to.

I'm used to being pushed by you.

"Why would I go mad?" Alex asked.

"Too much power at once can bring on madness," Merlock said. "Firstborn children get the power in our world. Corruption of power runs deep in our family. You cannot forget that, especially while learning. If you don't learn your limits, you'll destroy yourself."

Alex tugged Aaron's hand and looked up at him. She tried to speak but instead exhaled sharply. Aaron sat and hugged her. Everywhere they connected, she trembled.

I know you're scared, but you have me now. You're not alone in this.

"We agree we need those books. No one here will risk letting her teach herself," Aaron said. Jerome leaned over and whispered to Edward. They exchanged a glance and then turned back to Alex and Aaron.

"I'll give you three days to come up with a plan. Then I'm summoning your father, and *we'll* decide which plan we follow," Edward said.

"I accept your terms," Aaron said.

"We'll come up with our safest plan for retrieving the

books," Alex said, turning to the senior military men around them.

Aaron kissed her cheek, making her flush. Edward and Randal smiled at them. Jerome was stoic, but his eyes were sparkling.

Your eyes betray your pride in me, general.

As they walked toward the library, Aaron intertwined their fingers.

"Do you think they knew?" Alex asked.

"Knew what?"

"That when I accepted you, it would bring out the Datten in you?"

A loud thunk echoed as they entered the library. Upstairs, they found Megesti sorting books. They looked over the ones Megesti had gathered when Michael appeared in the stairway.

"I was told to report here because we're planning an adventure ...?"

A crack sounded as Merlock arrived.

"We're planning war," Aaron said.

"With whom?" Michael said, giving Alex a nervous look.

"Moorloc. We're going to war to get back my books," Alex said.

Michael took a seat on the bench beside Alex. "I'm in. Where's the castle?"

"I don't know exactly, only the area." Merlock rubbed his forehead, groaning.

"What about your premonition? Do you remember anything useful?" Megesti handed Aaron his book before he turned to face Alex.

"What do you mean?" Alex asked.

"Somehow, you pulled us into your dream, but we remember nothing now. Premonition gifts fall to the daughters," Merlock said.

Michael reached over and pinched Alex's shoulder.

"Ow!" Alex slapped him, making Aaron chuckle.

Michael raised a single eyebrow at her and rubbed her shoulder. "Concentrate," Michael said. "It's only been a few hours. That dream is still there. I know it is because if we were in the camp, you'd still be talking about it."

Alex closed her eyes and groaned. Then she placed her hands on the table, and when she opened her eyes, they were white.

"*There will be three armies before a crumbling castle. If you want to succeed, you need to find your Edward to become the king you're going to be,*" Alex whispered. "*Blood from the taken will show the castle. You will wield the blade of the fallen to vanquish the traitor. Beware the son who tries to atone for the father—he's not as he seems.*"

Alex went silent, and Michael gripped her shoulder so tightly his fingers turned white. Alex's head bobbed, and her body lurched forward, but Michael's hand kept her upright. When she opened her eyes and looked around, everyone was staring at her.

"Did it work?" Alex asked, and Michael nodded.

"I haven't seen a proper Cassandra vision since before my sister married your father," Merlock said.

"I don't understand," Aaron said, noting the fear on Alex's face. "You said to find my Edward? Isn't that you?"

"No." Alex laughed as relief filled her face. "I'm going to be your wife. Warren doesn't make your Edward. It's the faith and trust our fathers have in each other despite everything they've endured."

"Do you know who it is?" Michael asked.

"No. It isn't anyone I know," Alex said.

"What about the rest?" Aaron asked. "You said blood from the taken will show the castle."

"It has to mean Alex," Michael said. "They took you from Warren."

"I believe he's right, Alexandria," Merlock said. "You'll need to come with us."

"No," Aaron said, but Alex turned to him, clearing her throat.

"I will not be told how I'm allowed to help."

"But—"

"No," Alex said, glaring.

"Fine, but I'm going too."

They talked into the night, discussing options for finding the castle and what Alex's cryptic visions could have meant. By the time they headed for bed, exhaustion had set in, but Aaron couldn't leave Alex's side. Unconsciously, they found themselves outside his bedroom door. Alex grinned at Aaron, took his hand, and led him inside, closing the door behind them.

"I don't have expectations of you," Alex began. "I just—"

"Don't feel comfortable without Stefan there?" Aaron finished for her, and Alex nodded. "Stay with me. I love having you here." Aaron slipped his hands around her waist, pulled her to him, and kissed her. He caressed her back, found the ribbon of her corset, and loosened it.

"I have nothing to sleep in."

"You can sleep in anything you want—nothing, my shirt, or I'll fetch your nightgown." Aaron released her and grabbed one of his shirts.

Aaron couldn't help staring as she undressed. Noticing her skin flush, he turned his back to give her privacy, but she took his arm and turned him back to look at her. She touched his chest and leaned up to kiss him. With amazing speed, Alex pulled Aaron's shirt over his head and slipped out of her dress. While she did this, Aaron switched to his sleeping pants.

"So you learned," Alex teased.

"Learned?"

"To put on pants." Alex laughed. Aaron closed the distance between them in seconds, sliding his hand along the curve of her backside and kissed her. In his sleeping pants, there was no hiding what she did to him as the evidence pressed against her.

"Aaron." She swallowed hard, and then her eyes went wide. "I need a knife."

Aaron froze for a moment, but Alex squeezed his hand. "I need you to trust me."

Aaron nodded and, releasing her, grabbed his dagger from the table. Alex unsheathed it, and held out her hand. Exhaling, he placed his hand on hers, and then Alex sliced into his palm, before cutting hers. She interlocked their hands and whispered. "Blood of my blood, blood of your blood. Now both of us can see the castle."

Aaron's eyes grew wide as he looked down. A faint gold light engulfed their locked hands. As they pulled their hands apart, Aaron's palm was angry, but the cuts were already healing. He pulled her to him and kissed her more frantically than any kiss they'd shared before he led her toward his bed. After more vigorous kissing and caressing, exhaustion overcame them. Aaron wrapped his arms around her, clutching her, worried he'd wake up to her being gone and it all having been a beautiful dream.

CHAPTER 57
ALEX

Alex woke up feeling more rested than she had in months. She'd cocooned herself so fully in Aaron's arms that he grumbled when she wiggled and tightened his grip instead. One hand caressed her breast while the hand on her hip inched downward. Alex's body further warmed at his touch, and she moaned. The sound snapped the half-asleep prince out of his dreamy exploration.

"Morning," Alex whispered.

Aaron kissed her neck and hugged her. His muscular legs snaked around hers and locked onto them.

How are your legs so strong?

As if reading her mind, Aaron said, "Your legs feel amazing. Riding gives you a vise grip."

Alex swallowed hard, unable to chase away the image of Aaron at the jousting match on Thunder. When she shook it off, her brain replaced it with the image of him between her legs at the castle. Aaron nuzzled against her, and it took everything in her to resist Aaron's touch.

"What's wrong?" Aaron asked.

Alex grabbed his face and kissed him. "Nature calls."

Aaron laughed and kissed her more deeply before she scrambled out of bed. Aaron's room didn't have a bathing suite, so he always used the one in Daniel's room. When she opened the door to Daniel's room, however, she found Michael.

"Morning, princess. I'll let Edith know you're awake so she can bring you your dress. You can't very well go scampering around the castle in Aaron's shirt."

Alex frowned at having been caught sneaking out of Aaron's bedroom. Aaron arrived behind her.

"Prince Aaron," Michael said, nodding.

"Morning."

Michael looked at Alex. "With Stefan out of commission, protecting you will now fall on Randal, Matthew, and myself. The kings aren't taking any chances."

"Kings?"

"Our fathers will have insisted you're guarded. You're a Princess of Datten now too. It's normal."

Soon Edith arrived to get Alex into her favorite green dress. Afterward, she went to the library while Aaron snuck into the kitchen to get them something to eat. Alex found a spell book mixed into the stack of books they had pulled to review. In the time it took Aaron to fetch food, Alex had figured out how to unlock and lock a door with magic and could dry wet clothes while wearing them.

"Where'd you get that?" Aaron asked as Alex showed him some spells the moment he arrived.

"It was on the table. I suspect Merlock left it for me." Alex couldn't help but smile. Her powers felt like a raging storm that erupted out of her at will, but these minor spells let her feel that maybe she could learn to wield them one day. Alex took the larger baguette from Aaron's tray and took a bite, flipping through the book. Aaron looked over her shoulder at the words and chuckled.

"What?"

"The book's Megesti's. I'd recognize that chicken scratch anywhere."

"Then why is it here?"

Aaron wrapped his arms around her waist. "Megesti isn't so great with words either."

"Seems to be a Datten problem," Alex said, smirking.

"What I mean is, I think it's his way of welcoming you to the family. That's his first spell book. It was the one he was writing when my father was born. He was my age then."

Alex ran her fingers across the pages and smiled. "I'll be sure to thank him for it."

They spent the day in the library formulating a plan. Merlock had come up with a handful of possible locations for Moorloc's castle based on conversations with Victoria over the years. Alex noted anything else she could remember from her vision, but there wasn't much. She kept telling Aaron to find his Edward and laughing when he rolled his eyes. Megesti admitted to giving Alex the book, and she hugged him so tight he started coughing. That evening, Alex picked a new book to read to Stefan and said good night to Michael, Megesti, and Merlock before heading to her father's room. Aaron accompanied her as she read to Stefan from the Warren battle strategies book. When she finished reading, she sat on Aaron's lap for a bit.

"I'll leave you alone with him. I know you like to talk to him."

Alex squeezed him tighter. "Thank you. I didn't get to tell

him about the engagement before the accident. He saw the ring, but—"

Aaron let her stand up, and then he left the room. Alex sat back down on the chair and pulled it close to Stefan. She picked up his hand and stroked it.

"Stefan, I'm so sorry. You're going to be furious with me, but I *had to*."

ALEX CRIED the entire way back to Aaron's room, but she composed herself once she reached his door. He'd left his door unlocked, so she let herself in. Aaron rose the second she arrived. Her eyes were red from crying, but he waited until she was ready to come to him. When she did, Aaron wrapped his arms around her.

"I wanted him to wake up."

"I know." Aaron kissed her forehead and squeezed her. "What do you need? What can I do?"

"I don't want to wait."

Aaron stayed silent for some time before replying, "I have *no expectations*. I love you, and we are officially betrothed, so if you want to ..."

Don't blush. He needs to know you're serious.

Aaron kissed her and pulled her close, and as he did, Alex's body flamed with anticipation. Alex pulled back and stared at Aaron, and he understood. Holding her hand over her head, he spun her like when they danced then gripped her waist to stop her and untied the corset of her dress. Each gentle tug of the ribbon sent a desperate throb between her legs. After he finished, Alex turned to Aaron and pulled off his shirt, tossing it on the floor. She moved to kiss him, but his eyes went wide, and he ran to lock the door, making Alex laugh.

"My brother isn't here, is he?" Aaron asked, leaning against the locked door.

"No. He appears when he's needed or when he feels like it," Alex said.

Aaron reached for her hand. It was warm and clammy as he pulled her toward him. Standing before him, Alex leaned up to kiss him then stared into his eyes as she stepped back and slowly slipped her new red dress off her shoulders, letting it pool on the floor. Aaron's eyes widened, and he swallowed as he took in the sight of her. Her impatience brought a chill to the air despite the roaring fire, making her skin prickle with goosebumps and her nipples harden. Alex caressed his muscular chest as her heart hammered hers. She slid her arms around his neck to kiss him, but he scooped her up and carried her to his bed. Alex felt a flutter of nervousness run through her again. Edith's sisters had explained the mechanics but not the beginning.

Why aren't you just taking me like their husbands did? Is there something wrong with me?

"What?" Her voice was wavering. "I was told the man would handle ... things."

"Who told you that?"

"Edith's sisters. They said the first time will hurt."

"Those Nial sisters," Aaron said, shaking his head. He brought his knees onto the bed, moving toward her. She felt his eyes roaming from one part of her to the next.

"Not all men are demanding. I've overheard a lot of my father's men talk about their wives."

Aaron's arm looped behind her and slid her to the middle of his bed. Alex swallowed hard. "And?"

"I listened to the men who have had long and happy marriages. They all spoke of being gentle, never forcing, and making sure she enjoys it too. Did the sisters mention that?" Aaron pressed his lips softly to the little dip in Alex's neck.

Alex moaned before answering. "Yes. They said if you did *your part* right, nothing would ever compare."

Aaron kissed Alex's neck. "Then you know what to expect from me. At least once we've had the time to figure things out."

"What do you mean?"

Aaron had a mischievous glint in his eyes. "Cameron lied. I stayed away from maidens the same way they kept you away from men. There are no illegitimate heirs in Datten. It means after we have our proper Datten wedding, I plan to lock us in our bedroom for two weeks to figure out what makes you scream the loudest."

Alex grinned. "Why only two weeks?"

"I'm a quick learner—I intend to practice often."

Alex put her hand on Aaron's chest, feeling his heart pound as hard as hers. "I love you."

"I've always loved you." He slid his pants off and crawled across the bed toward her. Alex could feel his eyes soaking her in. When he reached her, she tried hard to stop trembling. He gently ran his fingers across her soft skin and kissed every part of her, tickling her.

"What are you doing?"

"Memorizing every bit of you," Aaron whispered. He kissed her neck, and she gasped. Alex felt Aaron watch her. He stared as her face flushed, and her nipples perked up from his every touch. He kissed her passionately and slipped his hand between her legs. Alex moaned at his yearning touch, and his blue eyes sparkled in the firelight.

"You can still change your mind. It's not too late to go back."

Stop being honorable.

Alex felt as if her heart would explode. "I'm not changing

my mind," she whispered and kissed him firmly, pressing herself into him. She encouraged his hand back, and he resumed exploring her. He kissed her all over, smiling at each sound he coaxed out of her.

Enough playing. I don't want to wait.

Her eyes locked onto his. "Aaron, I'm ready," she begged. Her hand trembled as she took his and moved it away, and, swallowing the lump in her throat, she spread her legs and watched his eyes travel down. Her breath caught in her throat as Aaron moved on top of her. The heat of his body made hers feel on fire.

The rest happened quickly. Alex felt Aaron's lips brush hers and his hand grip her breast. A strange pressure came, and then she didn't have time to cry out before he was in her. Alex whimpered and grabbed Aaron's back, squeezing her eyes tight to fight the pain. Glancing down, Alex gulped, realizing he had actually fit inside her.

"Am I hurting you?"

"A little, but I'll be okay. Don't stop." Alex kissed him, letting his tongue explore her mouth as it had done so many times while he let her adjust. When the pain lessened and Alex nodded, Aaron moved, thrusting slowly, trying not to hurt her. He held her as close as he could while he made love to her. The pain had dulled, and Alex kissed him—clung to him—tried to get as close to him as she could.

Soon they found a sort of rhythm, moving in unison as they did when they danced. Aaron's face flushed before he grunted and shuddered across his whole body, making Alex feel warm and sticky. He kissed her and collapsed beside her, panting.

Alex felt sore but loved. Aaron had been gentle and passionate and nothing like she'd imagined after her awkward tea with the Nial sisters.

I'll never forget tonight.

Running her finger across his arrow scar, Aaron wrapped his arms around her, gripping her to him.

Thank you for making me feel so loved.

Alex curled up in Aaron's arms, and she fell asleep, listening to his heartbeat.

CHAPTER 58
ΛARON

Λ click sounded in the room, startling Aaron awake. He reached for Alex and found her spot warm but empty. In the dying firelight, he caught two matching glimmers on his table. Aaron leaped from the bed and dashed across his room. Both his and Alex's crowns sat on his table. When he saw hers, his heart caught in his throat. Nestled inside it was his ring and a letter.

She gave herself to me because she planned to leave.

Aaron grabbed his pants off the floor and ran through the door still tying them. He wasn't sure where she'd go, but his gut screamed that there could only be one place. Barefoot and shirtless, Aaron tore through the courtyard. Michael was returning from rounds, and Aaron shouted. "Sound the alarm. She's gone!"

The full moon lit his path to her mother's garden, and Aaron reached the hedges that surrounded it before the alarm bells sounded. The gravel bit his soles as he forced himself to run harder. When he rounded the corner that led to the rose garden, he saw her at the end of the path. The gold lining inside the cape Alex had stolen from Aaron's room glimmered as her steps let the moonlight hit it. Aaron watched her stop at the end of the path before she turned to him.

Aaron moved toward her when a crack sounded, and Moorloc appeared.

"Alex, don't!" Aaron begged. "Whatever deal you made isn't worth it."

"I have to," she said. Her voice wavered, and she trembled as she looked at him.

"Why?"

A sad smile crossed her lips. "Because a week with you, even for decades of servitude, was worth more to me than centuries of freedom without you. You'll be a great king, Aaron. Just have the faith in yourself that I do."

Before he could reply, she took Moorloc's hand, and they vanished.

Aaron dropped to his knees. The pain of the gravel cutting his skin barely registered as the feeling of his heart being ripped from his chest overwhelmed him.

She's gone. What do I do?

He heard the crunch of footsteps behind him as he struggled to breathe.

"What happened?" Jerome's voice broke behind him. Aaron hadn't heard that tone since the day his brother died.

"She's gone," Aaron whispered. "I don't think Merlock healed us. I think—"

Stefan!

Aaron hurried to his feet and pushed past Jerome, running back to the castle. Inside he rushed past Randal and threw open the door to Stefan's room—the bed was empty.

"She's gone, isn't she?"

Aaron spun to find Stefan in the doorway leading to Alex's

room. Jerome caught up to Aaron and stopped when he spotted Stefan out of bed.

"Are you—?"

"I'm fine. Is she gone?"

Aaron could only nod as footsteps sounded nearby.

"No!" Edward cried, stepping off the stairs. His voice wavered as his entire body trembled. "She's not gone. She's in the stable, the kitchen, your bed, *anywhere*. Just tell me she's still in Warren!"

Aaron's chest heaved rough, ragged breaths as he stared at the floor. Edward collapsed, wailing. Aaron had heard that sound once before from his mother the day his brother died. Randal strode to Edward's side.

"Merlock!" Aaron shouted.

A soft crack sounded, and Merlock's eyes widened as he took in the chaos.

"She went with my brother, didn't she?"

Aaron nodded.

Merlock closed his eyes and sighed. "Did she go willingly?"

Aaron nodded again. The pain in his chest was unbearable. He needed to give his orders before he broke down. "I need my father. Bring us the King of Datten. We can't go to war without him."

"War?" Stefan asked.

"Moorloc took the books after the attack. We made a plan to get them back, but now we'll use it to get her. I don't care if she went willingly—he coerced her."

"She did it for us," Stefan said.

Everyone turned to him.

"It wasn't my healing, was it?" Merlock asked.

"No," Stefan said. "She told me everything before she left. She traded her freedom to save our lives. Without Moorloc's help, Aaron and I would be dead—a burden she couldn't bear. The guilt of hurting someone innocent would destroy her."

"I should have known," Merlock said.

Randal stood up beside Edward. "Jerome, accompany Merlock to get Emmerich. Aaron, Stefan—get dressed. You can't plan for war in dirty pants. I'll remain with Edward."

Aaron nodded and left to change; the crack of Merlock and Jerome leaving echoed into the hallway as he opened the door to leave. Back in his room, Aaron roared.

Why didn't you tell me? We could have figured it out!

An unfathomable rage exploded out of him so fast he had no chance to stop it. Aaron grabbed the door of his wardrobe, ripped it from the hinges, and smashed it into the bedpost, cracking it in two. Still furious, he charged into the wardrobe, sending it crashing to the floor. Finally, he picked up the broken bedpost and smashed his bookshelves, his table, his mantle, only stopping when he was about to hit his crown table. Her crown glimmered in the dying fire, and Aaron collapsed in tears.

A knock sounded, and Megesti looked down at him. "Is it safe to come in yet?"

Aaron hung his head in shame.

"Her goodnight tonight makes a lot more sense now." Megesti tossed a few pieces of the broken wardrobe into the fireplace.

"What did she say?"

"She told me to take care of you."

"Megesti, she's—"

"I know. You're falling apart. Which is why I'm here—to keep you together. We spent the last few days coming up with a brilliant plan, now we'll use it to get her back. But *you* have to sell your father on it. That means getting dressed and putting on that crown because sobbing messes on the floor don't get to lead the Datten army—only the crown prince can do that."

Aaron swallowed his rage. He squeezed his eyes shut and clenched his fists.

Count to ten. Daniel always said counting helps.

Aaron relaxed and stood as Megesti pulled clothes from the smashed wardrobe and held them out.

"I'll have servants move your things to Daniel's room."

Aaron opened his mouth to object but stopped. "Thank you."

Megesti smiled at Aaron. His green eyes sparkled like Alex's. "You're welcome, Your Highness."

WHEN AARON WALKED into Edward's room, he'd composed himself enough to the point where he appeared to be his most commanding self. Megesti followed with the stack of books from the library. The only other person in the room holding it together was Stefan. Employing his usual dominant stance, the power he exuded was enough to intimidate the younger knights, including Michael, but it had no effect on Alex or Aaron.

I grew up with the most intimidating Wafner, so you'll never scare me, but I hope you'll work with me.

Aaron swallowed hard, trying to think of something to say to Stefan.

Play nice for her.

Aaron sighed and smiled weakly as he looked at Stefan.

"She could have done better," Stefan said.

"What?" Aaron asked.

"Your engagement. She deserved better."

"Did you hit your head in that castle? There isn't anyone better for Alex than me."

"She could have gotten a better man," Stefan said, staring Aaron down. "You're welcome to prove me wrong, but I doubt you'll continue to show up when things get hard."

Traitor! Next time we're alone, I'll show you who's the better man.

"Enough," Emmerich growled.

"How're you going da find her? I can't wait anoder twelve yars." Edward's voice slurred as he sat in his usual seat.

Aaron felt for him. His own father wore his worried scowl, but Edward was destroyed. He was drinking straight from the bottle, and Aaron couldn't remember a time when Edward had drunk so much.

Where did he get that bottle, and how did he get this drunk so fast? He can't even stand.

Aaron crouched beside his godfather and took his hand.

"I swear on my crown, Edward. We'll bring her back. I won't leave my betrothed to rot in that castle."

"What do you plan to do?" Emmerich asked.

Aaron turned and faced his father. "We have a plan."

After they had all sat at the table, Jerome asked, "Where are Matthew and Sir Michael?"

"Leading the guards in the hunt for the princess," Aaron said. "They won't find her, but our men have to try."

"So what's the plan?" Randal asked.

"And how did you develop this brilliant plan?" Emmerich asked, crossing his arms.

Aaron ignored his father and spent the next hour filling them in on the plan he and Alex had come up with.

"It's clear now that Alexandria was helping develop the plan for us to retrieve her from my brother, and we didn't know." Merlock sighed and folded his hands.

"I'm going to go to the Betruger. According to my sources, a sorcerer caused the king's death, and I believe Lygari is the one responsible. Killing royalty seems to be a sport for him," Aaron said.

"Since when do you have sources?" Emmerich scoffed.

"People talk to you when they don't fear you. You hear more when you talk less," Aaron snapped. "If Lygari *did* murder the old king, his son may want revenge on the sorcerers too, and they might know the castle location."

What are you thinking, Father? I wish I could read you like Mother and Edward can.

"You intend to lead an expedition to the Betruger? *You?*" Emmerich looked at Aaron.

"Yes. It's time we try talking to the Betruger. I'll take a small group of our most skilled men. We'll go to Datten and from there, the Ogre Mountains. I'll do anything I have to—we need King Harold's help. Then we'll head to the northeast mountain range bordering the Oreean Sea and meet you there."

"Meet us?" Emmerich asked.

"Of course. I can't very well attack a castle of mercenaries with a small cavalry. I need the armies of Datten and Warren." Aaron looked from his father to Jerome as they eyed him suspiciously.

"Where did this prince come from?" Emmerich asked. "The Aaron I know is a pacifist."

"This is the Aaron the princess took to bed," Michael said from the doorway. "Alex always gets what she wants and seems to have had *quite* the effect on him."

Michael!

"You did what?" Emmerich's face turned red as he glared at Aaron. "You're going to save Alexandria and then marry her. I will not tolerate you dishonoring my goddaughter in this manner."

Did you just agree with my plan? Sneaky Michael.

"I'm about to mount an expedition to the Betruger to get her back. Nothing could make me give her up."

Aaron sighed at Michael before noticing Stefan had gone pale.

"I have my list of men prepared," Aaron said. "Michael, Jerome, or Merlock—since you won't let me go without at least one of them—and the best riders in both kingdoms, Caleb, Julius, and Cameron—if he's willing."

And speaking to me yet.

Stefan narrowed his eyes. "How do you know which men are the best riders?"

Aaron smirked. "Being the top jouster in Torian has advantages."

"Aaron," Emmerich began, "I think we need to *properly* consider this."

"I'm sorry. You seem to be confused because I wasn't asking. I'm going to get the Betruger, and I'm getting Alex back *with or without* Datten's help. The moment you signed that betrothal, I became a Prince of Warren, and Alexandria became a Princess of Datten, making her safety my responsibility. But this isn't about my crown or your legacy. It's about saving the woman I love from whatever nightmares her uncle has planned for her. If you deny me, I'll go anyway. I'll go alone if I have to."

Edward sighed. "Take any man from my kingdom you need. Just get her back."

"I'm coming," Michael said.

"As am I," Merlock said. "Should things go badly, I'll bring you, Baron Strobel, and Sir Michael home."

"I'm coming too," Stefan said, wincing as he moved.

"No," Aaron said. "You're not recovered enough for the ride across the mountains. You stay here and heal. When I have the Betruger, I'll send word. You and Randal can lead the Warren army to the castle. I don't doubt your loyalty, Stefan, but I know Alex would have my head if anything more happened to you."

Michael and Stefan smiled.

"Where should I go?" Jerome asked Emmerich.

"Let the young men head to the Betruger. We'll lead the Datten army when we receive word their mission was successful."

"How will we find the castle?" Megesti asked. "Victoria hid her castle so only Alex could find it. Moorloc's must be hidden too."

"It will be. He'll have protected it, so even if we were standing in front of it, we wouldn't see it," Merlock said.

Aaron placed his elbow on the table, turning his still bloody palm toward the group. "Blood of my blood, blood of her blood."

"She gave you her blood!" Megesti's eyes widened.

"What does that mean?" Emmerich asked.

Megesti grinned at Aaron. "It means if she's inside the castle, he'll see it because he's got her blood."

"Then we all have our duties to prepare," Randal said.

"Now let's get *our princess* back," Aaron said, marching toward the door.

EPILOGUE
TITAN OF MYSTICS

It was the same strange dream he'd had for decades. The girl stood at the water's edge and exhaled. Next, she removed her shoes, rolled up her pants, and waded into the chilly seawater. It would always end there. As soon as he'd speak to her, he'd wake up alone in his bed. He was no longer sure when it started or why he kept coming back to this beach, or this sea, with this *girl*.

Who are you?

Power flowed from her into the water and back again as her fingers skimmed the surface.

"What does a Poseidon sorceress have to do with the Titan of Mystics? With the next head?"

He straightened his burnt orange robe. It was hideous to look at, but that color marked him for what he was—an Ares sorcerer, known for their violence and ability to bring out chaos in anyone around them. Everyone knew to stay away from the orange robes.

He'd watched her long enough, and so he trudged into the icy water up to his ankles. Fire sorcerers disliked anything wet or cold, and he despised such things more than most. He cleared his throat and held out his hand. As her head moved, he waited to wake up, but this time was different.

She looked directly at him.

He recognized the cascading wavy brown hair, the perfect little nose, the beautiful full lips. He'd seen her face before when he was a boy, when he'd asked the black pearl a simple question. Her emerald eyes bore into him, looking through his dark soul. She was beautiful, but the power rolling off her as she looked back at him was exceptional.

His generation's heart ... was a girl.

He had asked the pearl to show him his equal, and now he knew she would be his.

TORIAN TIMELINE

Sorcerers arrive	No one knows
Founding of Datten	year 0
Founding of Warren	50
Founding of six southern kingdoms	50–200
Merlock arrives in Datten	1469
Megesti is born	1483
King Arthur of Warren is born	1484
King Emmerich of Datten is born	1503
Prince Edward of Warren is born	1510
King Emmerich is crowned king	1516
Prince Daniel of Datten is born	1522
Prince Aaron of Datten is born	1530
Princess Elizabeth of Warren is born	1533
Princess Elizabeth vanishes and Prince Daniel dies	1538
Present day of story	1550

KINGDOMS

DATTEN

Motto: Honor above All
Royal Family
King Emmerich (1503–)
Queen Guinevere (1504–)
Dead Prince Daniel (1522–1538)
Prince Aaron (1530–)

House of Wafner
Jerome (General of Datten) and dead Lady Gwendalin
Seven children: Patrick (Stefan), Jessica, dead Ryan, Arthur,
Samuel, Olivia, and David

House of Merlock
Merlock: royal sorcerer and king's advisor
Megesti: sorcerer apprentice and Merlock's son

WARREN

Motto: Prosperity through Courage
Royal Family
King Edward (1509–)
Dead Princess Victoria (1451–1538)
Princess Elizabeth aka Alex (1533–)

House of Nial
Randal (General of Warren) and Lady Judith
Three daughters: Abigail, Diana, and Edith

House of Bishop
Matthew (retired general) and Lady Lillian
Three sons: Marco, Aiden, and Julius

PRONUNCIATION GUIDE

Bernhard: Burn-hart
Betruger: Beh-true-grrrr
Datten: Day-ten
Ferflucs: Fair-f-looks
Lygari: Le-garh-ee
Kirsh: K-ear-sh
Kruft: K-ruff-t
Merlock: Mer-lock
Moorloc: More-lock
Nial: N-aisle
Ogre: O-grah
Oreean: Or-ian
Rassgat: Ras-gat
Torian: Tore-ian
Warren: War-en

ACKNOWLEDGMENTS

This story has been playing through my head like a movie for over a decade whenever I would run, and thanks to the help and support of so many amazing people, it will now be able to run through the heads of countless more.

Most importantly, I must thank my husband, Steve, and my children, Lillian, Katrina, and Zack. Not only did they believe in me but they also gave up time with me and sent me to the basement so that I could write. They listened to endless questions and second-guesses about characters and, in Lillian and Steve's case, read every version I wrote. Thank you for your endless love and support.

To my mom, Elke, and stepdad, Al, I want to say thank you for pushing me to never settle and for believing in all my crazy dreams.

To my dad, Hans Peter, thank you for giving me the ability to drink endless pots of coffee. It has been most helpful.

Next, I have to thank my friends. Selina R., thank you for reading my horrible first draft and giving me the hard kick in the tush I needed to take a hard look at the draft and rip it apart so it became what I have now. Kira B., my cousin, you didn't like fantasy books, but you read mine and loved it. That was one of the greatest compliments I have ever gotten. Mirabelle H., my fabulous friend who read that second draft after I fixed it thanks to Selina. I was scared to show it to anyone, but you loved fantasy so much I felt safe giving it to you, and I love all the love you have for my characters now! Dina, thank you for listening to my endless prattling on and on about my characters and for being part of the inspiration for my amazing characters. And Diana S., thank you for being such a creative and amazing force in my life for as long as Steve has been (and is being) so excited for me that I wanted to keep going even when it was hard. Carolyn L., my fellow fantasy lover, thank you for making me feel like I could do this and being excited about my book.

To my amazing online BookTok and Bookstagram friends, thank you for bringing a smile to my face and giving me a safe place to vent and talk books and cry when I needed. A special thank you to Brittany N., Codi E., Natalie, Santi, and Mia.

To my fantastic author friends I found online—you are shining lights in my dark days. You understand the pain and loneliness that comes with writing and also laugh and share stories about the craziest things we have had to google! Nikki, Tiffany, Amanda, Sonja, Penelope, Ruby, Rosalyn, Laura, Bekah, Jillian, Lynn, and countless more—you all make writing so much more enjoyable!

I especially want to thank the beta readers who took a chance on my book in January 2021. Because of your feedback, I have been able to turn this story into the book I have! So thank you, Xenia P., Anna S., Riannon S., Lauren C., Lillian A., Lizzie C. P., Ashely P., Brittany T., Danielle S., Kara N., Stephanie G., R. M., Alana F., Bevany S., Sarah S., Tashima G., Mary C., Erica E., Candis S., Candice N., Kristie M., Alexa B., Sarah A., Sarah B., Sarah R., Emma A., Oluwatison, Rebecca C., Rachel W., Angela N., Warda M., Michelle G., Emma J., Nessian L., Ricci C., Talya E., Elise Shauf, Jennifer L., Nina L., Stephanie I., Kristina P., Gabrielle A., Jessica J., Jennifer V., Rhian H., Nouria H., Valeria M., Natasha T., Shini K., Allie B., Amy A.,

Lindsay F., Sharon R., Alex T., Kylie D., Nakita A., Laura B., Summer B., Ricbre, and Rob.

I also want to thank my ARC readers and my street team for taking a chance on my story and helping to get my book out there!

Along with you all, I want to thank my alpha readers, Andrea Hernandez and Christine Hutton. You two have listened to all my crazy ideas, overzealous excitement, and always wanted to hear more. Thank you for your enthusiasm, encouragement, and your love for my characters, my world, and my story. And, Iliyan, I love my kingdom crests. Thank you for helping me embody what they each represent.

Thank you to my brilliant artists who helped my line marks and characters come to life! Casey (of RallyBirdBrand), your work is fantastic, and your series and sorcerer marks are just perfect! I love that I got to use them as chapter headings too. Hoang Tejieng, your renderings of my characters helped bring them to life for me!

To my author critique group—Stephanie Joyce, I found you at a conference and convinced you to be my friend by following you. Luckily, it was a virtual conference or that would be creepy! Amanda Terry Hamm, we pulled you into our crazy group as soon as we found you, and I am so thankful we did. Remember to be the lobster and ascend the hierarchy!

To my photographer, Brittany Nosal—I hate the way I look in photos, but you made the entire process painless and, more importantly, made me feel beautiful and gave me photos I love and can use knowing they captured the real me in all my happy, loving craziness!

I also want to take a LONG moment to thank the team of Lauren Taylor Shute Editorial.

Lauren, you are the CEO but so easy to talk to. I knew I found my editors when we started finishing each other's sentences at the first meeting. But you have become so much more. You are my guide in the world of publishing and book making, and I know I will never be lost thanks to you!

Shannon, you are an organization marvel. You must have as much information about author projects in your head as I do facts about my world. I love getting emails from you and can't thank you enough for your patience with my questions and reminders of everything that's due.

Sam, my amazing developmental editor! We broke all the rules when Lauren let me meet you in order to figure out how many books my first story should be, and I am so glad we did. Seeing the passion and excitement on your face was one of the best experiences I've had in my book work. I love knowing you are as excited about my books as I am! So thank you for being as picky as you are so that everything about my book is as amazing and concise as possible!

Brian, thank you for not letting my emotional attachment to my story scare you off. Your edits help my writing become more concise and ensure that everyone will know who is speaking and catch those missed confusions. Your enthusiasm and hard work are more appreciated than I can ever possibly express!

Jackie, you are a grammar guru! You took my crazy pauses and love of em dashes and made this book into something that people can read with ease and breathe where they are supposed to. Thank you for your patience with me and your phenomenal work!

To my cover designers, Alan and Ian—I cannot thank you enough for my gorgeous cover! I absolutely love it, and I so appreciate your dedication and patience with me helping me to get it just right. I love the final product and can't wait to see the next one.

S. E., I can't thank you enough. You speak editor, artist, and author and know how to make us all understand each other. It's so lovely to have someone I can run to when I'm confused or upset about my writing, and you always understand. Sometimes it feels like we are in each other's heads, and having that with my senior editor is a gift that I cannot say thank you for enough. But I try, so thank you!

Lastly, I want to thank all the amazing fantasy authors whose work helped me find a safe place to go to when I needed to escape the cold world—from Mary Shelley to J. R. R. Tolkien to Sarah J. Maas and Holly Black as well as Homer and the scholars of Greek mythology who gave me the inspiration for so much of this world. Thank you for changing my life!

ABOUT THE AUTHOR

Photo by Brittany Jean Photography

Alice Hanov was born in Germany and then raised on Pelee Island in the middle of one of the Great Lakes, spending her days imagining grand adventures in the woods around the island. She has never stopped writing and has a degree in rhetoric and professional writing from the University of Waterloo. Alice lives in Ontario with her hubby and three kids, various pets, and many, many books. You can visit her online at alicehanov.com.

Read on for a sneak peek at

BROKEN SONS

by

Alice Hanov

The second installment
in *The Head, the Heart, and the Heir* series

Gryphon
Press

ALEX

"Whatever deal you made isn't worth it!"

The desperation in Aaron's voice made Alex's heart break. She swallowed hard. "A week with you, even for decades of servitude, was worth more to me than centuries of freedom without you. You'll be a great king, Aaron. Have the faith in yourself that I do."

Please understand. I love you too much to let you die because I made a mistake. I can't live in a world that doesn't have you in it.

Alex turned and took her uncle Moorloc's hand. Wind sent Alex's chestnut hair swirling around her pale face as Aaron, her father's garden, and Warren's castle disappeared and the cracking sound echoed in a strange, massive hall.

Despite the late hour, Moorloc's castle hall was as bright as daytime without a single candle in sight. The scent of fire hit Alex before she heard the crackling. She glanced up and gasped, bringing her hand to her mouth. The entire hall was illuminated by flames dancing across the ceiling. Somehow, the room was still ice-cold, and she shivered. She was about to pull water from the air when a hand squeezed her shoulder.

"That won't do any good. I've enchanted the hall ceilings to burn all night to provide light. You can't douse it with water, and it creates no heat." Flickers of flames lit up Moorloc's ashen face as he released her.

How is that even possible? Pulling Aaron's cloak tighter, Alex carefully examined the room. The hall looked older than her mother's castle, and it was in nearly the same state of disrepair. Pieces were missing from the walls, floors, and ceilings. The weathered stones looked as if they had stood here for centuries. The wall opposite the door had an intricately carved throne with two smaller thrones on either side. Alex stepped toward it but froze and clutched her satchel strap as she looked back at her uncle.

Moorloc nodded and motioned for her to go look. He crossed his arms and stoically watched her.

The throne was larger than the ones in Warren and Datten and featured more elaborate carvings. The cushion was the same violet color Moorloc's cloak had been at the tournament. On the spindle was the same infinity symbol that was on both her uncles' necks. *The mark of Merlin for the Titan of Merlin.* Along the sides and the arms were smaller shapes. Looking carefully, Alex realized they were the other line symbols that Merlock had taught her— an ax for Ares, a leaf for Celtics, a grave for Hades, the Mire mountain, the clouded moon for the Mystics, waves of Poseidon, flames of Salem, and the Tiere fox head. Two smaller thrones flanked Moorloc's. On the right stood a simple throne with the Merlin mark and on the left...Alex's blood ran cold. The second throne was identical to the first, but the mark carved into the spindle was that of Cassandra. Alex bent toward the gold cushion sitting on the seat. *The same gold as Datten.* She moved her fingers across the fabric. It was softer than any material in Warren. Holding her breath, Alex moved her fingers to trace her symbol on the chair.

"Had Datten not interfered, we would have brought you here as soon as your mother died," Moorloc said.

Alex jumped back. She hadn't heard him come up behind her. "What do you mean?"

"This seat was your mother's. Anytime she visited, she sat beside me. In the place of honor."

Alex looked up at Moorloc's face. "What about Lygari?" *Do you not see how much you mistreat your son? It's no wonder he's so terrible.*

"I moved him to sit with the men."

"Wouldn't that upset him?"

"Nonsense. He realizes that the place at my side has always been for the most powerful sorcerer, and that, my little prophetess, is the daughter of Cassandra. The *Titan* of Cassandra. First, it was your mother. Now it's you."

"What exactly makes someone a titan?"

"A titan is the most powerful living sorcerer of their line. They each embody the entirety of their line's specific powers and wield them with a depth and precision others could only dream of. It's why our eyes shift to our line's color. When we harness that immense power, our eyes change because we become the living embodiment of those powers. Some even glow, depending on the situation and the sorcerer."

"How long is a sorcerer a titan?"

"Until death. Or another surpasses them in skill and power. It is possible for them to surrender the title, but it's rarely done."

"How can I be a titan already? I'm barely of age."

"More important is the level of power. By winter solstice, you'll have all of yours. So even though you're young, your powers are beyond your years."

You forced my remaining powers on me without ever asking.

What should have taken decades to arrive will now only take months.

Moorloc's smirk sent a chill down her spine. Turning away from him, Alex spotted the only two portraits in the entire room. They covered nearly the entire back wall. The first was identical to the one in her mother's castle and depicted Moorloc with a young Lygari. Their matching gold eyes and black hair against the gray stones around them made their skin look sickly pale. Beside it was a painting of Merlock, Moorloc, and Victoria. Her cousin Megesti resembled Alex and her mother, with the same chestnut brown hair and emerald eyes. Megesti's father, Merlock, was the combination of siblings with black hair and green eyes, but here, it was impossible to see since Merlock's face had been burned away. Alex looked identical to her mother, from the waves in her hair to the pale pinkish hue of her skin. The sight of Merlock's burned face made Alex swallow a terrified scream. She stumbled back and slammed into her uncle.

"Understand that he's the reason she's dead, and had you not chosen correctly, he'd have caused your demise too. Victoria served Datten for decades, but they abandoned her the moment she needed them. My brother is as guilty as they are. If it wouldn't strip me of my power, I'd have murdered him years ago," Moorloc said.

Goosebumps erupted along Alex's arms as a shiver ran through her core at Moorloc's icy tone. Even Aaron's soft cloak was no match for the chill that suddenly filled the room. Alex glanced at the ceiling. *How can it burn when the ground feels like ice? Wait ...*

"Strip you of your power? Is that the consequence of hurting your own kin?" Alex asked. *Does that mean you can't hurt me?*

"Not kin—*twin*. Sorcerer twins cannot seriously wound

each other without suffering the consequences themselves. Enough questions. It's late, and you're tired. Follow me and pay attention. I'll provide you with a rundown of the castle so you'll know where you will be expected to be at what time. Then I'll show you to your sleeping arrangements. I've procured everything you could need and left it in your room," Moorloc said.

Alex pulled Aaron's cloak tightly around herself when she realized Moorloc was watching her. *He must expect an answer.*

"A tour would be helpful."

Moorloc nodded and motioned for her to follow him. Terror burned in her chest as she swallowed the lump in her throat and obeyed. The only sound Alex heard was the crackle of the fire above and their boots on the stones as they entered the hallway.

The flames followed them down the ceiling of the deserted hallways as they made their way around the entire first floor. Alex noticed the bare stone walls as they passed. *Is the lack of decor because the fire would destroy it, or does he prefer it this way?*

The castle was mundane and not the magical structure she'd been expecting. Other than the fire lighting the ceiling, everything was ordinary. It was square, and the main hallway looped around the castle perimeter. Each corner had a simple square guard tower with a fifth in the middle of the castle. It required one to enter through the central courtyard. The outer hallway led to the various rooms, including the first hall they'd appeared in, guards' quarters, armory, kitchen, library, and two large bedrooms.

"This bedroom," Moorloc explained, pointing at a massive black wooden door, "is mine. Lygari's room is on the opposite side of the building. You'll be staying there while you are with us."

"In Lygari's room?" Alex asked. Her palms went clammy, worrying about how little she trusted her cousin.

"Yes. I need to ensure your safety while you adjust to life here. He's been moved to another room."

"But why—"

He raised his hand to show this conversation was over. "As I was saying, while you live here, you'll have access to most of the castle and the grounds, but a few areas are off-limits. My bedroom is one of them. As trusting as I am with you, I'm old enough to know that we all have our secrets. The Prince of Datten is finally aware of how good you are at keeping secrets."

At the mention of Aaron, Alex's pounding heart froze in her chest. Moorloc stared at her as she fought to push back the heartache desperate to escape her. *Please forgive me, Aaron. I had to.*

"I'll respect your privacy, within reason, as you find your footing here. And you will respect ours."

Silently, Alex nodded. Moorloc broke his stare and motioned for her to follow him down the hallway again. As they rounded the corner to the back of the castle, Alex looked longingly at the library Moorloc had shown her.

"The library is yours to visit whenever you desire. There are books that will help you with your studies and some for pleasure too. I'll assign you specific books and readings to go with whatever it is we are working on at that moment."

"Whenever I wish?"

"Naturally. Your mother kept odd hours when she was studying. Some days she would be up at dawn, and some days she would never sleep. I assume you take after her in that regard. Sorcerers are controlled by their mental curiosity and less by their primal need for sleep or food."

Alex exhaled loudly. Moorloc looked down at her as she tried to hide her face.

"You are my niece; you don't need to hide your feelings from me. Unlike my brother, I am the titan of our line, meaning I have the additional powers for our kin. I can sense when you have powerful feelings about something. For example, at this moment, you are feeling relief, guilt, and sadness."

Her arms twitched. *How? How does he know exactly what I'm feeling? I'm going to have to go back to hiding my emotions.*

Moorloc looked smug. "I presume you feel sadness at leaving the boy you believe you're in love with, but you'll learn you could never be happy with someone as simple as him. You feel relief at knowing that you are not alone in your strange behaviors. Lastly, you feel guilty about that relief because it tells you that your decision to come here was correct."

Alex avoided looking at him. *Aaron isn't just some boy I think I love. I gave up my freedom to save him and Stefan, even if my adopted brother will be furious I put his life above mine after everything he sacrificed to keep me safe. You may sense what I feel, but you don't understand the reasons behind it.* Wanting to end that train of thought, she spun around and scurried down the hall.

Moorloc cleared his throat, standing before another door.

Alex stopped and glanced over her shoulder. Without a word, he opened it and stepped inside. There were no other doors for the entire stretch of hallway at the back of the castle. *This room must be immense.*

Alex followed him and gasped. The lab was as large as Warren's main hall and dining hall combined. Mesmerized, Alex wandered around the room, desperate to take it all in.

It smelled the same as Merlock's lab: fire and strange herbs. Yet here the stench in the lab was potent despite the massive size. Moorloc had covered the wall closest to the door in a gigantic bookcase. Alex traced her fingers along the stiff spines of the journals, modern reference books, and ancient texts. Moorloc's footsteps moved away from her. A quick scan of the shelves revealed that none of the books were from her line. She crept to the next corner and saw another monstrous set of shelves covered in jars and tins filled with bizarre plants, herbs, and all manner of things. Despite being curious, Alex avoided getting too close. A jar had jumped at her once when she tapped it in Merlock's lab.

A giant white bear rug lay in the middle of the room. Alex stopped and bent over to examine it. Despite being on the floor, the fur was as pristine and smooth as the silk lining of Aaron's cloak around her shoulders. She'd never seen a white bear. The rest of the room had a large table and a fireplace with a pile of cooking pots stacked next to it, a wooden chest, and a giant wall of weapons and tools. *These would have fascinated Stefan.* She carefully examined the various lengths and styles of whips, daggers, swords, bows, and staves. None of them had red steel, so at least they wouldn't be toxic to her, only painful.

"I'll bring you back in here tomorrow when we go over the rules," Moorloc said from behind her. "Afterward, you'll have unlimited access so long as you follow those rules."

Rules? Alex exhaled to control her retort and slowly turned to look at her uncle. She kept her features stoic to not allow him to see her fear.

"Of *course* there are rules, Alexandria. Discipline is critical to the successful training of any young sorcerer. You, however, will need additional rules."

"Why? Because I'm a girl?" Despite her fear, Alex frowned at her uncle, making the flames on the ceiling crackle and light up more. She swallowed hard, worried her temper was about to get her into serious trouble.

"Yes, but not for the reason you think. Daughters of Cassandra hold the power of that line. It means that you carry more power than Lygari."

"More than *you?*" Alex gulped. The words had come out, and she instantly regretted it.

Moorloc's eyes narrowed, and his lips scowled for an instant. Had she not been watching him, she'd have missed it.

He stepped directly in front of her. Icy cold spread across Alex's chin as he tilted her face to look at him and smiled. "That, my little prophetess, remains to be seen and is precisely why you will have more rules. Are you ready to see the rest?"

Alex nodded and followed Moorloc out of the lab. At the door, she paused, looking back. Her mother had been in this room. *Maybe some small part of her is still here. Something that can help me get through this.*

Moorloc led her down a corridor, past more guard rooms and the armory. The entire second floor was just hallway after hallway of rooms for the mercenaries. The basement was damp and filled with old storage rooms.

"Now to your room." Moorloc led her back to the main floor.

"Where is the kitchen again?"

"Beside the hall. You are not to go there. The servants have too much work to do to entertain you. Meals are served twice a day at breakfast and dinner."

Once in the east hallway, they stopped at a large black door that matched Moorloc's bedroom. He turned the handle and pushed it open for Alex. Inside, the fire on the ceiling sprang to life. Cautiously, Alex entered, and Moorloc sent the fireplace roaring to life.

"The wardrobe is full of simple clothes—the ones you were so fond of while training in Warren. I had the servants sew them in gold and violet in honor of our lines."

Alex unfastened her cloak and hung it on the hooks next to the wardrobe. She removed her satchel and, after looking around, hung it up on another hook. The inside of the wardrobe was similar to Aaron's in Warren except it was all gold and violet. Something sparkled and caught Alex's eye.

"Gold thread to embroider your line mark," Moorloc explained before she could ask. He scratched his impeccably trimmed beard as he watched her.

"Is Lygari angry that I'm in here? I could have taken the other room. It wasn't necessary to move him." Alex closed the wardrobe and crossed toward him but stopped when she spotted a massive rug on the floor in the middle of the room. She crouched to examine it as Moorloc continued.

"This room has always been occupied by the second most powerful sorcerer in the castle. When your mother visited, she stayed here. Lygari has had it for decades, but he's aware you are more powerful than him, even if you lack focus and control."

Alex glanced up from the rug but couldn't read Moorloc's face. Merlock had never looked at her like that, so she had no basis to go on.

"It's a lynx," Moorloc said.

"I thought so. I've never seen one this large."

"It's from the Forbidden Lands. They grow larger there. I used this one to send a message."

"How? Why?"

"No more questions. It's early in the morning, and I'm sure you're exhausted. There will be enough time for all your questions in the months to come."

Alex's knees buckled as she stood up. *Months or years.*

"Until you get your bearings on how this place runs, remain in the castle and courtyard, but I expect the library will keep you busy for a while."

Alex looked up at her uncle, clenching her hands hard enough to hurt. The pain held back the sadness that threatened to engulf her.

"Welcome to your new home, little titaness. I'll send Lygari to fetch you tomorrow for dinner. Breakfast is early, and I expect you'll sleep through it." He turned to leave but paused. "I don't think I need to remind you that any attempt to escape or even leave the grounds without permission will forfeit the lives of both the lout and whelp."

I'm well aware Stefan and Aaron's lives depend on me behaving according to your archaic rules. Any slipup and you could undo the healing that saved them after I lost my temper and gutted them.

Alex nodded and looked down at the lynx pelt. When the door banged shut, all of her resolve drained from her. Droplets hit her legs as the tears ran freely. Only hours ago, she'd been with Aaron in his bed. Parts of her skin were still on fire and tingled from his touch, and the soreness between her legs meant it hadn't been a beautiful dream. She held her face in her hands and cried.

When she was drained of tears, Alex wrapped her arms around herself and struggled to stand. After her third try, she managed it and trudged to the hook where she'd hung her satchel. She pulled out a worn gold Datten tunic. As she carried it back to the bed, her tears started again. The wood was darker and the quilt was gold with her line mark on it, but the style was identical to those in Warren. She threw back the quilt and crawled onto the giant bed. The fabric was even softer than what she'd slept on back home. *Will I ever see Warren again?* After she pulled up the gold bedding, Alex curled up in a tight ball. Clutching Aaron's shirt, she breathed in deeply, smelling him, and cried, filling her chest with a burning pain until she fell into a restless sleep.

AARON

The church bells in Warren rang four times as Prince Aaron marched down the hallway away from the room of his godfather, King Edward. Despite Aaron's protests, the generals and kings decided they'd wait until after breakfast to summon the Warren knights Aaron had selected. They would embark for Datten on horseback and recover long enough to collect the chosen Datten knights. They'd remain in Datten until Aaron's father, King Emmerich, and General Jerome Wafner deemed them ready; then they'd begin the ride through the Ogre Mountains toward the kingdom of Betruger. If everything went according to plan, they'd be there in a month. Then all Aaron would have to do is convince King Harold to help him— or die trying.

It was early in the morning, and Aaron turned down the deserted side hallway and climbed the stairs that led to his room. Without thinking, he turned left and froze when he opened his door. He'd forgotten this wasn't his room anymore. One last time, Aaron crossed the threshold into his old room.

An hour before, Alex had been in here with him; she had shared his bed. *I was such a fool. What if she gave herself to me because she knew she was leaving? Does she even want to marry me, or did she say yes knowing she'd get out of it? Why did I let her do this to herself?*

"No. She said yes *before* the accident. She loves me, and I'm going to get her back," Aaron said out loud, surveying the damage of his room. "Please want me to find you. I need your love for me to be as strong as mine is for you."

Stepping over the shelf debris, Aaron could see someone had turned his dresser over and emptied it. The scattered books were missing, and so were Alex's crown and letter. *Did Megesti take them?* With a final breath, Aaron left his room and crossed the hallway to the room that belonged to his dead brother, Daniel—his new room. Until he had Alex back, he couldn't face the room they'd made love in. The taste of her still clung to his lips, and her scent would still be in that bed.

His new room was larger and had a balcony. He'd refused to use it after Daniel died. But with his room in shambles, it was this or a proper royal suite, and he intended to move his things one last time—when Alex returned and they were married. He'd move into her suite and never move again, especially knowing how she despised the idea of a king and queen sleeping in separate rooms. Aaron opened his wardrobe and realized that his gold cloak was missing along with his favorite training shirt. She'd loved his cloak when he'd given it to her all those months ago, and he'd insisted she keep it. But it had been ruined in that unfortunate training accident where she'd set herself and her father on fire. He smiled. *I hope you took them as reminders of me.*

He saw their matching gold crowns sitting on the side table. Aaron remembered how badly Alex wanted him to tell her how he could tell them apart. *Daniel threw mine at our father's head once. The royal goldsmith never could get that one prong perfectly straight again.*

The servants had moved both crowns since only he and his parents could tell them apart. Alex's crown would stay here, but his would travel with him. Nestled between them was his great-grandmother's ring, which he'd used to propose. Inside his crown was her letter. Exhaling, Aaron picked up the letter and sat down on his bed.

My dearest Aaron,

I love you. I love you more than I could ever tell you in this lifetime, and I need you to know that everything I said and did this past week was true. I meant all of it.

Please don't be angry with me. I know if you aren't yet, you'll be later when you wonder why I didn't tell you what I'd done. When I hurt you, Merlock took you away so quickly. I realized I couldn't live in a world without you, couldn't fathom a life that didn't have you in it, so I made a deal with Moorloc. He saved you and Stefan, and for that the price was giving myself over to be taught by him until he thinks I'm ready to return, however long that may be. But at least I was allowed a week with you.

Don't torture yourself wondering why I didn't ask for your help. I couldn't risk Moorloc learning that I'd told you. It would have broken my oath and undone your healing. I feel responsible for Datten losing Daniel. I couldn't let them lose you too.

I need you to know this: I trust you.

I trust you to become the man your father expects of you, to take care of Michael and Stefan now that I'm gone, to be strong and brave for my father, but most of all, I trust you to come for me. This entire week when we were planning how to get my family's journals, every hint and suggestion I gave you was to help you find me. Your strategies are always as sound as your father's.

Use that Datten piece of you and put everything together.

Be the crown prince you were born to be. Earn the loyalty of your men, discover your Edward, and convince him to join your side. Then come for me, and with my blood, you'll be able to find me. I'll learn all I can while I wait, so it will be safer for us all when I come home.

I'm not afraid of Moorloc or of my powers. The only thing I'm truly afraid of is a world without you. I took so much from you, and all I could leave behind for you was my heart. Guard it well.

Forever yours,

Alex

Tears streamed down his face as he read the letter over and over again. Finally, when he'd cried out everything he had in him, Aaron stood up and tossed his crown in the pile on his bed. He fastened his sword to his belt and began gathering things for the journey. He picked up a gold chain from his wardrobe, slipped Alex's ring onto it, and placed it around his neck. The second he got her back, the ring would be back on her finger and never leave it again as long as he lived.

He ran his hand through his golden hair as he moved to his wardrobe and took the old copy of *The Iliad* he'd stolen from her, his other favorite shirt, and a few necessities. As he moved to close the wardrobe, he paused. In the drawer, he spotted the green handkerchief Alex had given him at the start of the tournament. The stitching was so terrible he couldn't help but laugh. *Jessica needs to give up on teaching you needlework.* Alex's lady's maid had her hands full with that task.

He'd accepted her favor and planned to bring it to the joust, but after all the misunderstandings with Stefan and Cameron about the suitor business, he'd left it behind. More than anything, he needed to find Alex to make that right. Even a lifetime might not be enough to truly earn her forgiveness for not hearing her out when she needed him to. *No wonder she didn't tell me about making a deal.* Bringing it to his lips, Aaron kissed the handkerchief and placed it on the pile.

The church bells rang five times, and Aaron sighed. The kitchens would start breakfast, but he wouldn't wait. Dropping his plain shirt on the bed, he put on his formal Datten-crested shirt and crown. Then he grabbed his list of knights and hurried down to the stables.

Aaron pushed Thunder harder than he should have without a proper warm-up, but he didn't care. Even though he knew Cameron would help, part of him worried. *He might not do it for me but for his king and princess. He'll do it for Alex. He has to.*

When he arrived at the Strobel estate, he tied Thunder to a post and pounded on the door until Reginald, an elderly man in a long, tailored coat, answered it. The man gasped when he realized it was Aaron.

"Your Highness." He bowed to Aaron as he opened the door, and Aaron strode past him toward his uncle's office.

"I need to see my uncle and Cameron immediately. Don't even let them get dressed. And Thunder is tied outside."

"Yes, Your Highness." Reginald dashed upstairs after closing the door.

Bernhard Strobel's office looked like a small library. He'd covered the walls in bookcases except for the one with the fireplace. A massive carved desk stood in the far corner, and two large comfortable brown leather chairs faced the fireplace. Above the hearth were a pair of swords and a shield with the Warren crest.

Aaron stood staring at the shield when the door opened and Cameron trudged in dressed in his sleeping clothes. He snorted at Aaron's formal attire and crown.

"So it isn't my cousin who dragged us out of bed but the

Crown Prince of Datten. What do you *want*, Aaron?" Cameron bumped Aaron with his shoulder as he pushed past him to sit in his favorite chair. His blond hair sparkled in the glow from the fire, making his light bronze skin look almost as golden as Aaron's hair.

Aaron opened his mouth to say something when his uncle Bernhard arrived. At night, the man looked even more like an older version of Cameron, except his coloring was pinkish like Aaron's. Cameron's complexion came from his mother. Aaron hoped his uncle wouldn't be as upset. At least Bernhard had quickly changed and was wearing his less formal attire of black pants and a sea-blue tunic, the clothes he wore whenever Aaron came for dinner as his nephew and not crown prince.

"Aaron, what's happened?" Bernhard motioned to Aaron to sit at the desk, but Aaron held up his hand, lifted the empty chair beside Cameron with ease, and brought it to the desk. Bernhard gave Cameron a reproachful look before taking his seat behind his desk. Cameron groaned and moved the other chair next to Aaron.

"I need your help," Aaron said before Cameron even sat down.

"Aww, did Alex finally realize you're *annoying* and leave you?" Cameron crossed his arms and smirked as he leaned back in his seat.

"Cameron, behave," Bernhard said as Reginald arrived with the tea. "Thank you, Reginald. That will be all."

"Yes, sir." He bowed and slipped out of the room silently.

"All right, Aaron, let's hear what's so urgent that it couldn't wait for a civilized hour," Bernhard said as he poured each of them a cup. Cameron's blue eyes glared at Aaron.

"We need your help," Aaron said. He wiped his palms against his knees, trying desperately to stop their shaking.

"With what?" Cameron snapped.

"With horses." Aaron held his list out to Cameron, who snatched it. As soon as he glanced at it, his eyes widened and his body tensed.

"Why do you need fresh horses for fifty men?"

Aaron looked from Cameron to Bernhard. "Bernhard, within the hour, you're going to be summoned to an emergency council meeting where Edward and my father will explain that we're going to war with Moorloc. I'm going to Betruger with the men on that list."

"*I'm* on this list," Cameron said, looking from his father to Aaron.

"What happened, Aaron?" Bernhard asked.

"Moorloc took Alex. I'm going to get her back."

"What do you mean *took*?" Cameron was on the edge of his seat, suddenly interested in what Aaron had to say.

Aaron explained what had happened earlier that night, leaving out certain personal details. As he talked about the meeting between the generals and the kings, Bernhard listened intently while Cameron kept rereading the list of men.

"So I'm here to ask for your help. I'll even *beg* because I'm not asking as the cousin you're furious with or as the Crown Prince of Datten. I'm asking as the man in love with your future queen because if I could give up my crown and get her back *right now,* I would."

"What do you need from us?" Bernhard asked.

Aaron stared at Cameron, begging him to look at him.

"From you, Uncle Bernhard, I need horses. A lot of horses. Strong and fast enough to carry our men to Datten and then through the Ogre Mountains."

"And me?" Cameron asked as he looked up at him.

"I need your skills. I'm taking a cavalry of men to the Ogre Mountains to try to speak to the King of Betruger and need someone who can help with the horses. There's no one better than you—no one I *trust* more than you."

Cameron turned to face his father. Without a word, he leaned forward and picked up the tea his father had poured for him.

"The decision of whether to go is yours, Cameron. You're old enough. But if you're looking for my permission, you have it," Bernhard said.

Cameron took a long sip of his tea before he looked back at Aaron. "I'll go, but not for you. You and I are far from being all right. I'll go for Edward, for Warren, and for *her*. We lived twelve years without our princess, and if I can help make sure we don't go another unnecessary day, I'll do it."

"Cameron, you're welcome to hate me for the rest of our lives if you help me get her back." Aaron finally allowed himself to breathe deeply. Leaning forward, he grabbed his tea.

"Which horses are you thinking, Cameron?" Bernhard asked.

Taking a long drink of tea, Aaron listened to Cameron and Bernhard debate back and forth about which horses to take. When his cup was empty, there was a knock on the office door.

"Enter," Bernhard said.

"Beg your pardon, sirs," Reginald said. "The younger Sir Bishop was at the door with a summons from the king. I informed him of His Highness's presence and sent him off to the next estate with assurances that I would pass on his message."

"Thank you, Reginald. As soon as my son is presentable, we'll head to the castle."

"I'll prepare the horses," Aaron said as they all stood up and got ready to go.

∾

Arriving at the castle, Aaron, Bernhard, and Cameron headed straight to the throne room.

"Seems you beat us to the Strobels," General Matthew Bishop said when they arrived in the hall. His loose onyx hair fell against his rich brown skin when he nodded to Aaron.

"I did," Aaron said. "I wanted to ask for their help personally."

"We're happy to help however we can," Bernhard said. Aaron watched him strut over to Edward and Emmerich; they whispered together. Edward wore a simple Warren tunic like Bernhard, but it always looked better on him. His dark brown complexion made the blue and silver stand out. His own father always wore a gold tunic even though it washed out his pale complexion and was almost the same golden color as his hair.

"If I'm not needed here," Cameron said, "I'll head down to the stables. Gregory and I will need to see what they have before we send knights to get supplies from our estate or the shops."

"Cameron," Edward called, leaving Emmerich and Bernhard to join them. "Thank you. I know you and Aaron aren't in a great place, and I'm sure you're not thrilled with my daughter either about how things turned out, but I want you to know I won't forget this."

"Of course, Your Royal Highness. I don't blame her. You gave her the choice, and she made it. Regardless of how I feel about Aaron's actions, she's still my princess, and I couldn't live with myself if I didn't do everything I could to help get her back." Cameron bowed to Edward and hurried out of the room.

Edward crossed his arms and turned to Aaron. "You're going to have to find some way to make things right with him, Aaron. He clearly cares for Alexandria."

"She's always had that effect on people," Michael said, arriving in the room with Stefan.

"We're ready to help. What can we do?" Stefan asked.

Emmerich arrived at Edward's side. Aaron noticed the color on his father's pale cheeks. *Hitting the ale harder than usual?*

"Michael, find Randal and see who's missing from Aaron's list. Once they arrive, let us know so Aaron can address the men and see who volunteers," Edward said.

"Stefan, as the only son of Datten's general and the captain of the princess's guard, we'll need your help to convince the council this is what's best for the kingdom. Your link to both kingdoms will come in handy. Aaron, you'll need to convince a group of our best men to follow you on a mission without ever having been in battle—sorry, an *actual battle*, as opposed to the recent skirmishes."

Aaron smiled mischievously at the kings before looking at Stefan. "And last, Michael needs to ask Jerome for Lady Jessica's hand before we leave."

Edward's blue eyes lit up as he turned to Michael with a wide grin. "Is this true, Michael? I can confidently say I approve of the match."

"As do I," Emmerich said.

"You know Alex and I do," Stefan said, fixing his brown eyes on Michael.

"I'll make a deal with you," Michael said, pushing his shoulders back and glaring at Aaron and Stefan. The candlelight set off his light copper skin, making his blue eyes seem brighter. "If you two can get every man on Aaron's list to come with us, I'll ask Jerome."

"Done," Aaron and Stefan answered in unison before Michael swallowed and left to find Randal.

"Stefan, would you go keep the council members company? We need to speak to Aaron," Edward said.

Stefan nodded and ambled toward the other council members.

"It's alarming how quickly he became good at that," Aaron said, watching Stefan speaking to the council members who had already arrived.

"He's Jerome's son. Same fiery red hair, build, pale complexion, rationality, and military might. The Wafner name commands respect. I think being around Alexandria made him constantly have to fight to be in charge because she tried to take over. Since *you* took all of her attention, he's found his footing," Edward said.

"You said you wanted to speak with me? I assume it wasn't about the Wafners," Aaron said.

"Indeed." Edward grabbed Aaron's arm and pulled him closer. "I'm giving you the pearl to take with you."

"Why?"

"You're going to Betruger. We've been fighting them for six hundred years, and I doubt they'll trust you. It's likely they'll want to imprison or even kill you. I believe the pearl will be a tempting enough gift to get you an audience with the king."

"You're giving Betruger your pearl?"

"Aaron, I would give Betruger my kingdom if it got us Alexandria back."

"That's an empty offer," Emmerich said. "They'd never be able to defend it, and Datten would take it back in a month. But I agree. The pearl goes with Aaron."

"Why would they want it?"

"It's not about the gift itself. It's what it will provide for you," Edward said.

Aaron looked at his father, and it suddenly made sense. "The pearl's my *proof*—proof that I am who I say I am, that Alex means to me what I say she does. If the king uses it and sees his own past truths, he'll know mine are real too."

"Now you're thinking like a king," Emmerich said.

Aaron looked at the two men before him and couldn't help remembering Alex's words. *Find your Edward.*

Before They Transformed Their Kingdoms, They Were Children Bound by Fate

AVAILABLE NOW

Don't miss *The Spare Who Became the Heir and Other Stories: The Early Adventures of The Head, the Heart, and the Heir*, enchanting short stories that bring to life the fantasy kingdoms of Warren and Datten and the children who grow up to rule them— all leading up to what will come to pass in *The Head, the Heart, and the Heir.*

VISIT

alicehanov.com

FOR MORE INFORMATION